GETTING OVER CHARLIE

CHERRY MARTIN

A CIP catalogue record of this book is available from the British
Library from September 2021

ISBN paperback: 978-1-9168958-1-2

Proud to work with Print On Demand Worldwide who mirror my
environmental beliefs and are FSC® and PEFC chain-of-custody
certified, meaning this paper is sourced from sustainable forests. They
have also won multiple awards for their planet friendly approach to
print, production and every day working life.

Cover by creative bestie, Billy Allinson billyallinson.com
www.bestiestrilogy.com

ACKNOWLEDGEMENTS.

For all the besties who I laugh, cry, celebrate, deliberate and carry on carrying on with ...

Without fail, you make my days, weeks, months and years better. Thank you for making me laugh at points when all I wanted to do was cry. For pouring me champagne in the knowledge that one day I would sip it again and smile at how lovely life is.

You are all unique stars with unique superpowers, the shine that binds you all together? You choose to be kind. And funny. And give good hugs. Even the ones who hate hugs ...

My besties, you are the family that I have chosen. You mean the world to me.

To all of you: seek wonder, spread hope and keep shining.

To my family ...

For your unfailing love and belief, I love you. Mine is a different kind of legacy to having children - I hope between this and Golden Birdie you can understand that I'm heralding what I believe to be the best and finest elements of life. Acceptance, love, truth, courage, belief and hope. All with either a dash of nature or laughter - whichever is needed at the time. I can't bear the thought of anyone feeling alone so if my words can help in some way then I will always step up to the challenge.

To the reader of this book ...

Chances are we haven't met yet ... if you're looking for a rom com to tuck into then I hope this fits the bill. Pour yourself your favourite cuppa or tipple and get stuck in. Let me know what makes you chuckle the most.

If however, you're reading this and dealing with heartbreak then my heart goes out to you. I hope *Getting Over Charlie* provides you with a hug in a book and some laughter to distract your mind as you get to know Abby, Lucy and Woody. Perhaps there will be a golden nugget of advice hidden within, that reminds you that in time your spark will once again turn into a flame.

Abby realises that unconditional love is all around, not just in 'the one' as the movies would have you believe. You're never alone. Come and chat on @cherrymwrites or follow @bestiestrilogy for news of when book two *All The Vows* comes out ...

I wish you all peace, love and of course a truck-load of giggles.

xox Cherry

GETTING OVER CHARLIE

CAN TRUE LOVE BEGIN AT
HAPPILY NEVER AFTER?

CONTENTS

1

AN UNEXPECTED VALENTINE

ABBY FLICKED HER long hair out from underneath her shoulder and squinted through her lashes as she lay on the bed to see what was going on. Normally Charlie was all over her at this point; she was wearing the lingerie he'd bought her yesterday for Valentine's Day and knew that her sleek body was rocking it, so it couldn't be that.

She felt him shuffle down and perch on the end of the bed.

'Come on!' he muttered.

'Come on what? Charlie, are you OK?'

'Yes, it's fine. I thought I was in the mood, but it turns out ....' He trailed off.

Abby pulled herself up to move over to support him.

'No, no, stay right there,' Charlie gestured upon hearing her move. 'Come on, little man, we're a team, remember?'

Abby followed his gaze down; gosh, he was talking to his privates. 'Oh, is it not ...'

'Don't! Don't even say those words. He's just left me for a mo. He'll be back.'

Abby nestled back down under the covers, glad it wasn't anything more serious. She felt exhausted from a day of cooking and entertaining his friends, anyway. 'Charlie, you'll be fine. It's just one of those things.'

'No, it's not one of "those things", this is *my* thing, and it's not doing what it usually does, thank you very much.'

Abby smiled, maybe this was some kind of game play.

'Look, let me see what happens if I ...'

Charlie turned to her, his face contorted with angst. 'No, you stay right there,' he ordered.

Heck, he really did look worried, mixed with a look that she hadn't seen before. Was it desperation? 'Charlie, this is something that I'm sure happens to every guy,' she said in soothing tones.

'Oh really! Is that what you've found in your experience?' he snapped back.

'Well ...'

'In that case, maybe it's you.'

Abby rolled her eyes.

'This hasn't happened to anyone else, actually, and I'm sure if you let me help you, everything will be fine.' Abby moved off the bed and walked around to face him.

Charlie didn't look up, he remained sitting on the edge of the bed, hunched over. 'Just give me a minute, let me focus.'

Abby watched as his face turned red.

His manhood rose, then deflated, before rising slightly.

'It's like it's breathing,' Abby giggled.

'Silence. I'm focusing like all hell here.'

Abby shook her head and looked at it. It deflated again.

'Don't speak,' Charlie glanced at her. 'Don't even look at it.'

'Oh, for goodness sake.'

'Well, it hasn't happened with anyone else but you!' Charlie stared at her, his eyebrow rising deeply into his forehead as the latest realisation hit him.

'It's you! You've broken my cock! You gave me a Valentine's blowie yesterday, and that's what's done it. You're like that spider.' His face cringed, and he took a step back away from her as if he didn't want to get bitten again.

'What are you talking about? What spider?'

'That one that bites you and you remain hard for 24 hours and then you can't get it up ever again. Oh my God, is this going to last forever?'

Abby was horrified, 'But I hate spiders! Plus you've hardly been hard for 24 hours, Charlie.'

'Oh, rub it in, why don't you.'

Abby rolled her eyes. This was just getting ridiculous. 'Look I'll sleep in my lingerie, and I promise you by morning, you'll be better.'

Charlie looked down sorrowfully. 'Come on, buddy please! I've always treated you so well, gone wherever you've led me, don't fail me now.'

Abby lay back down in bed. 'Charlie, don't you think you're overreacting just a tad?'

'My cock, the one that I grew and loved all my life, talked to as a friend, which it is, just died on me. No, I don't think I'm overreacting!'

'Just come to bed. I'm sure it'll be fine in the morning. It's probably just had enough after the past 24 hours of Valentine's Day celebrations.'

'Enough. You're right.' Charlie slapped his forehead causing his cock to bounce. Abby joined him in looking down to see if it had made a difference, but it still hung in sorrow.

Abby felt confused. 'What do you mean "I'm right about enough?"'

'Abby, listen, I'm sorry – I really am – that it has to come out like this, but it's over. I've been meaning to say this for a while now. I just can't do it anymore. I'm sorry, you're just not enough for me, and this situation just proves it.'

'What? You didn't have this problem with me yesterday.'

'Well, yesterday you made me feel good about myself. Today ...' Charlie resolutely grabbed a bag and began picking up a few of her clothes and stuffing them in a bag.

'Charlie, be serious. This isn't funny.' Abby sat up straight now, her heart pounding ten to the dozen. This situation was escalating far quicker than she could have imagined.'Look, I'm sorry about your flaccid p ...'

Charlie covered his cock. 'Don't you dare utter those words to us,' he gasped.

'OK,' Abby paused. 'Look, I'm sorry I wasn't more sympathetic; I just thought that because you haven't had this problem before, it would go away. You'll be fine tomorrow, you'll see.'

'I'll be fine tomorrow because you won't be here. It's you, I know it is. I was meaning to say it sooner.' He raked his hands through his hair.

'Charlie, don't say that. It's really mean.'

'I was just trying to wait until after Valentine's Day because I'd paid in advance for the hotel, and I wanted to see you in that lingerie I bought you. Life is so unfair. I should have just manned up and ended it before. Jack was right.'

'Jack? So, wait, you've been talking about this with your friends?'

Charlie nodded.

Abby held her hands over her heart. She couldn't

believe what she was hearing.

'And they told you to end things with me a while ago?'

'Yes, and now this,' Charlie gestured downwards, 'is blatantly a cruel act of karma for me.'

'Oh my God ...,' Abby welled up, the tears instantly spilling over and running down her cheeks. She gasped for breath.

'Charlie, I know the past six months have been a little mundane, maybe.'

'Maybe?' Charlie exclaimed. 'It's nothing like it was. We're nothing like we were.'

'I know. I feel as though you've changed in how you treat me,' Abby was honest with him.

'Well, you've changed towards me, too. All you're interested in is cleaning the apartment and staying in.'

'I was trying to make it nice for you, for us to be here, together, and you said you didn't have much money and yet you wouldn't let me pay if we went out.' Abby felt desperate. All of her good intentions were being thrown back at her.

'Well, I do have some pride, you know. It doesn't matter anymore now, anyway, not after this.' He slung the bag of her things on to the bed.

'Of course it matters, Charlie. You're all that matters to me. How can you be saying this so callously?'

'Enough. I just need you to be on board with this. Honestly, Abby, I can't do this anymore.'

His cock leapt up immediately. 'See! I'm being honest again and my little buddy is already responding.' He gestured at the proof.

'But Charlie, I love you. Our future together, this is just a blip. Look, we can work at this.' She sat up straight in bed.

Charlie shook his head resolutely. 'It's all about priorities, Abby. My little fella comes first now, and I have to take care of his needs.'

'But we're in love,' she pleaded.

'No, you are.' His cock drooped. 'Abby, you need to leave. Your emotions are radiating their way over here and affecting me.'

Tears rolled down Abby's cheeks. 'Charlie, you're saying some really hurtful things here, but I'm going to put it down to the stress of this,' she pointed her finger to his manhood, and he leapt back.

'Abby you need to go.'

Abby shook her head defiantly. 'No, we need to talk,' and she tried to glean some more information on what she thought had been a lasting relationship: 'What did you say to Jack?'

Charlie stopped and stared at her. She covered herself up with the duvet.

'My mind is made up, Abby.'

'But I'm cooking tomorrow, the chicken's in the fridge,' Abby reasoned, pitifully.

'Well, of course you must take it with you. Wait here.'

Charlie disappeared and came running back with the uncooked chicken. Abby blinked. Holding it just above his privates made the bird look well hung. If he got a hard on now, holding a dead bird instead of her, what would that mean? He did love chicken, but that would be going too far. Every time he breathed, it moved up and down slightly under the bird.

He followed her stare and yelped, 'I said don't look at me!' As if her gaze was toxic, he moved the chicken lower to cover up himself up.

'Charlie, seriously, I can't help it; you've got your

schlong on my M&S chicken. It's free range, but I don't think it's that liberal.'

'Oh fine, I brought it in for you to take, anyway.' He threw the chicken across the bed for her to catch.

'Charlie, I'm not leaving you. I love you! We belong together, like you said in the card.' Abby said stubbornly, holding on to the chicken.

'Oh that, I copied that from a song on the radio.'

'Charlie! We need to work at us, make *us* better.'

'You're not enough for me, Abby, you haven't been for a long time. Great at the start, but not so much now. I'm not really quite sure when it changed ...'

'Charlie, please.' Abby was sobbing now, trying to juggle the chicken and a tissue to wipe her tears away. He was her world. 'You can't possibly mean this.'

Charlie finally came round to her side of the bed. 'Look, I'm sorry.' He stroked her hair out of her face. She moved to hold him, but he held her back at arm's length. 'No, you hold the chicken.'

She nodded and clamped her arms around it.

'Abby.' He was whispering now, 'Some people trust their gut, but, Abby, I've got to trust my little fella on this one. He's never steered me wrong before.' He pulled out a pair of her old pyjama bottoms from her bedside drawer and handed them to her. 'Let me help you put these on.'

Abby in silent shock, nodded, forced herself to get up from the bed and tugged them on. Tears choking her, she clutched the chicken and let him guide her to the front door of the apartment where he handed her her bag of clothes.

'Enjoy the chicken, Abby.'

Those were the last words she remembered him

saying as he closed the apartment door behind her, and she stood in the dark of the hallway, the sigh of relief she heard him exhale after the door closed sliced her heart in two.

*****

ONE HOUR LATER, she'd made it back to her apartment and was sitting at the table in her kitchen, watching her two best friends, who were normally the epitome of calm, stride around in fury at what she was telling them. Her house mate, Woody, had called her best friend, Lucy, straight over for backup.

'"His little fella's never steered him wrong"? It's got to be hard to steer anything at all. I sincerely hope you pointed that out to him, Abby!' Lucy's bone china complexion flushed with pink rage at Charlie's manner.

Abby shook her head feebly. She felt like a wilted plant.

'Seriously, Abby, what's happened to you?' Woody's voice got seriously deep when he was angry, which wasn't often.

'The old you would be spitting bullets at this,' Lucy reprimanded her.

'Lucy, he said I'm not good enough. He was the one! I had everything, and now I've lost it by trying too hard. I've somehow ruined my life whilst trying to make it perfect.' Lucy and Woody looked at her, utterly aghast. She avoided meeting their eyes.

'Abby! He is a complete dick, with a dick that doesn't work!' Woody exclaimed, fiercely protective of her. 'Look at how many women I date, and I don't take any of them for granted the way that he's done with you.' Lucy nodded.

'Although, to take someone for granted generally requires staying with them for longer than two weeks, Mr Woods.' Lucy pointed out.

'Well, either way, it works. No one's confused or crying.' He justified his behaviour. Abby stared at them, her eyes welling up again. How could this be happening? They'd made so many plans together.

'Abby,' Lucy cut in. 'What has he done to you? You'd never let anyone treat you like this before. And what's with this chicken?' Lucy nodded at the chicken on the table. 'Shouldn't it be in the fridge?'

'It probably should. He gave me it to bring home.'

'What?' Lucy and Woody simultaneously raised their eyebrows.

'Abby, literally nothing about this story makes any sense,' Lucy sighed.

'So your ex gave you a chicken to pacify you after dumping you?' Woody was aghast. 'I don't give women anything when I dump them. I've got to ask: is that what you want?' Lucy thwacked him over the head.

'Ouch! What? It's an honest question!' he exclaimed.

Abby stepped in. 'No, you guys, I was supposed to cook it for us tomorrow.'

Woody picked up the chicken. 'Bizarre how out of everything you have there, he thought of this,' he mused.

'Well, he used it to stop me looking at his cock for a while ...'

'This bird has had another man's cock on it?' Woody dropped it immediately.

'That poor chicken.' Lucy stared at it as though it had been abused, which upon reflection, Abby decided, it probably had.

'Well, it's going in the bin. I can't believe you brought

that home on the Tube.'

'I know, there was a woman sitting opposite me on the train giving me death stares the whole journey home.'

'Probably a vegan.'

Abby nodded at Woody's thinking.

'She made me feel even worse. Is that what I do, make people feel bad?' Tears rolled down her face again at the notion.

'Not at all,' Lucy grabbed her hand and held it tightly. 'Abby, you're normally the life and soul of the party. Apart from the past six months of being with him, you're happy ...'

'You're reasonably funny,' Woody proffered. 'For a girl.'

Lucy continued, 'You're there for people, you have a ton of friends, everyone loves you.'

'Then why did he say he wasn't in love with me anymore? How am I not enough?' She was desperate to know so she could fix this.

'Did you ever consider that maybe he's not The One?' Lucy said quietly.

'No, not at all, Luce. I love him. I'm just going to speak to him tomorrow, let him calm down. I can fix this.'

'I hate to break it to you, Abby, but you can only work at a relationship if he wants to, too, and speaking honestly, as a guy,' Woody softened his voice, acutely aware that his words may hurt her, 'it genuinely doesn't sound as though he wants to.'

Lucy nodded in agreement.

'Yeah, Woody's uncharacteristically right. One person can't sustain a relationship, and if you're honest with yourself, you'll admit that you've been carrying Charlie for a while now.'

'No, Luce, he'll message me back soon. I'm sure of it,' she sat up straight in the chair, feeling more certain. Even if he had been having doubts and talking to his friends about it, at some point, he would realise he needed to talk to her. She smiled. 'He's just freaking out after the issue in the bedroom; I'm sure you can understand that.'

Woody looked away, which she chose to ignore. She just needed to give Charlie a bit of time and reassurance that she was the one and there for him. This was just a blip. She looked at both of their faces, intently gazing back at her. Suddenly, she felt exhausted. 'You guys, thank you so much for being here, but honestly right now, I think I need to go to bed.'

'Have a bath and relax before you do,' Woody suggested kindly.

'Come here you,' Lucy pulled her into a hug. 'It's going to be alright, you know. Work will take your mind off it.'

Abby nodded. She'd forgotten all about work – and that it was even Sunday.

'Call me if you want anything, and I'll come straight over.'

'Thank you, Luce,' she looked into the eyes of her oldest friend. 'Don't know what I'd do without you.'

'Well, you don't have to worry about that. Just go and get some rest – you look beat.'

'Yeah, the sooner I sleep, the sooner I can wake up and speak to Charlie about sorting this all out. What a mess!' Trying to ignore the look that passed between Woody and Lucy, she moved towards her bedroom. Gosh, she needed to sleep.

2

WHO WOULDN'T WANT A 'NOAH'?

ABBY ROLLED OVER and pulled the duvet up and over her head in an attempt to block out the workmen banging around outside. It was weird, she could have sworn that one of them had used her name. Curiosity got the better of her, and she tossed the duvet off to listen closely. Heck, the banging wasn't coming from outside, it was coming from her bedroom door.

'Abby, will you get out of bed and let us in?' Lucy sounded vexed.

'Luce, if you're my friend, you'll just leave me alone.' Stuffing her head back under her pillow, Abby tried to block out Lucy's voice.

'Come on, Abs!' the deep tone of Woody's voice sounded out. 'I need my flatmate back.'

'Come on, Abby, please let me be there for you,' she heard Lucy sigh.

She groaned; Lucy's bossy tone did have a tinge of desperation to it, and she didn't want her to worry.

'We're not leaving you in there any longer, Abby. It's time to join the real world.' Even Woody was getting bossy now, too.

'No!' she called out. Staring up at the ceiling again, she knew every millimetre of it by now.

'Sod it, Woody, she's not listening to us.' Lucy's decisive voice was getting louder now. 'Come on, man up and push harder! We must be able to get in.'

'Perhaps she's locked it,' Woody gasped, obviously straining against the door.

'No chance,' Lucy proclaimed. 'She couldn't find the key to lock it.'

'Hey!' Abby called out. Harsh, but probably true.

'Let's push together; it's just her stuff,' Lucy said resolutely.

Abby looked at the pile of clothes and clutter surrounding the door – *good luck,* she thought; it was normally chaotic, to say the least, but now it resembled a war zone. Apart from signing for takeaways, the boxes of which were also propped against the door and scattered around the room, she'd been doing everything in her ensuite. Entering and exiting the room had become a mission in itself.

It had been two days since Charlie had told her that he didn't love her anymore. Two days after the world she had become accustomed to had stopped turning. Lying motionless in bed, she knew that her inability to leave her bedroom was insane, but it was as though her entire body had gone into shutdown; everything about her high energy and enthusiasm for life had just been sucker-punched out of her.

'Guys, seriously, I'm fine. It's not like I'm hurting anyone by being in here. Just let me be!'

'No chance! It's time to rejoin the land of the living,' Woody yelled back.

'One, two, three …,' they both cried in unison before spilling into her room.

Through the dust-filled gloom, she saw Lucy steadying

herself as she almost lost her footing on a pizza box then wrinkle her nose and sniff: 'What is that?'

'You see, it's safer for me to remain lying down,' Abby said.

Woody was clambering over her stuff to get to the window. 'Ergh, gross! Lucy, can you turn on the light please?'

The room was instantly illuminated.

'Nooo!' she moaned, pulling the duvet over her head in shame. She heard Lucy's muffled intake of breath.

'Go away!' she begged feebly, kicking the bottom of her duvet.

Lucy made it over to her, failing miserably to conceal her shock at her appearance. Tears welled up in Lucy's eyes: 'Look how he's left you.'

'You're meant to pretend that I still look great despite eating all of this takeaway.'

She'd noticed her rather grey pallor the other day but was helpless to change it.

'Come on, Abfab, we need to get you up. Woody, let's go and hang in the kitchen.'

'Yes to the kitchen and life beyond the cave,' Woody agreed.

'No,' Abby murmured.

Woody and Lucy paused. 'What's wrong with moving?' Lucy asked gently.

She covered her face with her hands: 'I can't explain it, Luce.'

'Well, please try, so we can help you,' Lucy pleaded.

Abby paused, why didn't she want to leave her room? 'Honestly, Luce, I don't know how to deal with this. And if I leave my room, then I'll have to.'

Lucy nodded.

'It's like time stands still in here. Every hour that goes by, I think it's getting closer to the time when he'll realise he's made a huge mistake and that I'm the girl for him.'

Lucy bit her lip.

'He told me that I wasn't enough for him, Luce. How can that be?' she dissolved. 'I did everything for him.' Tears rolled down her face, and she felt herself being pulled into a massive hug. She let herself sob.

'Look, Abby, time might feel as though it's standing still in your room, but it isn't.' Lucy's tone was softer now. 'How do you think we knew to come today?'

She shook her head. She actually had no idea.

'Your boss called Alice, and she called me straight away. She's really worried.'

'Why would my boss call my mum?' she said indignantly.

Lucy looked at Woody.

'Because it's been a week since you last went to work.'

'What?' She was shocked. 'A whole week?'

'Yes.'

'He thought you'd been in an accident because you didn't call in. He was worried, he called your mum, your mum called me.' Lucy said, concern etched on her face.

She nodded guiltily, seeing the double figure of missed calls – from everyone but the one person she wanted to speak to.

'And there's been some serious miscommunication on our parts, too. I just thought you were really busy and dealing with breaking up with Charlie in your own usual way. So I've left you to it. A mistake which I ...,' Lucy trailed off.

'Luce, it's not your fault. Gosh, the last thing I want is for you to feel bad.'

'I've never seen you this low.'

Abby nodded slowly, her friend's words starting to fade into the background. A whole week off? She'd thought it was just two days. How worrying was that? 'Do I even have a job anymore?' she whispered.

'You do, but you're going to need to go to it. We'll find out what your mum blagged for you, so your story is straight,' Lucy assured her.

'Really a week?' she asked, still incredulous.

Behind Lucy, Woody was looking all around him. 'What is that noise?' He asked with hands on hips – it was clearly bugging him. The repetitive strains of the menu page of the DVD she had inserted was playing over and over again in 12-second loops. His frown deepened as he realised what it was. He looked horrified.

'*The Notebook*'? Seriously? Look you're not going to find your Noah in here. Oh my goodness, I've got to turn this off,' he grappled around the clothes-strewn room, located the laptop and perched precariously on the mountain of clothes covering her chair.

'Right, that's it, Abby. This has got to change,' Lucy said. 'Just sitting at home and doing your normal break-up process when *you've* dumped *them* is not working this time round. The hurt is too severe. One week of *The Notebook* and you're still a blubbering mess.'

'But I like existing in a world where a guy can row me to a lake filled with ducks or geese or whatever they are. It's beautiful …,' she blew her nose loudly. 'Although, all the Noah's I found on Facebook looked as though they were already happily married, which makes sense, I suppose.'

Lucy was aghast. 'It *is* a beautiful movie, but if you're searching Facebook for Noahs then it's definitely not helping. So, Woody, you know what to do ...'

'Don't worry, this is being confiscated,' he held the DVD away from him as if he was in danger of catching feelings by having it any closer. Abby yelped.

'No!' Lucy held her back. 'Abby, I know it's the hardest thing to lose someone you've loved.'

'It wasn't like he was just any boyfriend, Lucy – I adored him. I wanted to marry him and make a life with him. He's the only man I want to have babies with.'

Woody sneezed loudly, interrupting her. He rubbed his nose before clambering up and opening the curtains, causing the dust in the room to circulate rapidly. He sneezed again. Huffing and puffing to push the window open, he finally managed it and collapsed back on the chair, panting.

'Well, you can't stay in here. None of us can,' he sneezed again.

Grateful for the distraction, Lucy nodded her agreement. 'Time to put the kettle on, Woodster,' she smiled.

'My pleasure, ladies,' he stumbled out of the room.

'Luce,' Abby whispered, moving slowly. Taking the first step out of her room meant acknowledging this situation was real. She'd lost the man she loved. It felt like a death she had to mourn, and yet he was still walking the face of the planet ... just not with her. She gasped, instantly feeling the warm arms of her oldest friend around her, drawing her in.

She let the warmth seep into her: 'I've needed this.'

'I'm so sorry I didn't come around earlier. I feel awful – I was just trying to give you some space.'

'Why would I need space from you, Luce?'

'Well, you know my opinion of Charlie.'

She sighed. Lucy had been quite upfront and frank about her feelings for Charlie.

'There was something about him that just didn't resonate well with me. But that doesn't mean that I don't care about how you feel to have lost him.'

'Look, Lucy, listen to me. You've been my best friend since pre-school.' It was true, ever since Amber Goldman had wrenched Abby's doll from her, and Lucy had practically grappled Amber to get it back, they had an unwritten vow to remain friends forever.

'You're here now and getting here any sooner wouldn't have changed anything. I feel exhausted; my brain feels like a fog, and the only thing I can honestly think of is the moment he dumped me. It's the worst Groundhog Day ever.'

Lucy looked at her resolutely, 'Well, come on then, let's go and have a cup of tea and begin to sort this out.'

She nodded, not arguing. Firm but kind, Lucy was usually right. She followed her out into the kitchen.

Safely ensconced on a chair, she gratefully took the cup of tea Woody handed her.

'Well, I think it's safe to say that I've been dumped for the first time,' she managed weakly.

'Yes, my lovely, you have,' Woody confirmed.

'How ironic that the one guy I want to spend my life with is the one guy that dumps me,' she tried to joke.

Lucy and Woody both remained silent.

'This sucks,' Abby concluded.

'Yes, it does,' Woody concurred.

'People always say that time's a good healer, but I'm just sitting here feeling worse with every hour I'm not with him. Honestly, it was music to my ears hearing how much he loved me whilst being spoilt rotten on

Valentine's Day. Then the next day ...,' she paused.

'Bastard. What a way to do things. Why lie to you the day before? It's just setting you up for an even bigger fall,' Woody fumed.

'I'm still furious, Abby, why aren't you mad at him?' Lucy demanded. Woody nodded.

'Me too, and quite frankly, Abby,' Woody ventured, 'We never thought Charlie was the one for you.'

'What?' She was shocked. They knew her better than anyone. 'Well, I know you didn't like him towards the end, but ...'

'No, I never really felt like he was really that into you,' Woody said, matter of factly.

'How can you say that? He was so well mannered and considerate.'

'No, he was at the start. That all vanished when he knew he had you.'

She remained silent. Woody continued. 'Look, Abby, you're a hot catch. You know, when you're not looking like this,' he gestured at her face. Normally a sunny fresh smile rested on her lips and her blue eyes sparkled with cheeky cheer, framed by her long brown hair that bounced around as she laughed. Her size-eight figure was still intact, but her eyes felt strange, all puffed up and swollen. She didn't even want to touch her greasy hair, and God only knew there was certainly no smile on her chapped lips. Oh dear, she hadn't really looked in a mirror in the last week.

'I think he saw you as a challenge, thought here's a super-fit woman who's actually nice as hell, witty and intelligent, and he wanted to claim you. Kind of like a prize,' he paused and looked at Lucy who nodded for him to continue quickly.

'So, he went out of his way to make grand gestures.'

'Did he make grand gestures?' Abby rubbed her forehead, casting her mind back to the start. It had been gloriously romantic. 'Paris,' she whispered.

'Because ...?' Woody prompted her gently.

'For our one-month anniversary.'

He raised his eyebrows.

'Oh, come on, Woody, men do romantic things when they fall in love, too, or are you saying the whole relationship was a lie?'

'Look, Abby, let me explain,' Woody said, in his nicest voice, 'if you put chocolate on a plate, you're going to eat it, aren't you?'

'Yes,' she said weakly. 'I love chocolate.'

Woody nodded. 'So, if you turn up wanting to cook for him, looking the best you've ever looked and are willing to make every effort to make his life exactly how he likes it, rounded off with sex on tap, well, I don't think even the strongest man in the world could turn that down. We're simple creatures. Please ...'

He didn't need to finish. She knew what he was going to say: 'Please don't end up like the girls that I pull.'

Stark honesty from Mr Woods.

Lucy nodded her approval at what he was saying, 'He hasn't been man enough to walk away from you, so he's been treating you like rubbish for months in the hope you'll do the dirty work and dump him. You haven't, so he's finally had to.'

Abby sagged and put her mug on the table, silent tears running down her face. She saw Woody's face darken. He hung his head then, without warning, slammed his fists on the table. Both her and Lucy jumped. It was totally out of character.

'Tell you what, Abby, I wish you could be in my head right now. Then you'd get over him pretty quickly.'

'Get over him?'

'Yes, well, that's what you need to do,' Woody stated.

'Abby, he's broken up with you. He's ended it,' Lucy confirmed.

She looked up at her friends; they were talking as if it was completely over. Of course, it couldn't be – she and Charlie had been in each other's pockets for a year, you couldn't just go from that to nothing. Her chest seized up, 'I can't let myself believe it's over.'

Lucy spoke tentatively, 'I, for one, am sorry that things changed with Charlie. I'm sorry that you're still hurting about it. But, from my point of view, I'm so glad you won't be with him because you weren't yourself when you were.'

Woody took over, 'Yes, you've spent so much time trying to be what you think he wants you to be that you've forgotten to be yourself.'

'So, are you saying that if I can be sparkling Abby again, he'll love me, again?'

'No!' Lucy glared at Woody.

'No, definitely not.' Lucy spoke clearly, 'Why would you want him to love you again? Look what his version of love did to you ... he used you. He sucked all of your positivity out of you ...'

'Charlie's a dementor,' Woody registered excitedly. He knew it would resonate with Abby, a diehard Potter fan. Abby caught her breath, Lucy carried on quickly.

'Yes, Woody, he's much like a dementor, but as I was saying Abby, he's left you empty whilst his confidence rose and rose, and then when you had nothing left to offer him, he got rid of you. And yet *he* was the one that made you that way.'

Abby shook her head in dissent.

'He did,' Lucy proclaimed. 'It was awful to watch. I tried telling you but ...'

'I really thought he got me ...'

'Yes, but he used that knowledge against you. It didn't transpire into anything real when you eventually had to deal with everyday life did it? Did he share the laundry or sort out the bills? It's all boring, but it's all stuff that needs to be done, and he didn't help you with it at all. He left you to deal with everything on your own. And then to top it off, he'd talk you down if you didn't do it all exactly how he wanted it. Heaven forbid he got up off his arse to do it himself ...'

Abby dissolved, feeling the tears running down her face, 'I knew it was changing – it felt different, but I just thought that if I was the most perfect lady for him, if I made his life easier and took the stress away from him then maybe he'd love me the way he used to. You know? And things would go back to the way they were at the start.'

'All he did was give you the maximum to get you, and the bare minimum to keep you. You should feel disgusted by that and make a decision to want more for yourself. You deserve more.' Lucy's eyes bored straight into hers. She knew she had nowhere to hide. 'You *have* to go back to work next week. Life goes on, and you don't want to be destitute because of this.'

'But I'd planned out my life with him. Now I've got to start from scratch again and I just ...'

'... don't know where to start?' Lucy paused, her lips moving into a wide smile.

'*How* can you possibly look relieved at that?' Abby

was incredulous.

'Because *finally* I know what to do,' Lucy jumped up, reached into her bag for her notepad and flicked straight to the section marked 'Abby.' 'You need a plan. And we both know that I'm the best planner in the universe.'

Woody nodded. As frustrating as her organising could be, Lucy did have a knack of pulling things off in a legendary fashion.

'How on earth can you plan me out of this mess?' Abby said dejectedly, unable to remember a time when she didn't feel like her whole brain had been ditched on the side of a road.

Lucy looked determined, already scribbling down and blitzing a number of ideas. 'By having your very own "Getting-over-Charlie" plan.' She held up the page for Abby to see.

'Should I feel embarrassed or privileged that you have a whole section in your notepad about me?'

'Of course, the latter. You, my friend, take a whole lot of organising, but believe you me, it's happening.'

'The freight train has left the station,' Woody nodded.

'Right, step one. Contact.'

Abby's eyebrow raised.

'Hand me your phone,' Lucy demanded.

'Why would I do that?'

'Because I want to block him on your Facebook. Have you been using it to stalk him?'

Abby looked horrified.

'So, that's a yes.'

She stopped breathing as she contemplated what Lucy was asking of her. She had been checking his social media every hour for signs of him missing her. The thought of not being able to do so ...

'OK, OK,' Lucy backtracked. 'Take a breath. So maybe not block him just yet.'

Abby shook her head. 'I just can't do that right now, Luce.'

'Have you been messaging him?'

'Not if you don't count the texts, calls, messenger ...,' she tailed off, looking at their faces. Probably best not to mention WhatsApp, tweets or the comments she'd been leaving on their Instagrams together. All positive ones, borne of love, of course.

'But I've spoken to him every day for a year and a half. How can I just quit that cold turkey?'

'Has he replied?' asked Woody.

'No,' she shook her head.

'Well then, *he's* managed to quit *you* cold turkey.'

She chose to ignore Woody's comment. 'It's ridiculously hard. You can't go from being in love and present in each other's lives to suddenly being apart. It's like quitting smoking.' She exhaled. 'Gosh, it sounds so casual when people say they've 'broken up,' yet it really doesn't explain the heartache of it all it, does it? I mean it's a whole mental battle in itself.'

'Abbster, will you promise me you'll at least try not to message him as much?'

'I'll try, Luce. I promise I'll try.' Actually, she should tone it down because he might get fed up and block her, which would be horrific. 'What do I need to do next?'

'Well, before we can do anything in the real world, you need a shower.'

Lucy stood up and gestured for Abby to follow her to the bathroom. Grabbing a fresh towel from the linen cupboard, Lucy hung it on the rail and turned the water on as Abby started to peel off her pyjamas.

'See you in a bit, beautiful,' Lucy smiled and left her to it.

Letting the water drift over her felt good. How long had it been since she'd even done this?

She still looked pale and drawn, though, wiping the mirror of its steam, surveying herself when she finally stepped out of the shower.

She had bags under her eyes – that had never happened before. How on earth do you cover those up? Trying to pat and flatten the inflamed skin did nothing.

Throwing fresh pyjamas on, she took a deep breath and walked out of the bathroom into her bedroom, which was now dimly lit with a few scented candles. Her bed was remade, and the washing machine was on. She was beginning to see glimpses of floor space and carpet, which she now remembered was pale green. Woody and Lucy were busy giving it a quick dust around. She smiled, something she hadn't done in a week.

'Wow.' Woody and Lucy turned to her. 'Gosh, how long was I in there?' gesturing to all their hard work.

Woody grinned, 'This is the one and only time I'm helping you out like this in your cave.'

She nodded, 'Fair enough, Woodster.' He moved over and gave her a gigantic hug, which Lucy joined in on.

'Thank you! I love you both so much,' she whispered.

'Just be happy Abby again. I know it's going to take a while, but you look like you're out of the shock now.' They wandered back into the kitchen.

'Wine?' Woody offered, waving a bottle of red.

'Yes!' Abby grinned. 'The shock has passed. I mean who dumps me, hey?' She said carefully, trying to joke. Still feeling quite weak, she held out her hand for the large glass of wine. As she took a tentative sip, her face turned serious again: 'Right you've got to help me – I've never had bags under my eyes before, what on earth do I do? Will they stay like this forever? They look even worse after the shower.'

Lucy pursed her lips, 'The steam must have made them swell up even more. Item one on your list is getting you looking like your normal gorgeous self again, so go and lie down on the couch. Woody do we have a cucumber?'

'No, we have a tomato. Half on each eye?'

'No chance!' Lucy vetoed it straight away.

'What about a tea bag?' Woody pulled a pack out of the cupboard.

'Mmmm, no, they're not a good brand.'

'Seriously, Lucy?' Woody paused. 'Ah, hang on a minute,' he bounded up the stairs to his room on the mezzanine area and came running back down, moments after thumping around. 'I forgot I had this,' he said, dropping a small tube of haemorrhoid cream into Abby's lap.

'Eewww,' said Lucy and Abby simultaneously. 'Gross!'

'No, it's not what you think – you use it around your eyes,' he dropped to a whisper: 'Bags run in my family; they're hereditary. This works perfectly every time.'

'Can we Google it to make sure this isn't the grossest stitch up of all time? The last thing I need right now is pink eye.'

'I'm on it,' said Lucy grabbing her phone. 'It's kosher,' Lucy proclaimed. 'You really are the definition of metrosexual, Woodster. Right, how much does she need of this?'

'OK, not too much, and pat it in to stimulate the lymph nodes. Don't use too much and whatever you do, don't get it in your eyes!' Woody directed.

'I'm going to do it for you,' Lucy said, grabbing the tube.

'Oh goodness, this wasn't even in the plan, was it?'

'Looking good is.' And in her most commanding voice, Lucy said: 'Lie back and prepare to be bum creamed up to the max!'

'Well, Luce, that's the voice that tells me you're a firecracker in bed.'

'You betcha,' she winked and got to work.

Woody coughed, 'I'm just going to pour some more wine.'

Ten minutes later, with a glass of wine in hand, Abby sat up.

'So, what's next in the breakup cycle? You said there were stages.'

'Ah, yes. OK, so you've already done the standard ones,' she got out her pen to tick the list off. 'You've cried so hard you needed rectum cream, watched *The Notebook* at least once and searched for potential Noah's on Facebook, your hair was freshly trimmed and it's amazing, so I'm not letting you chop it up, and you already own enough shoes to shoe a small school. So, the next thing to do is ... and it's a big one.'

'Go out, get drunk and snog someone?'

'Well, I don't think you necessarily need to snog someone as we're not seventeen anymore, however, yes, maintaining a general positive attitude.'

'It doesn't say that – give it here!' Abby launched for the book.

'I'm going to release the stages to you one-by-one, otherwise you'll stress out about them.'

Lucy said holding it out of Abby's reach. She kept reading. 'You must go to work.'

Abby raised her eyebrows, 'Yadda yadda yadda and ... you must go out and talk to other guys on Friday night. Or Saturday if Lucy already has plans for Friday,' she quickly added in.

'You have plans without me?' Abby mocked.

'Sometimes that happens – doesn't mean I don't love you, though,' Lucy winked apologetically.

'I don't know, Luce.'

'Now you don't need to go out to find guys, I just want you to go to a bar.'

'... of my choice,' Woody interjected.

'OK, of Woody's choice and just relax in society again. It's been ages since we just went out.'

Abby nodded slowly, 'In a week's time?'

'Yes.'

'I'll pick somewhere beautiful, my lovely,' Woody assured her.

'OK. I guess if you're in charge of my decisions with this list for the moment, I can't really say no, can I?'

Lucy and Woody smiled back at her.

'It begins,' they said in unison.

*****

ALONE IN BED, she dialled the house phone and her dad called 'Alice' the moment he knew it was her: 'I love you, Abby. Here's your mum to sort you out.' He passed her straight over and she felt instantly hugged by the warm sound of her mother's voice. She had obviously been waiting for the call, and Abby felt a tinge of guilt that she hadn't done it sooner.

'Don't worry, dear. I know what it's like to not have the energy to even know what to say.'

'This is awful, Mum. It's been a week, and he hasn't even called me back.'

'Well, he did say that it was over, sweetheart. Maybe he really meant it.'

Abby paused, 'Did you think that he was withdrawing from me? Was it visible?'

'My dear, when you came to stay a month ago, you looked like a couple on the rocks. You were exhausted, trying to make everything just so perfect for him whilst he did next to nothing, and it takes two people to save a relationship.'

'But how, how, how did it get so wrong? How has he slipped through my fingers? I don't understand what's changed.'

'Well, he knew he had you, didn't he? He bossed you around because he knew that you adored him, and he took advantage of it. That doesn't make him a nice person in my book.'

'Lucy reckons him breaking up with me is the kindest thing he's done in ages, but ...'

'I agree with her.'

'How can you say that, Mum? I'm utterly devastated. I feel as though someone's died.'

'Abby, as your mother, I want to see you with someone that adores you, that would never talk down to you or treat you badly. You're so beautiful.'

'Oh gosh, Mum, if you could see me right now, you wouldn't say that.' She filled her in on the bum-cream incident. Alice laughed.

'Lucy and Woody have sorted me out.'

'They're amazing friends, dear. I feel so much better knowing that you're in their safe hands.'

'Lucy's got a plan, Mum.'

'Yes, she called me up while you were in the shower. I think it's a wonderful idea.'

'I think she wants me to go out and meet other guys, but all I can think about is Charlie.'

'It's not about moving on to someone else. It's about showing you what's out there and giving you a chance to remember who you are in the process.'

'I know who I am.'

'Really? When was the last time you went for brunch with your friends? Or phoned me up happy because you'd had a really great find at Brick Lane market? You've been so consumed in trying to be the perfect version of what you think he wants you to be that you've lost yourself in the process. All those little things you used to do that made you bubbly and happy, you just don't do anymore. Someone has to love you for who you are, not who you break yourself to be, my dear.'

'But I don't want anyone else, Mum. I only want him. I don't understand.' Her voice crumbled. Alice held her breath, knowing full well that her daughter, who had sailed fairly blissfully through life, was now coming up against a big stumbling block. Rejection.

'No-one warned me I might fall in love and that the guy wouldn't love me back. I just took it for granted that ...,' Abby's whisper faded out.

'... that he would. Yes, I know. But we didn't say anything because it's a life lesson that you have to learn, and we were hoping that you wouldn't have to go through this.'

Abby was silent. Processing it all.

'Are you in bed, Abby?'

'Yes, Mum.'

'What I want you to realise, my dear – and really

think on this as you drift off to sleep – is that there are many different kinds of love in this world. Love doesn't need to just come from one person; the media and films try to make you think that that's the only way you get it. Love from me and your father, love from your friends to name just two types of the unconditional kind. I know you want someone special in your life, but right now, you've two people in the next room that think the world of you. You're so fortunate, and you're going to have to train your mind to focus on these good things. Fall asleep thinking of their smiling faces and of me giving you a gigantic hug.'

'I do feel loved, Mum, thank you. I love you, too,' Abby whispered.

'That's my girl. Now, sleep well ...'

3

IF YOU COULD BOTTLE ATTRACTION...

ABBY AWOKE IN her room. Rolling over, she remembered Lucy's plan from the day before and instantly felt sick. An involuntary shiver overtook her body at the mere thought of going on a date with someone else, or worse, that Charlie could be.

Ugh. She brushed the thought out of her mind straightaway. Hearing a clatter in the kitchen, she remembered that she had a flatmate who would probably make her laugh. Not trusting her legs too much – her whole body still felt shaky – she walked slowly into the kitchen and looked at Woody, who was standing, stock still, eyebrow raised, staring at the coffee pot.

'Woody, are you alright?'

He visibly jumped, startled to hear her behind him, and said quickly, 'Yes.' He paused whilst Abby stared at him, cocking her head slightly, wondering what he'd been thinking about.

As if reading her mind, he said, 'Well, actually, I was just wondering about the lasting effects of caffeine.'

'Right,' Abby nodded slowly.

'No, seriously,' he nodded fervently. 'Who knows what it might do to you.'

'And you've just suddenly wondered this after all

these years of drinking it?'

'Yes.'

'After filling an entire cafetiere?'

'Oh, yes,' Woody nodded seriously.

'OK,' Abby said slowly, aware she'd never seen Woody ever look so pensive before. 'Well I need the caffeine, so if you're not having it, can I grab it, please?' That seemed to make his mind up, and he pushed the cafetiere over to her.

'How are you feeling today, sleeping beauty?'

'Well, I definitely don't think I'm that,' Abby instantly wondered if the bum cream had worked its magic or not. Woody was obviously thinking the same and was scanning her face for improvement.

'OK, so it's halfway there. Keep applying it religiously and you'll be back to my gorgeous wingman. Now if I can't have coffee, what can I have?' he mused.

Abby took her mug and sat down at the table, watching him. 'Why can't you have coffee, Woody? You're not pregnant, are you?'

'Ha ha! Er, no, it's not that,' focusing on the gap between the floor tiles, he edged his feet nervously along it, avoiding eye contact with her, the same way a child would do when they knew they'd been caught out.

As he moved past her, the air in the room was displaced and a sudden wave of heat hit her. 'Woody is the heating on permanently at the moment? I mean, I know it's only early spring, but even so, it's baking hot.' Realising how warm she really was, she tugged at the arms of the giant cardi she'd pulled on until it was lying discarded on the table. Flapping her top, she was beginning to wonder if she was going down with something. Agitated, she looked at Woody: was it just her? No, he looked red faced as well, come to think of it. As she opened her mouth to speak, Woody raised a finger. He looked pensive and she could see that he was working out the best way to say whatever was on his mind, so for once, she waited patiently for him to divulge all.

'Well, I know you've been a tad occupied lately, but ...'

Abby steeled herself for bad news; she'd never seen Woody looking this serious before. Oh God, Woody couldn't be ill – guilt started to wreak havoc with her mind as she realised how self-absorbed she'd been. She stretched out her arm in an attempt to hold his hand, trying to ignore the fact that his skin was slightly clammy.

He took a breath: 'Do you remember me saying there was a girl at work that I liked quite a while back?'

'A girl has made you ill? Oh, Woody, no.'

'No, not ill at all, why would you think that? Well, she's called Sofia, and it turns out that she likes me back.' Woody puffed his chest out slightly, 'naturally she couldn't resist the Woods.'

Abby rolled her eyes, but she was intrigued, Woody was never out of luck with the ladies, so this Sofia must be quite a girl to have him in such a spin.

'This is about a girl?' He nodded. She squeezed his hand before letting it go, sighing in relief. 'Thank God, I thought you were about to tell me that you were ill or something. So why the heating? Does she feel the cold? She can borrow something of mine to keep her warm anytime she wants,' Abby proffered straight away, relieved that he wasn't ill and that it was a solvable problem. Gosh, her thoughts really were all over the place at the moment.

'No, no, no, it's nothing like that,' Woody seemed annoyed that his train of thought had been broken.

'Oh. Sorry. Continue.'

Woody looked around the room before he spoke, fixing his eyes on anything other than hers. She knew she had a tendency to blink a lot less when she was focused, and right now, her blue eyes were piercing straight into him, probably making him slightly nervous. She looked down at her coffee instead.

Sensing that her uncharacteristic patience was going to be short lived, he started to stammer around the issue.

'It's weird, OK? Which is why I'm kind of embarrassed talking to you about it.' He finally looked at her, a fatal mistake; she trained her blue eyes on him, and he knew he had no choice but to bare all.

'Well, Sofia ...,'

Abby nodded, gritting her teeth against the 'spit it out' comment that was rising up inside her.

'... is a woman that *notices* everything.'

So, she's normal then, Abby thought to herself. She raised an eyebrow at Woody and nodded for him to keep going.

'Well, Sofia said that she was drawn to me because of my scent. She's got a heightened sense of smell, you see.' Woody's voice got a little higher, 'It's true, I've actually done some research into it.'

'It's a good compliment,' Abby shrugged, 'she likes the way you smell. That's not a problem, is it? You just need to stock up on whatever aftershave you were wearing that day. Or get a new one – what's the one by Gucci? That's insane.'

'No, not my aftershave, Abby. Sofia likes my man sweat,' Woody stood tall, proudly now, 'she digs the smell of me.'

Abby bit her lip to stop herself from grinning as Woody babbled on.

'She appreciates the way that I smell on a day-to-day basis and, here's the thing, without aftershave. It's a constant battle to get the scent just right. I'm watching what I eat and drink as it comes out of my pores.'

'Hence no coffee?'

'Hence no coffee. I want this woman, Abby. The fact that my man scent has attracted her is completely primal. It's caveman instincts; we've dropped the fake fragrance smell and gone to the core animal need of, well, me,' he pointed to his bare chest.

Abby paused, taking it all in, very conscious that as much as she'd just like to reach over, pinch him and rip the mick out of him, he was deadly serious about this, and he deserved her being a good friend after the past few weeks. 'So, what's the exact problem you're worried about? She likes you, she likes the way you smell, what's the big deal?'

'She likes the way I smell but only at certain moments. I don't want her to catch me smelling foul.'

'Why would you ever smell foul?'

Woody shook his head, exasperated that she wasn't getting it. 'Because obviously, I'm a bloke, and I sweat, and I don't want to smell bad because I've given up deodorant.'

Abby wrinkled her nose.

'... you know, to ensure that I smell as much as I can of just me. But that's stressful in itself, so now I'm sweating more because I'm worried about it smelling bad and the scent is changing. I'm so conscious of her walking by and dropping into my booth for a sneak kiss and potential grope that I want to make sure that I smell just right.'

'So, it's mind over matter, Woody, no stressful worrying about the sweat, and you'll produce eau de Woody, naturally.'

'Mmm.'

'Doesn't really explain why the heating's on.'

'Yes, it does! So that I can produce more,' Woody excitedly gestured to his clammy armpits. 'It's on so I can bottle it and take it to work and then quickly apply it under my arms throughout the day, so I'll smell like me. Disguised in a cool box obviously so that no one knows, I've thought this through. I'm not crazy!'

'Obviously not!' Abby joked, finally unable to help herself.

There was silence as Abby took in what he'd just said. If you'd have woken her up and told her that she would be having a conversation debating the merits of armpit sweat, she would never have believed it. She sighed, 'Only you could ever have this problem, Mr Woods.'

Woody grinned, making his way round to his favourite chair at the other end of the table.

'Honestly, Woody, trust you to finally fall for a woman that has an issue like this. Everyone else just likes Chanel. With the heating on constantly I'm going to boil this summer.' Woody eased on to the chair, comfortable with the conversation now he was over the worst of it. He swung back on the chair, his hands interlinked behind his head.

'Well, not necessarily. If we're going steady, we'll be having a lot more sex by then I'd imagine, and she's already told me she likes the post-coital arm pit best, so I'll just have to scoot off and bottle that.'

'Oh my God!' Abby exclaimed, slapping her hands

rapidly over her ears to protect them from hearing anymore. 'Stop looking so smug, Mr Woods!' He grinned cheekily back at her. 'If you *ever* use the phrase "post-coital" with me again, I swear I'll push you right off that chair – that's something that my gran would say.' They both cringed at the thought. Woody slammed all four chair legs to the floor again, knowing full well she'd keep her word.

'Now do you promise?'

Woody held his hands up. 'No more use of the phrase "post-coital",' he winked and quickly asked, 'Abby will you help me?'

Abby cocked her head to one side, not fully understanding what exactly she could do to help.

'Come on, you owe me for obviously being the best roommate ever. I know that you wouldn't walk away from me in my hour of need. Especially after making me watch *The Note* ... nope still can't say it without welling up.'

Abby rolled her eyes at the one film that had seemed to penetrate her flatmate's thick skin.

'OK, OK! What precisely do you envisage me doing?' Despite feeling weirded out, she was now intrigued to see what Woody smelt like.

A bead of sweat was rolling down his chest. Pausing him to stay still, she wrinkled up her nose and grabbed a spatula, flicked the bead of sweat on to it and brought it up to her nose. Woody watched and braced himself for her to leap on him or ravage him.

Abby shook her head, 'I can't smell a thing. Except maybe salt,' she wrinkled her nose again.

'Damn it! I knew I shouldn't have had the kebab last night. Look, I've been doing my research into sweat.'

Abby finally lost it and started to giggle – the image of Woody staying in to Google sweat was just too much.

'Oh, fine, forget it! Woody muttered and got up to walk away. 'I knew you wouldn't be any help.'

'Oh, come on, Woodster, that's a bit harsh. You've literally just told me that you're dating a woman who's got a sweat fetish. Imagine me saying this to you! And now, because I'm such a *good* roommate,' she said punching him lightly on the arm, 'I'm now deliberating the best ways that you can consistently produce that same sweat because we both know that its aroma changes as time progresses, and I'm concerned whether post-run sweat will smell differently to post-shag sweat.'

'Argh, that's why you're my favourite roommate!' Woody was all smiles now and swept Abby into an immediate sweaty hug.

'Eeergh!' Abby screamed and pushed him off. People often hinted that because they lived together, they might get together, but it was moments like this that, whilst knowing that she loved him to bits, he would definitely always be the big brother she'd never had.

'Maybe it's time to bottle it.'

'I can't believe you're bottling it,' she sighed.

'Well obviously I'm bottling it – I'm not stupid,' Woody said earnestly, 'that's why I need your help because I'm wasting prime sweat beads. I've learnt that I sweat mostly on my back, and I can't reach it.'

As Abby raised up her spatula and gestured for him to bring her a glass, she said, 'You owe me big time, roomy. Simple as.'

'No way, this is just payback for all the soppy movies you've made me watch that give me nightmares that one day I'm going to fall in love and only ever be with one woman for my entire life.' Woody shuddered, 'One woman. Terrifying.'

'They're romantic!'

'They're horror movies.'

'Well, either way, if this is my punishment for them, it's working. And remind me to buy a new spatula ...'

'Now, what have you been doing since you've been actually dating? Do you still spray deodorant occasionally?

'Au naturel.'

'All day?'

Woody nodded. 'You haven't noticed, though,' he looked mildly offended.

'I've been in my bedroom,' *Thank God*, Abby thought silently.

Between them, they mapped out Woody's regime and figured out that Sofia must have first been attracted to him when he had showered, deodorised and sprayed his aftershave.

'Wait, before I do this, the plans need to go on hold for a second. I need backup.'

'Oh no!'

'No one else but Lucy, I promise.'

Woody shrugged, 'Only if you think she'll be able to control herself with this,' gesturing to his sweaty torso.

'I think she'll manage just fine.' Abby said mid-dialling.

'Luce, can you get over here, ASAP?'

Obviously assuming this was a Charlie-related call, Luce said immediately 'I'm on my way.'

Thirty minutes later, the intercom buzzed. Abby, a renewed sense of energy in her veins now she'd have someone sane to laugh at Woody with, flew down the stairs to let Lucy in.

'Jeez, it's hot. Your heating bill is going to be immense.'

Handing her a spare pair of washing up gloves, she said in her best Darth-Vader voice, 'Don your gloves, the Force is strong in here.'

Lucy wrinkled her nose: 'Something's strong in here, I'll give you that. Abbs, you've seriously got to start showering regularly again.'

'Er, it's not me, thank you very much. Come upstairs and meet the sweat king. Woody,' she called out, 'Lucy's here.'

'Lucy, you made it.' Woody spread his arms out in delight as he walked out of his room, glistening with a sheen of fresh sweat from where he'd been perched on his radiator downing water and trying to sweat it out.

Lucy, her nose still wrinkled, was clearly caught between wondering what the hell was going on, feeling slightly ill and being thankful to see Abby out of her bed.

'Don't go anywhere near him,' Abby wielded the spatula at her best friend as a warning.

'Don't worry, I won't. What the heck is going on in here? Seriously what is that smell?'

'Is it not good? Have I crossed the limit?' Both girls nodded now. 'I can't smell anything anymore, you've ruined my sense of smell,' Abby said forlornly.

'Believe me, *I* can,' Lucy took charge, striding over to Woody. She whispered, 'Well, it's a little extreme, but good distraction,' winking at him before nodding back to Abby, who, despite her pale appearance and bags under her eyes, was focussing on dripping eau de Woody into a glass jam jar.

'Now, Woody, I care about what you're doing, obviously, but please shower, and Abby will fill me in.'

He nodded and went off, eager to please and get it right.

Five minutes later, he emerged. Having been briefed on the task ahead, Lucy nodded, 'Let's just get this over with.'

After three full hours of repetitive showering, shrieks and spatula scraping, enough mini bottles of eau de Woody were lining up on the kitchen counter, cooling.

Desperately needing some fresh air, Abby opened the windows whilst Lucy went off to turn the dial down on the heating.

'Hey, what's the time?' Woody called out from his bedroom, turning his radiators back down to a respectable temperature.

'It's almost five, why?'

'Well, my cousin's coming to crash tonight. I'd better shower, again.'

'Oh, you should have said. If I'd have known that Rachel was coming, I'd have baked a cake,' Abby said waving her spatula, to which Lucy raised an eyebrow. 'Alright, I'd have picked one up from M&S on the way home – but that's not to say that I can't physically bake one. It just seems rude to the bakers in the shop, you know, when they've gone to all the effort, I don't want it to go to waste.' Abby pulled it off with the face of a saint, but it wasn't fooling either of them.

The buzz of the intercom interrupted Abby's retort, and Woody moved to answer the call.

'Woody? It's Tim,' a guy's voice came over the intercom.

'Hey, bud, come on up!'

'Tim? You didn't say your cousin was a guy; I assumed it was Rachel.'

'Yes, I know,' Woody said cunningly as he pressed the unlock button.

'For God's sake, Woody, spit it out: is he hot?' Lucy was pissed off at a potentially ruined meet-cute scenario. Abby, ignoring Lucy's knowing smile that her pride for how she looked hadn't completely dissolved with the death of her relationship, dived behind the fridge door.

Tim mounted the top step into the first-floor apartment and paused. Tall with a lithe build and wide shoulders, he moved a stubborn piece of his brown hair out of his eyes, clearly surveying the scene. Well dressed and smelling of a normal man's aftershave, he made Lucy grin naturally. He was hot.

Woody, being Woody, acted as if it was completely normal to be half naked in a sauna of a room with two women wielding spatulas. He stayed focused on the task at hand and was intent on screwing on the remaining lids on the jars of his eau de Woody.

Lucy thwacked Woody firmly with her spatula.

Tim's eyebrows raised even more. Abby groaned inwardly, wishing that she had some of her old wit and charm to lean on, painfully aware that it must look like an incredibly random date or some weird initiation process they had before letting people into the flat.

Tim took a deep breath and was the first to break the silence.

'Well, ladies, you're going to have to introduce yourselves as this bugger is apparently useless at that. And thinking about it, I might need a shot to get involved with whatever's going on here. Plus is anyone else starving? I grabbed this on the way here, if anyone's game.' Tim waved their local Chinese takeout menu in the air then backed away quickly as Woody moved to hug him in his half-naked sweaty state.

'No chance, mate!' His voice had a deep well-mannered tone to it, and Abby knew, without even speaking to Lucy, that as far as she was concerned, he'd ticked off every element of their wish list.

'Eager to be included, prepared to drink if necessary and not afraid of the Chinese down the road's menu. Yes, you can enter the apartment,' Lucy smiled, holding out her Latex-clad hand before thinking the better of it and waving, 'I'm Lucy, and this is Abby.'

'Abby's my roommate,' Woody chipped in.

'I'm going to shake your hand when I've showered and please take great relief in the fact that Woody, as your cousin, can explain what's going on here. My best friend, Lucy, here will make sure that you get the whole truth and nothing but the truth.'

'Well, I think we're done now, so Tim doesn't need to be bored with that story. Ignore my flatmate,' Woody said, grabbing a towel out of the dryer and trotted past Abby to beat her to the shower.

'Leave the Chinese menu out as I'm sure these girls will indulge, I'm taking you to the pub for a catch up,' he called before slamming the bathroom door shut.

Abby rolled her eyes.

Tim chatted amiably about his job as an architect, which lit Lucy's eyes up as she was in the property business, too. Abby smiled as they discussed some incredible buildings in London that people often walked straight past on their way to the more famous sights.

'And what do you do, Abby?'

'Oh me? I'm in HR – pretty dull really,' she shrugged it off.

'Well, I don't know, you're potentially making

people's job dreams come true and ensuring the country's workforce is good. I always imagined it must be a pressured job, having to judge a person's character correctly in only a few hours.'

'Wow, I hadn't thought of it that way since I wrote my job application. You're good,' she smiled. Then instantly thought of Charlie. If Lucy and Woody were right, then she'd misjudged that one completely. She went silent.

WHEN THE LAST jam jar had been labelled and placed in the fridge. Abby and Lucy sat down quietly. Tim and Woody had long since left, and now, in the silence, Abby was aware that Lucy's eyes were looking into hers with concern again. She suddenly thought of her phone, maybe Charlie had texted her ... Sundays always used to be their cosy date day before the onslaught of another week.

'Just checking my phone.'

Lucy nodded silently, knowing that she wouldn't be able to stop her even if she wanted to. As the screen flashed up, it revealed one text from her mum, wishing her well for the week ahead.

'There's nothing.'

Trying not to show how crestfallen she felt, she worked to hold herself tall again, desperately willing herself to think of how she had laughed today instead of wondering what Charlie was up to. Could he be with another woman, curled up on his sofa watching movies? She swayed with nausea at the thought.

'Hey, you. We need to eat,' Lucy snapped her out of it, giving Abby the perfect excuse for her light-headedness. She smiled at her best friend, in all honesty, she had had a good four hours where she'd enjoyed giggling over

Woody's random antics. However, just thinking about Charlie, it was as if a dark storm suddenly hung over her head. She felt Lucy's hand squeezing hers.

'Small steps, eh?' Lucy said softly.

Abby nodded as the tears fell to the floor again. She'd only been up for a few hours, but suddenly she felt exhausted again.

'Come on. I'm going to run you a bath, help you choose what you're wearing to work tomorrow and figure out which movie we can curl up in front of. Mind if I crash here tonight?'

Abby nodded and leaned forward for a hug: 'I feel like I'm losing it, Luce. How can I feel slightly happy one moment and, the next, be in tears?'

'Because you're a passionate person, and you feel everything in this life to the fullest. So, when you're feeling low, you exert more energy to be happy, which is exhausting, and when you're finally tired, you can't fight to keep the pretence up as well.'

Abby nodded.

Lucy smiled back. 'You did genuinely laugh today, though, I saw it. A little more of that every day, and we'll get you feeling more like yourself in no time. It's all part of the plan: ensuring you have a job to go back to is next. Come on, let's figure out your story.'

4

THE IMPORTANCE OF SELF-MAINTENANCE

HAVING SERIOUS BAGS under her eyes worked in Abby's favour – they made her look quite ill as she trudged slowly through the office doors.

She kept her head down to avoid the inquisitive looks she knew her workmates would be chucking her. She'd managed to change the expression of concern on her boss's face to one of instant dismissal by babbling on about 'women's problems.' Fortunately, he was a man who had no desire to know what constituted as 'women's problems.'

Woody had been cursing the women in his team for their 'women's-problems' days off, and she was glad that she'd finally used her God-given right to that excuse.

'Honestly,' Woody had said, 'I don't have 'man problems,' and the worst part of it is that I don't even want to know what they are. You could probably take a whole year off, paid, and use that excuse, and I still wouldn't want to know.'

The week was one long battle of brutal concentration and trying to manage the high turnover of staff in the insurance company. She'd convinced her boss she was perfectly OK to work, now she just had to prove it to him – and herself – that she could make it through a normal working week. Her line manager, Claire, was the only one she'd told about Charlie, and she'd been an angel: hugging her when she needed it and taking on some of her workload to give her some space.

When Friday finally arrived, she walked home slowly with her favourite Taylor Swift playlist on repeat, choosing to believe the beautiful lyrics would pertain to her love life again one day. Unable to recount even one of the names of the people she'd hired during the week, she thought of Charlie instead. She'd drifted off several times this week during interviews, waiting impatiently for them to be over, so she could check her phone once more. Still no word from him despite her diligently messaging him every day, assuring him that she still loved him and would be there after this blip.

Finally, turning the key in her front door, she breathed a huge sigh of relief to be home and alone with her thoughts at last. After kicking off her heels, she ran a bath, adamant she should put him out of her mind, convinced she did not need to think about what he was doing on a Friday night without her. She felt sick conjuring up images of him hitting the bars, chatting up random girls.

'Come on, Abs, you need to have a positive spin on this,' deciding to give herself a pep talk as she dried off. 'The more girls he meets, the more likely he is to realise they're not you and come back.' Did she believe herself, looking in the mirror at the tired eyes staring back at her? Not really.

Feeling exhausted, she dropped back into her safe routine of ordering a takeaway, slipping into her PJs and pressing play on a movie. Losing herself in a world of dreams, she just had to believe that if she just waited long enough, Charlie would see sense and call her. She sighed. Checking her phone for the millionth time, the fatigue of a week pretending she was fine hit her, her eyes closed and her thoughts drifted away.

Waking vaguely disorientated, she heard giggles and the door slam, signalling the return of Woody and his armpit-sniffer chick; she buried her head under the duvet to block out the sounds of them enjoying each other's company and fell back into a deeper sleep.

'Abby!'

Someone yelled at her in her dream.

'Abby!'

And now she was being shaken. Opening her eyes, startled, she saw Lucy standing over her with a vexed and totally disapproving look on her pretty face.

'What's up, Luce?' Panicking, she wondered how long she'd slept: 'Shit, is it Monday? Did I sleep through the whole weekend?' Crap, she'd be fired if she was late again, especially after her less-than-mediocre performance last week.

She jumped out of bed and began looking around – what could she wear?

'Calm down, Abs,' a slightly playful smile formed on Lucy's lips as she saw Abby's state of genuine confusion. 'It's Saturday, 1:45pm.'

Abby stared blankly at her before registering she still had a whole weekend left, still had her job and still had time to relax; her eyes flitted back to the bed.

'Oh, no you don't!' Lucy, reading her mind, positioned herself between her friend and the place of hidden solace. 'You've forgotten, haven't you?' she asked reproachfully. Abby grimaced and racked her brain to work out why Lucy should be standing here, looking as if she was ready to go somewhere else. But it was no good. She had literally no idea and hung her shoulders, defeated. She hated letting Lucy down.

'Sorry, Luce, I can't remember what it was or where we're meant to be going.' Lucy was dragging her by the arm into the kitchen – why did her friend feel the need to constantly get her out of her room all of the time now? An idea popped into Abby's head: 'Ooo, I know, we're meant to be meeting Woody's armpit sniffer of the south later.'

'Oi,' the indignant sound of Woody's voice emanated from his room.

'Sorry! I'll make sure she whispers her insults next time,' Lucy jumped in to save her.

'Cheers, make sure you do!' Woody yelled back.

Bustling around with the kettle, knowing how useless Abby was until she'd had her caffeine fix in the morning, Lucy looked at the wall clock. 'Did you not get my text?' Abby shook her head.

'Well, what it said, if you had read it, was that we've got our tests this afternoon and then we're going to have something to eat before meeting Woody's armpit sniffer of the south.'

'What tests, Luce?' Abby's brow furrowed.

'Hey!' Woody yelled over her again. 'You're going to regret saying that when you meet her.'

'Why, will she sniff us?' Lucy threw back, dramatically snorting under her arms to check her aroma. Satisfied, she turned her attention back to Abby standing motionless in front of the kettle, barely blinking, waiting for it to boil.

'Seriously, Abby, it's nearly 2pm and you're still in your PJs.'

Abby shrugged, 'You know, Luce, every day you sound more and more like my mother.'

'I'll take that compliment. Come on, Abby, wake up. We're going to be late.'

Abby's eyes finally opened wide. The penny dropped, 'Oh, heck, Lucy, I'm so sorry, I completely forgot.' They always got their smear tests done together as part of a girly ritual of health, and this had been booked for a while.

'You don't say,' said Lucy with her hand mocking aghast. Abby looked at her apologetically and after taking a quick slurp, she added some cold water, downed the mug and dashed into her bedroom. Lucy liked to be composed at all times and despised being rushed or late for anything. 'Damn it, you'd think that some of me would have rubbed off on you over the years, but no ....'

'You've got two minutes to throw something on and then we're out of here,' Lucy called after her, choosing to disregard Woody's harrumph emanating again from his bedroom, followed by a 'no chance.'

Thinking, Abby stood stock still in front of her chest of drawers.

'Stop choosing panties! Lucy was beginning to get shrill now, 'it doesn't matter if they match your bra. We need to go.'

'Damn it, you know me too well,' Abby said before managing to quickly match up a set from Ultimo. She had a real issue with wearing odd underwear. After graduating uni she'd got rid of all her old panties and bras, replacing them with perfectly matching sets. It had cost her a small fortune over a few months, however, she could now no longer stand to walk around knowing that they weren't matched.

Turning away from Lucy, Abby tore off her pyjamas, slipped into her underwear and pulled on the pair of skinny jeans that Lucy was holding out impatiently, then threw on her dad's old Bowie T-shirt and leather jacket, chucking a scarf to wrap around her neck to finish it all off. Tying her long brown locks into a Kate Moss-esque bedhead ponytail, she presented herself to her best friend: 'See?' she said, even slightly shocked by herself. 'Simple! And I'm ready.'

'Miracles will never cease.'

'Again, you're just like my mum.'

'Come on!' Lucy busied her out of the room.

'Shit!' she yelled, two feet from the Tube station barriers, Lucy waiting for her on the other side.

'What?' Lucy frowned.

'Lucy' she loud-whispered, rooted to the spot, 'I haven't shaved or waxed,' Abby's eyes were wide, blood drained from her cheeks.

Lucy rolled her eyes: 'Who cares, Abby? They do this all the time. They're not even looking at your legs.'

The attendant glanced over, listening in on their conversation, and a few irritated Londoners bumped into Abby, tutting at her blocking the machine.

'No, but Luce, I don't mean my legs.'

Lucy threw her arms up. As always, she'd had hers done two days before, on her lunch break, to prepare for the occasion. 'Oh, honestly, Abby, just get through here. How bad can it really be?'

'You saw the state of my room,' Abby said in despair. This was going to be hideous. She started plotting, maybe she could borrow a pair of scissors from the receptionist and tidy up in the bathroom.

She didn't mention to Lucy just how much she had let it go, but basically since the dumping incident, it would be safe to say she had applied climbers' rules and not looked down.

'Abby, we can't be late. It's rude. Come on, let's go.'

Making her way to the escalators, Abby grimaced at her best mate and decided she couldn't back out now, so she scurried down to the platform behind Lucy.

Abby sat in silence on the train, trying to ignore Lucy staring at her crotch, probably trying to imagine how big it had got.

'Well, it can't be that bad,' she whispered, 'your crotch looks flat to me.'

'It's the denim holding it down. Lucy, my foof is so overgrown it looks like a deadly-yet-still-protected mangrove reserve in the Everglades, where no man has trodden since time began.'

'How can it be that bad? It's only been a few weeks since you had it stripped off for ...' Lucy tailed off.

'Oh, you know how quickly my hair grows,' Abby snapped back. Annoyed, she counted back the weeks it had been, and Lucy was almost right, she'd actually been due for her regular wax two weeks before Valentine's Day, so ... four weeks. A lot can happen in four weeks, she moaned to herself.

'Well, even so, you must be exaggerating,' she paused. 'Have you really done nothing to it?'

Abby groaned: 'I couldn't see the point after what happened.'

'Well, if it were me, I still wouldn't want it to get out of hand,' Lucy said primly.

Abby raised her eyebrow. 'You could have texted me to make sure that I'd read your other text properly,' she whined.

Lucy stayed silent. When Abby was in this mood, silence tended to be the best option, plus she reminded herself, Abby still hadn't had any breakfast, which wouldn't help her foul mood.

'This is going to be awful.' Four weeks of no grooming, not even shaving her legs and she was a brunette, so they were dark, dark hairs. She started to sweat, trying to breathe slowly to calm herself with the rationalisation that nine times out of ten, it was a female doctor. It'd still be mortifying, woman to woman, to show how much she had let herself go, but nowhere near as much for a guy to see her lady bits looking like that.

Dear god, she needed to get a grip, Abby thought as she followed Lucy up the familiar Clinic for Women's Health steps. Inside they both instinctively looked at the clock to check they were on time. Three precisely. Abby rolled her eyes as she saw her punctual friend's lips relax into a big smile, knowing she could relax in some weird euphoric 'on-time bliss.'

'Ooo, which magazine do you want?' Lucy asked excitedly as Abby scanned the receptionist's desk for scissors.

'Um, I don't really want to touch any of them, to be honest. Luce, what is that smile for?'

'Well, compared to last weekend, you're now out of your flat and socialising again, so I'm proud of myself for that.'

Abby raised an eyebrow and looked at the other ladies around her. 'It's hardly socialising on any normal scale, is it, Luce?'

'Well, today was kind of a bargain because I'm also giving you the gift of safe sex.'

'What?'

'They said we could have the normal smear test, or book in and have the works as a bargain, so, of course, I got us the works – we're being checked for everything.' Patting Abby's knee with glee, Lucy sat back, beaming at her friend as if she'd bought a Prada bag at Harrods and found she'd been given a free wallet as part of a one-day promotion.

'Luce, seriously, I wasn't majorly up for having my bits poked around, but I was convincing myself that it would be alright because it's fairly quick. I'm not sure I'm up to all of the crude questioning and extended STI tests.'

'Abby Richmond for Dr Bennett.' Someone looking no older than an intern poked his head into reception.

'Oh, there you go. Enjoy!' Lucy winked.

'Just because it's the most action you've got in a while,' Abby muttered back, before picking up her tote and fake smiling the intern before following through the swing doors and into the consultation room where, utter disaster, stood a ridiculously good-looking male doctor alongside a knockout blonde female nurse. *Great. That just seals the deal then*, Abby thought.

The eager-to-please intern that had called her in, clattered instruments together enthusiastically, making noise over menial tasks as Abby nodded her hello and sat quietly on a chair, praying for this to be over as soon as possible.

Her uncomfortable body language was lost on the doctor. A tall silver fox with lustfully broad shoulders, he looked as if he took style notes from George Clooney; he leant across and pumped her hand enthusiastically, speaking in a deep well-heeled voice: 'Great to have you here – and for the full works. Glad to see a woman who knows a bargain.'

'Isn't it free, anyway?' Abby said but he carried on regardless.

'I'm Dr Bennett, and this foxy delight here is Felicity and, oh, do you mind having an extra pair of eyes on you today? We've got our helpful college intern Neil to assist us and learn his way around the female genitalia.'

Neil, who on closer inspection, couldn't have been a day over seventeen, beamed back at her: 'I like your ponytail.'

'Great,' she whispered. Looking for some sympathy in the eyes of the foxy delight, Abby saw the lithe blonde staring right through her, gazing at Dr Bennett, hanging on his every word, she realised that wasn't going to happen. Were they sleeping together? Abby wondered. Ugh, they'd probably just gone for it on the bed she was about to lie on.

'So, Abby, have you had a smear test before?' She silently nodded. He flashed her a winning smile, 'We won't keep you waiting on a Saturday. We'll just leave you to it for two minutes to strip off your knickers, normal procedures apply; make yourself comfortable on the bed and pop the paper towel over you if you want.'

Abby nodded: oh, yes, she would indeed be placing that paper towel over herself, without a shadow of a doubt. As they dutifully left the room, hoicking the still-grinning Neil with them, Abby drew the curtain and breathed. She pulled her jeans and panties down. Cursing in desperation, as without the tight restrictiveness of the denim pressing them down, her pubes now automatically stood to attention as if they'd never been flattened for even a mere moment.

Damn, it was a cruel irony that she could spend a fortune and waste hours of her life trying to convince the hair on her head to have that much volume and vigour and always with half of the effect.

Rummaging in her handbag for her phone, she called Lucy, hoping she'd be in the waiting room and able to pick up. Without even waiting for her to speak when the phone was connected, Abby flooded into panic: 'Shit, Lucy, I can't go through with this. I have a proper old-school bush... wait a minute, are you laughing?' Abby stood in horror at her best friend's inability to offer sound advice for the first time ever.

'Lucy,' she snapped, 'what on earth am I going to do?'

'Well, you can't possibly cancel it now,' Lucy said, chortling.

'Why can't I?' As it dawned on Abby that was all she had to do, she heard a dull knock at the door. 'I could cancel it!' she whispered excitedly before yelling out: 'one minute' to the medical crew waiting outside.

'Don't be ridiculous, they know you're here.'

'But ...'

'I've got to go, they're calling me in.'

'No, they're not!'

'Abby, you're not meant to have phones on in here, anyway – I'm getting dirty looks. Good luck,' and Lucy ended the call.

'Oh shit! Come on, Abby, focus.' Looking down, Abby realised that even she herself couldn't navigate it, so God only knew how they were going to. Rubbing her hands together to warm them up, with the aim of them acting like primitive hair straighteners, she started to smooth down the hair herself, but it defiantly sprung straight back up. 'No,' she moaned.

There was another knock at the door, and Abby knew she couldn't put this off any longer.

'OK, I'm ready,' she called out. In despair she hopped on to the bed, grabbed the paper towel and attempted to flatten it over her private parts.

No chance. Lying flat on the bed with her slim torso, only served to exemplify the height that her foof could reach, causing the paper to rise, into a tent like structure. She groaned as Dr Bennett pulled the curtain aside, revealing all her glory to Foxy Felicity and Neil the helpful intern. There was no hiding it now, Abby thought, as she felt her body go cold and mustered yet another fake smile. Damn it, she'd always had female doctors do her smears before. Why, oh why, did she have to have a cute male one today?

Standing at the end of the bed, Felicity whipped aside the paper towel and there was a long moment of silence as they all took in Abby's foof.

'Crikey,' Dr Bennett said. Felicity simply smirked.

'No, no, actually this is good.' Dr Bennett enthusiastically rubbed his hands together before snapping on some latex gloves. He gestured to Neil, 'I'm glad you got to see one looking like this.' Neil was silent, a tad shell-shocked, he clearly hadn't imagined her to look like that.

'Now, come around here. If you ever get a situation like, this where you can't see the entrance to the patient's vagina, we simply ask her to move her ankles together, like so and press her knees apart, like so.'

He manoeuvred Abby's legs into the correct position, and she obligingly parted her legs, trying to convince her knees to relax. Dr Bennett paused and looked at her: 'Now, come on, relax and let your legs go.' She bit her lip and screamed inwardly. Her legs had started to develop a tremor from her nerves. *Come on, please just relax, then this can be over*, she whispered to herself. Both knees were shaking uncontrollably in resistance to his efforts.

The long protracted 'Ah' from Dr Bennett stopped her internal pep talk in its tracks, causing Neil to pause in his note taking. Damn it, her legs were shaking rhythmically, and the room was cold, causing all the hairs to rise. *Oh no, I've got grizzly bear legs, as well. Just when I thought the foof was bad enough.* Dr Bennett let her bristly leg go and paused, obviously considering the next course of action.

He took his eyes off Abby's foof for a moment, winked and jovially said in his best Geordie accent: 'Well, this is our Bushtucker Trial for the day.'

She gasped.

'I'm not a celeb, but can I get out of here,' Felicity bitch nurse joined in. Abby swung her face to look directly at Neil's, flashing him her 'I will kill you with the nearest instrument if you speak right now' kind of face. Fortunately for Neil, he gulped and chose to remain silent. Wise.

'I hope there aren't any giant bugs up there,' Felicity joked. Dr Bennett guffawed.

Abby gestured wide open with her arms as if to say, 'I'm right here.' Oh, dear God, this was awful. She opened her mouth to explain that she'd been dumped a few weeks ago and had seen no need for a groomed foof, but when she tried to speak, no sound came out. Abby smacked her hands over her eyes and managed to stutter: 'Can we please focus on the task at hand?' Honestly, how was she having to pull up three medical staff?

Both legs were full-on shaking now, moving independently from her body – Michael Flatley would be proud – and she had no idea how to halt them.

'I feel as though I'm Indiana Jones trying to find the entrance to the Temple of Doom.'

'It's not *that* bad,' Abby stammered.

'Why don't we use these?' Neil the helpful intern suggested, excitedly pointing to the birthing stirrups.

'Excellent thinking, dear boy. You'll make a good doctor yet.'

'Pretty obvious suggestion, I thought, Neil,' Abby muttered sarcastically as the two of them each grabbed a leg and secured them into the stirrups, which now rattled against the bed as she quivered.

'Right, now I'm getting involved,' Felicity finally spoke up, removing her heels. 'I'm going to straddle her and hold her foof apart. There's no way that you'll get the instruments in the right place if I don't.'

Climbing on to the bed and straddling Abby's chest, her perfect arse in Abby's face, she led the way for Neil to shine the light where it needed to be for Dr Bennett to do his job.

'What a blinding team exercise,' Dr Bennett enthusiastically exclaimed.

Mortified, refusing to watch, Abby covered her eyes with her hands once more whilst her legs continued to jiggle around.

'Just to clarify, it'll just be the smear today, thanks,' she said, unable to bear a moment longer of this.

'Well, it wouldn't be safe to do anything else in this situation,' Dr Bennett confirmed, grappling with his scope.

'THAT'S IT, WE'RE leaving,' Abby said resolutely to Lucy as she strode into the waiting room, and, without breaking her stride, moved towards the doors to freedom.

'Gosh, you've been gone ages,' Lucy said. 'You just missed these two cute interns who came out saying the funniest thing about a patient with an angry growler and how ...'

As Abby stopped her in her tracks, with a glare, Lucy's face crumbled, 'Oh dear God, that was you. You're the one with the angry growler.' And she doubled up, holding her sides.

'How the hell am I the talk of the clinic already?' Abby was furious. 'I should be able to have any foof I want, without this. Do you know, I've got a good mind to go back in there and make a complaint about patient confidentiality. I swear that was so unprofessional.'

Lucy usually revelled in any opportunity to jump fully on her soap box about standards of care, so Abby looked expectantly at her friend, waiting for her to join in. Instead Lucy was shaking with the giggles. Abby was aghast.

'I think it would be easier to just change doctors. Or shear it,' Lucy giggled and coughed to cover it.

'I'm never going there again. Full stop!' Abby strode off down the high street. 'Right,' Abby said, looking for the nearest salon, 'that's done it. I'm getting waxed immediately.'

'Abby, don't you want to go home first and trim it down?'

'I'm paying her £35, she can bloody well trim it down. Yes, I'm getting the lot off and starting from scratch. Every last hair is going; otherwise I'll get nightmares. Maybe when I'm done with the wax, I could go back and wangle another smear.'

Lucy looked into her friend's face and started to

shake again, 'Honestly, Ab, you will laugh at this one day, I promise.'

'That was hand on heart the most embarrassing moment of my life. Nothing compares. Lucy, I swear, here and now, that I will never laugh at it.' Normally when Abby said that, laughter would follow as some random act of denial knee-jerk reaction. But this time, she waited for a few seconds and realised that what she was saying was, in fact, completely true.

Lucy's face had a wry smile on it; she was probably trawling through every other embarrassing incident from down the years. Abby halted in her tracks and pointed, there was a beauty salon across the street.

'Seriously? It looks like it belongs in the eighties.' Lucy was unsure.

'Doesn't matter. We're going in and it's coming off now.' She hauled Lucy across the road.

5

DEFINITELY NOT TINDER

'GOOD LORD, ABBY, I never thought you'd let yourself go to that extent.' Woody said disapprovingly.

Abby dissolved into giggles at his disgust, and Lucy joined her. It was 7pm now and both of them had forgotten to order any food in the wine bar Woody had recommended.

'Are you worried that she's lowering the tone of the place?' Lucy jibed. 'Because she's now hair free.'

'Hair free and carefree!' Abby held her glass of wine in the air and clinked Lucy's. 'My favourite wine in stock! Finally fate has dealt me a good hand today.' One bottle down and a second just started, she felt all warm and fuzzy. 'Woody, you look as though you're trying to blank out the possibility that women don't look any different in the flesh than they do in magazines.'

He grimaced.

'Having a big bush in the 70s was the fashion; I'm just trying to bring that back.'

'Yep - retro's in,' Lucy giggled.

'It's just a fact of life, Woody, all women are secretly covered in lots of hair,' Abby said fiendishly.

'Eeergggh! Enough!' Woody yelled before rising to greet his date.

Abby strained her eyes to check out the armpit sniffer of the south. 'Luce, what's her real name again?'

'I don't know, I can't remember anything when I've drunk this stuff.'

'Ladies, this is Sofia.'

'Wow, you don't look as if you have any hair anywhere. Well, apart from your head,' Abby winked.

Before Sofia could respond, Woody stepped in.

'Right, you look as beautiful as ever, my darling. Let's go to the bar and order you a cocktail.'

Abby giggled; Lucy was attempting to sniff them both behind their backs. She was about as subtle as a bull in a china shop.

'Sofia seems very well put together for an armpit sniffer.'

'Well, you never can tell.'

'Well, she's probably calm in the knowledge that, compared to me, she is perfectly groomed.' Even in her sozzled state, Abby could see that Sofia looked immaculate. Perfectly tinted blonde hair held in place by a sparkly pin and with a pretty oval, even-cheek-boned face and wearing a puff-sleeved shirt crisply tucked into a high-waisted slim-fit knee-length skirt and heels, she was something else. Woody had excelled himself this time, there was no doubt about it, she was incredibly hot.

'Perfect nails as well,' registered Abby subtly, hiding hers. 'Put that on my list.'

'Will do. How's it going with her over there?' Lucy had her back to the bar.

'From what I can see...,' Abby craned her neck for clues on Sofia's character. 'Well, she just seems to be standing there, looking perfect, whilst Woody speaks.'

Lucy pretended to yawn.

'You wouldn't be a tad jealous of Miss Perfection over there getting Woody's attention would you, Lucy dear?'

'Not at all!'

Abby raised a questioning eyebrow.

'No, I'm just intrigued what an armpit sniffer likes. I was expecting her to be more...'

'More 1960s Woodstock?' Abby suggested.

'Yes.'

'Well sssh, right now. They're coming back.' Abby tried to smile politely.

'So what do you do, scrumptious?' Lucy aimed her question straight at Sofia. 'Obviously you look gorgeous but what perfume do you wear?'

Woody looked alarmed. Abby laughed out loud; Lucy was definitely drunk.

'Well, I don't really wear one. I keep myself immaculate as I'm a firm believer in natural beauty and the pure attraction between humans based on their own animalistic scents.'

'See Woody? Natural. Let me tell you about my bush!' Abby proclaimed with joy, and Sofia's eyebrow raised into a perfect arch.

'No, no. I don't think we need to go there.' Woody interjected.

'Well, let me tell you that someone had to sort it out.' Sofia looked concerned.

'Don't worry, it's all gone now, though. The lot wiped off the face of the earth. Well, not the face of the earth, the face of ... my pussy.'

Woody put his head in his hands.

Sofia smiled sweetly and patted her arm.

'And let me tell you this,' Abby swigged her wine. 'Because although today may've been an absolute disaster, let me tell you what I learnt.' Taking a deep breath and batting Woody's hand away from her mouth, she mustered her best mock-wise sensei voice: 'Bad things happen to people with hairy pussy.'

'Abby!' Lucy cracked up, 'You sound like a wise mistress of the ages.'

'That's what I am Luce. That is exactly what I am. One with a hair free vagina, which will remain that way so that only good things will come to me.'

Woody sagged, grabbed Sofia who was speechless and took her round the corner to the far end of the bar again.

*****

WITH SOFIA SAFELY at Sunday brunch with her girlfriends, Woody was now cooking for Abby and Lucy, who were nursing stonking hangovers.

'Lucy, serious kudos, you've actually got me back to work, out in a bar and distracted me from Charlie.'

'Have you heard from him? Woody enquired.

Abby shook her head. 'Nothing so far.'

'I've also got you tested and waxed.' Lucy said proudly.

Abby harrumphed. 'Well, I'm trying to blank that out. So, come on, what's next on the list then? I've watched *The Notebook*, cried, stayed indoors eating ice cream and takeaways, I always listen to Taylor so that's a given, but I don't really want to change my hair to be honest.'

'No, you're good to go on that front.'

'Well,' Lucy paused, 'It's time to get you back into the dating scene.'

'Isn't that a little too soon, Lucy?' Woody stepped in, seeing Abby's face begin to lose its colour. 'We've only really just got her out of her PJ's.'

Lucy glared at him.

'No, obviously it isn't, I retract my comment. Right, let's download Tinder.'

'No!' Abby yelled, a little louder than she'd meant to. Either way... 'No. Way.'

'Whyever not?' asked Lucy.

'Are you on it?' Abby asked pointedly.

'Well I was...'

'Exactly. It's not the way I'd envisaged meeting someone, and it's all about hooking up. It's just not right for me in so many ways right now.' She tailed off. *God what if that was how Charlie was meeting people, night after night.*

'I can't go on it, Luce, what if Charlie's on there? That would kill me. He'd think I was over him and that I didn't care.'

'Or you could see that he was on there and be devastated again, knowing he was seeing other people,' Woody interjected. 'You're right, Tinder is a bad idea.'

'OK, OK, so Tinder is off.' Lucy crossed it off her list and tapped her pen on her lips. 'There must be other ways of meeting people that are more focused. I've got speed dating as the next option on my list ...'

'Speed dating? Really? Isn't that going back to the 80s?'

'Well, so many people are going back to it because online is so impersonal, plus if you don't want to go online...'

'Absolutely. I think speed dating is awesome,' Woody intervened, consumed with excitement. 'But these days, it's a lot more inventive.'

'Go on then, tell me all about it,' Abby sighed.

Woody was excited and animated, 'Well, now there's

speed dating salsa classes and some people do these nights where you get padlocked to someone else, the keys are mixed up, divvied out and you have to talk to everyone in the room to see who's holding the right key to unlock you.'

'And in the meantime, you're locked on to someone who might be hideous?' Abby grimaced.

'No chance!' Lucy said. 'Only because I'm doing whatever it is with you. Of course!'

'Or what about those nights where single people can go to the supermarket and meet people?' Woody suggested.

'I don't know, Woody, she'd be in a quandary over whether to stand in the chocolate aisle, the Champagne aisle or the steak aisle.'

Woody guffawed, 'You'd be knackered running around them all, checking for hot guys. It would be a good workout.'

Abby grinned at Woody. 'Er, Lucy, I always get more excited about the food than the men in the supermarket. Although, I guess at least I'd come home with loads of food even if I didn't meet anyone...' Abby was feeling better about this idea.

'No way. You're already more focused on the food. Plus, I don't think Waitrose do those dating evenings,' said Lucy, ever pragmatic. Seeing Woody's face, she explained, 'Well she's got to have standards with the next bloke.'

'Fair point!' Woody concurred.

'Now, I've written down hypnotism with this guy that comes highly recommended.'

Abby's eyebrow shot straight up: 'Really? I don't like the idea of someone messing about in my brain.'

'Worried that they might get lost?' Woody chipped and jumped out of the way as Abby swiped at him.

'Will you take this seriously, Woody?' Lucy reprimanded.

'I am ... but I'm worried for the guy doing the hypno; I need to protect my own.'

Lucy silenced him with a glance.

'Do they really do hypnosis for getting over your ex-boyfriend?' Abby enquired interested.

'I've found one place that does it. They said you have to exercise willpower after the treatments, though, so that's what initially put me off because that's Abby's whole problem.'

'Abby's got willpower,' Woody stood up for her.

'Yes, I know. But she doesn't have an endless supply of it. Trust me, I've read a book on it.'

'What's the book called?'

'*Willpower*, you doofus, it's by Penguin. It helped explain why I am the way I am. Made a lot of sense – you should read it. I'll let you both borrow it if you promise to wash your sweaty hands before turning the pages.'

'Oi, you two, I am here, you know!' Abby exclaimed. Honestly, they could be like a couple of kids. She never knew if it was pent up sexual frustration or just friendly banter. Abby was convinced Woody fancied Lucy. Lucy was gorgeous, her soft curls always seemed to fall perfectly coiffured around her oval face. Large breasts, shapely hips: she was just his type. Either way, she needed their focus as she could feel the urge to check her phone again coming on.

'Come on, guys, seriously! What's going to distract me next? As hard as work is, at least it takes my mind off it all for a bit.'

'Yes, sorry. Look, let's go with speed dating. If that doesn't work, we'll work up a plan B, but it's a start, an entry into the world again and ...'

'And it means that you might meet someone, too, and get bored of focusing on me?' Abby grinned at Lucy.

'We'll see. I'll book it up, Abby, and we'll see.'

Abby smiled. Any distraction was a good distraction. She squeezed Lucy's hand, grateful for her help, powerless to do anything but rely on it. She checked her phone. Nothing still.

6

SPEED DATING AND HATING

FOUR DAYS LATER. Thursday night. Abby stood awkwardly whilst Lucy appraised her.

'Oh my goodness, what are you wearing?' Lucy shook her head.

Abby grimaced as she watched her friend in obvious despair.

'You've got to change! You look like Sir Mix-A-Lot, circa 1992.'

'Oh Luce, don't hate on me,' Abby sighed. Her mind had been in a mess all day trying to prepare for the torture of speed dating. She'd covered herself up in baggy jeans, a plain t-shirt, a large leather bomber jacket and was seriously considering hiding underneath a Fedora, too. She couldn't shake the idea that when Charlie had dumped her, he'd rejected everything about her: her style, her personality, everything. It had spun her off completely. She had no idea how to dress to impress.

'I honestly don't know what to wear anymore, Luce. It turns out that mixing classic haute couture pieces with vintage accessories needs a certain amount of inner pizzazz to pull off, and I just don't have the energy for it anymore.'

Work had been much the same as the former week,

and it had drained all of her positivity. She looked longingly at the comfy pyjamas resting invitingly on her bed and sat down next to them.

'Luce, I can't seem to get back to my old self, so why not just let me be my new self? My new self is far easier, I kinda like wearing pyjamas, crying my eyes out, scraping my hair back and not feeling great. Wanna hang out?'

'No!' Lucy snapped. 'No, I do not. I want my old Abby back. The girl who not only felt fabulous, but who was fabulous. Who held her head high and didn't worry about one person not liking her because she knew that for every twit out there, there were twenty legends waiting to meet her.' She paused, 'The girl who'd walk into any bar or room with her head held high, confident in who she was and owning what she was wearing.'

Lucy put her arms around her and drew her in for a hug.

'I just don't feel confident at all. Charlie didn't want me the way I was, maybe he's right, maybe I'm not good enough.' Abby whispered.

'You are more than enough. My god, the sheer number of guys I've had come over to me asking about your status over the years is phenomenal.' Abby shook her head.

'Look at me, Abby. Just because one guy doesn't get you, that doesn't mean that there isn't someone else out there. I'm not going to let you slip backwards. So you need to get dressed because all the time you're moping about the wrong one, the right one might be right under your nose. You're not hiding out in here and bailing on me. We're going speed dating. I need you with me.' Lucy said firmly. Abby nodded dejectedly, raising an eyebrow, acknowledging the emotional blackmail to get her into gear.

'Ugh, I'm now obliged to come on your behalf, aren't I?'

'Yep!' Lucy smiled sweetly knowing she'd played it well, 'Let me pick something out for you to wear.' And in three short strides, she was rifling through Abby's wardrobe.

Abby grinned at her friend's sighs of despair at the state of her wardrobe. Lucy had tried and failed many times to convince her to categorise the contents either by colour or genre, but it still remained a complete mess.

'This would drive me crazy,' Lucy muttered as Abby stared past herself into the mirror, wondering how the hell she was going to find the energy to speak to complete strangers when she could barely initiate a new conversation with her oldest friend.

Lucy grabbed her by the shoulders and spun her round, grinning and pointing to the bed. She'd laid out her faithful leather skinnies and a black top with stud detailing on the shoulders. Girly but with an edge of attitude – All Saints had nailed it perfectly. Abby nodded and slipped into them, looking up nervously for approval, feeling that something was missing. Lucy didn't need to say anything; Abby forced herself to stand taller, managing to hold her posture straight for ten seconds before slumping back down again, exhausted. It was her confidence. How was standing tall so exhausting?

'He's killed your self-confidence, the bastard,' Lucy said through gritted teeth. 'Have you registered that yet?'

'I have,' Abby whispered, still unable to hate him for it. It was odd, Abby mused, looking at her reflection in the mirror; the clothes looked great and she was in pretty good shape, despite everything, but she knew there was something missing. She looked drained with her skin pale and hair limp. Feeling like crap for weeks on end had certainly done nothing for her looks. She needed to start taking care of herself again – Charlie would never take her back looking like this.

'Ugh,' Abby said, looking away from the mirror, chucking her hair into a scrunched bun. 'More blusher,' she rubbed some into her cheeks, trying to fake a healthy glow. Knowing that to get through this she just needed to do what she did at work: block out everything and focus on the job at hand.

'I'm not sure heels are the way forward tonight, though,' she said, grabbing a pair of matching studded ankle boots.

'Sassy,' Lucy approved,

'... and comfortable,' slipping them on, breathing in deeply and forcing a smile, she made her way out of the door.

'Let's go and meet some guys!' Lucy said excitedly. Linking arms with Abby, she started to wax lyrical about who they might meet.

An hour later, with two gin and tonics inside her, Abby felt lightheaded and sat lightly on the edge of one of the speed-dating tables – like those exam-room ones – to steady herself. To prepare for the evening's entertainment, the girls were all in a mezzanine area, by the circle of chairs and tiny tables, and kept completely out of sight of the guys, who were getting louder and more raucous in the bar below.

Abby twitched, moving from foot to foot, surveying the attendees. Some of the girls were dressed up to the nines, convinced they'd 'just know' and find their true love in two minutes. Others, the die-hard 'speedsters,' all well-polished in classic city clothing from work, were obviously a bit more realistic and playing the numbers game. She sneaked a look down at the army of guys below, some were incredibly good looking, and others were good at looking incredibly dull.

'Why are there good-looking guys here, for crying out loud? They should have no trouble pulling in a bar,' she rolled her eyes at Lucy.

'Are you *complaining* there are hot guys here?' Lucy giggled.

'No, I just think it's odd.'

'Well, maybe they're here for the same reasons we are: they haven't found the one yet. Maybe, like you, they've been through the emotional mill, too.'

'Interesting. That's a new way of looking at it.'

'I don't think it's just a meat market.'

'So how does this work? Do they each just come into the middle of the tables and do a mini presentation about themselves?'

Lucy looked shocked. 'Er, no. Abby, I thought you knew what happened at these things.'

Abby shook her head.

'Well no wonder you were nervous! Right the guys are essentially here for you to interview them; having good questions worked out is key.'

'What kind of questions? I haven't got anything prepared.'

'Just normal ones. With your job, you'll be fine.'

'Jeez, Luce, I'm used to having guys come and speak to me without this level of forethought and stress,' Abby felt panicked.

Lucy grabbed her hand, 'Look, come here,' she said, pulling Abby to one side and pulled out a pen and pad from her handbag. She paused for a moment, looked up, thinking, and wrote down four questions.

Abby read them and grimaced: one to ascertain what they did, what their morals were, what they were looking for and what they liked to do in their spare time. 'Ugh, it feels like a bland interview I'd conduct at work.'

'It's a start.' Lucy blushed.

'OK,' Abby fixed a smile on her face, finished the rest of her drink and ordered another round – a final round – for both of them. As she handed the last G&T to Lucy, her smile was genuine.

Lucy grinned, 'Now, you're getting into it. I knew you would.'

'I'll admit I'm intrigued, nothing more. I actually can't believe I'm doing this.' But her nerves, coupled with three gin and tonics on no dinner, were setting her adrift on a cloud of confidence. She giggled. This was ridiculous.

Separating the women from the men created an animalistic tension, and soon the gaggle of girls giggling on the mezzanine was as loud as the cavemen jostling downstairs. Eventually, a gong sounded, launching a wave of guys pushing and barging to make their way up the stairs first.

Abby, Lucy and all the other women took their seats in the circle.

Looking like dogs on heat, the men moved towards the clapping, whooping women and formed an orderly queue.

'I feel like I'm on a TV show,' Lucy giggled.

Abby sat pensive and wide eyed. Charlie wasn't one of them, thank God. What was he doing now, though? She realised with a jolt that she shouldn't be doing this; it felt like cheating to speak to these men. Her head was in such a spin that she jumped when Lucy touched her arm.

'Breathe,' Lucy reminded her. 'It's going to be fun.'

A bubbly 20-something organiser announced she would be sounding the gong every two minutes and that was the signal for the guys to swap seats, anti-clockwise until every girl had spoken to every guy. Each guy wore a name tag with their age in the top right corner.

First up for Abby was brown-haired Brecken, a terrified 19-year-old. That would never work Abby surmised straight away. As he sat down, Abby reminded herself that it was just like work – if she could manage to bullshit through questions there, she could here, too.

'Hello!' She adopted her passive work smile: 'Brecken: that's an unusual name, where are you from?'

Brecken grinned and instead of answering, stared at the studs on her shoulders. Following his line of vision Abby said: 'Don't worry I'm not a gothic S&M temptress who's going to stud you into submission.'

He looked taken aback.

'Well, unless you're a closet stud temptress, too,' she winked. Where the hell was this chat coming from? That wasn't very worky.

Brecken shifted uncomfortably in his seat and remained completely silent, with Abby staring at him in despair for the whole two minutes until the gong sounded. As Brecken moved on to Lucy, she told herself off for overcompensating her nerves with far too much abnormal chat. She looked despairingly at Lucy who she was sure caught the look out of the corner of her eye, but instead chose to lean in and chat intently to her two-minute conquest. Brecken once again remained in silence.

Abby rolled her eyes and that's when her brainwave hit. Sod talking to these guys as prospects; she didn't want to go out with any of them, anyway, so why not flip this evening on its head and do some research on her new favourite topic? Breakups. Everyone had had their heart broken, right? That's probably why they were all here, after all, so instead of boring herself and the men with interview questions, she could ask some real life questions and find out why they were here. One answer might even hold the key to understanding Charlie.

Beaming, she waited for the next man, Craig, 34, to settle in.

'Right, Craig,' she glanced him up and down. 'Why are you here?'

'Er, to meet beautiful women like yourself.'

'No, no,' she said impatiently. 'Come on, Craig, we only have two minutes. *Why* are you here...?' Craig looked bemused.

'In short, Craig, why are you single? And be honest. I'm trying to figure out the men from the bullshitters and I also want to know how you got over heartbreak. It's a lot to get through, so I ask again, with sixty seconds left, why are you single?'

'My girlfriend broke up with me because I was cheating on her. I have this compulsive need for sex to feel good about myself.'

'Well, off you trot, then. And, no, don't you dare say a word to her...,' she nodded her head at Lucy as Craig sat down in front of her best friend, red faced.

'Lucy, don't say a word to that one; he's a cheater.'

Lucy nodded and sat, her arms crossed and blazed pure rage and disgust across the table at Craig the Cheater for a two solid minutes. Abby cracked on.

'Ryan! How come you're single? And please note that I haven't got time for bullshit prepared answers.'

'I'm still in love with my ex, who dumped me for a hotter man, and I don't know how to get over her. I'm trying everything.'

'Oh Ryan, my heart goes out to you. I'm in the same place. Let's chat at the bar later, and we can compare notes. We can do this!' Their eyes met and they shared a look of mutual mental torture, which made Abby well up. Reaching over the table, she squeezed his hand until she realised it was slightly clammy. Touching was not a good idea here.

Brad, 29, an average-looking chap, sat down next, and she asked the same question to him.

'I wasn't ready to get married to my long-term girlfriend and broke up with her two years ago, thinking that being single would be better.'

'And is it?'

He winked at her, 'It could be if you meet me later. You're fit.'

Unperturbed by the blatant come-on and feeling a little sick, she was intrigued – this could help her with her problem.

'Brad, did this woman cook for you, clean for you, have sex with you, buy and wrap your family's presents, obviously reminding you of their birthdays in the first place?'

'Er, yes.'

'Did she love you completely and sacrifice everything normal in her life to make you happy?'

'Er, I guess you could say that. Yes.'

'So why on earth was that not enough for you? Are you mad, Brad?'

'I guess I may have been a tad cocky in what I thought I could get.'

'So you broke up with someone kind, who loved you because ... why?'

'Well, if she'd have been that perfect for me, I never would have let her go, would I? I was bored.'

That silenced Abby.

Brad was getting hot under the collar: 'Jeez, I didn't come here for this. I came here for some fun not a moral ear bashing. No wonder you're single.'

The noise of the gong and Brad's rapidly scraping chair drowned out Abby's less than polite response as he drew his chair up to Lucy. Abby gestured another 'saw across the neck' death sign, but Lucy shook her head and started chatting to Brad, regardless.

Abby launched at her next prey, David, 36, quickly stating why she was single and asking him the same only to be shut down.

'Look, Abby is it?' David said glancing at her sticker, 'I feel for you, I really do, you're obviously hurting, I can see it in your eyes but I am over my ex now, and I came here to chat to women, not provide counselling.'

'Harsh but true,' Abby snivelled into her tissue, nodding him on his way. David hopped up to move on to his next potential conquest in Lucy.

And so the evening went on. Before she knew it, she had single-handedly destroyed the mental wellbeing of over half the guys who had turned up and been left with a gaggle of men, all heartbroken like herself, to have a drink with in the bar.

'It wasn't quite the intention,' she admitted to Lucy in the cab on the way home, 'but the evening was a true testament to the old adage that misery does like company.'

'Abby, by the sounds of it, you didn't let them get

away with asking one question about you.'

'I know. It's quite a skill of mine. I'm proud to have avoided that many potential questions about my life in a clearly Q&A setting.'

'The concept was lost on you,' Lucy sighed.

'No, Lucy,' Abby didn't want her friend to feel as though her plan hadn't worked. 'It actually soothed me in a really unexpected way. It was comforting to know I'm not the only one that feels like death after they've been dumped. And in all honesty, Lucy, I was never going to actually meet someone, was I?'

'Well you never know,' Lucy shrugged.

'Well, I wasn't. I came to keep my promise to you and to show willing, but the truth of it is I can't think about kissing anyone else right now – let alone actually doing it.'

'True. What an experience though, eh?' Lucy nodded and accepted this was the most chatty and animated Abby had been in ages, so maybe it had done her good.

'Some of the guys just seemed to be out for a laugh, to see who they could lie to and go home with. Let's face it, Luce, they could have a perfect little story about themselves all made up and ready to go. Maybe if I was feeling better, I'd have had more of a laugh. We'll have to go back when I'm at mach speed again.'

'I dunno, Abs, I didn't actually think it was *that* bad,' Lucy went quiet for a moment, Abby waited for her to speak again.

'I know it's not conventional, and we always used to laugh at how desperate it seemed, but I can see how addictive it must be to keep meeting so many single guys in one evening to see if there's some form of spark. I honestly can't remember the last time that I did that.

And I prefer it to meeting someone online – at least you can get a taste of their character,' Lucy pointed out and looked away.

'Luce, I'm so sorry,' Abby berated herself. Her misery was so selfish; of course Lucy was excited about the chance of meeting someone for herself at speed dating. 'How was your night? Did you meet anyone you'd actually like to see again?'

'No,' Lucy said patiently, 'But I'd definitely do it again now I know what to expect.'

'I'm sorry, Luce. I'll pull myself out of this misery coma soon, I promise, and I'm definitely up for going again with you,' and she squeezed Lucy's hand. Losing Charlie was one thing, but losing Lucy's friendship by being a boring, self-involved misery guts just could not happen. She had no doubt that, unlike Charlie, Lucy would stick around, but that was no excuse for bringing her down, too. 'Actually, Lucy, forcing myself to focus on setting you up with a guy might prove to be more of a welcome distraction than you trying to set me up. How long has it been now?'

'The cheek. Mind you, it's been over a year,' she admitted.

'Look at you, you're stunning. It's such a waste.'

'I have standards and secrets.'

'Standards, yes, but secrets ... what are you talking about?' Abby was intrigued. She didn't think they had any secrets between them.

'Er, nothing much,' Lucy clammed up. 'Besides, this is all about you right now.'

'Alright, I'll let it go for now,' Abby accepted that Lucy clearly didn't want to talk about it in the cab. Grateful for the first bit of normal conversation, though, she said 'What was that quote of Voltaire's? Ah yes "I have chosen to be happy because it is good for my health" ... maybe I should start chanting that every morning and see what happens.'

'Yes, that's worth a shot. Good quote, Voltaire.'

'What's next on my 'getting over Charlie list?'

'Well, it's either dinner with the marrieds ...'

'Tarquin and Jane? Oh, god no.' Nobody was more married than Tarquin and Jane. Together since school, they perpetually tried to ensure that everyone around them a.) knew how happy they were and b.) got married as quickly as possible so that they could arrange even bigger dinner parties. You could watch *Bridget Jones* for an instant summary of the misery of joining them as a single person at the end of their dinner table.

'Ugh,' Abby shuddered again at the thought of it. 'Or ...'

'Hypnosis,' Lucy said firmly.

Abby paused. 'Crikey, what a choice. Lucky me, eh! I think hypnosis would be better. Anything would be better.'

'Ah, they're lovely people.'

'They are but ... yes, let's go with hypnosis.'

'Good, and in the meantime, you can help me out with a problem I've been having.' Lucy demanded.

'What problem have you been having?' Abby was curious. Shit, she'd been so out of touch.

'Nothing too serious, but I need you to be there for me, something to do with one of my secrets.'

'Of course!' Abby was intrigued. 'You want to talk about it right now?'

Lucy looked at the cab driver, who also looked interested. 'Not right now, but soon, definitely.'

'Whenever you want to talk, Luce, I'm here.'

'That's why we're such good friends because even when you feel like crap, you always manage to shove it to one side to be there for me.' Lucy hugged her tightly and Abby hugged her back.

'Always, Luce. Always.'

7

MASTER OF THE UNIVERSE, DAVE.

'OK, ABBY, ON my count of three, I want you to close your eyes.'

Abby tried not to giggle.

Dave had a funny accent, like he was trying to disguise his normal voice to sound more breathy and spiritual. And his breath smelt like Galaxy chocolate. Was this honestly for real?

She bit her lip and looked across at Lucy, who glared and mouthed 'focus' back at her. They were in Finchley, sitting in this guy's office-in-the-garage – sorry, his 'aura room.' He labelled himself as a hypnotherapist that specialised in breakups, the kind you keep going back out with the person, and promised he could 'get anyone over anyone.' Lucy had found him online, and now here they were, and Abby was about to trust this guy with, quite literally, her mind. Damn Lucy and her list.

Dave clicked his fingers. She drew her eyes level with his, his nose, 5mm from hers. This was weird – he was totally invading her personal space. It was the closest to any guy she'd been since Charlie. Plus he definitely had just eaten chocolate, which reminded her she hadn't had her chocolate fix today and now she was craving it.

'Are you ready, Abby?'

'OK, I'm ready. Let's just get it over with.'

'That's the spirit.'

Abby was pretty sure it wasn't, and she was doubtful it would even work, but she breathed in and out before trying to calm her thoughts.

'One.'

She breathed in deeply again.

'Two.'

That was odd, she felt dizzy.

'Three.'

Blank.

Darkness.

And yet … space. She was flying through space. A voice spoke in the darkness:

'Galaxy, you're now in the galaxy.'

There was a faint smell of chocolate in this galaxy, she realised. Excellent. She'd always wondered what space would be like. And now she knew. Chocolate. Now to find where it had come from.

'Mmmmm, Galaxy,' she tried to mouth. But her mouth felt tight. That's weird. I hope it opens easily when I find the chocolate, Galaxy was her favourite.

Master of the Universe, Dave flooded into her mind, telling her to find her happy place.

'Don't you worry about a thing,' she assured him, 'I'm on my way to it right now, just left of Mars.'

This was amazing, she had transported from Finchley to the universe in three seconds and discovered it was all made of chocolate. How had no one realised this before? Stephen Hawking had seriously overcomplicated matters; she needed to update the science community when she got back and remind them of what her mother always said: 'overthinking is the killer of all joy.'

She beamed as she flew past Malteser moons. How had she never realised each of the planets and all of the stars were chocolate bars, too? A revelation. This was one of the most prolific moments in her life, she was sure of it, but her face felt slightly wet. Space must be chilly tonight. She pulled her scarf around her tightly and then looked down, it wasn't a scarf at all, it was a cape.

Even better.

Best day ever. She beamed as she flew past the Milky Way, circling and whizzing around a cluster of Starburst.

'I know you have a Bounty of thoughts.' Master of the Universe Dave was speaking again. 'But you have an Aero dynamic mind.'

'No, Master of the Universe Dave, I never liked Aeros.'

'Either way, I want you to believe that you are no longer a Drifter. He's a complete Flake. You need to find someone who's Forever Yours, a real Old Faithful.'

'But I'm not craving any of those right now, Master.' Damn her mouth felt weird.

'Well, you might not know exactly what you want just yet, let's face it, it's been no Picnic, but it's a Marathon not a sprint.' This was why Dave was the Master of the Universe, he just knew what was what.

'You're right, Master, it's been a real Rocky Road but...' She could smell Galaxy again. Maybe that's what she should just trust her instincts and aim for. Yes, she left the last Rolo, swearing that it smiled at her choice.

Master of the Universe Dave spoke again: 'You just need to let go, Abby.'

'You're right, Master, I don't need any old Freddo. A Galaxy is far better,' she licked her lips in anticipation and launched herself in ...

8

EVERYONE NEEDS A CAPE

'HELP ME GET her on this chair,' a distant female voice was speaking. It wasn't Dave, Master of the Universe, anymore. She felt sad. Where had Master of the Universe Dave gone? She'd liked being part of his world. She licked her lips. The Galaxy smell had gone, too. She'd never actually got a proper bite, but she vaguely remembered trying.

'Wait, I think she's coming out of it.' There was that voice again.

'Why is she so wet?' A male voice now. It sounded familiar ...

'Oh my goodness, I'm never doing that again.'

Lucy, it was Lucy.

'I am doing that again,' Abby whispered. 'That was the best experience of my life.' She forced her eyes open to see Woody looking intently at her.

'Well, you're home and OK,' he said.

'I flew home? That's impressive.' She wasn't too surprised; today had been a day of atomic revelations.

'No, we bussed it back,' Lucy sounded sharp.

'A Double Decker?'

'Well, yes it was, but I don't know what difference that makes. It was bloody awful.' Lucy plonked herself down.

'They're not my favourite either, but I think that's a little strong,' Abby said. 'I flew around the universe today, Woody.' Abby pumped her chest up with pride, Lucy raised an eyebrow, which Abby chose to ignore, 'I had a cape and everything.'

'You're still wearing it,' Woody grinned.

'But I was wet' Abby stated, confused. Lucy exhaled with exasperation.

'It wasn't a cape, you absolute donut, it was Dave's tablecloth. He tied it around your neck because you were drooling.'

'Dave, the Master of the Universe?' Woody was in tears, laughing, 'Oh, I'm actually aching that I wasn't there.'

'Abby, you snogged the hypnotherapist because you thought he was Willy 'Galaxy' Wonka. I literally had to pull you off him.'

'No, Lucy, you've got it wrong. He's Dave the Master of the Universe, and he made me see I need to choose his Galaxy over Freddo.'

Lucy's jaw dropped, 'Did we just have the same afternoon?'

'Whatever works, eh, Luce?' Woody chimed in.

Abby grinned. She felt great. 'I knew you'd get it, Woody. Extraordinary to think that what we see as stars are just chocolates really, far, far away.'

'Really? And how much did you pay this guy to find that out?' He looked to Lucy, who buried her head in her hands.

Abby followed his gaze. 'Not enough. He was awesome. Come on, Luce, you must be happy, that's two things off the list, I've been hypnotised AND I've snogged someone new.'

'I don't think it counts if you don't get kissed back.' Abby looked shocked. All guys had enjoyed kissing her in the past.

'Abby,' Lucy exclaimed, 'you drooled so much, you literally slipped all over him. Then you just opened your mouth and devoured him.'

'Like he was a chocolate bar?' Woody finished.

'And she was a chocolate-craving octopus.'

'Oh my god! Lucy! Why didn't you stop me?' Abby pelted them both with cushions. Woody gave up and rolled to the floor in hysterics.

'Because I knew you wouldn't believe it *and* I was too busy filming.'

'What?' Abby and Woody shouted in unison.

'Don't you dare!'

'I've got to show Woody, Abby.'

'No, you don't!'

Lucy pressed play.

'No!' Abby sat mortified at the sounds of her naming all of her favourite chocolate brands while Woody clung to his sides in silent-laughter agony.

'Wait ... look at her go.'

'This is where she tells him she likes to suck and melt Galaxy first.'

'Abby!' Woody guffawed, in sheer heaven with this video.

'No, I'm not looking.'

'You've just launched at him. I'll narrate for you.'

'Thanks, Luce. Such a great friend,' she put her fingers in her ears but could still hear the muffled sounds of yelling, Lucy screaming at her to get off the guy and her moaning and groaning like she was having chocolate sex.

'You're now straddling him.'

'This is comedy gold.'

'Woody, this is never leaving this flat.'

'Dammit! That's it, I'm never eating chocolate again. There you go, you see, hypnosis works. Now, please, can we get back to Lucy's plan?'

'Give me a minute, I'm worn out.' Lucy looked broken. 'I was so worried he'd addled your brain and I'd ruined you forever.'

'Oh, Luce!' Abby rose to hug her, she really did look exhausted. Lucy sank into the hug and they both giggled.

'Maybe let's just focus on making sure your mind is fully back with us and not in some chocolate universe,' Woody said softly, wiping away tears.

'Yes, maybe. But can I still wear my cape?' Abby grinned. Wearing a cape felt fab. She'd have to save up and invest in one, they were definitely the way forward.

'Hey, Luce, I'll buy you one too as a peace offering for today.'

Lucy smiled and nodded.

'She'll be able to buy one herself from the money she makes with that video,' Woody sniggered.

Abby raised her eyebrow, 'No chance. Seriously, you two ...'

Her phone beeped. Charlie? She instantly hoped, leaping for the phone. But it was an unknown number. So the hypnosis hadn't done anything. Charlie was still her instant thought. Great. She checked the message:

'Hey, Abby! Nice to meet you the other night. Wondered if you'd like to meet for a drink sometime? James from speed dating x'

'Hey, Luce.'

'Yep, what?'
'This is going to cheer you up.'

9

WAS IT A HARD ON?

ABBY GRITTED HER teeth. Despite religiously messaging him every day, reassuring him of her love, Charlie still hadn't messaged her. She forced herself to clip a statement necklace around her neck for her evening date with James. It complemented her dark-green knee-length wrap-around dress.

Abby walked slowly to Angelique, a bar just off Regent Street. London never ceased to amaze her: you could go from hyped streets of chaotic crowds, turn down a side street you'd walked past for years, stumble on a great bar and feel like you'd discovered the crown jewels.

She marvelled at the boudoir-style decor and couldn't help but smile as James waved at her.

'I like this place already.'

'A great find, isn't it?' James stood up to kiss her cheek, pulled out her chair and pointed to two vivid green cocktails. Giving her coat to the waitress and whispering 'thank you,' Abby sat down and peered at her cocktail.

'Normally, I like to choose my drinks,' she said to James, not wanting to seem like a bossy killjoy. But she wasn't one of those girls who just accepted whatever their partner chose for them in life. Before you knew it, they'd ordered you a salad and you were never eating steak and chips again. Abby shuddered.

'Of course, but I just wanted you to start with one of these. It's their speciality and surprisingly delicious. And I wanted to see if you could guess what's in it.'

'Challenge accepted,' Abby's competitive streak surfaced, diluting her nerves.

Sipping some water to cleanse her palette, she picked up the cocktail glass like a wine connoisseur, breathing in heavily.

'Ah! Wheatgrass,' she fired instantly.

James nodded, impressed.

'That explains the colour, and at least I'll be getting some goodness from it.'

James nodded, 'Wheatgrass, what else?'

Finally taking a sip, she continued, 'Cinnamon, apple juice ... but what's the alcohol?' She could never taste vodka, but she'd swear to a judge and jury that it was just a healthy smoothie.

'It's coconut rum and a dash of Champagne.'

'Well, it's amazing. Woah, I can feel it going to my head, though, let's share some rosemary fries.'

'Glad you like it.'

James chatted about his job as an investment banker, then they moved on to sharing funny first-date stories.

'Had you ever been speed dating before?' James asked.

Abby laughed and dived into telling him about her abysmal attempt. James was cute. He was charming, he seemed genuinely interested in her. The only but, and it was a big but, was the complete lack of sparks flying between them. Still, he was treating her beautifully, and she couldn't remember the last time Charlie had taken her out and flattered her with attention and cocktails.

That said, James's mobile kept beeping. Abby wasn't keen on guys compulsively texting when they were with her. It was rude. Why meet up with someone if you're planning on spending the whole time texting someone else?

James's phone beeped again.

'Another date lined up?' Abby joked, trying to figure out why such a smart, well-spoken, eligible man was still single.

James coughed, 'Hardly, it's my mother wondering if I got here alright. Ah bless her! I'll just quickly text her back if that's OK. She lives with me and will be worried, I don't know what time I'll be back though ...'

Ah, question answered.

'So are you close with your mum then?'

'Oh, yes! I always joke that I don't get to make most of my decisions.'

'How so?' Abby cringed.

'Well I was told what to do through education, and at work, I follow such strict guidelines and red tape that I'm pretty much told what to do there. And for everything else, there's mum. She agreed I should date you tonight. I actually don't know what I'd have to do if I had to make a decision by myself. But women like that right? They want to take charge?'

Abby paused. She'd never thought about it that way. 'Um.'

James continued, 'I'm hopeless at interior design, for example, so Mum came shopping with me.'

Abby blinked, she loved her mum, but her interior design was a little dated.

'She likes to be involved with my life,' he shrugged.

'So outside work and education, your mum makes

all of your decisions?'

'Pretty much.'

Well that definitely explained why he was handsome and still single. She took a big swig of her second wheatgrass concoction.

'All done, I'll put it on silent now.'

'Ah right,' Abby said, wondering how she could wrap this up.

'Does it bother you that I'm close to my mum?'

'Not that you're close to her, gosh no; I'm close to mine, but, sorry, I just find the fact that she's so involved in your decision making a bit strange.'

'Look, Abby, my mother might make some choices for me, but she doesn't control who makes my heart beat faster just by looking at them.'

Well, that was nice to hear. She couldn't help but smile, 'OK, maybe it's not so bad.' She smiled again.

'You have an amazing smile. Actually, on that note, have you ever had any wisdom teeth out? I have an operation in two days to have all of mine taken out.'

'All of them in one go? Ouch!' Abby exclaimed. 'I had one taken out when I was fifteen, and my whole face swelled up like a basketball. I don't envy you that.'

'Ah, it'll be alright, Mum'll be there to nurse me back to health.'

'Not wanting to freak you out, but it's not like a fever to nurse. It's more a matter of time for the wounds to heal and really, really good oral hygiene. Cross your fingers against too much swelling.' Abby watched as his face paled. 'But what the hell, if your mum can cook soup you can suck through a straw then that's all good.' She added quickly. He was obviously more nervous than he was letting on.

'Exactly. And maybe you'd like to come and watch a movie with me. I won't be able to talk that much.'

'Bonus,' Abby grinned. 'Yes, that sounds chilled out.' What was she saying?

'I'll try not to drool too much.'

'I'll make a video of it if you do.'

'Perfect!'

The banter was light and not too serious, and after one more drink, Abby decided she was going to quit while she was ahead. He was lovely, but no real spark flew between them, at least not for her anyway, but James kept glancing at her, which she pretended not to notice.

Before going their separate ways, they walked together back to Embankment, strolling through Piccadilly Circus taking in the sights and sounds of London at night. James took her hand in his as they neared one of the fountains at Trafalgar Square and quickly pulled her behind one of the lions. He nestled into her, taking her face in his hands and slowly bent his head down to kiss her. As their lips touched, Abby was almost shaking, her mind was screaming for Charlie. Oh, dear god, there was no way she could back out now, she was just going to have to endure the kiss. Her hands automatically found his waist and rested them there whilst his lips gently pressed against hers.

He pulled back and stared at her deeply. 'I've been wanting to kiss you for hours now.'

That did it, she needed to be needed, she could worry about it later. She smiled a little and angled her head for another kiss, this time warming into it a little bit. Two seconds later he pulled her closer. Wait was James hard? Ergh, that was a bit much for a first kiss, especially with no extra spark.

'OK,' she said pulling back, 'tonight was nice.' Maybe it was just his denim zip, she reasoned. He smiled at her and pulled her into a hug. Nope, it was definitely not the zip.

'So the next time I see you, I won't be able to do this. One more smacker for the road.'

She obliged. 'Good luck for the operation, James, I'll jump into a cab from here.'

'I'll text you, Abby. Good night.'

10

WHAT'S WRONG WITH A RECCE?

'Guys, I'm not completely sure, but he may have had a hard on.'

'What?' Lucy exclaimed. They were back at Abby's for a post-date de-brief, with Woody in tow.

'Well, you are hot, Abby and maybe he just really, really liked you,' Woody grinned.

Abby grimaced.

'How were you even that close?'

'Well, here's the pathetic part: he leaned in to kiss me, and he'd been saying all this nice stuff to me and I couldn't remember the last time someone did that, so I leant in to kiss him, and he pulled me close. And that's when I felt it.'

'Ah, that's sweet,' Lucy smiled.

'Sweet? Lucy, it's not sweet. If this wasn't about trying to get me over Charlie, you'd be saying it was gross and never to see him again.'

'And are you going to?' piped Woody.

'No! When we were at the bar, I agreed to a second date, but now I need to cancel it, and seeing as you're my secretary and all...'

'Wait, what was the date going to be?' Lucy asked.

'Just a movie. He's having his wisdom teeth out – all

of them in one go.'

'Crikey,' Woody clenched his own jaw protectively.

'Yes, and I said I'd go round for a movie to chill out.'

'Well, where's the harm in that? You sit, you watch a movie, he's going to be high on painkillers, anyway. Why not go along and hang out, see how it goes?' Lucy reasoned.

'Maybe you should have just dived in at the deep end and brought him home? You know, get over someone by getting under another,' Woody suggested.

Lucy shook her head, clearly disgusted by Woody's tactics.

'God, no!' Abby said, resolutely. 'There was just no massive crush or spark. Plus, if I'd have brought him home on the first date, I'd have felt too slutty. You know I pride myself on making men wait – it makes them fall harder.'

Lucy nodded her approval.

Woody laughed, 'What utter bollocks! No, you don't make them wait until the third date for sex, you give them a BJ 'to check it all out down below,' he retorted.

Abby and Lucy glanced at each other and threw their heads back in laughter. It was true, they had vowed long before either of them had even had the slightest chance of losing their virginities, that to avoid being like some of the girls at school, they would remain aloof and do the BJ first, to recce the guy's manhood and decide whether or not they wanted to take it further.

Abby found over the years it was not only a massive turn on for the guy – especially if their past girlfriend had only gone down as a birthday treat – but if anything appeared untoward, she wouldn't bother with the BJ, make her excuses and leave. Far easier to leave when you're fully clothed than being naked and realising you don't want to go through with it.

'Well, I'm yet to bring home a girl who thinks the same,' Woody said playfully. 'Mind you, with me they just go straight for the sex.'

'We know that, Woodster. We can hear you!' Abby said, only part joking.

'So, anyway...' Lucy directed the conversation back to Abby and James. 'What did it feel like to be on a date?'

'I don't know. Luce, most of the time it felt wrong, like I was cheating on...,' she couldn't bring herself to say his name. 'I didn't kiss him because I had an urge to, I just wanted to kiss him because he was treating me so nicely, and I wanted to be wanted. Now I feel unbelievably pathetic.'

An image of Charlie flashed into her head. Abby felt crestfallen, the mini high of meeting a nice stranger who was interested in her had boosted her confidence, but she knew, really, it was just that she wanted Charlie to treat her that way again. But Charlie didn't want to take her for a drink, kiss her and give her a lovely night out. Clenching her eyes shut, willing those thoughts away, she opened them again to see Woody and Lucy holding their breaths. She tried desperately to form a smile.

'It's OK, Abs. Look how far you've come,' Lucy said softly.

Glad that she was in diving distance of her bed, Abby looked at her room.

'So, you want to stay in tonight?' Lucy asked.

Abby quietly nodded. 'Actually, if you guys don't mind, it's been kind of a hectic day, and I just want to crawl into bed. Sorry to get you round here.'

'That's alright, I can chill with Woody,' Lucy smiled

at her and got up to pull her into a big hug.

'OK,' Abby whispered, needing to get away before she cried. 'Look, I'm not going to lapse back into another pit of despair. I just need to mull tonight over...'

'I'm relieved to hear that. Go and have a bath,' Woody said. 'I'll leave a mug of tea in your room and see you tomorrow.'

'Best roommate ever,' she whispered. 'Thanks, Woody.'

SHE CHUCKED HER clothes over her chair, absentmindedly brushed her teeth and crawled under her duvet, tucking it all under her body. As her body relaxed into the warmth, she wondered how she could possibly flit from feeling so non-committal and jokey about James to feeling sucker punched about Charlie in the space of five minutes. She texted her mum and was not hugely surprised when her phone beeped a minute later. Alice came back with wise words:

'It's the comparisons. Comparisons you didn't think you'd have to make because despite how bad it was at the end, you secretly always believed that Charlie would turn it around and sort it out. Comparisons that you're naturally going to make with the first guy you kiss. But you don't need to rush, and you must try not to compare them. The next person will always be different to the last because everyone's unique. You need to train your mind to work out whether each person is right to be in your life based on their own merits and not based on a comparison to a past relationship.'

'Ooo, good point. Epic answer, Mum, thank you, love you xx'

James was a distraction from thinking about Charlie, but the bottom line was that was all he was: a distraction. Thinking back over all of her boyfriends, she'd always been the one to dump them, so she'd never felt the need to do the whole rebound thing, if that's what this even was...

Abby was so confused she wanted to scream and let out all the messed-up tensions in her head. She'd never analysed herself so much in her life. Pulling the duvet over her head, mainly so she couldn't reach her phone and text Charlie, she curled up on her side and lay in the darkness, thoughts mulling over in her head. Battling what she knew Lucy, her mum and Woody were all saying, with the natural ache for the past still inside her, she eventually fell into a restless sleep.

WHEN SHE AWOKE in the morning, Abby still felt quiet and pensive. She wandered to the kitchen and found a note by her favourite breakfast mug: 'Love you, Ab Fab – have a great day – I'm cooking tonight if you fancy it.' Woody's notes always started her day in a good way. 'Hell yeah,' she wrote back and added a smiley face. With a grateful smile on her lips, she made herself a big mug of strong tea, decided today was indeed a new day and it was going to be a good one. She had wasted too many days being miserable about something that she couldn't change. Other men clearly found her attractive, and she should focus on that. More to the point one hot guy found her extremely attractive. She giggled, remembering how he had struggled to contain himself. Pushing aside the reliable black dress she'd planned to wear to work, she dug out a bright white wiggle dress with a tiny black belt that emphasised her curves.

James texted her and at first she ignored it, not knowing what to say. Then after taking a deep breath, she replied on her lunch-break, wishing him well for his operation. What the hell, she thought, even if he is only a distraction from Charlie, that's a good enough reason to see him again – and she'd had a nice time really. She heard the familiar ding as he replied straight away:

'Keep Sunday free for movie night, I think my mum's going out.'

He ended it with a flirty wink, and Abby slid the phone back into her bag, smiling to herself.

Sunday, that was good. It meant she could spend the weekend with Lucy, maybe get a vintage market fix: Brick Lane on Saturday and a lazy brunch on Sunday before seeing James.

She messaged Lucy immediately with her idea and a minute later her phone pinged again:

'It sounds like a perfect date! Why can't I find a guy like you?'

Done. Plans for the weekend sorted, Abby forced herself to get back to the task at hand, work.

11

WHEN YOU TRY TO DO A GOOD THING

'I THINK SHE's in shock, Woody,' Abby heard Lucy say, she sat still, bolt upright in the chair at her kitchen table in the flat. It was Saturday. Post-date.

'Well, of course she's in shock, the poor girl's covered in jizz. That's bound to shock anyone,' Woody pointed out.

Lucy gave him a look that clearly said 'What would you know?' before moving aside to let him wipe away a bit she'd missed on Abby's neck. He had to rub hard. He frowned.

'God, it's like concrete! Thank god you didn't swallow this, Abby, it might have killed you.'

Lucy rolled her eyes, 'Woody, that's just what it's like.'

'Impossible,' Woody shook his head, grimacing, 'Abby, this is going on the excessively long list of favours you've accumulated over the past two years.'

'Oh, for goodness sake,' Lucy tutted and pushed him out of the way. 'Right, missy,' Lucy bent down so one of her hands was resting on each chair arm, 'You're in your apartment, you're safe, so tell us, what on earth has just happened to you?'

Abby pondered what Woody had said. On reflection, maybe that was why her mouth felt paralysed. Looking at Lucy through, she rhythmically moved her head from side to side, looking first into Lucy's right eye with her left and then moving her head slowly so her right eye was then looking into Lucy's left.

'Nooo,' Lucy translated helpfully.

Woody rolled his eyes.

Abby knew she could keep this up all night if it meant not talking about what had just happened.

Lucy sniffed. 'I can smell wine on her breath, Woody. Maybe she's just plastered. None of this makes any sense. I've never seen her like this before. Should we call a doctor? I'm worried.'

Woody shrugged, 'What are we going to tell the doctor? I've just wiped off the evidence,' he proclaimed holding up the tissue then realising what it was and gagged.

Abby started to draw a breath in, and Lucy and Woody leaned closer to her.

'His mum was there,' she whispered before clamping her mouth shut, visibly shuddering.

Woody tried Lucy's eye-level tactic and kneeled in front of her. He spoke tentatively as if speaking to a child. 'Did his mummsy wumsy see you giving her boysy woysy a blowey?'

'Yes, yes, she did,' Abby whispered very quickly as if saying it quickly would make it no longer true. Woody guffawed. Lucy swiped at him.

Abby rocked on the chair.

Lucy frowned, 'Right, Abby, I've just got to ask, why are your hands covered in blood?'

Abby looked down to see her left hand was, indeed, covered in dried blood.

'Oh my god, Abby, have you killed his mum?' Lucy exclaimed.

'Oh my god, have you eaten his cock?' Woody almost screamed.

Both of them cupped their hands over their mouths in horror, looking like they were about to go into shock themselves.

'Are you both on drugs?' Abby snapped out of her shock, suddenly feeling the exact opposite to what she felt before. Now she didn't want to hide it, she wanted to share it as quickly and as loudly as possible, then it was out of her and over. Forever.

'Are you sure you really want the hideous details? I wasn't going to say, but really.'

Abby was shaking.

'Woody!' Abby yelled – he'd zipped off to the bathroom to wash his hands. 'Get in here now, and I mean immediately.'

Abby was like a plane taking off, gaining more and more speed, adrenalin surging around her body. She stood up to tell her story, her breathing getting faster. Woody hurtled back in.

'Woody,' she barked, 'sit down exactly where you are.' Woody obediently dropped to the floor, crossing his legs. Lucy grabbed a dining chair. If she wasn't feeling so wired, Abby would have laughed, they looked like two young kids at story time.

'Well, the evening was going well, gorgeous apartment, fabulous wine, I was funny, he was you know drugged up from the operation, bandages all over his face and in his mouth. He couldn't kiss me, but he pulled me between his legs to massage my neck whilst we were watching a movie and, I don't know how, to cut a long story short, I drank my wine and gave him a BJ,' Abby paused.

'Why?' Lucy asked, open mouthed.

'I don't know, I just panicked and thought it would cheer him up after his op.'

'So considerate, I'm proud of you Abby,' Woody nodded.

'So, the wine had gone to your head and you freaked out. What next?' Lucy wanted to get to the traumatic bit.

'I'm getting to it Luce,' she sighed. 'I was concentrating on what I was doing, in the zone, as it were. He was moaning, everything seemed fine, his hands were in my hair, you know how they do.'

Lucy nodded.

'Well, they suddenly started punching the bed, either side of my face. I was nervous you know?'

Both Woody and Lucy silently nodded.

'But then I figured, some people have come faces, maybe James has come fists.'

'Everyone's different,' Lucy reasoned.

'Go on,' prompted Woody.

'He was screaming, well as much as he could with all of the gauze bandages in his mouth. I swear I didn't know what was happening until I looked up.'

Abby closed her eyes at the memory of the vision, 'his stitches had burst from the BJ, he had blood bubbling from his bandages and pouring down his face. I was shocked so, of course, I stopped, but he reached down and kept going himself.'

'Kinky bastard,' Lucy exclaimed.

'Honestly, every thrust seemed to fizz more blood out, but that's when it got really bad.'

'It gets worse than this, I'm wincing over here?' Woody had his hands protectively over his privates and looked visibly in pain.

'Not for much longer, but through all the commotion I heard another scream, I knew it wasn't me and when I turned around ...'

'His mum was there! Oh my God, Abby!' Lucy shrieked. 'Surely that made him stop?'

'You would think! But no, he didn't. I don't know where he thought he was or maybe he was high on painkillers, but she hit me over the head with her handbag thinking I was murdering her son and letting him have one last shot at a good time, but as she was pulling me off the bed, he came.'

Woody gasped. 'Did he come on his mum's face?'

'He came on her face. And over me. I could barely see.'

'Oh my god,' Woody exclaimed. 'Abby, this is the worst-best thing that's ever happened to you,' and he started to laugh.

'What?' Abby's eyes widened, looking to Lucy for support.

'Oh, Abby. Oh dear!' Lucy's shoulders began to shake, 'I'm sorry but ...,' the giggles overtook her.

'It's not funny, Luce, she thought I was a hooker!'

'What did you do?' Lucy gasped through tears of laughter.

'Well, I was trying to be polite, so I said "Hello, I'm Abby!"'

'What? Abby, no you didn't introduce yourself!' Woody howled.

'Yes, I did, and she grabbed my bag and thwacked me with it, so I wrenched it off her. She couldn't see very well because of the ... you know ... so I did the only respectable thing and ran away.'

'What did James do?' Woody gasped.

'He just kept screaming. And his mum was screaming.

It was all very loud, and I never want to go back there. The end.'

'I think that's fair enough,' Woody wiped his eyes.

'I don't know what I was thinking. In honesty, all I could think about was Charlie's face, so I just knew I had to get thoroughly tipsy and go for it.'

'Well, I think you succeeded there,' Lucy said still giggling.

'Yes, Abby my lovely, no one could ever accuse you of half measures,' Woody applauded.

'I will take that compliment, and I hereby swear that is the last time I'm ever doing it. I'm never giving anyone else a blow job ever again.'

Woody wiped a tear from his eye. 'Oh, Abby you must. You just burst a guy's stitches because he was about to explode with pleasure; you're too good at them not to do them again, it would be a criminal loss to society.'

'Tough. It's not happening. Plus he had a slightly wonky cock – that should have been a sign something was going to go horribly wrong. I should have known something bad was going to happen.'

'What were you doing giving him a blowjob on the second date anyway?' Woody asked.

'I wanted to see if I still had the knack.'

'I don't think anyone is going to doubt that. Now all this blow job talk is making me feel hungry. Sushi anyone, or have you eaten enough?' he said pointedly at Abby.

'Well, yes, it does sound like you'd be quite full,' Lucy grinned.

'No way! Chinese for me. I need some calories and buckets and buckets of wine. I want to drink until I stop shaking and remembering his face and his mum's.'

Abby began to smile, 'Oh my god, his mum … she had come in her eye too … I definitely need wine,' she said giggling, starting to relax more now. She felt Lucy's gaze on her.

'I don't care how unhealthy that attitude is, we both know I'm not an alcoholic, but on this occasion, it's the only thing that's going to help me sleep without nightmares, honestly his mum was a dead ringer for the nanny in *The Omen*,' Abby shivered.

She took the large glass of red wine Woody handed her and, taking long sips, she let the red liquid slowly slip down her throat. Twenty minutes later, she felt a giggle. Putting her glass out of her reach on the table, she giggled and giggled some more. Woody's shoulders started to shake, and Lucy let herself go again.

'I'm loathe to give you another task on the list. They all seem to be going horribly awry,' Lucy chuckled.

Abby grinned, 'I burst his stitches! I must be rather good … perhaps I will do it again.'

'I knew it,' Lucy grinned.

'I'll drink to that,' Woody said, and laughing they all clinked their glasses together. 'To James!'

'Ugh, yes. So, Lucy, what's next on my list?'

12

IT BLOODY SUCKS

As MUCH AS Lucy's mind always shifted back to worrying about Abby, right now she had one of her own issues to deal with. One that was far more embarrassing to her than anything else, and one that had governed her life for the past six years, especially at work. She looked around the plush interior of the bespoke property company in Knightsbridge where she was lead consultant and thought, as she did every single day at this time, how if anyone here knew of her issues, they would never be tolerated in any way.

Lucy placed a hand on her stomach and held her breath, she knew from the familiar gurgle and hot sensation passing through her body that she had an absolute maximum of ten minutes to get to the loo, hope that no one was around and then let her IBS (It Bloody Sucks) explode. Just as she eyed the door, her phone flashed with a call from the MD. 'Shit,' literally she thought. 'Clive, darling, how can I assist?' she answered in smooth tones, holding the phone as far from her stomach noises as she dared.

'A new house in Chelsea, fabulous I'll head straight over there after the Mathiesons.' She put the phone down and checked her watch, damn it, she was two minutes down, eight minutes until a potential Armageddon situation. She needed to purge her bowel. Glancing over the top of the glazed glass partition, she saw that her new potential clients were walking through the front door. She wiped the bead of sweat off her upper lip, bent over with a cramp and held her breath. 'Oh my god.' This was a bad one. She'd had all of that wine and Chinese last night with Abby, and now she was paying the price for it. Gaviscon had done nothing.

'Are you alright? The Mathiesons are here.' Clive popped in and left her office as quickly as he'd entered it. Heck, come on, Luce, seven minutes left. She sucked her stomach in and strode out as confidently as she could.

'Mr and Mrs Mathieson, it is so lovely to meet you. Let me escort you through to our lounge. Glenda will get you some drinks and you can freshen up after your flight. I'll be with you in just a few minutes.'

With them safely ensconced in the lounge, choosing fresh pressed juices, she turned as elegantly as she could, praying her stomach wouldn't rumble again. Her bowels in turmoil, she tried holding her breath in a bid not to send more air into her system for her body to contend with.

'Damn that egg fried rice,' she took baby steps in her heels. God, she felt awful. It was like a sea of fire rolling in waves of anguish over her, instinct told her to bend over, which offered a sweet release from the cramping, but she couldn't get away with that here. Oh dear god, don't fart. Keep control, she begged her body, just focus on getting to the loo. Clenching her backside as hard as she could, she surveyed the open reception and the toilets all the way over on the other side. God only knew why they'd put the staff loos in reception. It meant you

couldn't even relax fully when you got in there for fear
someone would hear.

Looking right, she clocked that Julia, the ever-
observant receptionist, wasn't at her desk, and a mini
wave of relief passed over her. Julia took great pride
in knowing everything that went on in these walls,
and whilst she'd never mentioned it, Lucy knew she'd
probably guessed her dirty little secret – there was no
way she could sit there day in, day out and not have
spotted Lucy's contorted Ministry of Silly Walks and
belly rumblings on the way to the bathroom. Julia had
to be one of the most insanely annoying people she'd
ever had the displeasure of working with, one of those
girls that always managed to catch you at your worst
and judged everything. Plus, she looked like a modest
Gisele Bündchen and probably had perfectly functioning
bowels. Ugh, life was cruel.

'Oh hello, Lucy, are the Mathiesons alright? I wouldn't
leave them too long if I were you, new clients and all.'

'Yes, thank you for the advice Julia, glad to see you
back at your desk again,' Lucy answered through gritted
teeth.

Shit how long could she leave them? Tough, she
decided. She had to go to the toilet first.

As another wave of acid rolled her stomach over, she
bit her lip. Pretending to admire the old art on the wall,
she breathed and tried to control it.

'Haven't you looked at that picture before?' Julia
asked. Inane question number two.

'Yes, Julia, but I figure the more I look at it, the higher
the chance is that one day I'll like it,' Lucy snapped back.

'You won't find it so much fun to test my patience if
you're having to clean up my mess when you distract

me again,' Lucy said under her breath.

'What was that, Lucy?' Julia said pointedly.

'Nothing, Julia,' Lucy managed to sing through clenched teeth.

Julia gave her a look that clearly said she deemed Lucy mentally unstable, with no ability to find a man and nothing more to look forward to in life other than dying alone.

For god's sake, let me stand here screwed up in a weird position and clench my arse together as tightly as possible and just shut up for one moment, would you? Lucy screamed inwardly.

Sod it, Lucy thought, I don't care what she thinks, and she put her hands on the wall and bent to rest her forehead against it, continuing to clench, closing her eyes to focus even harder. She just needed this wave to pass before she could move again.

With that, Julia rolled her eyes and went back to organising her pens in order of the rainbow.

Feeling the wave subside, Lucy gritted her teeth. If she could just manage to walk in a straight line to the bathroom without having to breathe and clench so hard, she'd make it.

At that moment, Julia chose to rise and saunter across reception and into the bathroom, giving Lucy a polite smile, batting her eyelashes as she went in and locked the door.

'The bitch, she knows,' Lucy's breathing got harder. God, she couldn't take this anymore.

Her and Julia went through this rigmarole every day. Every single day, she pretended to look at the art before running into the loos and then, five minutes later, she strode out ready for business as normal.

She slowly positioned herself next to a filing cabinet close to the toilet, ensuring her spot as next-in-line.

Julia eventually came out thirty seconds later, touching her eyelashes delicately. Lucy faked a smile and grappled with the door handle, her insides sensing that now was almost time to purge. As she pulled the door wide open, Julia spoke loudly in her most patronising voice: 'Oh, I've replaced the air freshener in there, Lucy. Don't be afraid to use it, please.'

Lucy bit down on her gums and slammed the door shut.

Thirty relieving seconds later, Lucy sat in her own stench and put her head in her hands. She wanted to sob. Instead, she blotted off the sweat with a tissue and tried to calm down. She couldn't take the stress of this anymore. Products prescribed by her doctor had worked for about a month, but they ended up having the opposite effect, and she'd had the worst constipation ever. Destroying all hopes of living an elegant life, she'd had to shove those torpedo things up herself to force a movement. Even though no one could see her doing it, she still felt embarrassed having to explain what they were to the spotty faced teenager on the chemist counter.

'They're for my mother,' Lucy had lied, instantly met with a face that said, 'yeah right.'

On an average day, her belly would swell up to the size of a pregnant whale and the wind that came out of her was nothing short of hideous. It had the potential to wipe out entire nations. The only time that she'd spoken to Abby about it, she hadn't taken it seriously, giggling at her: 'Oh Luce, maybe your mission in life is to be Britain's most lethal weapon. We should just feed you milkshake and send you to the front line; there'd be white flags everywhere in a week.'

'This isn't funny, Abby,' she's said to Abby, who had laughed, clutching her perfect digestive system as she did so.

'Spend a week – no, better yet, a month – living like I have to and the stress of it all would kill you,' she'd said, knowing it was pointless. Abby would never understand how it affected her decision making. Her life. Every day, she had to rigidly plan her activities around it; swimming, jump-rope training, adult trampolining classes were all out of the question.

She'd even selected her job because of it. Even though she'd got high grades, the idea of being a surgeon or a pilot was out of the question as she needed easy access to toilets.

After getting her MBA, Lucy had contacted this extremely niche Knightsbridge property search company and given them a list of improvements that could make their good idea, great, and they'd hired her immediately to implement them all. Four years later and she was close to becoming a director herself. She loved scouting London for hidden gems so when the next client wandered through the door with a list of requirements, she could instantly source the perfect property for them. The properties they had on their books were highly sought after, to the point where the deals were done before they even went to market. They were highly selective and dealt only with high net-worth individuals.

It was only a small set of people that could enjoy their services, and Lucy loved every aspect of it – from delving into mood boards for properties to getting the go ahead for a piece of land that wasn't even technically for sale to bartering prices. Most of all, she loved snooping around other people's homes and, when it came to her IBS, well, the millionaires' bathrooms were always beautiful.

As her breathing returned to normal, she realised how close she'd been this time. She sat resolutely on the toilet. She couldn't carry on like this, sweating about going to the loo – it just wasn't normal. Julia's crass note Sellotaped to the door was both patronising and hurtful. If anything, Julia was there as her junior, to filter calls through to her. She shouldn't be taking this kind of crap from her. That was it, she was taking control of the situation. She was going to walk out with her head held high, go straight to her desk and find a solution to this problem once and for all. Bowel replacement surgery, if that even existed. She pulled her panties up, refreshed and ready. Never again would she endure another moment of Julia's sneering.

After washing her hands, she pressed the air freshener, which made a loud hiss she was sure Julia would have heard. Damn, she should have just left the smell and made her walk in to deal with it, that would have been a great payback.

But no, she reminded herself she needed to be the bigger person here. Straightening her skirt and feeling like she'd lost four pounds, which she probably had, she walked straight past Julia, flashed her a brilliant smile and sat down at her desk. Jiggling the mouse to jump her PC to life, she searched for the IBS clinic she'd seen in the back pages of a health magazine. When was it? Next Thursday? That's fine, she thought, writing 'IBS Clinic 7pm' in her diary and underlining it twice. She would most certainly be attending. Brilliant. Bring it on she thought ... and then remembered the Mathiesons were waiting. She strode into the lounge, glowing with confidence, ready to wow them with her property prowess.

13

ALL IN A DAY

ABBY HADN'T HEARD from Lucy for a bit – she'd backed off a bit with the 'getting over Charlie plan.' Abby was actually relieved, life was just too raw right now. Since Charlie had left, her usual day-to-day calm had disappeared, and in its place extreme emotions and random events had exhausted her. She walked slowly back from the Tube station after work, moving along the pavement in her own little world. A few steps from her apartment, she automatically rummaged for her keys.

'No, I don't believe it.' She rifled through her bag, but she knew exactly where they were: resting on the breakfast bar. Buzzing the intercom for ages gained no response. Woody wasn't home. She was locked out.

'Bollocks!' She exclaimed.

'Hello, there!'

She jumped and spun around to see who the male voice belonged to. Tim chuckled. 'Sorry, I didn't mean to make you jump.'

Gosh, he really was gorgeous. Say hello, she willed her mouth, but a gurgle of sound came out. Traitor. She nodded and managed a smile.

'You look better every time I see you. The gloves were hilarious, though,' he carried on, oblivious to her state.

She breathed a sigh of relief.

'Ah yes, the gloves,' finally able to speak. She smiled fully now.

'Very endearing!'

'Especially when covered in your cousin's sweat.'

'Argh, no more!' Tim stuck his fingers in his ears and laughed. 'Why are we still standing outside?'

'Well, here's the good news: we're locked out. When are you meant to be meeting up with Woody?'

Tim just grinned at her.

'Of course. Now! Why else would you be here?' She smacked her forehead.

'Well, if I know Woody, he could be anything from five minutes to five hours. Let's go get a coffee. Shall we go where we went last time?' Tim suggested.

Abby nodded, 'Sounds good to me.'

'You're looking a tad stressed, are you OK?' Tim said kindly as they settled into two comfy seats in the local coffee shop a couple of minutes around the corner. Woody'll be back soon, and I promise I haven't made it on to the UK's most wanted list ...'

'Yet!' Abby quipped.

He smiled, '...so you're safe with me.'

'No, it's not that,' she smiled at him. 'Honestly, I'm just wondering what the heck's happened to my life,' she said quietly.

Tim nodded, 'We all have those moments, Abby. You're not alone.'

'It used to be this vaguely predictable existence. I had a pretty clear future mapped out and now, all of a sudden, I'm in this crazy world of dating – which I really don't want to be in – and the future is all uncertain.'

'Well, it can't all be bad. Although Woody *might*'ve

mentioned how your date went with that guy. James, was it?'

'Oh my god, Tim! I'm going to kill him.'

'It's alright! You came off quite favourably as I recall.'

'I'm blushing under my makeup.'

Tim chuckled.

'Literally six months ago, I was a woman who not only knew what she wanted but thought that she had it. Dating nightmares just didn't happen,' she shuddered at the memory. 'Now I seem to jump from one embarrassing incident to the next.'

'Well, it's great fodder for your friends to laugh at, though right?'

'Yes, I'm definitely doing them a good service.'

Tim paused for a moment and looked straight into her eyes, his big browns locking on to hers, and she couldn't tear herself away. 'I still think you know what you want. You've just learnt in the last few months that you're not always in control of it.' He play-kicked her leg. 'Plus, I've loved hearing about your antics.'

She couldn't help herself and a smile exploded across her face.

'I'll bet you have.' She play-kicked him right back. Sipping on her coffee: 'I can't believe we're locked out.'

'We're probably not really,' Tim said.

She raised an eyebrow.

'We both know Woody's probably in there right now doing some ungodly thing to a woman he's just met and fallen in love with on the Tube.'

Abby grinned at that, surprised she hadn't thought of it sooner herself. Being self-absorbed in her misery was doing nothing for her instinct. She looked at Tim. There was something utterly reassuring about him one minute, and the next he'd surprise her again.

He grinned right back, surveying her, 'You're looking really well, Abby. It's good to see you looking like this.'

'Thanks, Tim, I keep forgetting you've only known me since the whole break-up thing with Charlie. I've been trying to be healthy again and get myself back into shape.'

'Ah, the classic post-breakup slim down.'

'It's weird how emotions can affect your eating habits, isn't it? I never ate much junk food but the moment Charlie-boy broke up with me, I didn't eat anything but. It was like I was punishing myself for losing him.'

'How did your body take it?' Tim joked.

'Not well, my body almost dumped me as well,' she giggled.

'Well, when Catherine the not-so-great broke up with me, I didn't eat anything sober. My mates were doing the guy thing and taking me out constantly, so I lived on dodgy coloured shots and kebabs for about a month and looked positively awful. When she called me to tell me she 'might' have changed her mind, I went running to meet her without looking in the mirror. Her eyes said everything she needed to say. She just looked me up and down, and I could see how appalled she was,' he threw his head back and laughed at the memory.

''Might' want you back? She didn't even know?'

'I know.'

'She sounds hideous.'

'Yes, it's funny how at the time you can think someone is truly amazing ...'

' ... and you make excuses for their behaviour...

'... and think it's you, when actually neither of you bring out the best in each other.'

'How long did you two go out?'

'Six years.'

'Wow. That sounds serious,' Abby gulped. That was considerably longer than all of her relationships put together.

'Yes, it definitely was a while.' Tim drifted: 'We met on a work project and things kind of fell into place from that. It was a textbook romance on the surface, and I did have some good times with her initially, but it was always quite predictable. I kind of assumed a deeper love would override the need for a spark after the initial excitement wore off, you know?'

Abby nodded.

'So I took our predictability as normal. She had the guts to want more of a spark, I guess, and she found her fuse with the guy she dumped me for, but not before seeing him behind my back for the last six months of our relationship whilst spending every penny of mine that she could.'

'Crikey,' Abby was open-mouthed. 'How could anyone do that? That must have been hideous to deal with.' She hadn't even considered that Charlie might have cheated on her...

'Mmmm, yes.' Tim nodded thoughtfully, 'I think I went through every single emotion in the book: hate, betrayal, sadness, self-doubt, wanting revenge. I questioned everything to try and figure out how someone I'd treated so beautifully could treat me like that.'

'Because she's bloody horrible. Nothing to do with you!' Abby exclaimed.

'But then I was gutted I'd lost her. A man thing I guess, we don't like losing, especially to other men.'

'No, I think that's an across the board thing. I don't

enjoy losing either.'

'But do you know what the weird thing is?' He paused and looked at her again, honesty pouring out of his eyes. 'Right now, I can't remember what I ever saw in her. She's pretty to look at initially, but you need to be beautiful on the inside, too. I think it shines through. The more she lied, the uglier she became.'

Abby sipped her coffee. At least Charlie had been honest and talked to her. You see he wasn't all bad, she told herself. He was just wrong in this instance, and she was right for him. She shook herself to focus on Tim, who was still talking.

'... and now I know her true character, I think she's kind of repulsive.' He took a big swig of his drink and put it down. 'This feels like a therapy session,' he joked.

'My mother would be proud.'

'Is she a therapist?'

'Yes, and a damn good one. She's my rock really. Always there with the good advice, it's just my poor form in not taking it.'

'Ah, but you have to learn these lessons in life, that's how you grow.'

Abby nodded.

'So Tim, what made you get over Catherine the not-so-great in the end?'

Tim smiled. 'Well, despite loving the shots and kebabs ... I don't know really; it was a whole mixture of things. I think time does give you perspective. My friends played a big role. They all liked her to start with but then they saw me sort of quieten. They all said I wasn't myself, afterwards of course. And I gradually spent time doing the things I used to love. Oh, and I got rid of anything she gave me, and suddenly my space and my life were mine again. And that felt good ...'

Abby listened intently. He'd dealt with it and become a better person. Maybe if she focused her intentions on being like that, she'd be better all round, but that would mean accepting it was over, which it wasn't. Her mind had drifted again. She forced herself to focus on Tim. 'Not much fun at the time but you've come through it alright?' she asked.

'No, it wasn't much fun. The boys just wanted me to go out and drink, but to be honest, I just wanted to hide away. Not very manly really on that score, but it was the first time I'd been dumped, and I just didn't know how to deal with it.'

'Yes! I'm the same!' Abby exclaimed, excited to have found someone else who could share her exact pain. 'No one tells you when you're growing up that you might meet someone and it *not* work.'

'So it comes as a complete shock and then you think the grown-up thing to do is to keep working at it.'

'What a nightmare!'

'Damn fairy tales,' he rolled his eyes dramatically.

'Yes. No one gets dumped in those. Plus the pain of rejection just seems to get worse, doesn't it?'

'Yes, everyone told me it would get better with time, but those first few weeks ... ugh.'

'I know! Completely hideous. It's like every second offends more than the last,' Abby was delighted to have met someone who shared her view.

'I wish it could have happened sooner to me, to be honest. Then I could have moved on and found the woman I'm meant to be with, instead of thinking it was her for so long'

'Oh gosh, Tim, I'm so sorry you felt like that. Mind

you, if that's the way she was, then I'm glad it happened before you married her, when it would have been far more complicated and heart-breaking to go through.'

'Yes, so everyone says. It didn't help at the time, but now, I completely agree,' and they both stared at their coffee cups.

'Woody's told me a bit about what happened with Charlie.'

Abby hung her head, almost embarrassed. 'He just didn't love me anymore. Rejected me and now, I guess, I'm just left trying to figure out what it was that made his feelings change, what it was I did wrong.'

'Maybe you didn't do anything physically wrong. You've broken up with guys before because they're just not right for you, right?'

'Yes.'

'Well maybe he just felt like that.'

'It could have been so perfect, though.'

'But it wasn't, and you need to take your own advice. I'm glad it ended before it got more complicated to breakup.'

'True,' Abby shuddered. 'I don't know how people cope with divorces. It must be brutal to have to start again after thinking you've sworn your life to one person and made all those plans.'

Tim smiled at her, 'You're going to be A-OK, Abby. As much as you might have signed yourself off to him in your head, there's going to be a much better person for you who'll actually put a ring on it,' Tim mimicked Beyoncé's hand flourish.

'Oh wow,' she giggled, 'that was something special.'

'I will take that compliment and add it to my CV,' Tim chuckled.

Abby looked out of the window before drawing her eyes to meet his again. Her voice was lowered to a whisper: 'How do you know I'll meet someone else, Tim? You say it with such certainty.'

'Because you seem like a good person, you've got a lot of good people around you and, at some point, if you keep being true to what you want and who you are, you'll meet someone who feels the same. But you can't hide yourself away if that's what you want. Although it sounds like you're making a pretty good job of getting back out there.'

Abby rolled her eyes at that, 'You've got your cousin to thank for that. My normal way of dealing with any life problem – ice cream and movies – just wasn't working this time.'

'Speak of the devil,' Tim held his phone up to show a text from Woody. 'Ten minutes and he'll be back. We can finish up here and wander home.'

*****

BACK IN THE apartment, Abby scurried off to her room, eager to call Lucy. 'Lucy, Tim told me how his ex cheated on him, spent his money and then left him, that's pretty brutal compared to what I've been through, don't you think?'

'Yes, that's awful, but how is it relevant to what you've been through?' Lucy asked.

'Well, it kind of looks as if I got off lightly, doesn't it? So I don't understand why you and everyone are so vehement about me getting over Charlie. It wasn't as if he did anything like that to me.'

'Tim?'

'Woody's cousin, you know the gorgeous one,' why was Lucy being so slow off the mark today?

'Yes, THE lovely and gorgeous one. Here's a question: why don't you go on a date with him?'

'Huh?' Abby said, 'but he's Woody's cousin.'

'So?'

'Isn't that off limits? No. Besides I think we're in the friend zone. I don't get any kind of vibe from him.'

'Maybe if he's been hurt too, he wants to take it slowly and is just getting to know you first. You know dipping his toe in the water a bit to see what your ethos is.'

'Well, me blathering on about Charlie was probably not the best option then.'

'Nothing about Charlie is the best option. Tim however ...'

'Well, I was going to say that at least Tim knows I'm honest and upfront,' Abby paused to imagine it. He was lovely. People always had two sides to them, though, and she shuddered, not having the strength to take a risk and find out what his dark side was, so she shook off the notion.

'Genuinely, Lucy, I know what you're doing and, believe me, I love you for it. He is gorgeous, but I just don't think he likes me that way, we only talked because I got locked out, plus,' she said matter of factly, 'right now I can't afford to emotionally put myself on the line again.'

'Yes, well, of course the sensible option is to keep thinking about the guy that hurt you, chipped away at your confidence until you weren't yourself anymore, made you perpetually unhappy and insecure. ... Mmmm nice guy, that Charlie. Yes, what was I thinking suggesting you go out with someone nice!?' Lucy raged in a rare moment of sarcasm.

Abby paused before speaking. 'You see, Lucy, here's the most frustrating thing. I can hear you saying it, and even I'll admit there's a part of my mind that knows it to be true. I can't argue with you. So why in god's name, *why* can't I get over him? Why can't I break the habit? If anyone else had treated me that way, I'd have deleted them from my life in minutes, but with him I still live in the hope that he'll realise what he's lost. Why do I still check my phone waiting to see if he's contacted me again and wants me back? I was my best self around him, Lucy. My. Best. Self. I literally couldn't have done more, looked more toned or tried to please him, and it still wasn't enough.'

She heard Lucy breathe in. 'Because that's just it. He's manipulated you into believing that it's all your fault. So you think every day 'what can I do differently to win him back, for it to go back to the way it was before. But actually, it's him who changed, he's the one not making the effort anymore and why you fail to see that I don't know.'

'But at the start it was so good.'

'Of course, it was good, it was all for show, and you enjoyed falling for it. The real Charlie then came into view, and you spent all your energy trying to convince him to be the charming version of himself because you prefer that, but he had no need to because he already knew he had you, hook, line and sinker.'

'No! I don't buy it.'

Lucy groaned.

'You're wrong, Luce, it's not *his* fault our relationship changed, it was mine. I was so happy to play girlfriend that I turned into cook and cleaner. I'm the one who changed – I got boring. Maybe if he spent some time with fun Abby again, he'd come back to me.'

'Abby, life with you is never boring. You can't take 100% of the blame for the relationship dissolving. He had to fight for it, too, but he didn't.' There was silence as they both weighed Lucy's words.

'I hate that he didn't,' Abby said, softer now.

'Because you're not used to losing the guy. You're used to getting what you want, and in every other part of your life, work, even money to some extent, you're used to just trying harder or being tenacious so eventually you hit your goal. But you can't control human emotions.'

'But I see other women turning on the charm and winning their boyfriends back, and they end up happier than they ever were before. That's what I want – I want my old life back.'

Just then her phoned chimed a text alert through.

Charlie.

Charlie had just texted her.

'Oh my god, Lucy, he's texted me. Charlie's literally just texted me.'

'What really?' Lucy couldn't hide her surprise or her dismay, 'How come?'

'Well I might have texted him.'

'When?' Lucy prodded.

'Every single day, sometimes more than once,' Abby confessed triumphantly to Lucy's groans. 'You can't deny it's worked, though!'

'What kind of thing have you been texting him?'

'Positive affirmations of how I feel, I wanted him to know that despite the distance, he is the only person on my mind and that I believe in us.'

'Well, what's he said?'

Ignoring the cautious tones in her best friend's voice,

Abby flicked through to the message, her fingers shaking slightly over the screen.

'He wants to meet, Luce!' Abby's voice was high and felt estranged from her body. It was the most energetic voice she'd squeezed out in months.

'What did he say after two months of blanking you?'

Abby, high on her newfound energy, blanked Lucy's darker comment, 'Well, he said that all my texts had made him realise we need to delve more deeply into the state of ourselves, and we should meet next week. He's suggested Green Park.'

A moment of silence told Lucy it was alright to speak now, so she did. Somewhat pointlessly, she asked: 'And are you going to go?'

Abby shrieked, 'Yes! Oh my goodness, Lucy, I'm so relieved. I can't live happily without him Luce, I've tried.' How she was ever going to wait until next Thursday, she didn't know. The excitement was too much.

'OK, I have seven days to preen myself and make sure I'm looking my absolute best for our triumphant reunion. Hair, nails, legs waxed, you name it.'

Lucy was silent on the phone.

'Lucy, you're wrong about Charlie, he didn't suck the life out of me, he makes me feel alive ... listen to how much more energised I am just from one text!'

'And just how worrying is it to me that your entire energy and happiness levels can fluctuate based on his one measly little text. Your confidence should not be so linked to him,' Lucy said in despair.

'I'm instantly more myself, Luce. I haven't been myself since he broke up with me.'

'Well, the Abby I know didn't exist in the last six months of your relationship *with* Charlie, so to me, you've not been yourself for a lot longer than that. You're only feeling alive because he took your confidence from you, and now he's decided to breathe some back ... It's all in his control. It's so wrong.'

'Right, that's it, Luce, we need to change the conversation because I know we're not going to agree on this one. Before I forget, are you still good for breakfast tomorrow?' After chatting a bit more to Luce and advising her on what to do next at the gym, Abby hung up, eager to start turning her life around. After coming out of the fog that had surrounded her for two whole months, she could see her 'nothing else matters' attitude needed to go, and she finally admitted that her room was in an awful state. 'Pigs would die if they were trapped in here,' Woody had said seriously, 'either of depression or lack of oxygen,' before he'd covered his mouth and walked back into the kitchen with his best 'have you no shame' face.

'Right,' if she was going to look good, she needed a nice room to look good in. Four hours and a bin bag of rubbish later, her other copy of *The Notebook* was back on its shelf in the living room and she resolutely threw her 'getting over Charlie' comfort pyjamas into the black bin bag of the past as well. Her laundry was drying, and making her bed was the last thing to do. Looking around the room, she was pleased with her handiwork. It really was a beautiful bedroom – high Georgian ceilings, a deep pile carpet she could now see and, from behind the piles of dirty laundry, she'd unearthed her fireplace, which now looked gorgeous covered in candles and flowers. Candles. Where were her scented candles? Sod it, she'd have to buy one tomorrow. Texting Lucy, they arranged to meet on the Kings Road, between Jo Malone and The

White Company she was sure she'd find something ...
her tidying antics had done nothing to calm her mentally
charged nerves, so she grabbed her freshly laundered
gym kit. Step two: preparing her body.

*****

LUCY PACED THE floors of her own already-pristine
apartment, extremely concerned for her friend. Having
scraped her off the floor two months ago, she knew that
to the world Abby appeared to be back to her normal self,
but Lucy knew she was still balancing on an incredibly
thin edge that Charlie had the power to push her off of
again. It was a chilling thought.

The only person Lucy knew that could calm her
nerves about Abby was Abby's mum, and although
she didn't want to worry her unnecessarily, she found
herself dialling her number. Within moments, Alice was
distilling her soothing tones down the line.

'She's always been so confident in what she likes and
what she will and won't accept in life. To have someone
place doubt on every single aspect of who she is, how she
looks and what she enjoys has made her question who
she really is. For the first time ever, really.'

'She's just so vulnerable right now. I don't want him
to hurt her.'

'Oh Lucy, you know she's like a freight train, there is
no stopping her when she's mid-journey. As hideous a
process as it might be for her if he derails her again, she'll
have the self-awareness to get through it and be proud of
who she is and not let anyone dismiss it so easily again.'

'That's assuming, of course, it doesn't go well. I'm
petrified they're going to end up back together, and I'll

have lost my friend to a bastard, sorry, idiot once again. I can't bear seeing her personality so damped down.'

'Abby believes he's perfect. But no-one's perfect. Her father drives me crazy sometimes, but it's never about the big stuff.'

'Yes, the respect is there.'

'Respect and values – we both share and want the same things in life. I think Abby's going to need to see that she and Charlie don't have that. He does nothing for her. Maybe she'll see him again and realise that she's placed him on far too high a pedestal.'

'Maybe. She's just so excited ...'

'Well, it's up to Abby. As emotionally charged as she can be, she's not stupid, and believe it or not, she's listened to what you've said over the past few months. All that will be flying around her brain as well.'

Lucy paused to take it in.

'Thank you, Alice.'

'Well, thank you, Lucy, for being there for her. You're the sole reason I've felt so calm about this. You're an amazing person and an amazing friend. Now tell me, what's new with you? Let's end this on a good note ...'

*****

ALICE LAY AWAKE in bed next to John that night, glad that Lucy had called her. Abby needed to know how fortunate she was to have such a good friend. Although she believed everything she'd said to console Lucy earlier, her natural maternal instinct was creeping in, and she stared at the ceiling with her worries.

She hadn't shared the latest with John yet, but after all these years of marriage, he obviously sensed something was bothering her and had probably guessed it was a matter of the heart with Abby, as he was holding her close. She would tell him if it was serious, but for now, she just looked at her husband's smile as he lay holding her. Family life all seemed to be a constant cycle of calming down loved ones' emotions when life chucked them a curveball. Funny how just some human kindness and touch could make you feel so much better and warmer. Alice leaned into the crook of her husband's arm and cherished his calming presence. She wanted that warmth so much for Abby and prayed with all her heart and soul that her daughter would find the courage to block Charlie out and move on. It was 50-50 at the moment. She prayed something would happen to make her realise she was fine the way she was, and there actually was something wrong with the way Charlie treated her. Until then, she'd follow the advice she'd given Lucy: be patient. And if her daughter was going to go full-steam ahead with seeing Charlie again then all they could do was be ready and there for her after he said what he wanted to say ...

14

OH NO HE DIDN'T

ABBY'S HEART HAD been pounding since Charlie had texted her a week ago, and it was showing no signs of slowing. She'd had her hair sliced back into her normal style, kissing goodbye to the dry ends of the last two months. After a leg wax and having her nails done, she'd emerged from the salon feeling altogether fabulous, and that feeling had stayed with her until now.

Now here she was, moments from seeing him again. She paused at the entrance to Green Park to compose herself and slip on her new heels. Her hands shook slightly, so she breathed slowly, trying to calm herself before walking the final few steps to the park. Sunlight met her square in the eyes, blinding her for a second as she scanned the park for him. She gasped: there he was. Standing, dressed impeccably in a suit, he was even more handsome than she remembered him. He'd obviously dressed in his best suit for her. Her heart swelled.

'Abby, how the devil are you?' She ignored the fact he was speaking as if he was welcoming a long-lost cousin into his home and quickened her pace to throw herself into his open arms. As she neared, he closed them abruptly and instead, grasped her hands as he kissed each cheek. His touch sent shock waves through her body.

'Crikey, if you're not the one, I don't know who is,' she whispered. No one else had ever made her feel that way, ever.

'Abby, come, let's walk.'

She smiled up at him, breathing in his scent. He smelt like home, and she was utterly transfixed. She didn't move. Her heart pounded as Charlie pulled her gently along to a quieter corner of the park. Feeling his hand press on her arm sent another jolt through her body. The love she felt for Charlie, the love she'd been desperately trying to suppress over the last two months, came flooding back and hit her like a truck. Her feelings hadn't faded at all – she'd been exhausting herself trying to force them out of her.

'Well, what's the plan?' She beamed, 'you sounded so intriguing on the phone.'

'You always were so impatient. Wait and see,' he said with a hint of a knowing smile.

Abby paused in her tracks. She just needed a moment to take it all in. Looking up into his eyes, she started to smile a slow smile, and when his blue eyes gazed back down at her, she tried not to gasp. It was like they were piercing straight into her heart – god she'd missed them. She turned her body to face his, waiting for him to draw her in. She was longing for him to kiss her now.

Why wasn't he kissing her? Maybe he wanted to talk first, she reasoned. Sod it, she'd take it as slow as he wanted; they had all the time in the world now. There were so many questions she was itching to ask him: what had happened to make him realise she was the one? Had he seen other women? Ugh, maybe she didn't have the resolve to ask that – she didn't really want to know the answer either.

She realised she'd been staring up at him and not talking for way too long. She snapped out of her thought coma, giggling nervously. 'Sorry I just, well, it's just ...,' she told herself to breathe, '... well, let's just say it's nice to see you again.'

Charlie's lips curved into a charming smile, 'Yes, I can imagine it is for you.'

Abby felt awkward – what a strange response. She inhaled to speak again, but before she could, he continued.

'Let's walk,' he gestured towards the right with his free hand. Abby followed his lead.

'Er, how far are we going?' Her feet were beginning to hurt in her new heels.

'Not far,' he nodded his head in the direction of the tall Victorian townhouses opposite. She looked up at him again trying to read his face. He was being very quiet. Probably taking in the severity of what life would have been like had he not realised his mistake. Don't take him back without a bollocking, she thought, however fake it might be – that way he'd be put off ever deserting her again. Despite the rubbing on her sole, there was a slightly victorious spring in her step again. She saw their reflection in a window and checked out their perfect height proportions. They really were a handsome couple; they would have cute babies for sure. She looked relaxed and younger somehow, the tensions from the past few months dissolved away, and she smiled broadly.

'It was worth the time apart if we're going to be stronger than ever now,' she halted her steps. 'Stop, Charlie, I need to say this,' and somewhat reluctantly, it seemed, he paused. It didn't matter, after months of trying to suppress her emotions and change them to follow everyone's advice, it felt good to finally be so honest: 'I love you so much, Charlie, I knew what we had was different and special and worth it. I know I was a mess at the end, and you do need to listen to what makes me happy more,' she reprimanded him. 'But hopefully time apart is what you needed to figure that out. I knew you would be worth the wait.'

Charlie loosened his hand in hers and she held it tighter. He gently shook it off and tilted her chin to his. This was it, he was going to kiss her again. Closing her eyes lightly, she waited for the softness of his lips to meet hers.

A second later, no kiss. Abby squinted through her long lashes and he spoke: 'We're actually here.'

Abby pulled back playfully to see where they were, it just looked like a normal town house to her. Oooo, perhaps it was like one of those posh members' clubs like at Grosvenor Square, which looked like a normal house on the outside and then up the steps, through the huge wooden doors, a butler would emerge to guide them through to an exclusive world of boutique luxury.

The promise pleased Abby no end. He'd gone to so much trouble to make their reunion special, so Abby flashed a fabulous smile up at him, excited to her core, 'Lead the way, sir...' Still holding his hand, she walked up one step behind him. He glanced down at her and pushed open the door.

Almost wanting to close her eyes and open them once the door was open, she stopped next to him and followed him inside, looking expectantly up at him, like a dog transfixed by its owner, full of trust and belief something good is about to happen.

Instead of plush carpet underfoot, she almost instantly caught her heel on a worn rug, a faded and tired remnant of someone's holiday in Morocco at least a good ten years ago. Charlie tutted. Abby did a double take – did he really just tut at her tripping up? She looked around the entrance hall, a completely dark room save for a beam of light coming from one large window on the first floor landing, which was covered in tracing paper and had a vase of fake flowers dumped in front of it by someone who perhaps cared once. The light streamed determinedly in through it anyway, illuminating the dust their arrival had thrown up. An oak staircase stood proudly in the centre of the room, polished only by the oil on people's hands sliding down it over the years. Clearly once a beautiful place, it had been left to fade.

'Where are we?' She asked as her eyes adjusted to the darkness and making out an old-school reception desk set behind a sliding window. She followed his gaze down to their hands: his hand was wide open and hers was curled tightly around it, clutching him. She let his hand fall away from hers, and he didn't fight the movement. Her mouth closed, mirroring his silent awkwardness as she looked up at him. Free from her grip, he moved to tap on the receptionist's window. And moments later, a lady, who Abby put in her mid-fifties, with the name tag 'Belinda' bustled through with her notes.

'Ah, yes, Charlie, you can go on up. She's expecting you,' Belinda gave Abby a quizzical look over her glasses. Abby moved uneasily from foot to foot, a childhood trait and a sure sign that she was uncomfortable.

'Brilliant, thank you Belinda. Nice to see you again,' Charlie proffered in his most charming voice. Surely that was the voice he should be speaking to her in if he was trying to get her back?

'Come on then,' he moved to stand just out of hand-holding reach. The mood changed entirely. Suddenly his eyes weren't sympathetic, they'd hardened as if preparing himself for what was to come next. What was coming next? An overwhelming sense of dread crept over her and Charlie offered no reassurance as he bounded up the stairs and waited at the top of the first floor for her. His brow furrowed as if she'd deeply annoyed him. This wasn't the Charlie who had smiled so genuinely at the park, and he certainly didn't look like the Charlie who had slobbed around the apartment, taking her for granted.

No, he actually looked slightly deranged. She felt her body move automatically towards him while her mind raced. The silence in the large building amplified the click of her heels, emphasising the torture that the right one was giving her foot. With one hand on the wooden bannister, Abby pulled herself up the stairs.

Finally reaching the top, she steadied herself. 'Charlie, what exactly is going on?'

At the sound of her voice, a door to their right swung open and a woman in her late 40s dressed in a smart grey suit with her hair tied up in a tight bun crisply said: 'Good afternoon to you both, please come inside.'

Charlie practically ran through her door. The woman, unphased by his eagerness, remained standing where she was, gesturing for the concerned Abby to move forward, which she duly did.

'Hello, I'm Abby,' she held her hand out to shake, 'you'll have to forgive me, I have no idea what's happening here.'

'Never mind, dear, all will be explained in the next

hour or so, I'm sure.'

Abby frowned and she moved into the room to see two chairs opposite a desk and a chaise longue by the window. The fireplace had an array of framed certificates resting on it. The penny finally dropped; they were at couples counselling. No wonder Charlie was on edge, he hated talking about his emotions at the best of times, let alone in front of a stranger. That explained why he'd been so tense with her – he was nervous. Bless him.

She felt so relieved and smiled at Charlie supportively, grateful he wanted to work on their relationship to this extent. Lucy could not fail to be impressed by how seriously Charlie was taking their reunion. They were going to get through this. She relaxed. The space was clean, bright and comfortable; it felt like an oasis in contrast to the dark dankness of the rest of the building.

'I'm Miss Esther. Please address me as such. Everything you say stays within these four walls and I'm pretty sure there's no one listening down the chimney.'

Abby sat on the edge of her chair, poised to listen attentively.

'So let me start by asking what you know of me,' Miss Esther prompted.

Abby simply shook her head gesturing a big fat zero.

'Charlie has asked me to set aside an hour and a half for you, Abby, today.'

'*Us*,' Abby corrected her looking at Charlie kindly, trying to reach his hand, 'Charlie set aside an hour and a half today for *us*.'

'Ah, no,' Miss Esther looked directly at Abby, 'an hour and a half, for *you*.'

Abby looked confused and turned to Charlie, 'What? You got *me* this? OK, so, well we're wasting valuable minutes of *my* time here, will one of you please tell me what's going on?'

Miss Esther looked at Charlie, waiting for him to speak. Abby was getting impatient. 'Charlie? Oh dear god, is this what I think it is?' She felt her cheeks flushing red with shame. She'd so blindly believed he wanted her back that this was both mortifying and gutting at the same time.

'Charlie,' she hissed, 'if you didn't want me back, why didn't you just say so?'

'Well, I tried when I broke up with you almost three months ago, but your feelings had grown so strong for me that you put a mental block against hearing it.'

Abby held her head in her hands. It was true, she'd completely misread every single signal Charlie had given her in his text, judging it on what she wanted it to be and not what it actually was.

'Anyway, Abby, don't worry. This is on me,' he leant over and patted her knee. 'You have 90 minutes to get over me.'

Abby's eyebrow moved disturbingly close to her scalp.

'Listen to Miss Esther. She's helped many women get over me and live happy and fulfilled lives.'

'What?' Abby's blood was boiling.

'Well, I'll leave you to it then,' Charlie clipped and jumped out of his seat, Abby rose in fury.

'No, no you stay there, like a good girl,' Charlie pushed Abby back down. 'No, my dear, you need this, OK?' Charlie spoke to her if he was addressing a six-year-old having her first tetanus shot. He turned to Miss Esther.

'So Miss Esther. To get you up to speed, *this one* told me outside how much she still loved me and this time apart had only confirmed that.'

Abby hung her head in shame: 'this one'? How many

others had there been? How could she have thought he was the one? She had put him on a pedestal; he'd put her on a list. She wanted more than anything to just leave, but one part of her wouldn't let her.

'The way you looked at me when you saw me again, Charlie – you felt it. I saw it in your eyes. You blocked me out the second we entered this building. You're just scared of loving and being loved. You're nothing but a scared little boy.'

'Major denial, too. Extreme case, this one,' he nodded to Miss Esther. 'Try and wrap it up in an hour,' he concluded before crossing the room.

'Oh, we're going to take all night here, Charlie,' Abby yelled. 'Don't you worry about that. Come on, Miss Esther, let's watch a movie and get takeout 'on Charlie.' I'm definitely not leaving now.'

'Goodbye, Abby.' And with that he strode out of the door, probably straight back to his dingy apartment to put his boxer shorts back on. She knew his real truth. She was furious.

'She believes we had time apart to reassess our feelings and not because it was over,' Miss Esther quoted her notes.

'I can't be the first person to go through a breakup and feel that way, surely?' Damn it, why hadn't she been dumped before so could have behaved like a teenager when it was vaguely acceptable, even expected?

'So have you been calling him?' Miss Esther cut to the chase.

'Yes,' Abby said, 'and texting, tweeting, WhatsApping, Facebooking and emailing – all the 'ings,' not to mention the odd #throwbackthursday on Instagram. Oh, the shame,' Abby hung her head.

15

THE RESCUER

'RIGHT, WELL, LET'S get down to it,' Miss Esther pragmatically powered ahead.

Abby nodded.

'Great. First a few questions. One: did he love bomb you at the start?'

'Love bomb?' Hadn't Lucy used that phrase?

'Shower you with affection and grand gestures?'

'Yes!' Yes, he had and Lucy had clocked it.

Miss Esther wrote something down and checked something off a list.

'Would you say that you were more confident before you met Charlie than afterwards?'

'Definitely, yes.'

'Would you say that during the process of your relationship, you said to yourself: "I can't do anymore for him and yet nothing I do is good enough or makes him happy?"'

'Yes, definitely,' Abby felt a tear trickle down her cheek at the memory. 'He actually told me when he broke up with me that I was not enough for him.'

'Did you feel exhausted or mentally drained?'

'Yes, absolutely,' where was all this leading, she wondered.

'Don't worry, this will all make sense in a moment,' Miss Esther must have read her mind – but of course, this was not her first time.

'Did he share with you a moment from his past that made you feel considerable sympathy for him?'

'Yes, he told me about his father not loving him.'

'And that made you hold him closer and promise to protect him?'

'Yes,' Abby spoke quietly. 'Before you go on, does that make me a fool? Why is sympathy relevant here?'

'Because if someone views kindness as a weakness, they create situations to induce sympathy. It's very hard for a kind person to resist taking care of the other person. You naturally feel closer because they've shared something private with you, and you swear to yourself you're going to be so caring that their pain will dissolve. In that moment, your existence becomes about them.'

Abby nodded, taking it all in.

'Now, that's not to say that anyone who shares a dark memory is manipulating you, you just need to weigh it up with the rest of their intentions.'

'OK,' Abby paused. 'Was anything real or true with Charlie?'

Miss Esther paused and looked at Abby over her glasses. 'That's not for me to say, I can only analyse what you tell me.'

Abby nodded again.

Miss Esther continued: 'Tell me, what were your hopes when you met Charlie?'

'I wanted to fall in love and make a life with someone.'

'You wanted a life partner?'

'Yes, but he said the same to me,' Abby justified.

'And maybe he meant it, or thought he meant it at the

time. You can never be wholly sure with Charlie. You see the problem with people like Charlie is that whilst they may want those normal things, there is one overriding factor in their minds that rises higher than any other thought or wish. Do you know what that is?'

'No, honestly, I don't. Please help me understand who I fell in love with.'

'He wants to win. It is his only fuel. You're a beautiful woman, smart, no doubt talented, a lot of guys would like to be with you. An excellent prize to have on his arm.'

'But he won me, he absolutely got me! Why would he then leave?'

'Because he'd won. And he needed to win again. He knew he had you. It's all about the chase with him. He is a narcissist. He's not genuinely kind. He adapts to situations and plays you until he's won. He follows very different thought patterns to the rest of society. We all have a bit of narcissism within us, but we have the ability to control it and weigh it up when comparing it to other elements of life. He doesn't. And crucially he is *never* going to change.'

Abby sat in silence, trying to take it all in.

'It's a lot to take in initially, but I'm trying to whizz through it so you have some understanding of what you've been through. Let's push on for now, you can always come back and see me again if you need to.'

'OK,' Abby whispered.

'Have you tried to date other people and fail?' Miss Esther enquired.

Abby nodded.

For the rest of the hour, Miss Esther churned through questions and explanations. It was all stuff her mum, Lucy and even Woody had told her, to help her see

Charlie for who he really was, but somehow hearing it from someone so unbiased made it all the more real.

An hour later, Abby sat on a park bench outside Miss Esther's, not knowing if she was in shock or not. What she *did* know was that she was livid. Utterly and uncontrollably livid. Annie Lennox sung about a thin line between love and hate, but Abby was well beyond that line. She was furious. She yanked off her uncomfortable heels and slung them in her bag, savouring the relief of her foldable ballet flats as they instead kissed her sore feet. She just wanted to get home.

'What a complete prick!' Abby voiced loudly, startling a few dog walkers.

Unapologetically she carried on voicing her frustrations. 'Am I more mad at Charlie or myself?' A lady walked past, shook her head and tutted.

'There's nothing I can do about this face, it's just the way it is when you find out you've been dating a narcissist,' Abby responded. The lady moved on. Others walked past her, avoiding eye contact nervously. A pigeon landed right by her.

'Oh my god, what has happened to my life?' She yelled at the pigeon, who flew into the nearest branch and took a large crap.

'Yep,' Abby nodded, 'that's exactly what happened to me. He shat on me from a great height and I sat under it, taking it. An abysmal state of affairs, Abby,' she reprimanded herself and the pigeon flew off.

Abby groaned in exasperation thinking back to Miss Esther's words: *Don't feel bad, he brainwashed you; he's done it to loads of women. He's very clever, very manipulative. He's hopelessly insecure, so to make himself feel powerful, he likes to take confident and beautiful women and beat them down so that they rely on him, but ironically in doing so, they change their character and no longer become attractive to him, so he spits them back out. It's rather unprofessional of me to tell you this because, in some ways, he's one of my best clients, he brings in a lot of referrals,'* she paused here to look over her glasses, *'but I can see in your eyes that you're ready to go and need get on with your life. Don't let Charlie bring you down any more.'*

It was weird. As wholly embarrassing as the whole episode had been, it really had done the trick. She felt different. She'd been living in a state of fake hope that she could control the situation and turn it around herself, when really Charlie had controlled their relationship, every second of it, from beginning. Lucy had called him a parasite once, and she'd been right. He had literally devoured every good thing about her, wrung her dry and was no doubt moving on to the next poor victim. He should come with a warning.

ABBY MADE IT home and let the hot water wash the last salty tears from her face. This time, no one was seeing her cry. She pounded the wall in the shower with her fists, the way she'd seen people in movies do.

'Ouch!' It really hurt, so she stopped that straight away.

She watched the shower water drain away, willing herself to stay still until the last drop had gone, washing away the last memory down the plughole with it.

She rubbed herself dry with a fresh new towel and dressed in different clothes. Nothing tainted by Charlie would touch her 'fresh start skin,' and with her reborn resolve she stepped into the hall. Hearing music in

Woody's room, she banged on the door and, when he opened it, went straight in for a hug. Holding his warmth to her tightly, she managed a grin. 'Drink?'

Woody raised his eyebrow at her, remembering the text from Lucy earlier that day warning him to be in.

'I've got a Sancerre chilling in the fridge, me lady, if that satisfies your craving?' Woody's butler voice was always hilarious.

'It'll be a start,' she giggled. 'Come on then, Jeeves, start pouring.'

'So how did it go?'

Abby walked into the kitchen with him, 'Well, it's over.' Holding her voice steadier, Abby said it more firmly. 'It's over.' She had not been able to utter those words over the past months, but now she said them, a numbness she hadn't felt before travelled over her. It was actually true.

Woody pushed the glass of chilled wine towards her. Abby took two sips, opened her mouth to speak, thought about what to say to Woody, looked at him again, then guzzled the rest of the glass. Woody pursed his lips together, nodded, gestured and refilled her wine glass.

'It takes a lot to shock you, Abby, despite it happening quite often these last few months. Is that what this is? Shock?'

She nodded. She knew he was intrigued, but he'd have to wait a moment before she could even know where to start.

'Oh, spit it out! Abby what happened?'

She looked at him and shook her head again, 'Oh Woody, you just wouldn't believe the audacity of that man.'

'You wanna bet? He's a grade-A tosser. I would totally believe it.'

A polite knock on the door signalled Lucy's arrival, and Woody ran to let her in.

'What have I missed?' Lucy pulled Abby in for a massive hug, her eyes full of concern.

'Nothing, she hasn't told me what happened,' Woody spoke, frustrated as anything.

'I will do now. Lucy, what are you doing tomorrow?'

'Nothing much, why?'

'Well, I need to go shopping.' Abby stressed 'shopping' in the way that Lucy would know that by hook or by crook they would be shopping from 10:30am till however late it took. 'Help me go through my clothes tonight will you? I mean everything: underwear, the lot, you name it. I'm chucking out anything that I ever wore with Charlie.' Pausing as she realised that that would mean a considerable amount of her favourite collectables, she rephrased. 'No, scrap that, I'm chucking out everything I bought to wear *for* him when we were going out. Yes.' Happy with her decision, she nodded and tapped the table with her hand, 'Take a seat people. You would not believe what he did to me earlier.'

Ten minutes later Lucy shrieked: 'The sheer audacity of the man!'

'That's what I said! Woody, what do you reckon?' They both looked at him.

Woody looked awkwardly uncertain of what to say when two women were borderline neurotic. It was so much easier with guys – if one of your mates crossed the invisible line of friendship, you either never spoke to them again or socked them in the jaw. Women, from what he could tell, smouldered and plotted and literally seethed until one day they'd wake up and not only be completely fine and laughing off the severity of the situation, they'd go one step further and tell *you* off if you expressed outrage or anger to it as well.

After a brief silence, he spoke: 'Solid twat. Better off without him,' and punched his hand down on the table.

'Yes!' They both cheered.

Lucy beamed at Abby, 'Let's drink to counsellors, new shoes and new dresses. And new guys.'

'Definitely. Whoop! I made it out the other side!' Suddenly she felt that old thrill of wanting to meet someone without any fears or doubts.

'Wow. I'm back, you guys, group hug,' she drew them in close to her. They were her best friends in the whole world.

'I couldn't have got through this without you both. Thank you so much! You're the best friends a girl could ever wish for. I love you both very much.'

'You know we love you, too,' Lucy looked emotional from the sheer relief that she had her friend back and out of Charlie's reach.

'Ha ha, you just went to counselling organised by your ex to get over him,' Woody laughed, breaking the emotion with a classic piss take.

Abby nodded, 'Ah well, at least it worked.'

'Should have done it months ago,' Woody suggested, which earnt him two sets of raised eyebrows.

'I'll get more wine,' he said, moving out of swiping reach.

LATER, WOODY HAD gone to meet some friends at a bar, Lucy and Abby sat curled up with a mug of tea in bed.

'Was Alice pleased when you told her?' Lucy asked.

'Yes, she said she was relieved and proud of how I was now,' Abby looked at Lucy. 'Thank you for keeping her in the loop.'

'She calmed me down the other night.'

'I'm so sorry to have worried you, Luce, I really didn't mean to,' Abby bit her lip. The last thing she wanted to do was stress out the people that loved her. She really needed to think about her decisions in the future before flying right into them. As good as the heads on approach had always been for her, lately it just didn't seem to be working.

'So how do you feel now?' Lucy asked tentatively.

'It's weird, Luce, I guess this is what getting over him feels like. I don't really feel anything anymore. I feel...'

'... sad?'

Abby nodded.

'You're mourning him and that's fair enough.'

'That's exactly how I feel. I don't ache for him finally. He's really not the man I thought he was and, though it pains me to say, he didn't love me how I want to be loved.' Abby looked at Lucy: 'You were right, I wasn't truly happy.'

Lucy stretched out her hand and held Abby's: 'For once, hearing the words 'you were right' doesn't actually make me happy. I wish to god he'd proved me wrong and you hadn't gone through this. I never want to see you that upset or low again.'

Abby nodded. It had been such a mental journey of self-doubt and heartache, the realisation she was coming out the other side of it was definitely good. 'How ironic, Luce: the nicest thing Charlie ever did was to help me get over him.'

'Breaking up with you might be the only honest thing he's done,' Lucy agreed.

Abby did feel freer now. Her head had been a cloud

of hurt, waking up every single day aching over him, worrying about him and what he was doing, berating herself for letting him get away. Battling emotion from the second she awoke to the minute she lay down at night was utterly exhausting. It would be nice to just wake up and have something other than pain to look forward to. Maybe she could go out on a proper date now, one that she wasn't forced into.

'It's making me wonder what I'm going to feel next for him.'

'Well in time, you'll feel nothing, I guess.'

'I sort of do already,' she whispered.

'Well that makes sense ... you've felt every other emotion, which would explain why you have nothing left to feel.'

Abby nodded and stared out of the window, 'It's kind of scary in a way. I feel like I'm just starting out all over again. I know I went on that date but really my mind was on Charlie, so my heart wasn't in it.'

'I know.'

'It was a good distraction, though,' Abby nudged Lucy's foot to let her know that all of her 'getting over Charlie' attempts hadn't been in vain.

Lucy paused, then grinned wickedly, 'What even vampire dude?'

Abby was aghast, 'Gosh, did that really happen to me?' she giggled.

'Oh yes, Miss Abby! Oh yes it did.'

'I still can't quite believe it.'

'Well I, for one, won't *ever* let you forget it.'

'Cheers, Luce.'

'Anytime, Abs. Actually I might need your help with something. Can you keep next Tuesday night free for me? I'll text you the details.'

'Is this to do with the big secret you've been meaning to share with me?' Abby said gleefully wondering what it was. 'I can't wait ... I'm in.'

Lucy grinned back at her.

'Something I'm definitely looking forward to indeed ...'

16

AVERSIONS GALORE

IT WAS TUESDAY evening and Lucy waited nervously for Abby to arrive. She stood right by the Tube station, at the corner of the large stone building that must have been a bank, back in the day. Knowing her best friend's weird issues when talking about bowel movements, the text she'd sent her asking to meet here had been deliberately secretive, but after all the weird scrapes she'd been there for Abby, she knew Abby owed her. There was no backing out now.

She saw Abby's tall frame rise out of the Tube station and look around to get her bearings. Waving her hand high in the air, Lucy caught her attention, and Abby flashed her a big grin in return.

'Keep calm,' she whispered to herself. Lucy's legs felt shaky, she was so nervous.

'Phew, just made it in time,' Abby said. 'Hello lovely,' as she trotted over the road, narrowly dodging a taxi hogging the road. As she stepped up the kerb, one of London's homeless people burped loudly and held out a cup for change.

'Charming!' Abby said to Lucy then looked down: 'I'm so sorry, I don't have any change.'

The old man grunted and unapologetically checked

her out.

'OK, come on then,' Lucy linked arms with her and took a deep breath.

'You've been very mysterious, Luce.'

Lucy remained quiet, trying to ignore Abby's eyes boring into hers.

'Seriously, you're beginning to make me worry now. I thought you were about to tell me about a guy or something.'

Lucy twitched, aware she was developing a sweaty upper lip, which Abby was scrutinising.

'Um,' now the moment was here, she didn't know where to start. For once, Abby was silent waiting.

'Abby, I have something to ask of you.'

Abby nodded hurriedly, 'Anything. Luce, are you alright?'

'Yes, I'm good, I just didn't want to do this on my own.'

'Do what?'

'This.' And with that, Lucy firmed up her grip on Abby's arm and yanked her in the direction of the corner building. This was it; she was going for it. She tried to ignore Abby's frown as she squinted at the poster nearby.

'What is it that poster is declaring? War on what ...?' Lucy felt her best friend's weight drag against her.

'It'll be fine once we're in there.'

'Lucy, stop!' Abby protested.

Lucy paused, not loosening her vice-like grip on Abby's arm. She turned her head to look at her and saw Abby's eyes wide open.

'Wait, Luce, where are we? Why are we here?'

Lucy sighed, halfway up the steps. She shouldn't have looked into her eyes – she couldn't stand seeing people look worried without wanting to soothe. The homeless guy still watching them slowly rose to his feet, pointed at Abby, leaned back and laughed his head off.

'Why am I getting laughed at by a homeless guy?'

Abby closed her mouth and gave him her best 'don't you dare' face. Lucy watched as her best friend craned to read the IBS clinic's poster in its entirety.

'Are you kidding me?' Abby's face filled with horror, 'Lucy, you know my aversion to poo. It makes me sweat … even thinking about, let alone talking about it.'

'Abby, calm down.'

'There's no way that I can go in there. Lucy, I feel for you, I really do, but I'll be physically sick. Even the notion of it is making me feel ill. I close my eyes when I do one, let alone talk about other people's.'

'There's no way you can have an aversion to poo,' Lucy said, matter of factly.

'Everyone has an aversion to poo.'

People were stopping and staring now; Lucy lowered her voice and hissed, 'Abby sort yourself out.' Her friend was breathing rapidly. 'You told me once how your mum had to take you to the doctor to convince you that you weren't a princess and you needed to poo.' Abby nodded.

'You'd held it in for two weeks, thinking it was smelly and brown and shouldn't be in the world.'

'I just couldn't believe I'd created it…,' Abby said to her woefully.

'Well, trust me, Abby, you need this class as much as I do,' Lucy was beginning to feel panicky herself now and this stress wasn't helping her stomach.

'But it really does make me sqwuirm, I was brought up never to discuss it, so I never do.'

'Are you meaning to tell me that with all the open and

frank discussions you have with your mother about sex and literally everything else in life, you *still* can't talk about poo?'

Abby grimaced and nodded her head. 'Absolutely, she's worse than me. My dad used to change my nappies and take care of that side of things. Please, Luce, don't make me go in there,' Abby pleaded. 'I'll vomit.'

'Abby all you've done is convince me how much you actually need to go in there too; it sounds like you have issues to deal with. Along with the rest of us IBS sufferers.'

Abby shuddered.

'This is important to me,' Lucy looked at her. 'I need you. You owe me, Abby.'

'OK, just give me a moment to steel myself.'

Lucy rolled her eyes.

'Wait, wait, wait ...' Abby was grabbing short breaths now, looking like she was going to hyperventilate, 'Just tell me what happens so I'm not scared.'

For god's sake, I really do wear the trousers in this friendship, Lucy realised. 'So, it's a room where we go round in a circle and discuss our problems and share solutions. Well, that's my understanding, anyway.'

'Because it's a clinic for poo, Lucy, everyone will think it's alright to just let rip right? It's going to smell awful. I won't be able to breathe.'

Lucy tightened her grip again and continued walking up the steps.

'Lucy!' Abby hissed in horror, 'I read that every smell has a weight to it, so technically if everyone does fart, we're going to breathe in the gas of twenty people's IBS sufferer's poo. It'll be overwhelmingly toxic.'

'Well, you travel on the Tube, don't you? It can't smell

any worse than that. Now suck it up,' Lucy said calmly.

'Oh my god, I'm going to contract it. Is that how it works? Is IBS airborne?'

Glad she hadn't loosened her grip anymore, Lucy strode up the remaining five steps with Abby behind her, looking like a panicky gazelle about to spring off in the opposite direction to evade certain death.

A high-pitched squeal spun their heads around; the homeless guy was now hysterical: 'Even *I* wouldn't be seen dead going in there,' he guffawed.

It stopped Lucy in her tracks; she was being judged – who the hell else was seeing her walk into the clinic? 'Let's just hurry this up,' Lucy muttered, nerves piling on. Thank god Charlie had dumped Abby – she had more than enough favours to call to get Abby in here.

She could hear Abby whispering a pep-talk to herself, stammering her way through it: 'I'll be alright, I just won't be able to breathe. I just won't breathe.' Lucy ignored it, and with the judgemental laughter ringing in her ears, she practically dragged them both through the door and gave a bright 'Hello there' to the lady waiting inside.

'Welcome!'

Lucy looked at Abby: 'See, she sounds normal,' she hissed.

'I'm Hilary.' She had a big smile and a big body, which she moved around the little table to shake their hands, 'And you are?' Hilary said, closing the door and drowning out the outside world.

'My name is Lucy, and I booked two places for me and my friend, Abby, for tonight.'

'Ah, yes, that's five pounds each, please.'

Lucy handed over a tenner. 'It's on me this time,' she

side-mouthed at Abby, who rolled her eyes in response. She certainly wasn't going to pay for this experience. Ever. At any time.

'Right,' Hilary ticked their names off a list, 'you're the last two to arrive, so come on in and we'll all sit down. I'll just lock the door. No escape after that,' she giggled.

Lucy felt Abby flinch at that, she elbowed her and smiled at Hilary.

'Wait, wait, wait,' Abby panicked, breaking free and bolting for the front door.

'Abby!' Lucy was shocked, surely she wouldn't really abandon her in her hour of need.

'One sec, Luce.'

Lucy watched as Abby stuck her head out of the door for one last breath of fresh air then spun back in: 'Sorry Hilary, we're ready now.'

It was exactly as Lucy had imagined, a circle of 16-or-so people sitting on plastic high-school chairs. Lucy beamed at everyone, so excited to eventually be here, happy at last not to have to suffer in silence. They all smiled back. At last, this is going to be great. She sat down and patted at the empty seat beside her to Abby who shuffled over to it and sat down, hunched over and arms crossed.

Reading Abby's body language, Lucy groaned inwardly. In intimidating situations she didn't want to be in, the normally loud and confident Abby went into herself. She let everyone else do the talking and barely spoke unless to answer a direct question. It was rare for this to happen, but her familiar confidence drained away, replaced by an anxious quietness. Never mind. She'd survive this. She patted her knee and winked. Eager for what came next.

*****

ABBY MADE UP her mind there and then not to talk. She would be there for Lucy, of course, but simply sit in silence and try not to breathe too deeply what could potentially be the acrid weight and smell of these random people's bowels. Aware they were the two new girls in the group, she noticed everyone was staring at them. Slowly she reached into her bag and pulled out her scarf, which she wrapped around her neck, covering her nose and mouth, breathing through the silk. Her eyes peered left to right above the scarf, taking in her surroundings. She noticed that every single person in the room had their legs crossed, probably a safe option to hold everything in, she reasoned. Keep them crossed people, keep them crossed, she silently willed.

The group were mainly women, from 18 to their early 50s, she guessed, but there were also three guys. Two vastly overweight and one who looked normal enough. Abby studied him: he was sandy haired, blue eyed and wore a suit. Appearances are so deceiving, Abby mused, I wonder if any of my exes ever had an issue with IBS? She'd never thought to ask and had always instinctively avoided the bathroom for an hour after they'd ventured into it.

Hilary finally spoke, 'Good evening, everyone. You'll notice we have two newcomers this week. Shall we start by finding out what their problems are?' The whole group nodded adoringly at her.

Hilary turned to Abby, and Abby felt her eyes widen in horror. She looked at Lucy, then back at Hilary.

All she got from Lucy was a smile and quite attention. Wow, Lucy was loving this, Abby thought. She put her hand over her mouth and shook her head.

'You're afraid of your own shits?' Hilary joked, 'Jeez, they must be bad.' Her congregation laughed.

Mortified, Abby covered her face with her hands and turned away.

'OK, it's OK to just listen this time.'

Abby nodded, pulling her scarf further up for protection.

She figured the only person she had to listen to was Lucy, who stood up willingly and smiled.

'Wow, it's so good to finally be here. I've been trying to summon up the courage for weeks, and now I'm here, it's good to know I'm not the only one struggling with this.' Lucy regaled her near miss at work, it had been the catalyst for her decision to finally come along: 'I just don't want to live like this anymore. I feel like it controls my life – I can't be spontaneous and make any decisions off the cuff because I'm worried about how my bowels might react; I'm constantly so worried about toilets being nearby or the food I can eat. Camping and trekking in the mountains would be an issue to say the least.' Fervent nods of appreciation supported her admissions.

Lucy took a big breath: 'The amount of time I spend worrying about this, and the weird looks I get from people who don't understand why I'm suddenly sweating, well, I came along tonight because I wanted to know that I wasn't alone in feeling like this, and I wanted to see if anyone had any help or advice.' Her voice shook a little as she sat back down.

Abby watched as a tear rolled down Lucy's face; it had clearly taken a lot for her to do this tonight. Reaching out, she grabbed her friend's hand and held it tightly. Lucy squeezed it back.

Two of the ladies approached her, hugged her and a huge smile of relief and acceptance spread across Lucy's face. And as one of the ladies sat down, a mini fart popped out.

'Ooops,' the lady said in a small voice.

Hilary made no such apologies. 'That's Maria that is, it happens every time she sits down and sometimes when she stands up. You'll get used to it.'

Lucy giggled. Abby felt her mouth open in shock, but then quickly clamped it shut when she realised she was about to inhale the aftermath of Maria's release. *Every* time she sat down? Good lord, that could easily be 50 times a day! Where on earth did she work? Urgently looking around for the nearest window to dispel any potential fart fumes, Abby jumped up and moved across the circle to jiggle open one of the windows. It was one of those old-style window fastenings with metal dials and pulleys which were tricky to adjust. Panting desperately, she managed to free the old window letting in some fresh air.

'Better now?' Hilary enquired.

Abby nodded her thanks and grabbed a seat to sit right next to it, breaking the circle and gaining a scowl from Lucy, which she ignored and silently curled her legs up on the chair and kept listening.

For an entire hour, everyone introduced themselves and explained how their IBS affected them. After that, they each shared one thing they had tried and found helpful. Sylvie, a bright university student, found her stomach gave her so much pain she'd be doubled over in lectures. She was trying a new herbal drink every morning but had only noticed a difference if she failed to eat breakfast – but then she got really sleepy. This opened up a discussion on what was best: food high in fibre to slow the process down left half the group completely constipated.

Maria was something else, instead of communicating her thoughts by speaking, to show her seal of approval she rose and sat down, nodding every time and squeaking out a mini-fart. Every time she got a smile of affection and approval from someone in the group. Abby was appalled every time, without fail. She gagged and willed herself to pass out as each person discussed their bowel movements in minute detail.

To help her through the ordeal, Abby focused on Lucy. Damn, she looked gorgeous. Bless her for going through all of this, Abby thought. The group drew her in, proffering ideas and asking her tactics, before coming to a consensus that she should try herbs and colonics. At that, Lucy grinned and raised an eyebrow in Abby's direction. Abby's stomach grumbled in fear.

'Ah, I think we have someone excited to go with you over there,' Hilary piped up with a big smile and a wink.

Abby glared at her stomach in shock – how could it turned on her, here of all places? On top of the nerves of the last hour, it had been ages since she'd eaten and her stomach rumbled again, nagging her to leave and get some food. Mortified, Abby just sat there tightening her stomach muscles, desperate for this to be over. Lucy just smiled sweetly at her.

Abby closed her eyes. How much longer was this going to last?

When the wall clock ticked round to 8pm, she was sure it would be over, and she could finally leave. She had learnt more about digestion than she ever wanted to know; she just put food in her mouth and never worried about it coming out at the other end. Fast or slow, she didn't care, it happened, never to be spoken of.

Hilary stood up to address the group, 'OK, everyone, Lucy, has this been a help?' Lucy nodded appreciatively and smiled at everyone again.

'I don't know if you'll be back with your friend?' Abby blinked. As cringeworthy as some of the discussions on random strangers' bowel movements had been, Abby swore to herself she would come along again to support Lucy if she wanted her to, so she nodded along with her best friend.

'Good to see, well, next week we're going to discuss holidays and how to deal with foreign food and plane flights ... all ideas welcome.'

OUTSIDE THE BUILDING ten minutes later, she felt dizzy, unsure of whether it was the fresh air or the exhilarating rush of freedom.

'I'm so sorry, Luce. I had no idea how bad it was. I had no idea how much it affected your daily life.'

'That's fine. Thanks for coming in.'

'Oh, come on, Luce we both know I was rubbish,' she admitted, linking arms with her best friend. 'I had no idea just how much the digestive system makes me want to be sick, I've definitely got these issues from my mum.'

'Well, thank your lucky stars you don't have any IBS issues. If you did, you'd be screwed.'

'So, are you going to go again?'

'Yes, definitely, and I'm going to try everything they suggested.'

'I promise I'll come every week if you need me, too, even if I am pretty useless. I might spot something I can help with. And, actually, when I opened the window, it wasn't so bad. My treat next time,' she winked. 'Come on, can you stomach a drink?'

'I refuse to let this run my life, so yes, for wine I shall pull through.'

'I applaud your strength,' Abby grinned.

'Thank you. I thought you might ...'

'Well, just as long as you don't ever fart when you sit down...'

'Would our friendship be over?'

'Yes, totally.'

They giggled and pushed the door into the bar. Abby had some change after buying the wine, so instead of leaving a tip, she nipped over the street and knelt down by the homeless man: 'I have some change now,' she whispered, placing it all in his palm.

'So, you survived?' he said.

'Yes. It wasn't as bad as I thought it was going to be.'

'Most things aren't,' He said kindly.

'Have some new wisdom for me next week, please,' she said, grinning.

'Ah so, you're coming back?'

'Yes, to support my friend, of course.'

'Of course,' he nodded.

'You're a soft touch,' Lucy said as they entered the Tube station.

'Well, whatever put him on the street, it's going to take an awful lot of effort to get him off again, and at that age, who knows if he will. It makes me sad.'

'That's why I love you,' Lucy smacked a huge kiss on her cheek.

'I do have a heart, you know, I'm just rubbish with poo.'

Lucy gasped.

'What?'

'That's your new dating profile statement right there!'
'No chance,' Abby retorted. 'Come on, let's go home. You're coming to mine.'

ONE DOUBLE HELLO

ABBY WOKE UP on Saturday to a text message from Charlie:

'So I take it that the counselling worked, you're over me now?'

'Ugh, what a loser,' she flung the phone on the bed, unanswered, behind her. 'Right that's it, I'm going to the gym.'

Two hours later, she'd sweated and stretched her body and was feeling good about herself. Walking home, she saw Tim, once again sitting outside the flat.

'Oh, hello again,' she smiled naturally at seeing him.

'Hey,' he leaned down to kiss her cheek. She smiled when his lips touched her skin. He smelt of deep musk and caught her completely off guard.

'Hello, right back,' she beamed.

'You already said hello.'

'Ah yes. You've been double helloed, you lucky thing. Good things will happen.' What the heck was she saying?

'Excellent,' he smiled.

'How come you're outside this time Tim? Is Woody not home again?'

'Well, actually, he's just told me to give him another thirty minutes.'

'What, so he can have a bit longer with his latest conquest? Are you serious?' Abby was open-mouthed.

'Ah, it's Woody. Anyway, it does mean that I've got thirty minutes to kill. Fancy another coffee?'

'Yeah sure, it's turning into a bit of a ritual,' she smiled.

Tim took the gym bag off her shoulder, 'Here let me hold that, you've already had a workout.'

'Thank you!' Thank goodness she'd showered at the gym, at least she looked vaguely respectable.

'I need to get back into my gym routine,' Tim said, swinging her bag on to his shoulder. 'Maybe all I needed was a gym bag like this to get me psyched up for it again,' Tim said cheekily, a gentle smile on his face.

'Yep, that's definitely what's been missing,' Abby chuckled, appraising his physique. 'Although you don't look as though you've let yourself go.' He stood a good few inches taller than her, with broad shoulders and no belly fat from what she could tell. Gosh, what was his aftershave? It wafted her way again. She shook her head slightly to bring herself back to the moment.

'So, how's the dating going? Any more vampire moments.'

'None, you'll be pleased to know,' she pushed him playfully.

He laughed, 'Damn that was funny, getting my Abby update from Woody.'

'You guys do that?'

'Yep, it's not just women that talk you know.'

'Well, why would you want to know about me anyway?' She smiled innocently and giggled as he held the door open to the coffee place.

Abby breathed in the aroma of the freshly ground beans, 'Gosh, I love this place for breakfast,' she said.

'Got time to eat?' Tim enquired.

'Well, I'd better not have too much as I'm having lunch with my mum in a few hours, but a cappuccino and a piece of cake would be ace. They're all good here. You choose ...'

'Right, you go and get a seat.'

Abby wandered over to the comfy chairs, two had just come free. This was all very relaxing.

Tim reappeared, 'They're going to bring it over.'

'Perfect. So have you had a busy week at ...'

Tim stood grinning in front of her.

'Hey, what's this?' Abby exclaimed.

The waiter was walking towards them with a slice of apple cake complete with candle.

'Happy birthday, Abby,' Tim smiled. He bent down to kiss her on the cheek again and she beamed. Again.

'How on earth did you know?'

'Woody may have mentioned it.'

'Well, I'm blown away,' Abby said blushing. 'Thank you, Tim, that's really sweet.'

'Well, the cake's for me. You can have the candle though.'

'Wow, thanks. You're so generous,' Abby giggled.

'Yup, pretty much,' he laughed.

'Well, in that case, it's incredibly late notice, but if you're free tonight, I'm having some drinks in the Oblong Bar. It's pretty cool, if you want to come along?'

'Um, awkward. Woody already invited me, hence me knowing it was your birthday.'

'Oh, did he now?' She winked, 'Well, that's all good

then.' She was enjoying this chat. It was flowing easily. How had she dismissed how gorgeous he was before?

She tucked in, 'Gosh, this is good.'

'You like your food, don't you?'

'Hell, yes. I'm not one of those women that doesn't eat,' she paused, not wanting to look like a cave woman shovelling it into her mouth, but she was suddenly ravenous after her workout.

'It's good to see,' and for a moment, she thought he was going to draw a comparison between her and his ex, but he didn't say anything else. Relief. Their exes had been the hot topic of conversation last time they'd had coffee, and it was nice to have silently buried them in the past.

Tim smiled at her and she smiled back at him. She felt completely relaxed in his company, warmer somehow: 'I should have invited you anyway, Tim, I'm sorry.'

'Well, we barely know each other, so you're forgiven.'

'I suppose you should have my number really,' she pulled out her phone.

'Yes, I suppose that would be easier than hanging around outside your apartment.'

'It would definitely make sense, but I did enjoy the spontaneity of coming home and seeing you there.'

Tim paused as she looked at him. He spoke quietly now, 'Well, actually I was going to ask you for your number anyway, Abby,' and he very slightly bit the inside of his lip, 'to see if you would consider going out on a date with me some time.'

A flurry of butterflies in her stomach and a warmth in her cheeks told her it was a good idea. 'Well, that would be lovely,' she smiled and reached for his phone. What a great day this was turning out to be. She typed in her number and handed it back to him.

'OK, cool,' she suddenly felt shy and hot. What was happening to her?

'Well, I'll catch you later on this evening, then,' Tim beamed.

Abby smiled back. Tim turned the conversation around to wondering which woman Woody was seeing currently. They chatted easily as they sipped on their coffees together before Abby noticed the time.

'Heck Tim the time! I'd better run because I need to meet my mum. But seriously thank you for the cake. I hereby promise to eat that with you at any time.'

'I believe you! Enjoy your lunch Miss Abby, see you tonight.'

Abby walked away trying to hide the fact that she was grinning ear to ear. Now she was doubly excited about tonight.

*****

'HEY, Y'ALL, HERE'S the birthday girl,' Woody said, proudly twirling her around. Walking in with Abby and Lucy on either arm was no bad thing. It made him look amenable and desirable to any onlookers, so he put on his best, most gentlemanly voice.

Abby looked stunning tonight. Her mum had been so delighted to see her looking so fresh and happy that she'd taken her shopping. She wore a backless halter-neck black dress which ran down to just above the knee. She'd paired it with black croc Louboutin's and red lipstick. Even Lucy had done a double take when she saw her.

'Phwooar. That's my girl.'

'You look fabulous, too, Luce.' Wearing a lacy V-neck

skater style number from Reiss, Lucy was ready to dance as well. It had been ages since they had gone out like this and they were buzzing.

Abby had had butterflies every time she'd thought of Tim for the rest of the day. She wanted a moment without Woody around to tell Lucy, but so far it had been so hectic, she hadn't had a chance. Her mum had kept looking at her inquisitively all afternoon, clearly gagging to ask her what – or who – had lifted her spirits so much, but she managed not to pry.

She worked the room, hugging and chatting with all her random cousins and friends, including Claire from work who'd been a legend these past few months, and still the only one to know why she'd been off work. Tim smiled at her from the bar before wandering over with four G and Cs.

'What's a G & C?' Lucy asked with glee.

'It's gin with Champagne instead of tonic, they're obligatory on every birthday,' Tim grinned.

'Wow. That sounds dangerous,' Abby said, reaching out for her glass and brushing Tim's hand as she did so. Their eyes met and she caught her breath. Tim looked away quickly.

But nothing got past Lucy, Abby knew she'd noticed.

Utterly oblivious, Woody took a sip: 'Well, it might help your dance moves Tim,' he joked.

'It's delicious,' Lucy sipped, a quietly entertained look on her face. 'How have you not brought him out for drinks before?' she chastised Woody.

'Yeah, Woody! Worried it wouldn't be all about you?' Abby instantly joined in.

'Naturally ladies, that's all I worry about,' Woody mocked.

'So, what's the verdict on the G&Cs? You can have something else if you'd like,' Tim said, his eyes only on Abby.

'Gosh, no way. It's delicious,' but she knew full well she'd have told him that broccoli vodka was delicious at that point. 'A birthday treat, indeed. Come on, let's dance. Lucy could you tuck my bag under the coats, please?' Abby grabbed Tim's arm, and they joined a bunch of her friends already on the dance floor.

LUCY SMILED AS she watched the pair flirt their way to the dance floor, then returned her attention to Abby's clutch and tutted, seeing that Abby had forgotten to close it. How she didn't lose everything she owned on a night out she didn't know. As she was grappling with the clasp, the screen flashed – a text from Charlie. Her heart almost stopped. 'I thought she'd slashed all contact with him?' she whispered. Unable to curb her curiosity, she read it fully.

'Missed hearing back from you earlier. Happy birthday beautiful. I've been thinking a lot about us lately. Perhaps I was wrong. Either way, I hope you remember my present to you last year...'

Lucy's heart beat fast, what on earth was he playing at? Was this the first time he'd been in touch after the whole counselling debacle? She needed some space to think about what to do. She hurried to the loos and, safely in a cubicle, she keyed in Abby's code and flicked to see the message in all its rubbish glory. She gasped as she saw the string of messages, all sent from Charlie to Abby, since the counselling session to now.

Lucy's mind was whirring; why hadn't Abby mentioned this to her? There was not one reply from Abby, and there would be no point in her deleting her own responses and not his texts. Was it even significant now after everything that had happened? She felt sick at the thought of him. And even if it was insignificant, an ex was still a powerful evoker of emotions, and a person only had so much willpower.

Scrolling up further, she began to read through text after text after text that Abby had obviously sent to him since Valentine's Day. Crikey. Abby never did things by halves. Each text was ridiculously long, assuring him of her constant love and belief that they could still have a future together. Viewing all of these messages to Charlie only made Lucy's decision that much easier.

Holding her breath for the fraction of a second it took to delete Charlie's message, she nervously looked around as if someone might see her dirty deed. Not that dirty a deed, she told herself. She was doing her duty in not letting that arsehole screw up her best friend's mind again, or ruin her birthday evening.

Back in the bar, with Abby's bag safely packed away with hers, she laughed when she saw Abby larking around on the dance floor with her friends from work. She realised she wasn't the only one watching her; waiting in line at the bar, Tim's face reacted to every move Abby made. Every time she threw her head back to laugh at something someone said, he smiled too.

Lucy nudged Woody in the ribs. 'Ow! What?' he said, rubbing them.

'Look, he's staring at her,' motioning across the bar of busy people at Tim.

'He's totally checking her out,' Lucy said excitedly

to Woody.

'No, he's not,' Woody brushed her away, 'he's my cousin, he wouldn't look at her in that way.'

'Is there such a thing as a cousin code?'

'I'm just telling you I'm right' Woody glared at her.

'OK, OK,' Lucy said, backing off. She was certain that she was right, though. She sipped on her drink and waited until Woody had gone to the bathroom. Tim reappeared with another round from the bar.

'Her highness requires more gin, apparently,' he smiled.

'Abby's ruin,' Lucy joked.

'I doubt that. She's having too much fun to be completely ruined. I'll help you get her home though if you need it!'

'Thank you, Tim. She looks amazing, doesn't she?'

'Always. I mean, she does have a birthday glow about her.'

Lucy nodded. From what little time she'd spent with Tim, he seemed lovely. That was a good start. She caught him looking back at Abby and his smile widened again. Yes, she was definitely right. Now all she needed was to see if Abby felt the same.

Giggling and on a high after a night of no worries, just good times, Lucy linked arms with her best friend as they weaved their way home in a cab.

'You looked like your old free-spirited self tonight, Abbster.'

'Gosh, Luce, for the first time in ages that's how I felt,' Abby grabbed her hand, 'I've been waiting to get you alone to tell you this.'

Lucy beat her to it, 'Tim likes you.'

'Yes! How did you ...?'

Lucy grinned.

'You're good. He asked me out when I saw him earlier today.'

'Amazing. Abby, he's lovely. Just let yourself enjoy it.'

'Yes. I must try not to freak out.'

'Well, I hope Charlie makes you wiser, not jaded. You know, able to spot when someone's not all that they say they are. Strong enough to walk away, not change the essence of yourself again.'

'Oooo, check you out after G&Cs.'

'Yes, they were fabulous, weren't they?'

'A definite tradition now.'

Lucy grinned, 'He asked you out,' she sang.

'Oh my god, I really wanted him to kiss me. And he didn't. I'm desperate for our first date now!'

'Arrrghhh,' Lucy shrieked. 'This is so exciting. He's gorgeous. Is he going to tell Woody?'

'I'm not sure.'

'Woody seemed quite anti the idea when I mentioned that I'd seen Tim looking at you earlier, as if there was some cousin code or something.'

Abby frowned. 'I've never heard of a cousin code.'

'Oh, sod it Abby, go for it. Just don't mention it to Woody until it gets serious.'

Abby's eyebrows raised.

'*If* it gets serious. *If...*'

Abby nodded at her, 'Good plan. Should I be different around him, Luce?'

'Different how?'

'Well, different to the way I was around Charlie?'

'Right, let's get one thing straight. Tim is not Charlie, period. No one is. The key to you finding your eventual Mr Right is being yourself, regardless of what they're like. Yes, in time you may have to compromise on a few plans or ideas, but you shouldn't change who you are for anyone. You're a good person, you need to meet someone who likes you just the way you are.'

Abby nodded thoughtfully.

Lucy tried again, 'Think about how many people came tonight, Abby. If the essence of you was really that bad, no one would have shown up. It was Charlie who was wrong, not you.'

Abby paused, 'True.'

'You've got be yourself.'

'I suppose he did like me when I was at my worst.'

'Exactly.'

'Plus, it sounds like he's been through the mill a bit, love wise,' Abby pondered for a second. 'Yes, OK, you're right.'

'Phew,' Lucy smiled.

'Now, let's make cheese toasties to snack on, and I can fantasise about what it's like to kiss him.'

'Well, don't think about it too much – I don't want you all over me when I'm trying to sleep.'

'In your dreams, Lucy. In your dreams.'

'Nightmares, Abby. I know way too much about you.'

'Hey, I thought you said I was nice!'

'Oh whatever. Come on, the cheese is calling me...'

18

ONE OF THOSE DATES

ABBY MET TIM in Canary Wharf. She'd opted for her Pepe skinny jeans with some cute Hudson ankle boots in the end as he'd said there may be some walking involved. Leaving the Tube station, everything looked familiar somehow, and she realised she'd seen it in so many movies, with its high skylights and dramatic detailing. She smiled in anticipation and walked out of the station into the sun, and there was Tim standing there, waiting for her. He smiled instantly when he saw her.

'Hey, there!' he beamed, and she smiled back at him.

'Hello!' she whispered, surprised again by his effect on her. Holding her breath as he rested his hands lightly on both of her arms and bent down to kiss her cheek, she caught his scent again. Her heart skipped a beat. How on earth was he doing this to her?

'Let's have a wander.'

'Let's.'

'I thought we could walk to Greenwich, do the market and maybe I'll show you something I love.'

'It's been ages since I've been to Greenwich!' Abby exclaimed excitedly.

'Ah, brilliant,' Tim looked relieved. 'I know a cut through the Isle of Dogs, so seeing as the weather's fine...'

'Perfect, let's stroll,' Abby found herself linking her arm naturally through his before wondering what the hell she was doing, but he didn't seem to pull away or mind. The bustle under Canary Wharf skyscrapers quietened almost immediately as they turned on to a path along the waterway.

The pair meandered along, exchanging stories about each other's week as they passed the yacht club and on to the River Thames. They headed to the bottom peninsular of the Isle of Dogs and passed the transformed warehouse apartments and fisherman's cottages, before dropped down to the tunnel beneath the waters of the river above it.

'That was way better than taking the train,' Abby exclaimed as they emerged in Greenwich, the other end.

The sun glinted off the glass protecting the hull of the Cutty Sark, and they marvelled at how it had survived that fire years ago, then strolled through the Old Royal Naval College and all of its glory.

'Shall we have a look at the market?' Tim suggested.

'Um, something tells me that you already know the answer to that question! Hell yeah!' Abby chuckled. 'You know about my penchant for antiques and old finds.' They dodged the London cabs and crossed over the little road to enter the marketplace. Artisans and antique traders peddled their wares from every corner, and the shops around it were home to those Greenwich inhabitants that could afford the high rents and practice and sell their craft every day. They mooched through the marketplace, with Abby stopping at almost every one of the antique jewellery stalls. 'I was hoping to find something to match my necklace,' she showed Tim the pretty bird and feather on a chain, which he studied carefully.

'I found this at Spitalfields and wondered if the artist might be here. No joy today, I'm afraid,' she said after a thorough search.

'It just means we'll have to come back,' Tim smiled.

'Exactly.'

'Come on,' said Tim, 'we could spend forever rifling through this lot, and there's something I want to show you before lunch. But it's another bit of a walk. Are you up for it?'

Normally being dragged away from the stalls would have been torture, but Abby was having such a lovely time, she looped her arm automatically through his again.

'Lead the way!' He squeezed it and grinned, 'You're going to love this. At least I hope you are. Either way, it'll work up your appetite.'

'Well, that's fine with me,' she chuckled. The thought of food made her stomach rumble, but Tim didn't seem to notice as he led the way up past the Maritime Museum to the expanse of Greenwich Park with its diagonal pathways. The sun shone down on them and Abby turned her face into it, closing her eyes for a moment to soak it all in.

'It's very nice to see you like this,' Tim said to Abby.

'What do you mean?'

'Well, you just look so relaxed.'

Abby knew he could see the sparkle in her eyes, there was no way she could hide it. It was such a contrast to how she'd been the first few times they'd met. She just felt so comfortable with him. Play it cool, Abs, don't be too full on and scare him, she whispered to herself.

'Well, I might be having an OK-ish kind of day,' and she nudged his ribs with her shoulder.

Nearing the hill in the centre of the park, they had to walk single file to get through the crowds of tourists coming down the other way. Tim had unlooped his arm from hers and she missed the feel of it. Will he kiss me today? She wondered, realising she hoped with all her might he would. It wouldn't do for her to make the first move – Tim clearly prided himself on being a gentleman, and that was, at the end of the day, what she wanted, so for once in her life, she'd just have to be patient and enjoy the suspense. Gosh, Lucy would be proud.

Snapping her out of her reverie, she felt him slip alongside her again and retrieve her arm.

'Right, as we walk up the hill, look to your right so I can wow you with the view to the left at the top.'

'Phew,' she puffed. It was steeper than it looked.

'Keep looking right, Miss Abby.'

'Argh, the suspense is killing me, I want to look left!' Abby exclaimed, laughing.

'Don't you dare!' Tim warned as they neared the top and met a hoard of people taking photos either side of the Meridian line at the Old Royal Observatory.

'Good old GMT. Wow, I didn't realise you could see it like this.'

'It's even better at night when they shine a green laser beam into the sky.'

'That sounds cool, I hope I see it.'

'I think you might, but first ....'

'Ooo, can I look now?'

'You can in one, two ... oh, sod it,' Tim said as she felt herself being scooped up in his arms. Laughing, she placed her hands over her eyes: 'Tell me when I can look.'

Tim set her down gently, stood behind her with his hands resting lightly at her waist and whispered: 'Now.'

Abby dropped her hands and smiled as she was met with a vast sweep of London that took her breath away. In front of her, the park rolled away like a giant green skirt patterned by people moving across the diagonal criss-cross of paths. Her gaze drank everything in as Tim whispered out the landmarks:

'I love the cacophony of architectural styles and history ... you've got the traditional lines of the Old Royal Naval College, then the modern skyline of Canary Wharf and the tower 'One Canada Square' – did you know it was the tallest building in the entire country for years? Then...,' he swivelled her to the left, 'you've got ...'

'The Gherkin,' Abby interjected.

'... and of course The Shard, and if you focus in over there, you'll see...'

'St Paul's! Wow! Anyone who loves London needs to see this view, it really is breath-taking.'

Tim nodded, 'This is one of my all-time favourite views. I don't just share it with anyone, but something told me you'd get it.'

'When did you first come here?' Abby asked, eager to find out more.

'My uncle brought me when I was a teenager. He was researching influences of the Maritime ages and he brought us to the museum. I fell in love with the place, I guess,' he paused, Abby realised she was hanging on his every word.

'For me, it's the one place in London I always feel completely calm, yet totally inspired. All of the amazing landmarks we've just looked at seem so large and domineering up close, but from up here, they just don't seem as big, and I guess that's what this place does for me: it gives me a sense of perspective and calm. Here,

I'm above all the tiny things I do and stress about on a daily basis. If I ever have a problem, I head straight here and mull it over and ...'

'And the problem doesn't seem so large?'

'Exactly.'

She followed his gaze back to Canary Wharf.

'It's crazy to think every single day that one square mile has over one million people passing through. Everyone's in a rush, no-one stops; it's just so intense.'

'Yet here, you can't see any of them.'

'Nope,' he agreed, 'instead you just see what people are capable of when they embrace their imagination and create something that was once nothing more than a dream.'

Abby couldn't add to that. He'd put it perfectly. 'Thank you for sharing this with me, Tim ... it's so special.'

Both of them had dropped their speech to whispers, as if not wanting to disturb the beauty of the scene in front of them.

'It's extraordinary you've shown me this view of London,' Abby said.

'Why's that?'

'Well, it's just that over there, way in the distance, can you see another patch of green on the horizon? It's Hampstead Heath, and if you go to just the right part of the heath, guess what you'll see.'

Tim's face lit up, 'The same view from the other perspective.'

'You're still smiling,' Abby whispered.

'That's because I think that you get me, Abby. And now I'm itching to go there and see it.'

Her heart was doing triple backflips. Stay cool, stay cool, stay cool. 'Well stick with me, Tim, and maybe if you're really, really lucky, I'll take you there. The heath is massive and you need to know the *exact* bit.'

'Well, maybe that will be date two,' he bent down and kissed her cheek. Her body leapt as if someone had set a firework off inside her. Right on cue her stomach rumbled. She blushed and coughed.

'Gosh, I'm starving you. How terrible!'

She giggled still blushing, 'I do feel a bit peckish.' Absolutely ravenous more like it.

'Well I have a reservation for a place I think you'll like back down in the village. Come on, let's go and eat.'

'Music to my ears, Tim.'

'To your stomach more like!'

She giggled and chased him back down the hill.

BAR DU MUSEÉ had one large burgundy room, oak panelled against the bustle of Greenwich Village outside, and it transported them to a backstreet in Paris. It delighted Abby, who fell quickly for the old black and white French photos and the back-lit wall of wine bottles, all French the waiter assured her. Through a curtain at the back, she spied a courtyard covered with a pergola holding a well-established vine.

'Gosh, it must be beautiful to come here in summer as well,' she said, her eyes finally adjusting to the darkness of the room.

Tim let her take it all in, 'It's a gorgeous hideaway, isn't it? And trust me, the steak is phenomenal.'

'Well you had me at steak,' Abby giggled as they opened the menu. She sniffed, 'It even smells tasty in here,'

'I think it's the cinnamon candles,' Tim said. It was only 1:30pm, but every single candle added to the warm amber glow.

She looked at him as he perused the menu – he intrigued her. She'd been excited about this date but only in the hopeful way that it would turn out alright. She knew she could trust him from what little time they'd already spent together, and she obviously found him physically attractive, but she didn't know if they'd really gel. He seemed to notice the same things she did, which was a positive sign that maybe they shared similar values and mindsets.

Cutting through her thoughts, Tim reached across the table and took her hand – he'd obviously stopped looking at the menu while she was thinking. His hand was warm and masculine and large enough to fit hers safely in, and it was all Abby could do to contain the bolt of electricity that startled through her at his contact. He looked at her, clearly hoping for her approval at his impulsive gesture. She squeezed her hand and beamed naturally.

Tim breathed with relief, 'I've wanted to hold your hand properly all morning. I've been stuffing my hands into my pockets to try and be cool.'

'I just thought you were cold,' Abby giggled. 'I almost bought you those gloves you tried on!' She took great pleasure in his smile, which widened as he realised she had wanted the same. He laughed and let out an exaggerated sigh of relief.

'How hungry are you?' he asked, and Abby raised her eyebrow in response. 'Ah yes, your stomach rumbled.'

'Well, I was planning on doing the polite ladylike thing and just going for a starter, but my stomach gave my eating habits away. What steak would you recommend?'

'Thank goodness for that! It's no fun to sit with someone picking at a salad and looking miserable whilst

I chow down on some excellent food. It makes me feel like a caveman.'

She grinned, 'You're going to be very happy with me then.'

'Well, in answer to your question, they're all good, but the fillet with the red wine jus and field mushroom is exquisite.'

'Sold.'

'Me too! I always vow to try something else, but it's just too damn good to miss.'

'You can't have food envy either, for I will fight and protect my meal by any means possible.'

Tim chuckled, 'That could be funny to watch. How do you like it?' he asked as the waiter came over.

'Two steaks, medium rare with a jug of the ... peppercorn?' he paused for her to answer.

'Actually, Tim, I'd love the Béarnaise.' Truth be told, she'd have been perfectly happy devouring the peppercorn, but Charlie had always ordered for her, and she was determined to do things differently. Her opinion mattered, no matter how small the decision. She wondered how he would take it, nervous all of a sudden. Tim didn't even blink.

'So, a jug of each please and all of the trimmings. Would you like red wine?'

'Yes, absolutely. Do they have a French Malbec by any chance? I've only had Argentinian,' this was all just so calm and lovely. Sharing her own opinions and making her own decisions, however minute, wasn't scary at all. How had she ever fallen into such a weak spiral? She squeezed Tim's hand again, grateful for how naturally lovely he was.

With the wine ordered and poured, they pulled hands

away for a moment to lift their glasses: 'Cheers!

'Here's to a wonderful day so far,' she said.

They both drank and she peered at him over her glass as he enjoyed the wine, full bodied yet insanely smooth. She wanted to know more about him.

'So, you've already heard quite a bit about my life from Woody, tell me about yours. You're an architect, inspired by Greenwich, but how did that come about?'

'I've wanted to be an architect since I was six. I would draw houses on any scrap of paper I could find and turn old cereal packets into cardboard buildings. I had a whole town at one point. I think it stemmed mainly from my grandfather, who took me on weekends away when my parents were arguing – they're divorced now – and we'd explore castles and walk around the towns, and he'd ask me what I thought each building was trying to represent. Modernity, character, austerity. It's an amazing way to see the world, to delve into each design and see how it heralds a particular place in time. Each one has their own story. I find it fascinating.'

'Wow,' Abby was impressed. 'I've always just taken in the buildings as part of the overall scene, but now, well maybe I'll have to look closer.'

He nodded, 'Definitely do, but I warn you it gets addictive, and it makes you want to build your own.'

'And have you?'

'Not quite yet, but I've just made partner in my firm, and it'll happen one day.'

She genuinely wanted to hear more – his eyes lit up so much as he talked about his passion.

'They hired me after uni, and I've grown with them.'

'Do you want to branch out by yourself one day and have your own firm?'

'Yes, absolutely, in fact there's three of us that have been discussing how we can do it.'

'Gosh, my work story isn't like that at all. I needed a job to earn money, so I got one. That's it. Done.'

'Ah, you need to rethink that, Abby. Of course there are days you don't particularly enjoy working with the clients or something else will stress you out, but on the whole you can go to bed happy knowing you're living the life you've chosen and love. You need to be inspired.'

The waiter set down their steaks, Abby nodded her approval – the fillet looked fat and juicy.

'Is that really possible?' She said, never having met anyone who knew it to be true. She picked up her knife as Tim picked up his.

'Well, obviously nothing's perfect, but I'm being true to myself, so the feeling of accomplishment is always real, and I want to leave my mark on this world. You'll have to see some of the images from my portfolio so far.'

'I would love to.'

'Sorry, I'm gassing on, it's one of my favourite topics. Do you love what you do in any way?'

Abby paused, taking the time to think about it. 'I wouldn't say I love my job, but in the past two months, I've definitely taken a lot more pride in it, which feels good actually. Can't instil pride in others if you don't have it in yourself' to coin the phrase that I've made the HR team's mantra.'

'I'll drink to that,' he laughed, and they clinked glasses again.

'This steak is incredible, by the way,' she added, loving every mouthful.

'I'm glad you like it.' Tim paused, 'I didn't mean to be rude about your job, Abby.'

She looked directly at him. 'It's just that you're such a passionate person, I don't want it to go to waste. There must be a way to unleash that on the world somehow.'

'Maybe the world's not ready,' she started to joke. 'But seriously Tim, thank you. You're making me think.'

'Oh no, on your day off and everything.'

She pretended to throw her napkin at him in jest.

'I guess I don't want to feel as though I've wasted my time on something I don't love.'

'Love and believe in,' Tim corrected her. There was that jolt of electricity again as he took her hand and looked earnestly at her.

'One thing I do know with absolute certainty,' she whispered.

'Yes?' Tim whispered back.

'I need more Béarnaise sauce.'

He threw his head back and laughed.

'What's so funny about that? It's a serious situation over here.'

It was 4pm by the time they emerged from Bar du Museé, and they both squinted to adjust their eyes to the sudden sharpness of the daylight.

'My gosh it feels as though we've been in another world,' Abby exclaimed.

Tim had a firm grip on her hand and as long as it stayed that way, she didn't care where they went next. They moved in a comfortable silence along the busy road leading into Greenwich Village before making a left at the far end of the Royal Naval College.

'There it is,' he said, pointing straight ahead, 'The Trafalgar pub. Winston Churchill used to come here and loved the whitebait apparently.' It was right on the water's edge.

Abby looked up at him, 'Gosh Tim, I'm so full from lunch. Do you mind if we walk along the Thames for a few minutes; I'd just like to see it from this angle, close up in case the light goes?'

Tim smiled down at her, 'Sounds good.' They meandered past the pub and along the Thames Path to the Royal Naval College.

'It's beautiful,' Abby said, staring up at the grand buildings.

'You are,' Tim murmured, swinging her round so she was facing him, he drew her into his arms. Instinctively, her hand moved to his chest covered with his deep navy wool coat, and she swore she could feel his heart beating or was that hers?

'Abby, I've just got to kiss you. Is that alright?' he whispered.

She nodded as he bent his head down to hers. Her heart was hammering in her chest as he drew her closer into him and their lips touched. Finally. She leaned into his warm chest, enjoying the feel of his muscular body beneath his coat. He kissed her softly at first, then let out a moan as she moved her hands into his hair, forcing his lips harder on hers. Their lips matched every movement, locked together, for what seemed like an hour. Abby finally drew away and gazed into his eyes.

'You have such incredible eyes,' Abby whispered. They were a beautiful hazel, mellow and mesmerising. Resting her forearms on his shoulders and running her fingers lightly into his hair, she brought his lips back to hers. Exploring each other with their hands as their tongues met for a long while more, Abby felt her need for him rising inside of her. Tim's breathing became more ragged, and they pulled away slightly at the same time.

'I want to savour every moment with you Abby. Do you mind if we don't rush?'

'I was about to say exactly the same to you,' Abby giggled a little, burying her face into his chest, breathing in his cologne.

'I've waited a long time to feel like this.'

'I feel the same,' she said drawing her face back from his chest and smiling up at him. 'I've had the best day.'

He'd seen her cavorting around on so many random dates that she didn't for one second want him to think she was doing the same with him, but when she looked into his eyes, she could see she had no reason to worry. He looked totally at peace being there with her.

It was so strange, in one day the dynamic between them had totally changed. They had gone from joking around buddies with no chemistry or touch between them to staring like they'd never seen each other before. Maybe in some ways they hadn't.

'Come on, let me walk you home, or at least to the Tube,' Tim said.

They sat on the Tube in silence, their arms still interlocked and Abby's head resting on his shoulder, tired but happy after a fantastic day.

Before they neared the stop where they'd go their separate ways, Abby smiled and kissed him gently. He placed his hands in her hair and kissed her passionately, honestly, beautifully.

She realised that she was dreading the moment she'd have to part from him. He felt like a reminder of everything that was lovely in the world.

'You're beautiful, Abby. Full stop. I'll call you soon, I promise.'

*****

As she walked the ten minutes from the Tube station back to her apartment, Abby beamed at everyone along the way. This is what love should feel like. Goodness, did she just think the 'L' word without balking in fear or analysing? 'Yes, I believe I did,' she said almost skipping. Her heart was filled with butterflies.

She realised there was no way she could disguise the look in her eyes if she saw Woody, so she crept through the door, hoping to avoid his merciless quizzing of her about her day. Seeing the flat in darkness, she relaxed. Woody was probably out on a date. What was the point in sitting in a dark flat by herself? None. She messaged Lucy immediately.

'Lucy are you in?'

'Yes - come on over.' The text pinged straight back.

She scrolled through her phone, checking messages, and there was one already from Tim at the top. She savoured it:

'I'm still smiling. You did that to me. Thank you. I can't wait to see you again ... are you free next Saturday?'

That was almost a week away, but she jumped around the kitchen, full of elated energy. Absentmindedly her eyes dropped down the list, bypassing the one she'd just seen from Lucy and going straight to the three from Charlie. Her heart pounding now, she pressed to view them, each one more emphatic than the last:

'Abby my little lady, how are you? It's been ages since you replied to me.

I still think of you. Care to meet? Xx'

She drew in a sharp breath and went on to the next one:

'Abby I need to be honest with you, you are the only girl that's managed to stay inside my mind. It just got crazy and mental for a while didn't it?'
And one final one:

'Abby I've tried dating other women, the only one I need is you. I need you Abby.'

Shit. She really needed Lucy.

19

CONTRADICTIONS

LUCY BEAMED AT her from the moment Abby arrived at her apartment.

'So how was it?'

'Oh. My. God.,' Abby said.

'Oh my god good?'

'Oh yes.'

'Really?'

'Oh. My. God. I'm blown away by today. Was that even real?' Abby almost gasped at the memory.

'What was even real? What did he do? Where did he take you?'

Abby looked at Lucy, she was hopping on the spot, as utterly beside herself as she was.

'This is so amazing. I want to hear everything, tell me everything.'

Abby nodded, her movements still felt slow to her as if she was wrapped in a haze of loveliness.

'Wow,' Abby recounted every moment of her day, she didn't want to leave anything out to Luce. This was important. There had been such a seismic shift in her view on love and its place in her life this year already, and today just backed up her new way of thinking.

'It's like we were equals on the date, you know?'

'How so, did he make you go halves?' Lucy looked perplexed.

'No, I don't mean like that, he was the perfect gentleman where paying was concerned. No, it was far deeper than that. We talked and we were both interested in each other's stories. With other people I've dated, they've just been keen to sell themselves and be the big man that they drown out anything interesting and I don't even want to listen to them. I just assumed that was normal, but with Tim, well, we just talked. He gave me a glimpse of how his mind works. He's just so genuine. I can't wait to see him again to find out more about him.'

'Wow,' Lucy was transfixed, 'What did he do differently to make you feel like that?'

Abby thought for a moment, wanting to sum it up perfectly for her friend.

'Well, instead of just bragging about what he did, he told me why it inspired him, why he'd made the decisions that he'd made to get him to where he is today. So now I feel as though I understand his decision making. And it's considered. He's thoughtful. And, my goodness Luce, when his hand touched mine.'

'Aaargh,' Luce shrieked, 'did he kiss you?'

'Oh boy yes.'

'Arrrgghh,' Lucy jumped on her couch Tom-Cruise-on-Oprah style. 'Tell all!'

'He kissed me by the Thames for, well it felt like an hour, and I just ...'

'Melted into him?'

'Yes. Absolutely. Completely.'

'Perfect!' Lucy, satisfied, sat back down.

'I know. I'm walking on air.'

'I can see,' Lucy grinned at her. 'This is incredible.

What a lovely first date. Long may it continue. So where and when is the next date?'

'I told him I'd show him the view east from Hampstead Heath next Saturday. I think I'll tell him to meet me at Camden Lock first and we'll wander up by the canal for a bit.'

'Oh, how nice. Abby, I'm so excited for you.' Lucy drew her into another big hug. 'My god that's nice aftershave.'

'What? Oh, of course, I've got his scent on me. He smells good, doesn't he?!'

'Yup. You're not going to wash, are you?'

'Probably not,' Abby grinned. 'I feel giddy. How am I ever going to wait until next Saturday? I can't wait to see him again. It's just ...'

'It's just what?' Lucy enquired, a slight frown on her face.

'No, it's silly, it's nothing really.'

'Abby, tell me what you're worried about.'

'OK, well admittedly Charlie and I didn't talk as much as Tim and I did today, but he still made me feel special, and we had some really romantic, lovely times ...'

Lucy nodded.

'And look how that ended up.'

'I know,' Lucy sighed, 'but the only thing you can do with matters of the heart is to recognise where someone might be taking you for granted and be stronger with the next person. You know this. We talked about it on your birthday – admittedly you'd had a few G&Cs by that point.'

Abby smiled, 'Indeed I had.'

'It's all about the standards you set for yourself this time. You know what's acceptable, what makes you feel good inside, true?'

'True,' She had learnt a lot about relationships and herself these past few months.

'Just be a bit more aware with this one and don't let your feelings cloud your instincts. However nice you might want something to be, if it isn't *actually* that way, then you voice it, see if they agree and if the situation doesn't change, then you walk. Simple really.'

'So simple,' Abby rolled her eyes.

Lucy raised her eyebrow right back at her.

'OK,' Abby agreed. 'I think sometimes we can overcomplicate things because we have a certain result in mind. I definitely did that with Charlie.'

'Exactly and were you happy?'

'Nope.'

'Was he?'

'Evidently not,' Abby said wryly. 'You get a good vibe from Tim, don't you Luce?'

'Yes, actually I do ... He seems considerate. And not in an over the top way. Although weirdly, saying that Charlie *wasn't* happy ...'

Abby's mind drifted back to the messages.

'Have you heard from Charlie?' Lucy looked instantly stressed.

'Ugh yes. He messaged me on my birthday to ask if I was over him. 'I take it the counselling worked' to be specific.'

'What an idiot,' Lucy shook her head in disgust.

'Then actually, I just checked my messages and he's now saying that he can't get me out of his head,' Abby paused. 'It just made me wonder ...'

'Wonder what? He's just missed your attention.'

'I know, all the same, he hasn't said anything quite like that before. What's up, Luce, you look awkward as hell.'

Lucy stood there silently. Clearly debating what to say.

'I deleted one of his birthday messages to you Abby. I've been meaning to tell you but ...'

'What? You did what? What did it say?'

'You'd just gone to the dance floor with Tim, and I could tell that he liked you, and I didn't want anything to ruin the night. I'm so sorry.'

'Lucy, what did it say?'

Lucy breathed, 'Just remember how you felt today with Tim.'

Abby was getting impatient. 'What did it say, Luce. Does he still love me?'

'It said 'I hope you remember my birthday present last year to you and something about missing hearing from you.'

'He misses me?' Abby felt a familiar twinge inside of her.

'Yes,' Lucy's voice trembled.

'Did it say he still loved me?'

'I can't remember.'

'Try.'

'I honestly don't know,' Lucy welled up.

'Luce, you shouldn't have done that.'

'I'm so sorry, Abfab.'

'I trust you with everything, Lucy. You need to trust me to make my own decisions, whether you deem them to be right or wrong.'

'I know I should. I'm in the wrong completely. I had the best of intentions though.'

'He misses me...,' she pondered that.

'Does he miss you or the attention that he got from you?' Lucy pointed out.

'I take it you saw my other messages then?'

Lucy stopped talking.

Abby grimaced. 'Well, back down to reality with a bump, aren't I?'

'Oh no, crap, I shouldn't have said anything. I'm so sorry I did it – and now I've ruined your day with Tim, too.'

'You haven't ruined it at all. But I am going to go now. I need to think about what to do.'

'About Charlie?'

'Yes. About Charlie and about Tim. He's never said that he misses me before. Not once in all this time.'

'It's only when you've stopped contacting him.'

'Yes, well maybe that's what was needed.'

'No, he's manipulating you again. Remember the counselling session,' Lucy begged. 'Remember how you felt today with Tim.'

'But Charlie and I have a lot of history. Sometimes you need to work hard at things. If that's what he needed to realise how he felt about me. Plus what do I really know about Tim? In six months he could make me feel as bad as Charlie did.'

'You don't believe that, surely,' Lucy went red in the face. 'He's no good for you. He doesn't bring out the best in you or make you feel worth the stars and the moon.'

'That's a fairy tale, Lucy, and those don't exist,' Abby snapped.

'No, it isn't,' Lucy pushed back. 'You felt like that today.' Tears streamed down her face, and she moved to grab a tissue.

'I'm going,' Abby grabbed her jacket and put it on. A waft of Tim's aftershave on her scarf made her feel heady all over again. She blocked it out and headed for the door.

'Abby, calm down.'

'No, Luce,' There were tears in her eyes now. Damn

it, why was she welling up?

'Be true to yourself, Abby. That's all I ask.'

She nodded, unable to think of anything other than Charlie.

20

DECISION TIME

THIS WAS IT, Abby thought, looking down at her phone, her heart knew which road she had to choose, and she was going to listen to it and finally be happy, once and for all. Shoving a few things into an overnight bag, she breezed past Woody, who wolf whistled at her.

'Someone's got a new hair-do, and I like that skirt. Where are you off to?'

'Charlie texted me, don't wait up,' and with that she bounced down the stairs, out of the front door and headed straight for the Tube station.

Rapping her knuckles on Charlie's flat door, thirty minutes late because she'd stopped off at a shop on the way, she heard Charlie thumping around. He opened the door in his underpants and some old t-shirt he'd obviously slept in. The complete opposite of his polished attire at the counselling session and in stark contrast to her gleaming self. She didn't care, though. How he looked wasn't relevant.

'You look good, baby,' he turned to give her space to enter.

Patience, Abby told herself, patience, you need to be very clear with what you want moving forwards.

'I'd offer you tea, but I haven't got any milk.'

'I'll get myself some water,' Abby's throat was dry from the adrenalin running through her body – and the stale air inside the apartment.

'Hey, would you chuck in the laundry whilst you're at it? It's next to the washer.' Charlie called out, already taking up his position on the sofa.

Abby automatically leaned down to pick up his dirty washing off the floor. As she was scooping up his boxers and shirts, she stopped. Rooted to the spot, she held her position. A conversation she'd had with Lucy came flooding back: Charlie had said goodbye one Sunday morning, without even remembering to kiss her goodbye or make plans for when they would see each other again. She'd been really upset about it and had said so, in tears, to Lucy.

'*I just don't know what I've done wrong, Luce.*' Abby had sobbed. '*Honestly I'm doing everything I can. Nothing about me is good enough. He told me he was 'marginally impressed' with me the other day when I cooked you all that roast ... and it was a good roast wasn't it, Luce?*'

'*It was an unbelievable roast Abbs. Michelin-star quality. I meant to ask you, what had he done to you that was so special to deserve you cooking it?*'

It was a good question and one that Luce had obviously already known the answer to – a big fat nothing. He'd sat on his arse all day as he had done the day before, playing PlayStation before going out with his mates.

'*And what did he do after the roast?*' Lucy had then asked.

'*Well, we hoovered the flat.*'

'*It takes two of you to hoover?*'

'Well, he was loading the dishwasher, and I didn't want to look ungrateful.'

Luce snorted. 'After you'd cooked and he'd given us the big drama about how he would wash up "you sit down, darling, I'll get you a glass of wine," all of that was bollocks, was it?'

Again Abby had remained silent. Lucy had been absolutely steaming with rage. 'Abby what on earth has happened to you? When and how did you let this 'relationship,' and I use the term loosely, come to this?'

'Are you saying that I've let it slide? Because I've really tried ...'

'No I am not.' Luce cut in firmly. 'He has let it slide. Not because of you but because of the lazy, arrogant person that he truly is. When was the last time he treated you nicely let alone like a princess?'

Abby remained silent.

'What has happened to my friend Abby who wouldn't let anyone boss her around? He's drained all of that vigour from you. You are literally a shell of who you used to be.'

'He doesn't hit me and isn't horrible to me, though.'

'No, but he doesn't do anything good. He doesn't do anything nice 'just because' he loves you or he's thinking of you and wants to make you smile. He's made you dependent on his choice of when he's going to be kind.'

'He used to,' Abby cried harder.

'I'm sorry, Abby, I'm not going to be sympathetic this time, 'used to' is not enough. This guy is using you; you've become his personal maid not a girlfriend. In fact, actually it's worse than that because if you were his maid at least he'd pay you. You're using all of your free time to tend to his needs, and he thinks nothing of *yours. THAT'S NOT A RELATIONSHIP.'*

Lucy had let rip. *'Look at what he's done to you. You don't even walk tall anymore, you hang your head and constantly apologise. He's made you into a wet rag that he can wring out and use again.'*

'Lucy, I know it sounds mental, but I just feel like we're going through a rough patch.'

'For five months?'

'Yes, for five months, all couples have them. And no, I'm not myself, but I love him, and I'm committed to making this work.'

'Is he though? He looks like he's doing flat zero to make your life as easy as you're making his.'

'Oh, he's just busy. He's quite caring when you're not around.' A little white lie.

'Do you love him or the idea of him; the way he was at the start when he was trying to woo you and impress you. We all liked him then, but that's not who he really is.'

'I love him, and I know that person is inside of him, I just need to bring it out again. He's the one Lucy.'

Lucy sighed and dropped her head in defeat.

'Look, Abs, I didn't come out today to upset you. I say what I'm going to say because you're my all-time best friend, and I'm only going to say it once, just please promise me that you'll think about it.' Abby had nodded in silence.

'You cried over the fact that you feel like you're losing him, but from my point of view, it would be no great loss. Except to him. Playing the perfect little housewife requires a loving husband who appreciates the efforts she goes to. You haven't got that, he doesn't notice, thank you or treat you well. You've become at best his mother

and at worst a doormat he just walks over. I can't bear it.' Lucy had welled up at that point.

Abby had said nothing. What could she say to that? She felt so deflated. Any pride she had always disappeared when Charlie withdrew his affections. She was mentally exhausted by it all now. Why wasn't she good enough for him? Everyone else would say he didn't deserve her, but if she was so great then why didn't he treat her well?

She'd said goodbye to Lucy, and automatically picked up a mug and a beer can he'd left in the lounge and taken them to the kitchen.

'Are you alright in there?'

'Um,' Abby was rooted to the spot with her memories.

Abby clenched her fists against the urge to wretch, the sheer sight of him and all that he'd put her through repulsed her.

'You disgust me,' she murmured.

'What, babes?' he said, leaning acrost the soda, surrounded by his own muck.

She raised her voice, 'I said: You. Disgust. Me.' It was a voice even Abby had never heard herself use. Rising out of the depths of her stomach and curdling into a putrid mass against him. He disgusted her for treating her and her friends that way – because by proxy, he'd upset Lucy and she never let anyone do that – and he'd almost made her lose her job. Yes, it had been her decision to wallow in thoughts of him and make him a priority, but he could have encouraged her, like a good boyfriend would, to take pride in her work and still be a good friend to the people who had stood by her for years. But no, it had all been about him.

Charlie was leaning up on the sofa looking at her with a dumb look on his face.

Raging, she clenched her fists around the dirty boxers, leaned down and grabbed more laundry, rank and limp from sweat and god knows what, and stormed over to him, throwing it all as hard as she could into his face. Charlie fell off the sofa, landing on his breakfast plate.

'What the ...?'

She chucked the rest of his dirty underwear over him. Yuck. There was a lot of it – he'd obviously been saving it up for her, or the next poor girl to do.

'Don't talk,' she yelled. Not caring who heard her, 'I never want to hear your voice again.'

Charlie peeled his crusty boxer shorts from his face and remained silent, stunned.

'Do you know, I hated you for sending me to that counsellor, but in the most ironic way, it was the nicest thing you've done for me in months. Because I realised what everyone has been saying about you was true. I hung my head in shame, but it did what you wanted it to do: it got me over you. Completely.'

Charlie smirked, desperate to say 'as if.'

Abby squinted at him. 'You don't believe me, do you? Do you know how many times during the last four months I've been humiliated to the point where I just wanted to crawl home and hide under the bed covers? Yet even in those moments, no one has ever, ever made me feel as worthless as you made me feel, Charlie.'

Charlie yawned, grabbing the PlayStation controller. The suave man that dressed well and stood tall in public was nothing more than a slob and a lay-about at home.

'No, you're not going to play on that. You texted me, you got me over here, you *are* going to listen to me.'

He kept his face turned to the TV, as if she wasn't there.

Abby would not be ignored. She strode over to the wall, wrenched the plug out of the socket and ripped the plastic plug off the wire.

'My next boyfriend will not have one of these. He'll be able to hold a conversation, and if he wants to play pool, he'll go to a bar like a normal person and play it there, not on one of these, like a complete loser, sitting here in a pit by yourself.'

She saw his horror as she eyed up the TV, but instead, she grabbed her bag and turned it upside down, tipping all the contents over his head.

'There. Have these back, I don't want anything of yours. Your message said you need me. You need a maid. You don't even know me.' She was bright red now.

'I've met someone really lovely. A true gentleman, who treats me beautifully, naturally. Abby's throat curdled into a snarl. She was so angry. She shook the bag – something had wedged in the seam; it was a photo frame of them both. She held it high, looked him straight in the eyes and flung it into the corner where it smashed, shards of glass flying everywhere.

'There. That's what you did to my heart. You didn't just break it you smashed it to smithereens. I was utterly broken.'

'I know, my little Abby, but if you loved me, you'd forgive me.'

'You're a parasite. I don't love you. You are nothing to me. Suck on that.'

'All this emotion is proof you still care. You're mine, up here.' He gestured to his head.

She felt the rage boiling within her.

'I am not yours. Don't even pull that one on me. You don't love me. You just tried to manipulate me with insecurities and guilt. You're a selfish bastard.'

'Oh, come on Abby, you were so quick to fall for it, admit it, you enjoyed yourself. It's not my fault you changed. You hurt me by changing, but I do still love you.'

She looked at him in horror.

'Come here, baby,' he gestured for her to lie on the dirty laundry and cuddle.

'How deluded are you?' She felt sick. What a hideous life she would have had.

Completely indifferent to the words, she'd just been speaking, Charlie shrugged.

'I'll text you later, babes.'

'No, you won't, you're not going to get me like that either.'

Grappling around in the inside pocket of her smaller handbag, she grabbed her phone and snatched the SIM card from it. Coming prepared for that kind of crass comment, she'd nipped into the first mobile phone shop she'd seen and picked up a new SIM card to use until she could officially change her number. She snapped the old one in two.

Charlie frowned, 'What are you doing, you crazy girl?'

'Not crazy actually, I'm saner than ever before. This is something I should have done a long time ago,' and she chucked the broken SIM on to the pile of everything he'd ever given her.

'You must have liked the way I treated you Abby – you wanted me back.'

'I didn't like anything. I fell for the man you pretended to be in a bar not the dickhead you are at home. Do your own fucking laundry, and when you've finally grown up and realised what you could have had, don't bother coming crying to me because I wouldn't even blink at the memory of the worst sex of my life with a man with a wonky penis.' Abby had actually quite liked his dick, but there was no harm in giving the guy a complex – he'd messed with her head enough.

His look of shock at her last comment almost made her laugh out loud – trust that to finally hit home. With that, she swung her handbag over her shoulder. Something hard hit her back. What was that? Reaching inside, she saw the final piece and smiled with glee as she clasped the frozen chicken left over from Valentine's Day.

Charlie's eyes flickered with recognition, 'Is that the ...?'

'Yes. Yes, it is,' Abby confirmed. 'I was saving it to cook and celebrate our reunion, but you can sod that and have it right back.' With that, she held it over her head and aimed it straight at Charlie as hard as she could, and he yelped as the solid frozen lump hit him square in the face. Without wasting another second, she turned on her heel, strode out of the door and ran down the stairs. She felt bad for leaving the chicken to fend for itself in Charlie's apartment, but she banished those thoughts and slammed the front door with as much strength and gusto as she could muster. Beaming her brightest smile, she walked away.

She was over Charlie. It had been a long time coming, but the complete and utter closure she'd granted herself was as restorative as a thousand-hour spa treatment. She almost skipped to the Tube, hellishly late for her date with Tim but confident he'd understand when she told him. She whizzed him a message from her new phone and hoped he would amuse himself at the Lock – there was plenty to do in Camden whilst he was waiting for her.

21

THE FEAR

TIM WAITED OUTSIDE Camden Tube station for Abby to show up. He'd done his research and the stall owner Abby had bought her necklace from had a sister stall at Camden Lock, so he'd arrived an hour early to ask her to set aside the matching bracelet as a surprise. He couldn't wait to see her smile when she found out.

He was desperate to see her, he'd thought about nothing much else since their first proper date. She'd seemed so fresh and genuinely happy and it had been years since he'd felt like this. If ever.

Looking at his watch again, he wondered if he had got the meeting place wrong. Twenty minutes late and no response on her mobile. Was he really meant to meet her here at the Tube station or did she mean meet at Camden Lock? How could he screw up the meeting place? Maybe he should check the Lock again, she could be pottering around the stalls before their date. He knew she wanted to have a wander up the canal to Primrose Hill.

'Shit,' he exclaimed has he neared the Lock and grimaced at the number of people all jammed around the stalls, bars and kiosks, finding her in this rabble could be tough. He moved as quickly as he could through the busy crowds, but it still took him about fifteen minutes to check every stall and shop for her.

His phone pinged with a message saying, 'Running, literally running x,' but it was from an unknown number so he ignored it and carried on looking. Standing on the bridge overlooking the bustle of happy people, Tim felt frazzled. He scraped his fingers through his hair. He'd looked everywhere, there was no sign of her. Pushing all thoughts that he'd been stood up out of his mind, he knew he had only one option left. He had to go to her apartment. Worried something might have happened to her, he quickened his pace.

*****

'TIM!' WOODY SWUNG the door open, looking surprised but happy to see him.

'Are you alright?'

'Yes,' Tim said abruptly before pausing, he'd honestly been expecting Abby to open the door. Then he realised that he didn't have a clue what to say to her if she did. 'Er, is Abby in as well?'

'No, she isn't mate. Good timing to pop round though, I'm definitely up for a beer.' Woody turned to get his jacket.

'Wait a moment, where is Abby?'

'Argh,' Woody grimaced. 'Charlie texted her.'

'Charlie?' Tim felt his insides start to sink.

'Yes, and she left straight away. That man,' Woody spoke through gritted teeth.

'So, she ran to him the instant he texted her?'

'Yes, of course, well, it's Abby and Charlie, isn't it?'

'Abby and Charlie,' Tim nodded. He was suddenly finding it hard to breathe.

'The boy can do no wrong, he's sodding perfect in her eyes ...'

'And she just ... went?'

'Yes,' Woody sighed, 'she was all dolled up with an overnight bag. But let's face it, it will all be wasted on him, she'll come back in tears at some point.'

'No doubt,' Tim managed before steadying himself on the doorway. My god, he'd been so foolish to think she preferred him and was ready to move on.

'Sorry, mate, I'm just shoving this worry on you. I thought she'd turned a corner – she's been really happy lately.'

'Well maybe being happy meant taking a risk with her heart, and she wasn't ready to do that just yet ...'

'Maybe,' Woody looked at him curiously. 'Are you alright?'

Tim knew he had completely sagged in the space of five minutes and likely gone a pale shade of grey. Woody probably hadn't seen him like that since Catherine had upped and left him.

'Tim, come in,' he gestured, 'let me sort you out with something.'

'Er, no, it's alright, I just feel ill all of a sudden. I must be coming down with something. I think I'll be better off just going home.'

'OK mate, whatever you want,' Woody was confused. 'Give me a buzz when you're better, and we'll go out for that beer.'

Tim nodded and turned away, his head swimming with the thoughts of Abby kissing Charlie, clashing with the memories of her kissing him last week. He almost swayed over at his own quick-hearted foolishness. That 'The heart is a vital organ, you were so foolish to lay yours up for the slaying' quote had never been so true. With no energy to walk, he hailed a cab and slid dejectedly into the back seat. This is why he hadn't wanted to date her – the fear of feeling like this.

22

KEEP TRYING

ABBY MADE IT to Camden, cursing, 'Shit, shit, shit, Tim, pick up,' she willed, still trying to call him, but for some reason, it kept going through to voicemail. She was so late. She broke into another run, pushing through the crowds as quickly as she could to get to the Lock. Craning on her tiptoes, she stood on the bridge and looked across the stalls, trying to catch a glimpse of him. Thank heaven he's tall, she smiled, sure she'd see his smile soon...

She grabbed a coffee after ten minutes, and kept her eyes peeled for the sight of him.

Anxious now, it was coming close to an hour she'd been there.

What to do? Should she call Woody and ask? What if something had happened to him? She was getting worried now; it seemed so out of character for him. She decided against calling Woody; Tim had wanted to keep this private for a while, and she had to respect that. 'I guess I'll just go home then,' Abby said to herself, more confused than anything. There had to be a logical explanation for this. She looked down at her new phone again. Maybe he was rejecting the calls from her new number. She started to make her way back to the Tube station, her brow furrowed. This was not how today was meant to be panning out.

Sod it, I'll just try one more time. She told herself. Still keeping an eye out for him, she dialled his number one last time. He answered on the second ring.

'Tim! Oh, thank god I was worried something had happened to you. Where were you today, are you alright?'

'Don't lie to me, Abby,' Tim's clipped tone came as a complete shock, she'd never heard him sound that brutal before.

'Don't make out like you're worried about me.'

'I *am* worried though!'

'I was there, Abby.'

'So was I, Tim.' Abby's heart hammered faster and faster – what was going on? 'Tim, why are you so upset? I was 40 minutes late ... I'm really sorry. I promise I'll be more punctual next time, but I did text you.'

'Next time? No chance. Abby, I told you what I went through before, please do me the courtesy of telling me the truth. Please, stop lying to me.'

Abby stopped dead in her tracks. He didn't believe her. What on earth was going on?

'Tim, please listen to me, I was at the Lock, I tried texting you...' And then it dawned on her: he didn't know she had a new number, so he'd probably dismissed it. 'Tim maybe the confusion's come from me having a new number. I had to get rid of my old one.'

'Oh right, so do you have one phone for him and one for suckers like me?'

Abby was quiet.

'I know you were with Charlie today Abby.'

She remained silent.

'Stop lying to me.'

'Tim, you've got this completely wrong.'

'Have I?'

Tim's tone was brutally sarcastic, she could tell he was hating himself for having been seemingly stupid.

'Tim, Charlie has been texting me non-stop for the past two weeks, so I went over there today ...'

'Yes, glowing, all dolled up, with an overnight bag.'

Woody! Abby thought. Shit, he must have spoken to Woody, and with Woody not knowing the whole story, he'd put two and two together to make six hundred. She suddenly felt cold with the fear of how this was panning out.

'This is all a huge misunderstanding.'

'You must be so happy he wanted you back, was I just the catalyst to make him jealous?' Tim sounded rejected and forlorn now: 'I feel so stupid, Abby. I thought we had a special connection, but you were just using me to get back with that rat.'

'Tim, stop, you've got it so completely wrong. I went there ...'

'I don't want to hear it, Abby. I may have been a complete fool to fall so quickly for you, but I did ...'

'I've fallen for you, too.'

'Bollocks. Are you calling me from there? Are you there now?'

'No, Tim, I went to Camden Lock after I went to Charlie's, you weren't there, I'm still here waiting,' Abby was in tears. 'Woody just ...'

'Don't bring Woody into this. At least he was honest with me.'

'You have to let me explain. Tim you have to believe me – I swear it's the truth. I'm texting you from a new phone because I didn't want him ...'

'How do you think I feel, Abby?'

Damn it, he wasn't hearing her – things were spiralling out of control: 'But you're not believing me.' Somehow, from all that Tim had been through, he was even more fragile than she was. His issues were overriding everything. 'What do I have to do to convince you?'

'I don't think there is anything you can do. Please leave me alone now. Goodbye, Abby.'

Tim hung up, leaving Abby listening to a devastating silence.

Abby gasped. People around her moved in slow motion, all sounds were blurred. Tears streamed down her face, ruining her makeup, but she didn't care. How could this have gone so wrong so quickly? Last weekend had been so beautiful. She'd felt like fragile porcelain when he held her so carefully; he's seen right into her, understanding she only wanted him to hold her again. She knew it was crazy to feel like that so soon, but her instinct was right. He was one of the good ones. How could this have happened? Someone bumped into her from behind, and she spun around, loosely hoping it was Tim.

'Don't stop in the middle of the walkway,' the stranger cursed her.

'Sorry,' She muttered – she also hated it when people did that.

'Right, I need to get home,' she whispered to herself, 'I need to speak to Woody.'

ABBY SAT IN the same spot, staring at her silent phone until darkness fell. Woody came home hours later. Walking past her open door, he peeked in and jumped out of his skin when he saw her sitting so still, ghost white.

'Abby, what's happened? Oh no, has Charlie hurt you already?'

'Sit down, Woody, I need to tell you something,' Abby's normally animated voice was now a monotone whisper.

'The reason I've been so ridiculously happy this past week is because I went on a date with Tim.'

Woody looked taken aback.

'Please don't be mad,' Abby rushed her words, 'he's utterly lovely. He made me feel I was walking on air last week.' And she filled him in on the events. Woody looked completely crestfallen when he heard about his role in the outcome. He put his head in his hands.

'Oh my goodness, Abby, I'm so, so sorry. Everything you've been through, and then I do that.'

Grabbing his hands, Abby hurried to console him: 'It's not your fault in the slightest Mr Woods, we should have told you.' He looked up at her. 'Seriously, it's my fault, I should have been more upfront about what was going on, but I just wanted to keep it quiet until I was more sure of how I felt, you know?'

Woody nodded.

'Can you call him though?' Abby asked.

'Yes, of course, I'll do it now.'

Woody dialled Tim and was instantly put through to his voicemail. And over the next hour, he called him ten times. But Tim didn't pick up. Abby was beside herself. She couldn't have lost him because she'd gone to Charlie's flat before their date. Why on earth did she have to be so impulsive and do it then? She could have done it any other evening this week and not have ended up with this issue. She'd still have Tim's respect.

She thought about him sitting at home hating himself for letting his guard down and feeling hurt because of something she did.

'He's still not answering,' Woody said, cutting into her thoughts. 'It's almost 1am, Abby, I've got to go to bed. I'll keep trying in the morning, though, I promise. Are you going to be alright?'

Abby smiled weakly at Woody and nodded. 'Thank you anyway,' she whispered.

'I'll back you up. Don't worry, Abfab. Just let him calm down, and you'll be able to speak to him. Tim is nothing if not reasonable,' and he kissed her on the top of her head and left her to her thoughts.

Abby wasn't so sure. He's only just started letting his guard down with her, and he seemed fairly resolute when it came to right and wrong. It must be even harder after he'd been majorly burned – of course his reaction would be to clam up completely. Even in the short time they'd spent together, she knew this would be black and white for him. The way it used to be for her, too, she reflected. But over the past year, she'd seen there were so many shades of grey, that you couldn't have just one simple rule to apply to everything. Matters of the heart needed more emotion when dealing with them *because* they were emotions. If Tim followed his normal black-and-white thought process and simply blocked her out ... she shuddered.

She couldn't go from feeling so god-damn awful about Charlie to having a glimpse of how it could be and then have to mourn the loss of something that had the potential to be beautiful.

She glanced at her watch again, it was too late to call her mum without worrying her. 'Bugger. What would her advice be?'

She'd say one of three things, Abby reasoned. One: make sure she spoke to him. Two: sometimes people come into your life not forever but to show you a lesson which you need to learn and be grateful for. And three: go to bed and it will seem clearer in the morning – classic parent advice.

She leant back in her chair and pulled her knees to her chest. If Tim really was meant to only be in her life to teach her a lesson, what would his wisdom be? She looked up, of course: it would be restoring her faith in herself and how she should expect and demand to be treated. She was worthy of being treated beautifully, and that's what he'd done because he wasn't a douche. He was one of the good ones, god damn it.

She considered her mum's logic some more: what would my lesson be to Tim? She couldn't have him thinking that all women were the same. She had to make him feel the way that he'd made her fee: utterly worthy of being treated beautifully. 'That's it. I just need to keep telling him until he believes me. I refuse to believe that it's over because of bloody Charlie. I'm not letting that idiot make anything in my life negative ever again.' She felt resolute. Lucy and pretty much everyone had been right all along. She did deserve better; she deserved a shot at being with Tim, and he deserved her. That was it, she decided, standing up. Tomorrow, she would keep trying to contact him until she got through. She was not going to let this one go without a fight.

23

IT'S THE TRUTH

'ABBY, I THINK you're going to have to be altruistic about this one,' Lucy said to her kindly but firmly, 'It's been two weeks now.'

Abby pursed her lips and shook her head, 'No chance. I know where you're coming from, Luce, believe me I do. But there's something about him.'

'Abby, he's not even taking Woody's calls on this, and he's his cousin. Maybe he's more messed up than you realised.'

'He's definitely more fragile than I realised,' Abby agreed. 'But that only makes it all the more important that I speak to him.'

Lucy closed her eyes at her, exasperated.

'I know what you're thinking, Luce, that I've merely transferred my feelings from Charlie to Tim and going from not getting over one guy to not getting over the next.'

Lucy just looked at her.

'Luce, I just know. You have to trust me, Tim is different. He's worth it.'

'You said that about Charlie.'

'Yes, and I've been through a lot since then, and I've learnt a lot since then. About human nature, about love and about myself. And about guys. I can tell a true gentleman when I see one ... and Tim is one. I have never, in my life, felt that way.'

'What way?'

'Safe but electric. Completely calm yet completely happy. I only ever want to feel that way!'

'Well what about at the start with Charlie?' Lucy was quizzing her now.

'No, it was thrilling with Charlie because he went crazy and made all of those stunning grand gestures. Tim quietly listened to what I said I liked and organised a date that was thoughtful. He started to open my eyes to see the world in a different way.'

'In that short time?' Lucy looked doubtful.

'Yes,' Abby nodded, tears glistening in her eyes. 'Yes. He captures everything in such a beautiful way. I just want to keep talking to him. He's the man to make me think differently without losing who I am. He never talked over me, not once. He was genuine and interested.'

Having been so emphatic that Charlie was the one for her– she could see 'I've heard all this before' in Lucy's eyes. But she pushed on: 'Tim is special, he will come back. I just have to be patient.' Lucy's jaw clenched as she breathed out steadily.

'Luce, look at me, look at the way I am. I'm not climbing the walls, not not working or eating myself to death with junk food. I'm not rolling over screaming and crying, I'm not anxious or depressed. I'm calm because I know he's been hurt just as much as me, but he's never really let it out and dealt with it, unlike me,' she winked.

'Yep, you let it out alright,' Lucy gave her a sideways glance.

'Well, I'd rather get it out and not have it come back

to bite me. He's fighting his old demons here – he's not fighting me.'

'But I don't want him to make you part of those old issues.'

'He won't, I won't let him, but he needs me right now. I know that for sure.'

She paused as Lucy puffed out her cheeks, lifted her eyes to the ceiling and sighed, 'OK Abfab, I believe you.'

'Good! Now, tell me what I need to do.'

'Well, if you do get him back, you need to have a conversation about communication because you certainly can't have this ghosting treatment every time he disagrees with something you do.'

'I agree. Noted.'

'So, have you been round to his place?'

'No, doesn't that seem stalkerish? Plus, I don't know where he lives.'

'Woody will know ...'

ABBY STOOD OUTSIDE Tim's apartment building that evening, waiting for someone to come out so she could pop in. Soon enough, she was outside his front door, ringing his buzzer. Her resolution to speak to him pounded through her mind as strongly as her heart thundered. Even if he never wanted to see her again, he had to know the truth – for his own good. She heard footsteps padding towards the door and drew a breath as Tim opened the door ... and slammed it straight shut.

'Go away, I don't want to talk to you.'

'Tough. You have to hear this, Tim. It's the truth.'

'I just want you and Woody to leave me alone for a while.'

'I'll leave you alone if you want, but first I have to

tell you this.'

Abby paused. He was obviously considering it. 'Good enough trade?' Silence met her, then footsteps padded away from the door. Another door slammed. 'Fine,' Abby said. 'I'll wait.'

She'd brought a magazine and a smoothie just in case, so she settled herself down. It was a good 40 minutes before there was any sound. She heard footsteps softly making their way to the door again.

'Can I speak now?'

'Jesus, Abby!' Tim exclaimed.

She grinned, having clearly startled him.

'You know I could get you removed from the building?' he threatened.

'Ten minutes of your time, Tim. Please. That's all I'm asking for,' Abby rose and placed her fingertips lightly on the door as if being closer to him might somehow alter his decision, 'then I'll go. I promise.'

Again, silence, but she could swear she could hear him breathing softly, inches away. She took a breath and started talking.

'Tim, those moments with you meant the world to me. You've shown me how life and love should feel. Our connection was real ... ' She touched the door between them.

'Until you flew back into Charlie's arms.'

'I went over there to tell him to completely sod off. Maybe I should have told you before I went, but he filled me with rage – he started trying to manipulate me again – and I only saw him for what he really was because you'd treated me so beautifully. I just didn't think to tell you. For that, I'm so sorry.'

'So how do you explain the overnight bag?'

'A bunch of his stuff I didn't want in my flat anymore. I don't want anything of his there. Ask Lucy! The other week we went through all my clothes to get rid of any that reminded me of him. He utterly disgusts me.'

Still silence.

'Tim, I never ever want to see or hear from that man-child again, that's why I changed my number. I'm not Catherine. I'm not going to hurt you.' She paused. 'I want to go on the date that we planned together. I want to feel how we felt that day in Greenwich. *That's* who we both are. *That's* what was real,' she rested her forehead against the door.

'Look, Tim, opening up to someone is a risk. Loving is a risk. But I can honestly tell you, I am neither of the things your ex was. I would honestly never, ever do that to you.' For goodness sake, Abby thought, how ridiculous must she look talking to a door? She didn't even know if he was still listening. What was she doing?

'Right, Tim, I'm standing here right now, and you're being a complete wuss, trying to block me out because you're scared opening up will hurt you again. But you're only hurting yourself,' she blurted. 'Have you done this to other girls? Do you find something wrong with everyone you date so you have an excuse to back away and not get hurt? Misery and fear are safe, but they're path ...'

'Safe?' the door swung open. He *had* been listening.

'Yes, safe. Feeling sad is easy because it holds you in a place that can't change: the past. It takes far more courage to pick yourself off the floor and move on.'

'I don't think sadness is easier to deal with than potentially being hurt,' Tim defended his choice.

'Yes, of course it is. You can fill your time and mind to distract you from being hurt and screwed over, whilst neatly avoiding it happening again,' his eyes bored into hers.

'But look at me, Tim. I've told you I'd never treat you like that, so really what have you got to lose? You just need to get to know me, and you'll realise that.' He blinked at her, staring straight into her eyes. She definitely had his attention.

'And am I right in thinking the only reason you've acted so strongly to me seeing Charlie ...'

Tim winced at the sound of his name, and Abby made a mental note never to say it again, whilst hurriedly moving on.

'... well, you would have only reacted that way if you cared about me. And caring about me is a *good* decision,' she felt her voice beginning to shake as she spoke softly. 'I always have the best intentions, Tim, just not always the best execution of them.'

'I *did* really like you.'

'Then you must still do,' she said desperately, before tightening her resolve. 'Come on, Tim, I'm not just some random girl you met in a bar. You know enough about me to know I'm telling you the truth.'

He looked her square in the eyes, holding her gaze. Was it past memories of pain he was reliving or was he processing everything she'd just said? Either way Abby knew better than to speak until he did. His face was unreadable. His shoulders sagged.

Instinctively she reached out for his hand, 'You holding my hand was real,' she whispered. 'Our talking about anything and everything was real. I only want to date you, Tim. I am not your ex.'

Tim dropped his eyes to the ground.

'No, look at me. You owe me at least that,' and she

waited. When he raised his eyes level with hers, they were filled with so much pain she ached to wrap her arms around him, but it had to come from him. He needed to give her a sign.

'It's me, Tim, your initial instincts were right. Our kiss said everything I needed to know ...'

'God, Abby, what have you done to me?' He whispered gruffly, pulling her into him and reaching his lips to hers. She kissed him back as hard as she could, holding him so tightly. His lips moved to her neck as his hands clung to her waist. He moaned as she moved his face to hers, their lips searching for each other. They clung to each other, pushed against the hall banister. Their tongues touching, exploring each other, confirming everything that they both needed to know.

Abby broke away, 'I have to know that you believe me Tim.'

'I do,' and he kissed her again. His chest pounded next to hers, his arms pulling her in tightly against it.

She felt a tear roll down her cheek.

'No, have I made you cry?' he looked devastated.

'No, I'm just so utterly relieved,' she smiled, exhausted: 'What a mess!'

'Not made any easier by the way I handled it. Abby, I'm so sorry, I should have listened to you. I should have believed you.'

Abby nodded and bit her lip, 'Yes, you should. So, can we learn from this and say that if we're ever confused about something with each other, that we just have a chat about it and be like, "hey, I'm not so sure about this". Rather than doling out the silent treatment and breaking each other?'

'Absolutely. And I need to realise you're not like her.

Because you're not, and I know that. You were right – I was just scared.'

'I was right,' she smiled. 'I love hearing that.'

'Don't love it that much,' He grinned.

'No,' she snuggled into him, burying her face into his chest.

'I'll always be honest with you, Abby. I promise you that.'

'I promise you the same, Tim.'

He held her so tightly, not wanting to let her go. She breathed in his cologne, knowing she'd done the right thing.

'So now can we go out on another date?' She asked, giggling.

'Yes, absolutely, well actually in one moment ...' Bending his head to hers again, they kissed and kissed and kissed.

'Let me get my jacket. We're going to a wine bar for a big fat glass of red and then I'm walking you home.'

Abby's cheeks ached and lips quivered from smiling, and while Tim grabbed his coat and wallet, she jumped around a few times in the hall. Her knees almost weak from the kissing. 'Wow, just wow,' she said to herself. Everything just felt right. She grinned at him as he tried to shift his hair into a better state after her hands had been in it. He sighed, gave up and held out his hand to her.

'Come on then. Date two ...'

24

NO HALF MEASURES

RELIEVED THAT ABBY had rectified her issues with Tim, Lucy was looking forward to a good Saturday night out with the IBS clinic crew. They were heading to Rosemary's, on Woody's recommendation, for an evening of gluttony and eating everything they all probably shouldn't.

After rising at 10, she enjoyed a light breakfast and read her favourite magazine, which had been batting its glossy eyelids at her since Tuesday. Inspired by the interior's section, she cast her gaze around her apartment. Right, time for a change. What could she do in a weekend to give it a different feel? Her furniture was mainly neutral – light grey upholsteries and white woods made her apartment feel calming and light – so she could change the look just by adding different accessories. A dash of colour here and there would be no bad thing, so she decided on a bit of shopping and finished her coffee.

She dressed in her old gym gear, thinking she'd do a pre-dinner workout on her way back home from shopping, and was on her way to the door when she caught a glimpse of herself in the mirror.

'God, I look dreadful,' she exclaimed, pulling at the old saggy t-shirt she'd worked out in for years.

In a moment of clarity, she pictured Abby in her dating prime, captivating men left, right and centre. Whether or not she ended up going on a date with them, she certainly got their attention for the best possible reasons – and one of those was she always made an effort to look her best, no matter what she was doing.

'Sod it,' Lucy voiced out loud. Maybe what she needed to do this weekend was channel her inner 'Abby,' to test out her theory that if she acted a little more like her best friend, she'd get more attention from guys.

There was no better time to start than right now. When Abby had been dating Charlie in the early days, they'd gone shopping and she'd impulsively purchased a load of Nike training gear. Abby had then shown her a load of toning exercises she'd been doing religiously since then, and in the shower, she could tell they'd been working. Ripping off her old gym clothes, she stood there in her undies and surveyed herself. Her toned curves didn't look half bad, very Dita von Teese. Why the heck hadn't she shown them off in that new gear yet?

Yanking the labels off the capri pants and top, she slipped them on, swishing her hair back into a high ponytail instead of the usual scraped back, harsh bun. Then she lightly dabbed some cream blusher on her cheeks, glossed her lips and did a double take when she looked in the mirror. Her normal gym attire made her look ten years older than she was and hid the figure that she'd been working so hard to achieve.

She sighed, for once Abby had been completely right: she did have to work it a little bit more. Her opinion of letting a guy see her at her worst and fall in love with her anyway to prove it was true could be shelved – it clearly just didn't work. 'Only ever let them see you not looking so great when they're already in love with you and even then, sort yourself out!' had been Abby's retort to her comment. 'Seriously, Luce, you have to draw them in. If they think you're going to let yourself go *after* you're married and you already look a state before it then it's not going to bode well is it?'

It had only taken her a few more minutes to fine tune herself, there really was no excuse. Slinging her gym bag over her shoulder, she grabbed her keys and left her flat.

Lucy strutted around Selfridges, forgetting about her home interior needs and instead purchasing designer goods on impulse, which she would only normally do after weeks of deliberating the market and choice and finding the best price. Still if she was going to act like Abby BC (before Charlie), then her new mindset determined her need for a new wardrobe as well as a newly decorated apartment, so she invested in an Alexander Wang dress for her evening out and when she twirled around in the changing room, it spun out like a ballerina's. 'Would it be too much for tonight?' She mused. 'Oh, what the hell. These people see me every week talking about IBS for crying out loud' – she had to look pretty to counteract it. Next she went all in and thoroughly smashed her Selfridges card on a pair of Jimmy Choo's heels. The final piece in the puzzle would be the perfect Anya Hindmarch clutch Abby had given her for Christmas, so she was sorted.

Half of the ladies going were already married and had little ones and were really excited about a night off, and she was sure they'd be making an effort, too, and all together they should have a great laugh. Even if the group hadn't found a miracle cure for their shared problem, they had really bonded and found a means of laughing about it whilst swapping cures. Laden with yellow bags holding tonight's outfit and a few more for next week, she paused at Givenchy, picking out a new lipstick, then Bobbi Brown for a shimmering new eye colour.

'Right, that's me done for now,' she said to herself. She felt fabulous, even if the active wear was now getting quite hot. She held her head high and worked her sports chic out of the store, her ponytail swinging high from side to side as she smiled, noticing people were actually smiling back. Wow, people in London do have the ability to smile back. She must just be radiating happiness.

Good lord, she noticed the time, how was it was 5pm already? No time for Tottenham Court Road's interior shops. Still, thrilled by how her day had turned out, she Tubed the short distance home and ran up the stairs, jumping a little higher than was needed on each stair, figuring it was her substitute for not going to the gym after all. She would go tomorrow she promised herself –today was her day of indulgence.

Hopping into the shower and applying a hair masque, she buffed her skin with a body brush, breathing in all of the essential oils as she did so, loving her day. Glowing, she emerged from the bathroom 20 minutes later, in a towel and slippers, ready to run some serum through her hair to style it for the night. Booking a taxi for 55 minutes' time, she turned on some music and dried her hair off before opening her new makeup. Clapping her hands with excitement, she took a sip of her wine before smoothing some tinted moisturiser over her creamy white skin, setting it off with a rose pearl blush. Adding the sparkly eye powder really made her eyes come alive and with her expertly applied mascara, she was good to go. Unwrapping her clothes, she hung them up to survey once more. Phew, she thought, she still loved them all.

Right how to accessorise tonight's attire. Flicking through rows of bracelets and necklaces, she found two that went perfectly and decided to layer them both. Tiny pearls and a gold pendant swung around her neck, and on her wrist, she wore Abby's favourite piece of hers, a Cartier Love bracelet in yellow gold. It had been her mother's, who never wore it anymore, so last Christmas she'd slipped it to her and told her to make it shine. 'I hope it will bring love to you, my dear,' she'd said. Lucy smiled as she remembered. 'I should really wear this every day then,' she murmured to herself. She was always a bit conscious of how much it was worth just hanging on her wrist. Was it a bit much for a meal at an Italian?

'Oh, sod it,' she smiled, fixing it on. It seemed to be the phrase of the day – she'd said it with every purchase. With ten minutes to go, she slipped on her dress, smoothed it down and stood in front of the mirror again. Suddenly missing Abby. The two of them would be dancing around and laughing, probably a bit tipsy by this point. She took a selfie to prove to Abby she'd made an effort and waited for the doorbell to ring.

Arriving at the restaurant she tipped the driver, and unlike the normal black cabbies, he got out and opened the door for her.

'I'll dress like this all the time if I get treated like this,' Lucy said to him, giggling and loving it. Escaping the cool evening air, she entered the bubbly atmosphere of Rosemary's, where, almost immediately, she saw her table of eleven waving and smiling. It warmed her up instantly and she beamed back. The waiter took her trench coat off to wolf whistles from some of the girls.

'Oh, you know I always dress like this,' she said playfully. Maria got up to give her a hug, sat down and promptly farted, drawing cheers from everyone at the table. Lucy laughed and cheered as well. They were all really good fun. The only rule for the night was to not mention how they met. This was a night to just be normal, which indeed they were.

Giggling, discussing clothes, shoes, men and enjoying the sumptuous sauces and pastas that appeared dish after dish, Lucy was having a great night. She shared some of her and Abby's antics trying to go out with guys. Abby's latest 'getting over Charlie' drama provided great fodder for conversation, and it was only when the eleventh bottle of wine dried up and dessert was brought out that Rachey, the devilishly pretty but fortunately taken girl sitting to the left of Lucy spoke up.

'Hey ladies, who's still single? We're forgetting that we have a hot guy in our midst.'

Lucy looked down the table and, sure enough, Will had tucked himself between the other ladies.

'Come on, girls. If there's only one guy here, you need to share him around a bit,' Lucy said, patting the seat next to her, not knowing where that uncharacteristic outburst had come from.

Will looked like a bunny in headlights. He was majorly outnumbered and didn't want to argue with a table of wine-fuelled raucous women, so he threw his napkin down and grinned to whoops of approval. He stood up grinned and wiggled his butt a little to work it for the ladies, who clapped and cheered as they all shuffled around the table to make space.

'Sit next to me, there's just about enough space,' Lucy said, flashing him her best smile, hoping she didn't have blue teeth from all the red wine. To make sure he had room – and more importantly could check out her outfit – she stood up and pretended to move her chair around a bit.

It worked. He lifted his chair around the table and sat it down next to hers. Perfect grouping thought Lucy, nicely between me and a married woman. Excellent. As she took another sip of her wine, she giggled to herself: what had got into her tonight? Maybe this is why Abby shops so much; it had turned her into a rip-roaringly fabulous confident version of herself.

'So, it's Will, isn't it?' she took the lead: 'Welcome to our end of the table.'

'Yes, let's see how it compares to the fine ladies at the other end.'

'Well, we need to show him a good time, girls. Come on, we need to win,' Lucy quipped and raised her glass. In between bad jokes and more crazy stories, they piled through more and more wine. Holding her head as upright as she could, Lucy looked around the table, not understanding for a moment why it was such a struggle to keep her head still. Gosh, she realised, she was smashed. Happily smashed and surrounded by lovely people. Spurred on by the love she felt for everyone, she pushed her chair back.

'A toast to all of you amazing people. May this be the first of many, many epic nights.'

She was met with whoops and hollers.

'Drink up everyone, we need to find a dance floor!'

Everyone got to their feet, somewhat precariously, and clinked glasses swigging the remainder of their drinks back as quickly as they could. Lucy and Will clinked and finished their drinks in one. Caught in the moment, Lucy almost threw her glass over her shoulder but caught herself in the act. Hysterically laughing to Will: 'Would you have believed it if I'd have done that?'

Will laughed loudly, 'Well in Greece they throw plates, so maybe in Italy it's wine glasses.'

'That was close, you'd better get me out of here quickly,' she giggled.

They paid the bill, leaving a decent tip on the table, and with well wishes from the management to come back whenever they wanted, they held on to each other and staggered their way outside. Spotting a bar across the street, Lucy whooped and ran in her heels.

'Come on, everyone, I'll get the shots in ...'

25

HELL IS NOT WHITE

LUCY FELT HOT. All over. Ridiculously, boiling hot. Was she burning? Oh my goodness, was she dead and in hell? She felt like she was. No, hell wouldn't be this white, she reasoned. Where was she? She leaned her head up as much as she could bear, and her eyes took in the familiar surroundings.

Oh, thank god she'd made it home, she exhaled from the sheer effort of holding her head up and let it slump to the pillow again. Her body was suffocating under her 13.5 tog quilt. Touching her chest, she cringed – she was completely covered in a sheen of sweat. She lay utterly still to see if that would make it any better. The room spun around her. Literally everything was in white. Was this really her room?

Yes, it was. She'd just been in such a rush to get out of the door, she hadn't put her quilt cover back on. She tried to lift her head again but only managed an inch this time. She felt scorched, her head was pounding and what was up with her mouth? So dry. And fixed wide open. Wiggling her jaw as best she could, she gurned, she put a finger on her tongue and ran it along her gums: dry. Slightly spooked by the arid state of her mouth, she tried to think what she'd done last night. She'd ruined her saliva glands and now they wouldn't work anymore. Panicking was doing absolutely nothing to help her sweat situation. Peeling one part of the duvet off her skin only seemed to make another part stick to her even more. She moaned a dry garbled noise.

Oh my god, this day was already awful, and she'd only just woken up. How was she ever going to survive it? She had to get out from under this duvet for a start. Her whole being depended on it. She'd read somewhere that the stupid sex noises tennis players made when they went to hit the ball actually forced more energy from their muscles. Well, she was desperate and willing to try anything now to make her body respond. Taking a deep breath through her gaping mouth, she exhaled a deep wail from her stomach. OK, at least she could form some form of noise to give her strength. With her mouth still hanging open, she breathed in again and willed every muscle in her body to move the duvet.

'Raaarrrghhh,' she wailed. 'Raaaarrrgghh,' again. Four times and she finally managed to kick the duvet off. Exhausted from the exertion, she lay panting on the bed, preparing herself for her next move, which would be to get to the bathroom at the other end of the room. Eyeing it up, she reckoned it would take her 15 minutes, but once there she could finally get some water inside her. At the thought of water, her stomach turned. Lucy rubbed her stomach gently, pacifying it with her thoughts. Milk? It groaned again. No, nope, not milk. Black tea perhaps? She paused, black tea seemed alright – there was no tension inside her at the thought of it.

Her legs felt floppy, and Lucy wasn't sure how much weight they could hold. Instead she rolled slowly on to her front on the bed summoning up her strength to use her moaning tactic to moan herself off it and to the floor.

She breathed in, gave one long exhale of a 'Raaaaaaargh' and she slithered like an ancient dehydrated snake on to the floor. Taking a moment to catch her breath, still unable to close her mouth, she focussed on the bathroom door with a steely eyed gaze that she imagined Sir Ranulph Fiennes had when looking up at the final ascent of Everest.

'Raaaargh,' she moaned again, pulling herself half a foot along the carpet. It was going to take her an hour at this rate. Stopping to regain her breath, still shocked by her lack of saliva, she heaved herself to her hands and went for it again. 'Raaarrrgh,' she made it two pulls before pausing to wonder what her mum would say to see her one and only child in this state. God, what a thought. Just as she took a deep breath to moan and pull herself along again, she lifted her head to see two feet sticking out of the bottom of the bed.

Totally paralysed, unable to scream, shock shook her to the core – there was an imposter in her bed – her body began to tremble all over and another layer of sweat emanated across her body. Quick as a flash, the feet moved and were suddenly standing there, right in front of her.

'Raaaargh,' Lucy moaned, throwing her hands haphazardly about in a weak form of self-defence. But as she looked up, all she could see were a set of cock and balls just dangling down. She could try to use primitive swipes at those. Crikey, they were a ginormous target, or was that the alcohol marring her vision?

This was probably the most vulnerable, she'd ever been in her entire life. The only factor to counteract her fear, she reasoned was that in her current 'unable to close her mouth' state she closely resembled Edvard Munch's *The Scream* painting. So in terms of being attacked for her looks, she wagered that she was probably going to be alright - No one wanted a sweaty scream shag. And if he did, then he truly was sick. She then almost smiled that her stellar reasoning skills hadn't been soaked up by alcohol, even if her saliva glands had been and her mouth couldn't move.

'Good morning!' The balls spoke. A voice she recognised. She tried lurching her neck up to catch a glimpse of his face but only caught another angle of ballage before flopping back down, face first.

'Oh dear, oh dear,' the balls spoke again ... Will, she thought. Will from the IBS clinic. Oh well, at least it wasn't a complete random.

'Raaaaaargh,' she managed to moan, and he knelt down, concerned. Cock and balls now nearer her face. She grimaced.

'Oh dear,' he said with a sunny voice. 'Well, it's only right you should be suffering – you were putting it away last night, and you're only tiny. Come here ...'

Rolling her deftly on to her side, he scooped her up in his arms. Lucy flung her arms over her face, sure she must look terrible. When he placed her back on the bed, she almost cried and just gave up. He must have assumed she'd fallen out unintentionally. Flopping on to her back, she pointed at the door and mimed turning on a tap for some water. He pretended not to understand her, but she moved to swipe his manhood and only narrowly missed.

'I'm on it. I'm on it,' and he moved towards the door.

'Raaaarghhh,' Lucy moaned to herself, finding comfort in the now familiar sound. She snapped back to reality, berating herself instantly: What have I done?

I've slept with someone and I can't even remember it. Oh god and in front of all of her new friends at the IBS clinic, she could never go to the meetings again. That was final. She must look like such an alcoholic whore, turning up for their first social gathering in her finest glam and slamming literally the only eligible guy there. She was never allowed out without Abby again, she simply could not be trusted on her own.

Starting to overheat again, she tried to regulate her breathing and focus on surviving the moment. Right now, though, she just needed Will to bring her some water. She could hear him clattering around the kitchen, he seemed to be taking ages to fulfil the slightest of tasks. Men honestly, she raised her eyebrows in sheer frustration – get some water, how hard could it be? It can't be taking this long. It was just as well that she couldn't really speak or else she'd boss him to high heaven. Coming into her flat and taking advantage of a clearly obliterated woman. She'd have a word with him about that, if her mouth would ever work again.

Eventually she heard water hitting glass and breathed a sigh of relief. As he padded back into the room, she held out her hands, narrowly missing the swinging cock and balls. Damn, they were huge, they were beginning to resemble some form of jungle creature. If she just craned her head, they'd look like ... no focus. Lucy your mouth is still fixed wide open, at this rate he's going to get the wrong idea.

Will clearly thought her staring meant she was interested and promptly swayed them around so they were swinging. Lucy began to laugh, thinking no woman alive would find that attractive, but with her mouth still wide open, she made such an awful sound, she reached quickly for the water again.

Will looked dejected, 'I was trying to hypnotise you to help with your hangover.'

She sipped the precious elixir down and swilled the rest into every crevice of her mouth, flexing her jaw three times in relief.

'I thought you said you were a lawyer not a hypnotist,' she croaked. She gulped a load more water down. Then regretted it as her stomach turned over, probably in shock at receiving something pure and non-alcoholic.

Will jiggled his balls again. She giggled at his attempts to make her laugh. Mental note: must *laugh* at jokes, not sleep with people who make them, she chastised herself.

'Look, in all seriousness, how are you feeling?' He actually looked concerned now.

'Still drunk,' Lucy answered lolling back on her pillows, trying to pull herself up a tad. Not sure if she really was still drunk. She was in the worrying half state phase between being drunk and being horrendously hungover. It could all go wrong in an instant. Better to stay still. Now she had to figure out how to get him to leave in a kind, quick and polite manner.

'Did we *do it*?' Was all that left her lips. Brilliant.

'No,' he replied calmly.

'Really?' she grinned, thoroughly relieved.

'No. We didn't 'do it.' It was far more than that. You and I made a physical connection in an atomic manner.' He paused looking thoughtful, obviously trying to find the right words. 'Seriously, it was incredible, it's like your vagina was CERN, you know the ...'

'Yes, I know what CERN is. Your manhood certainly ain't an atom, though.'

Will's face broke into a proud beam. And Lucy buried

her head in her hands. Oh god, she was joking with him and saying 'ain't.' She wasn't the type of person who said 'ain't,' what was going on with her?

Will snapped her out of it: 'Right. Now you've the power of speech back, I'm going to tell you about my morning.'

Lucy frowned. He carried on...

'I thought I was dreaming and had landed on a desert island, where in the nearby shallow waters, a beached whale was drowning slowly, smacking itself to move to deeper waters. Then I awoke. I realised it was you.'

Incredulous someone could be that rude, Lucy's scrunched her eyebrows up and scowled at him. Surely a gentleman would never say such a thing? He leapt off the bed, shaking it violently, and she clenched her stomach muscles in desperation. Oh god, he wasn't hungover at all. Die, she willed inwardly, outside my apartment, stop swinging your manhood jungle around and just die or, failing that, just let me die in peace, please, until I feel better and want to live again. What was he doing now?

'This is what you were like,' he eagerly demonstrated Lucy's flopping and slithering naked off the bed with sound effects, making the beached whale sounds of 'Raaaaargh' as he made his way back to her.

What was happening to her mouth? The corners were beginning to rise. No don't laugh and encourage this mad behaviour. Lucy couldn't help it as Will fixed her gaze and made the whale noise again. Perched inelegantly on a pillow, Lucy began to laugh as hard as her stomach would allow her to. 'Save the whale,' she whispered.

'Greenpeace would be proud,' he grinned.

Seeing her finally relax a tad seemed to have a calming effect on him. He climbed back on the bed, but she held her hand up to him to be still.

'Goodness. You're really suffering, aren't you?'

'Yes,' she whispered. 'From what I do, putting emphasis on the 'do,' remember of last night, you were drinking just as much as me – I know you're a guy, but how come you're not even a teeny bit hungover?'

Will smiled at her, 'Oh well, I always take milk thistle supplements before, during and after a night out, and they stop me being hungover. I tried to get you to try one, but you spat it out and threw it in my face saying you don't do drugs.'

'Literally spat?' Lucy was horrified. She didn't even chew gum because she thought it looked vile and made a hideous noise. Now she was spitting. She covered her face in utter despair again. 'I'm not normally like this,' she reasoned with herself and Will.

'Oh sure,' Will jested back.

'No, really I'm not. Abby, she's my best friend ...'

'Is she the really quiet one that came to the meeting?'

'Ah yes. She's not normally that quiet.'

'Well, it can be difficult for some people.'

Lucy didn't have the energy to disagree or explain that Abby was the outgoing one. Not that she would spit or chew gum either for that matter. Unable to remember what her point was going to be, she rolled her head towards him and, as politely as she could manage, she said quietly, 'Would it be possible to have ten minutes in my room just to get cleaned up a bit?'

'Yes, of course. I'll do the same. Is there another bathroom?'

'Straight down the hall next to the spare bedroom.'

He left the room, and Lucy groaned as she pulled herself out of bed again and crawled to the bathroom.

Still unable to stand properly, she curled over like an old lady. Her brain was pounding, she had stomach cramps and she was still sweating for England. This is why I don't drink much, she thought. If it makes me boring, I don't care.

She didn't trust herself to stand up long enough to have a shower, she'd do it later when, if ever, she felt better. Clutching on to the basin stand, she cleaned her teeth, retching at the mint taste in her mouth. She grabbed a wet wipe out of the packet and rubbed it over her face and another one over her body. Had they used a condom last night? Had they even slept together? They must have done – she was naked and so was he. My god, why couldn't she remember even the tiniest detail?

Unable to stretch to reach her deodorant, she sprayed her Balenciaga perfume under her armpits and scraped a brush through a bit of her hair before feeling dizzy, giving up and grabbing her silk bathrobe then slowly making her way back to bed. Snuggled back up in a ball, she focussed on her breathing, trying so hard not to be sick.

Her stomach turned over in a familiar manner, indicating purge time, 'Oh heck. Just when I thought it couldn't get any worse.'

Will knocked on the door gently and pushed it open. He was wearing his boxers now and looking at her, concerned.

'I'm only hungover, I'm not going to die,' Lucy tried to joke, but even she wasn't so sure of herself.

'Well, I'm a bit concerned you've got alcohol poisoning,' he said, kneeling down so they were face to face. His eyes were as kind as she'd remembered from the beginning of last night. 'Lucy, as mental as the last not even 24 hours have been, I'd like to take care of you, or at least call someone to come over.'

Lucy shook her head and groaned; she didn't want anyone else to see her in this state.

'That's really sweet, Will, but I'll be OK, I just need to rest and fall asleep and re-awaken as my sweet, non-whale-like self later, I think.'

'Well, have some more water. I'll get dressed.' He slipped on his trousers and shirt.

'Guys, really have no walk of shame, do they?' She mused. Thank god she was at her apartment – even the thought of seeing daylight made her curl up even tighter, holding her stomach, which was moving the air inside of her around to create knots of excruciating tension. Oh dear god, Will has to go now. She needed to be alone if she was going to fart and let all of this air out.

'Yeah, we kind of lucked out, I guess. All dressed and ready to go,' he was far too cheerful. He bent down to write something on her magazine. 'Right, this is my number. Call me if you need me, or text me and let me know you're alright. See you at the meeting this week.' He paused. 'I had a great night, Luce, hope you feel better soon.' He knelt down to kiss her on the cheek and instead made a whale noise.

'Get out of here,' she laughed with a mock seriousness.

The relief that hit her when she heard her front door open and close was immense, almost as strong as the wave of nausea. Her attempts at slowing her breathing down and being calm had lasted as long as they had needed to whilst he was in her apartment and now her body was ready to purge itself. Unclenching her stomach muscles, she knew she had a minute to make it to the toilet. She made it to the bathroom in time, vomiting into the sink whilst her ass emitted the world's loudest and longest fart echoed round her ensuite.

'Phew,' she breathed in satisfaction. That felt incredible to finally set free from her body. Thank god he'd left.

'Got my keys now. Sorry, I'll be on my way now ... bye.' A voice emerged from the hall. She gasped in shock. Will must have forgotten his stuff, held the front door open and not actually exited the building. That was it, all dignity gone. She had nothing left, she must never see him again. Lucy mournfully hung her head. How awful.

Staggering back to her bed and collapsing, she took a further hour to gather the strength to tiptoe around her apartment to find her handbag from last night. She knew she must have brought it home because she had the keys to get in, but she still feverishly checked the contents. Happily, even her new lipstick was there – a small plus but she'd hang on to it. Her phone battery had died, so after being sick again, she summoned the strength to find the charger. All in all, it had taken her nearly two hours to find and turn her phone on, compared to two minutes on a normal day.

Drinking really does slow your reactions down, she thought. And wow, that was the deepest thinking she'd done all day. Did that mean she was feeling better? Her stomach growled again, the answer being a catastrophic and resounding no. 'There can't be much left,' she wailed. Damn this, she couldn't possibly blame this on the IBS. She looked at her bed from the loo. Had they used a condom? She assumed so as there were no tell-tale signs on her sheets. Clambering back inside the covers, feeling feverishly chilly, she willed herself to sleep.

Six hours later she awoke, resolute she had to shake this off. It was 5pm and she'd been sick all day. She hadn't done any of the shopping for the apartment she wanted to, and she'd had sex with a guy she didn't really know, which went against everything she believed in.

With her head in her hands, she figured she had to pull herself together - this was just an average Saturday night for some people. She picked up her phone to send a text:

Abby I'm never EVER going out without you again. Please get over here, it's urgent...

hope your weekend was good... xxx

26

MAN JUNGLE

'DON'T BEAT YOURSELF up for having carnal aspirations, Luce. We both know, deep down, you're a saucy bugger,' Abby teased her.

'Oh, Abby it would be fine if I could remember anything, even the tiniest bit of detail. I don't know if it was any good, if I was any good! That's essential knowledge.'

'Well, any sex is better than no sex for most guys, and it's not like it was your first time. You were hammered, so you either acted like a porn star, or at worst, you lolled around and let him take over. He was drunk as well remember ... I think he sounds quite sweet,' Abby concluded.

'Dangling his man jungle in my face when I'm trying not to throw up? Sweet?' Lucy was horrified.

'Ha ha, did he really do that? Well, he sounds like he has a sense of humour, too.'

'He has actually,' Lucy defended his one worthy quality. 'Although it takes him ages to get water.'

They sat in silence, sipping black tea.

'Abby, I can't face going to that meeting again. I'm going to look like such a slut. It was our first going-out session.'

.

'I know you've explained that,' Abby sighed. Lucy always beat herself up about stuff she couldn't change. Over the years, she'd given up trying to convince her otherwise and just listened.

'All the other women must be judging me. I turned up wearing all this over the top stuff and then went mental. They're all going to think they know why I've got IBS if they think I act like that all of the time.'

'Lucy, from the sounds of it, *everyone* was pretty messed up. There's only one way to find out, though ...,' Abby walked into Lucy's bedroom and instantly regretted it. Trying not to breathe in the rank hangover air, she retrieved Lucy's phone as quickly as she could, opened a window, retched and dashed out. Taking a deep breath in the hall to head off a projectile vomiting session between them, she handed the phone over to Luce and told her to text both Will and Hilary.

'Go on, you can't feel any worse.'

'Will's number is on the magazine next to my bed,' she mumbled from the couch.

'I'll give it five minutes before going back in there.' Lucy didn't look capable of texting, so she quickly typed out a message:

'Hey Hills, thanks for a wicked night. How on earth are you feeling today?'

'Best to play it safe, Luce, and not give too much away,' Abby reasoned.

Lucy dropped her head and sat in a funk, her eyes on her phone, while Abby pulled out a selection of DVDs, attempting to distract Lucy from waiting for Hill's text back. Playing it safe ruled, and within minutes, they heard a beep on the phone.

'Just what were those shots we were drinking? I have

memory loss from that point.'

Abby threw her hands up, beaming:

'Hills can't remember anything either and feels awful STILL,' Lucy exclaimed victoriously, looking slightly pious – at least she'd managed to contemplate eating food again.

'Don't gloat when you answer her,' Abby said as she finally risked going back in for the magazine and Will's number – happy to find the room already smelt better.

'Of course not. I'll send her smiles for feeling better soon. How fabulous that she can't remember anything,' Lucy beamed, and Abby rolled her eyes.

'So, Luce was Maria there last night?' wondering how the woman who farted all the time could cope with a night out.

'Yes,' Lucy giggled, 'and she really is a bit of a legend.'

Abby raised an eyebrow: 'How so?'

'Well, imagine how hard her life must have been for her, farting all the time uncontrollably.'

'School must have been hell,' Abby agreed.

'And yet it's somehow made her into a strong and confident person who's happy in her own skin.'

'I suppose she is living proof that she who farteth when she sitteth down, still has many friends.'

Lucy groaned and held her tummy, trying not to laugh too hard. 'I need to tell her that. It's true though!'

'Definitely,' Abby grinned, 'However, right now, it's now time to text Will.'

'Really, Abs?'

'Yes, I've been in that room now, so God only knows what it must have been like earlier on.'

Lucy grimaced, 'Ugh, I hate myself sometimes. What do I say?'

'Why don't you just keep it short and sweet and thank him for a great night and for taking such good care of you?'

'He took five minutes to get me a glass of water!'

'Yes, but big him up, make him feel good, then he'll associate you with feeling good. And yes, I *have* read that stupid book on positive management that you lent me.'

Lucy stuck her tongue out, the last of her hangover dropping away.

'Careful, you can't remember where that tongue's been,' Abby taunted her.

Lucy opened her mouth to give a retort and obviously thought the better of it.

'OK so I've typed out pretty much what you said.' She had been in a mortifying 'Scream' state this morning. She remembered the noise from her bowel and shuddered. Signing off with 'the whale is swimming again,' she handed Abby her phone. Moments later, it pinged, and Abby looked at Lucy, confused, her eyebrows raised.

He's texted back saying, 'Free Willy!'

Lucy snorted.

'That was all, though,' Abby was bemused.

'That's enough,' Lucy sunk back in the chair, relaxing.

Abby shook her head, not understanding the in-joke but glad Lucy seemed cool with it. And the phone pinged again. 'Ooo now you're talking,' she grinned at Luce.

'What?' Lucy tried to grab the phone from Abby's hands but failed.

'If you fancy a drink before the IBS clinic on Thursday let me know ... he didn't end with a kiss, but he did give you a smiley face.'

'Is that good or bad?'

'All things considered, you either put on a great show

or he's into girls who fart! But then we knew that already, look where you met.' Lucy looked murderous, so she quickly added: 'He's cute though and a good dresser, I'll give him that.'

Lucy remained silent.

'Don't go on a date with him unless you really want to, Lucy.'

Lucy stared back at her solemnly.

'I know what you're like,' Abby continued. 'You'll go on a date and be ultra-frigid towards him to try and prove last night was a one-off.'

'And what if I happen to like him?' Lucy spouted, surprising herself as much as she'd surprised Abby.

'Well that's perfect then, isn't it?'

'Oh god, I can't worry about it now. I'm all het up. Let's just order Chinese and I'll text him back.'

'Flustered and food? Excellent – you're feeling better. Thank goodness for that' and even though Abby had had a roast, she could never turn down duck pancakes.

Waiting for their food, Lucy texted Will back:

'That would be great - give me a buzz the night before and we'll figure it out.'

She, too, ended on a smiley face.

'It seems ridiculously shy to be acting like this after parading around the flat naked together earlier today, Abs.'

'Yes, but you're just mirroring his text tone. Let's see what happens,' Abby narrowed her eyes at Lucy, trying to work it out: did she like him, or was it that she just hadn't been with anyone in a while? Abby was more than happy to help Lucy especially as she felt oddly guilty for spending all weekend away from her.

'Right, now that's all sorted, tell me about your

weekend, Abster.'

Abby recounted her weekend of walks and talks along London's waterways with Tim, and Lucy listened with tears in her eyes.

'Oh, Abs,' Lucy grabbed her hand, slightly sticky from the hoi sin sauce that had arrived halfway through their catch up, 'He's special, isn't he? I thought so the other night when I saw you at the bar.'

'It's just so ... calm. Calm, simple, yet special and exciting, all at the same time. But I feel so relaxed because I genuinely feel it's right this time – and I'm not bothered about it being 'perfect' because I just think that he's perfect for me.'

Lucy looked as taken aback as Abby was saying it. It was the first time she'd properly admitted to anyone just what an impact Tim was having on her.

'I haven't shared that with anyone else yet. I didn't want to jinx it. Oh gosh I hope I haven't now,' Abby looked worried for a second.

Lucy shook her head and smiled. 'You just don't know who's around the corner, do you? Are you in love with him?'

'What?' Abby shrieked, picking up a cushion and whacking her bestie with it.

'Well, that means yes.'

'It's way too early to commit to saying that.'

Lucy stared back at her. Abby had wondered if her heart was going in that direction. But they were big words, and they still had a lot to learn about each other.

'Wait for him to say it first.'

'Shut up! I can't even think seriously on that level yet,' and Abby changed the conversation quickly: 'Luce, I felt awful you weren't there this weekend. I know how we've bitched about our other friends ditching us when they find a guy they like, and I couldn't bear it if you ever felt like that about me. If you ever feel that way, you need to kick me. Hard.'

Lucy nodded, 'I did miss you this weekend, I'm not going to lie. We're always together. It's been me and you for years, but as much as we talk about finding 'the one,' I guess we never realised it would mean spending a little less time together.' She breathed. 'I love you so much, Abster, I just want you to be happy. It was awful seeing you so sad before. You're the truest friend I know. You've had a great weekend by all accounts, and when I texted you, you still came running without hesitation. That tells me you're not going to be an ass.' She paused, 'But don't worry I'd tell you if you were.'

'I love you, Luce. I'd hug you if I didn't remember how bad your room smelt.'

Lucy drew breath sharply. 'Don't remind me. Oh my god.'

'You've got to get to know Tim more now. I've done the groundwork, and it's time he realises if he wants me, he gets you as well,' grabbing her friend's foot and grinning.

'Phwoooar, what a deal that is,' Lucy said, gesturing down to her current state.

'Yeah, maybe not today. That might scare him right off.'

27

I WANT YOU

ABBY FELT AS though she was in a fairy-tale version of her life. Since convincing Tim to let her back into his life, they had spent almost every evening together. Wandering around London, eating, sipping red wine and talking, discovering all the little things about each other, they'd barely been apart. Managing to restrain themselves, she'd kissed his lips a million times already. It felt real, the talking, the kissing, and in truth she knew she was falling for him hard.

Tonight they were sitting on his balcony, sipping Malbec and chatting about the countries they'd visited, enjoying a quiet Thursday night in – a million miles from the clubs and bars she'd usually be frequenting at the end of the week.

'Is this really happening to me?' she wondered, pulling Tim closer to her and snuggling into his warmth. It was such a contrast to six months ago that she just couldn't believe the journey she'd been on to get here.

Dropping her off at her apartment at the end of every date, Tim kissed her, their hands searching, their bodies touching, their lips exploring, before letting her go inside. Waiting for sex was getting unbearable. As much as 'taking it slow' showed respect, the build-up was rising to intolerable levels. From the moment his lips touched hers tonight, Abby's entire body screamed for him.

Abby pulled back from his chest to look into his eyes, 'I'd like to go away somewhere with you.'

'We can figure that out,' Tim smiled back.

'Tim...,' Abby stood up, slowly reached out and took his hand. Tim remained silent, closing his eyes for a second. She traced her fingertips over the palm of his hand and moved closer towards him. He opened his eyes and she moved so she was staring directly into his eyes. Almost black with desire, her dark chocolate eyes bore into him, not blinking. Her gaze flooded him, and his eyes widened with the same intensity, but Abby was suddenly tongue-tied. It seemed like she had a million questions, a million answers that she wanted stemming from a million fears.

'I'm right here,' Tim said softly but with as much certainty as he always had, holding her hand tighter in his.

Abby smiled; it was so simple – he was right here with her. All of him, his kindness, his calm assuredness. All of that was there with her and she'd done nothing but be herself to gain it. It was time.

'Yes, you are right here,' Abby whispered back, 'but there's one problem: you're not close enough.'

Tim peered up at her before catching his breath, as she stood tall in front of him, pulling her top lightly over her head to expose her perfectly formed full breasts. And there she stood in front of him on his balcony, utterly beautiful, her nipples taut with a mix of desire and the cool night air.

She looked down and saw Tim simultaneously clench

his fists and his jaw. A slow alluring smile played on her lips, safe in the knowledge she had a captive audience and closed the gap between them. She pushed her hands into his hair, letting her fingers trace rhythmic motions over him before pulling his lips to hers and kissing them. Fervent now. That was it.

No more games. She wanted him. Right here, right now. Her nipples were tense, aching for his touch, her breasts moved up and down with her increased breathing. Tim had been sitting with his arms locked at his sides, but he could hold back no longer, he drew in a ragged breath and rose, ripping his sweater over his head exposing his chest to her, lean and defined. He clasped her waist, drawing her close to him, moaning as her nipples grazed his chest, mirrored by her moan as their skin finally met each other's.

The night air had cooled her down, magnifying every movement his warm hands made as they travelled from her neck, down over her breasts, fanning out over her stomach and swooping low over her back and back up into her hair. He ran his fingers over her nipples and tweaked them hard, she threw her head back gasping his name, 'Tim,' she murmured for him. He let his lips taste the soft skin of her breasts, holding her body close to his, grinding into her. She could feel the extent of how much he wanted her, she ran her hands over his shaft through his jeans. God she was aching for him. Without caring who could see, he spun her away from him, twirling her round on the balcony, admiring her form as she stood there radiant in the moonlight.

'My god, Abby, you're so beautiful,' and he pulled her back into him, travelling his lips down her chest and up again until their tongues met in urgent need, his hands moving over every inch of her skin. Her heart beat faster, making her perfect breasts rise to meet his chest as she gyrated into his hardness.

Finally, she could stand it no longer. She forced the buckle of his belt undone, sliding it out, Tim scooped her up and she wrapped her legs around him. Her tits were in his face and she could feel his hastened breath on them as she bit into his neck. Tim moaned and moved her through his apartment, kicking the door to his bedroom wide open and placing her down. They pulled each other's jeans off and gazed at each other, perfectly naked. Abby's eyes took him all in: his toned chest, the light dusting of dark chest hair, his smooth stomach and his perfect cock, hard, erect, ready to take her whenever she gave the signal. Abby moved closer running her fingers over his hardness, she heard him gasp as her hands travelled the full length of his shaft and found his balls, knowing she was wet enough to take him whole.

Tim groaned with desire and picked her up again, this time placing her on the bed. Unable to even consider any other kind of foreplay, Abby widened her legs and wrapped them around his body. On top of her at last, the sound of her rapid breathing mirrored his. Clasping her hands on his butt, she pulled him towards her, he looked down at her, deep into her eyes as his cock found her. He moved slowly at first until he was fully inside her and she gasped.

'Tim,' Abby moaned, letting herself breathe deeply, drinking in the sensation of him finally being inside her. She clenched every muscle and he groaned, she arched her back, willing him to move deeper, wrapping her arms around him tightly to make it so. Rhythmically her hips moved over his shaft, pausing to watch it slide into her then lying back and pulling him so his whole body crushed into her. They moved together, their hips as one, he had conquered her mind and now he was claiming her body.

'I am yours, Tim,' she whispered. 'I am yours.'

*****

'OH MY GOD, you guys. You guys!' Lucy was beaming at her. Abby giggled. You'd think it was the first time she'd ever had sex the way she was clapping, but Lucy could obviously sense as well that Tim was completely different to anyone else.

'Gosh, Abby, you're glowing.'

'I feel like my entire body is sparkling, Luce, it's madness!' It was Sunday night and she'd rounded up Lucy and Woody to meet her at the bar for a few hours before she headed over to Tim's.

'So,' Woody said returning from the bar with a bottle of Barolo, 'tell us how it happened, and I'll try to imagine it's with someone other than my cousin.'

'Ah Barolo,' sighed Abby as Woody poured, 'delicious.' The entire world was like poetry to her at the moment, she couldn't shake the feeling, and she didn't want to either. She leaned back in her seat.

'Abby, if you don't start to talk soon, I'm going to throttle the happiness out of you,' Lucy joked through gritted teeth.

Abby started to fill them in on how the dates had been going, 'It's been lovely getting to know each other, and I really meant to sleep with him on date four, but he took me to Rosemary's Italian after you recommended it Luce, and I just couldn't resist the food there, I ate waaaay too much.'

'It *is* a good date place,' Woody nodded enthusiastically, 'What did you have?'

'Sod the food,' Lucy said, 'when did you *finally* have sex?'

'Well not after Rosemary's because I was just so full. But actually, last night. Date twelve.'

Abby was proud that she'd held off that long. 'I created an updated version of Romeo and Juliet's balcony scene,' she grinned wickedly and described how last night had begun.

'You were topless on the balcony?' Lucy shrieked.

'Absolutely,' Abby grinned.

'But anyone could have seen!'

'It was just my breasts, the cold made my nipples perfectly taut – they were like a homing beacon. I knew he wouldn't be able to resist.'

Woody took a big gulp of wine.

'He twirled me around at one point just to check them out from every angle...'

Lucy's jaw dropped and she grinned. Abby was enjoying winding her friends up, after all of the embarrassing antics of the past few months, having a positive story to tell had been a long time coming.

'Your breasts are perfectly formed,' Lucy pointed out. Woody coughed.

'Right then, this is like hearing about my sister. Can we skip your breasts? I think we get the idea.'

'So, did you do it out there?' Lucy quizzed her.

'No, that was our foreplay. So, we're both topless, kissing, I started to unbutton his jeans, at which point he scooped me up.'

Lucy sighed, 'That's the dream, right? Most of the guys in London just don't seem to have the scoopability factor in them, despite going to the gym. What happened next?'

'I wrapped my legs around him, he carried me to his bedroom and there ... two became one.'

Woody turned a pale shade of green.

'I won't put you through the gory details of your cousin, Woody.'

'I don't want to hear about the sex. I'm going to leave you ladies and get another drink.'

Abby paused for Woody to shake his head and walk back to the bar.

'Gosh, Luce, he's so gorgeous. I just gazed at him when he was naked, and he was gazing right back. He stood there in his moonlit bedroom, naked and hard. I can't get that image out of my brain.'

'And now neither can I,' joked Lucy. 'Tell me about the cockage. Good length?'

'Delicious length – found my g-spot instantly.'

'Girth?'

'Perfect not to suffocate on a blow job, but big enough to have kids with, lose elasticity and still enjoy sex afterwards, I reckon.'

'Wowsers!' Lucy was impressed. She was also quiet.

'You know when you take it slowly at first because you want to discover each other...,' Abby tailed off.

'Are you in love with him?'

'Oh, please, we've only just done it,' Abby answered a little too quickly and glibly. Could you be in love this quickly? It had only technically been twelve dates, but they had spent all of Sunday in bed.

'Let's not leap ahead of ourselves here, and certainly

don't say anything to Woody. Luce, it was just beautifully honest and raw, he just seemed to know how I wanted to be touched. Now listen, before Woody gets back, have you met up with Will yet?'

'No, we're catching up on Thursday, and thank you for not mentioning it to Woody.' Lucy smiled, squeezing her hand grateful for the saved embarrassment.

'Of course, you need to let me know how it …'

Abby cut herself off as Woody walked back over. 'Is it safe now? I think the wine has kicked in, so I can participate in the conversation now.' To prove it he asked: 'So was Tim treated to the obligatory "check the manhood out blowie" before two became one?'

'Actually, no I haven't done that yet,' Abby replied. 'There was no need.'

Woody and Lucy raised their eyebrows simultaneously.

'No need and I didn't want to waste any time, I'd already made us wait for what felt like forever,' Abby justified. 'Plus, I kind of just knew that everything was going to be alright.'

'He's made you feel that way from the start, hasn't he?' Lucy smiled in relief.

'Well, he is related to me, so of course he's a legend,' Woody said smugly.

'Oh, so now you're on board with me dating your cousin?' Abby and Lucy laughed.

Abby left the bar an hour later and went straight to Tim's, texting him from the cab. He was outside, waiting to pay for it, and immediately scooped her up in his arms, taking her indoors and stripping her bare.

'Good night?' He asked breathlessly.

'Yes, now fuck me,' she ordered.

Tim needed no more encouragement and the blood rushed to her head as he hung her over the side of his queen-sized bed. Tim stretched her legs across his shoulders, seizing her thighs and looking straight into her eyes as he fucked into her. He held her tightly and she screamed as she came, unable to control herself as she looked up at him. They both gave themselves to the moment, and as he came, he bent down and yelled her name into her breasts, holding on to her as it passed over him.

Still inside her, he moved her so her head was on the bed once more, then he collapsed on her. Abby lay buzzing, and they panted together. They'd only been apart for four hours, how the devil was she going to cope with ten hours at work tomorrow?

She couldn't bear to be parted from him. She pulled his face towards her and kissed him as their breathing slowed down.

'Stay inside me,' she whispered. 'I need you as close to me as possible.'

'I'm with you for as long as you want me, Abby. I'm yours.'

Abby welled up as he mirrored the words she'd spoken before. Maybe, just maybe, it was real this time ...

28

ALTER EGOS

DESPITE HAVING WINE with Abby, Lucy had been to the gym on Monday, Tuesday and Wednesday religiously to try and work off the effects of Saturday. Will had texted her the name and address of a bar around the corner from the weekly Thursday meet.

Now minutes away, she strutted down the street, trying to draw confidence from the sound of her heels clicking on the pavement. To make up for how awful she'd looked on Sunday, she'd power dressed today to meet him before the clinic. Abby had been right on the money with her attempts to convince him that she didn't normally act like that.

She paused and took a breath. She was almost trembling. She'd been so embarrassed all week and had probably built up seeing him way more in her head than she needed to. That she couldn't even remember getting home shamed her more than anything else. But not recalling anything had left her intrigued about Will. In her drunk state, she had found him irresistible, who knows what he'd be like sober.

He rose to kiss her on the cheek and gave her a massive smile. She was shocked: he was wearing a pin-striped suit and nice tie. Come to think of it he'd always been quite smart the few times she'd seen him. Just a complete contrast from the massive man jungle image she'd had in her mind all week. She caught herself staring at his crotch and blushed, bringing her face up to meet his eyes.

'Well, you're looking more like your normal happy self,' he grinned.

'Oh my gosh, don't remind me,' she tried to joke. She didn't think she would ever come to terms with her behaviour that night. Even thinking about it four days later, it felt like it had happened to someone else.

'I've just got here, too, I thought I'd wait to see what you fancied drinking.'

'That was thoughtful, thank you,' she nodded.

'So, are you in a wine mood or fancy chilling with a cup of tea?'

The part of her brain that wanted to prove him wrong screamed sparkling water, whilst her mouth betrayed her by saying: 'Shall we risk a wine?'

'No risk there, I brought protection, just in case.'

'Protection?' He brought condoms for a drink in a bar? She felt herself beginning to blush.

'My bike helmet, in case we start dancing on tables again,' he grinned fiendishly.

'Oh, OK,' she sat down, her legs had started to shake. Meeting up was such a bad idea. She couldn't place where her head was at at all.

'So, what do you do?' She cut straight into his conversation, breaking his flow, wishing immediately she hadn't. For some reason she couldn't focus on what he was saying, instead she kept wondering, did we do it? Was he good? Was I good? What tables were we dancing on? Where were we?

She was starting to get clammy just thinking about

it. Shit, and now she wasn't listening again. She was never like this, 'Oh my god, come on, Lucy, pull yourself together and listen to him.'

Whatever he'd said was obviously funny to him as the corners of his eyes crinkled and lit up. God, he had gorgeous eyes. And a massive schlong. Lucy laughed to herself.

'Ha, ha, ha,' the sound came out strained, and she gestured to the wine as if she had a dry throat.

'Oh, I'll get you some water.'

Lucy downed the rest of the glass before he could order.

'No, turns out you don't need it,' he widened his eyes and topped her glass up a tad.

What the heck had she just done? 'That's better' she said, a bit of Dutch courage before she could launch into what she needed to say: 'Look, so, the reason I wanted to see you ...'

He smiled.

She forced herself to concentrate. '... was to tell you that the woman you met on Saturday night wasn't really me. I don't really act like that at all.'

'You don't always look gorgeous and have incredible sex?'

'Um...,' damn what was he doing to her?

'Well, that's a shame. I liked your alter ego,' he grinned, and she found herself grinning back.

'No, I meant ...'

'I know what you meant. And it's cool.'

'Let's change the subject,' Lucy shook her head, trying to keep up with the pace on a disastrous mix of wine, no lunch, nerves and not listening to him earlier. If she wasn't careful, this meet up would end in disaster, too.

'So, you're a ...'

'Lawyer.'

'A lawyer? Fantastic.'

'Tell me, Lucy, what do you do with the rest of your time?'

'Oh, I'm a bespoke property consultant.'

'But that's work,' Will gestured with his hands and she caught a whiff of his aftershave. It was delectable. She leaned back, out of reach, keeping focussed.

'What else keeps you entertained?'

'Well, recently I've been helping my best friend get over her ex. I constructed a list of events she had to go through to take her mind off it, and I think it's actually worked. She's met someone.'

'How fantastic, you could sell your secret formula!''

'Well, some of the things, actually all of them haven't really turned out as I planned them to but ...,' Lucy grimaced.

'But that's life, and you can't control people's reactions or emotions, you just have to roll with it and see how you feel when you're with them,' Will debated.

'See if it's comfortable, yes. That's exactly what I was trying to explain to her,' Gosh, this wasn't that bad.

Will broke the conversation by looking at his watch, 'Look, I don't want to rush this, but we need to make a move if we want to get to the clinic in time. Unless you'd like to stay for another bottle of course,' he smiled.

'Oh god, no,' Lucy downed the rest of her glass.

'Right, well, let's go then,' he clipped, turning away from her. Shit, it had completely come out the wrong way, again!

'I meant because otherwise I'd be drunk again, not because I don't enjoy your company.'

He looked back at her, paused and nodded silently.

They walked around the corner and up the steps to the meeting room.

'Do you think they know?' Lucy paused.

'Only one way to find out,' Will said, pushing the door open.

Cheers sounded the moment they walked into the room. Lucy felt her face turn bright red.

'She's only had two glasses of wine tonight, so she's safe I promise,' Will joked.

'We'll move the tables just in case,' Hilary smiled. 'Well, you sure came out of your shell.'

'And ended up feeling like hell,' Lucy smiled tentatively.

'Well last Saturday night definitely settled the topic for today's discussion: what does alcohol do to our digestive system? Let's look closely at the effects.'

'Will,' Hilary's voice boomed, 'how were you the next day?'

Lucy could feel Will's gaze on her: please don't say 'Free Willy,' please don't mention my state, she begged inwardly.

He grinned, 'Well I felt terrible and wasn't quite right for a good few days. Wednesday I returned to normal, I think. I always take milk thistle, but I'd be interested to hear if there are any other foods that stave off hangovers or their effects? Besides kebabs, of course.'

Gosh, he's really lovely, Lucy thought, watching how he interacted with the group. How had she not noticed that before? To be fair, she had been more concerned with sorting out her gut.

The evening panned out the way it normally did with a bit of group chat afterwards before she hopped on the Tube home. She called Abby the instant she walked through the door.

'So how did it go?'

'I think, somehow, I kind of like him, but I've also somehow kind of given off the vibe that I don't want to date him.'

'Lucy, I despair. How the heck have you done that?'

'I don't even know. I was just so nervous and hell bent on him not judging me for Saturday night, which actually I think he quite enjoyed.'

'Of course, he did! You looked smoking hot.'

'Oh dear god, Abby, I meant to order water and be the perfect lady, but I ordered wine and downed a whole glass of it.'

Abby's laughter came down the phone, 'I love this guy already; he's bringing out a totally different side to you.'

'I must look like I should be going to AA meetings not IBS ones.'

'Maybe you'd see him in both, you never know.'

'I doubt it, he's a lawyer, well spoken, nice dresser ... anyway, I've mucked that up.'

'You haven't necessarily mucked it up, you get to see him every week and you can charm him back again, just give it time.'

'I guess. So how's Tim?'

'He's good, he's here now, we've just cooked with Woody, pop over if you like.'

Lucy looked at her flat, it was home, but tonight she didn't fancy being alone in it, worrying about Will.

'Can I stay on the sofa-bed? That way I can go straight to work tomorrow?'

'Of course.'

Lucy needed a hug and a distraction, 'In that case see you in a bit.'

29

HEELS STAY ON

LUCY LOOKED AT her watch. She arrived 20 minutes early for work, which had given her time to straighten out the client's home she was showing – rearrange the flowers and throw open the curtains and blinds. It was in Fitzrovia and an absolute literary lovers' gem, with lots of reading nooks to hide away in. The viewing went well, and she closed the house after flicking through some of the books on the shelves. She had an hour to kill before she had to be back in the office. As she pulled the front door shut, she toyed with grabbing a drink for elevenses.

'Lucy!' She spun around, hearing Will call her name from the other side of the street.

'Will!' She smiled instantly, 'What are you doing in this neck of the woods?'

'Just on my way back to the office after seeing a client,' he bent down and as his lips gently grazed her cheek, she caught a waft of his aftershave again.

'I think I may have just sold this place. Do you want to come in and check it out?' she whispered impulsively.

He raised his eyebrow.

'I've just shown the house, but now it's empty ... perhaps you'd like to view it for yourself?'

'Perhaps I might, I have always loved this area.'

What the heck was she doing?

He glanced around him.

She felt her chest rise in anticipation of his answer

'Yes actually, Lucy, I do want to see the house if you have time.'

I'll make time, Lucy thought.

'Excellent, come this way.'

She sashayed back down the tiny pathway to the front door, her pencil skirt accentuating her hips and heels. What the hell was she doing?

She pushed the door open and entered the hallway, chucked her bag to one side and outstretched her arms to him.

He entered the hallway, slammed the door shut put his arms around her waist and kissed her.

'Bedroom?' he whispered coarsely, unbuttoning her shirt.

'Up the stairs and on the right,' she breathed, kissing his neck.

They made it up the stairs, pausing when he crushed her against the banister, grinding into her.

'Oh my god,' she murmured breathlessly. He really was huge.

He ripped off her shirt whilst she released her skirt and pulled at his belt.

'Keep the heels on,' he said hoarsely, his hands exploring her, everywhere. 'Stockings? You saucy minx! They're staying on, too.'

She drew him into the bedroom and pushed him down on the owner's silk sheets.

She wanted to taste his cock and fuck him senseless. Every nerve in her body was on fire. Will moaned the second her lips hit his shaft, but she couldn't bear it.

Before knew it, she was sitting astride him, riding his cock, her nails running over his chest.

'Lucy, fucking hell,' he called out, his hands clasping her stocking clad thighs.

'Bite my nipples,' she ordered desperate for his lips to be all over her. 'Holy fuck,' she cried out as he did. His hands, grabbed her ass as she rode him, drawing himself deeper inside of her. Her pussy clenched tighter and tighter over his manhood as she devoured him, riding him fast and hard. She felt like a queen, a god.

'Oh my god, I could sit on your cock forever,' she moaned.

'Don't stop. Ever.' He moaned thrusting deep inside of her.

She came twice before he finally relented and came, groaning with ecstasy as he did so, his hands moving to hold on to the headboard Lucy had been clutching for extra support.

Lying in total silence, listening to the sounds of their breathing slowing down, she giggled.

He giggled. She giggled some more.

'Oh my god, Will, is that what it was like the other week?'

'Yes. Totally,' he said between breaths. 'You moved gracefully like a swan but screwed me like a porn star that had to pay rent.'

'Argh,' Lucy threw her head back laughing, 'I'm going to take that as a compliment.'

She felt him quiver still inside of her and she clenched her pussy tightly across his cock enjoying her power over him as his pupils dilated and his breathing became more ragged again.

'Oh my, your pussy is insane.'

She clenched it again and he jolted.

'Seriously, woman. Did you mean what you said, during...?'

'Which bit?' Lucy leant down low and whispered the words to him clenching her pussy at the same time. Will grabbed her arse and forced her to remain in the same spot – it was obviously working for him. 'I was ... wondering ... if ... you would sit on my cock forever.' Trailing her tits over his chest and clenching again, she felt him shudder and get hard.

'Fuck, yeah. See?'

'Oh my god,' Will exclaimed as he drove back into her fully. 'How is this even happening? You're never leaving me.'

Lucy threw her head back and enjoyed the sensation of his manhood against her g-spot.

'Shhhh, no more talking,' she gasped.

Will obeyed. He grabbed her waist and rolled them both to the middle of the bed, then holding her legs high over his shoulders, he pounded his shaft deep inside of her again. Lucy clutched the sheets and gasped, letting herself go in the moment as he consumed her entirely once more.

30

GET A GRIP

'WHAT? I MEAN seriously WHAT?' Abby was beside herself. Lucy had called her for an emergency meeting in the café, and she was bowled over by her story.

'Lucy, what if your client had come back in?'

'I KNOW!'

Abby grinned at her.

'And do you know the honest truth? I wouldn't have stopped! Fuck, it was so good. I swear.'

'Oh my god, I'm speechless,' Abby sat beaming at this new version of her friend.

'It's been so long, Abby. I mean how long exactly? A year and a half?'

'Good lord. No wonder you're unleashing on him.'

'I think I was already obsessing with seeing him again to see what it had been like. I know we'd obviously had sex because he'd said so, but to me it didn't feel as though we had, because I couldn't remember it.'

'Maybe it was so good you actually blacked out during?' Abby giggled. 'Gosh all of this sex talk is making me hot for Tim.'

'Let's text them,' Lucy said.

'One hour, I need you inside of me,' Abby wrote and showed Lucy, who giggled. 'I'll do the same. We're such blokes! This is what guys do when they want a booty call.'

Both of their phones pinged back within thirty seconds. 'Where?'

They cracked up.

'Gosh...,' Lucy said before trailing off.

'What?' Abby looked up.

'It's like my breasts are alive somehow.'

'You do have a cracking pair.'

'That's what he said. He actually slapped them midway through, and they bounced together. It made my skin tingle and from that moment on it's like they've got a mind of their own. Before they were these boulders I'd shove into my bra, now it's like they're a radar for anything that might turn me on. My nipples stand to attention and I have to obey.'

'Oh my god. Luce, you crack me up.'

'I mean it, Abs. Maybe this is how it feels to be a guy who thinks with his dick. I thought it was just a phrase but actually my breasts could get me into a whole lot of trouble right now. God everything is turning me on, and guys are asking me out. But the weirdest thing is I can only imagine his touch on my skin. Seriously, anyone else and it just wouldn't work.'

Abby looked shocked as her best friend then collapsed in tears.

'Lucy, what's up? This is amazing, don't cry.' She jumped up to give her a hug, shielding Lucy from the stares from onlookers in the cafe.

Lucy sobbed. 'I don't know where all of these tears are coming from, I can't seem to make them stop. It's just... I just feel...'

'Breathe, Luce, and tell me what's up,' Abby waited patiently.

'It's just I feel like he's making me come alive. All my life, my mum has expected a certain standard from me, and I've always tried to meet her expectations and be what she wants me to be, what my work colleagues need me to be, what the clients expect me to be. I'm myself around you, but obviously we don't sleep together. Around Will, I feel like I'm the 'me' I am around you, only times ten million. I feel as though I am a planet that's combusting and only he can make sure all my pieces remain in the same sphere. Does that make any sense?'

'Yes and ...,' Abby agreed, but Lucy was on a roll.

'... well it's only been a week and already I'm terrified of losing him. You read all these magazines about how empowered you should feel, and I thought I had that feeling with my good job and Louboutins, and I strut around doing my thing. But the real power comes from within, doesn't it. Well how weak am I that I needed a man to unleash it?'

Abby watched as her best friend dissolved in tears again, 'Lucy no, you've got it wrong.'

'How have I? I'm a complete mess, and I need him to make me the person I want to be. I need him Abby, and it's been a week.'

'You don't *need* him to be you. He's just unleashed a different side of you. There's a massive difference. Your power and personality have always been there, maybe you've unleashed two thirds of it on us and the last third is a private part just for guys?'

Lucy contemplated it.

'Guys that can handle it, of course,' Abby nudged her.

'I guess. Maybe. So, you don't think I'm pathetic?'

'Far from it. I've never thought that. Ever. Not for one single second. You're incredible, and I'm glad that you've discovered someone who makes you feel that way, inside and out,' Abby added wickedly.

Abby watched as Lucy pondered her words.

'Well how vulnerable does that make me now? I'm doing exactly what every confidence coach in the world tells you not to do.'

Abby drew a blank. She'd never paid too much attention to those people – the most she'd done was like their quotes on Pinterest, 'I'm intrigued, what's that Luce?'

'I've gone and put my self-confidence in someone else's control instead of having it for me,' she sobbed harder. 'How pathetic am I? It only took me a week to do that.'

'Oh my god, Lucy, you need to get a grip.'

'What?' She could tell Lucy had been expecting sympathy and was shocked.

'Lucy, you're one of the most forthright people I know. This guy may have unlocked a deeper side to your character, but he doesn't own that. You do. It's your character. If you never saw him again that part of you still exists. He may have unlocked it, but you still hold the key. You're incredible, now you need to dry your eyes, and we need to toast this man for creating this new chapter in your life.'

Lucy nodded and dried her eyes.

'It's like what you said to me about Charlie: people come into your life to teach you a lesson sometimes. Will has already shown you that you can be more confident, break away from society's expectations and hopefully live more freely, within the realms of the law, of course.'

'Naturally.'

'Just enjoy it, Luce. You're worth ten million Wills. Just fix your makeup first ...'

Lucy giggled, 'Thanks, Abster,' she whispered.

'Word on the street is that I might just owe you a few

conversations about guys. Hey, I could make you a list.'

'No chance. Now, I'm going to fix my face and then we're going to meet our men.'

GHOSTS

NEVER HAD ABBY found sex to be so deeply erotic before. Even the mere thought of Tim's name had her pining for him. She couldn't wait for his reaction to her surprise tonight. This weekend was their four-week anniversary, so she'd booked a hotel and was wearing Agent Provocateur to work. She'd gone for the whole sexy-secretary-meets-sex-maniac look and had blown £350 on the full stockings and matching set. But what the hell, life was too short not to fulfil a whole night of fantasy.

The hotel she'd booked was the Shangri-La in the Shard. One of her fantasies was to be taken from behind at nightfall whilst pressing her hands against the floor-to-ceiling windows. Right now, Abby didn't care who was watching – if anything, that would make her perform even better. She felt like a seductive temptress as she moved around the office. Her pupils were wide, sexed up, her hips swayed and she swore her voice was huskier. She was using the whole experience of going to work to get into her role play for later.

All seemed to be going well as she checked the hotel booking again, it looked gorgeous.

'Abby,' her boss, Derek, cut through her reverie. She looked up. 'Can you join me in my office, please?'

Heck, she needed to get out of sexy secretary role play – apart from the hip swaying, which was the only way she could physically walk in these heels – the last thing she needed was Derek thinking she fancied him.

'Abby. Please sit down.'

'I'd really rather not, Derek, I've got plenty to be getting on with today,' she breathed, berating herself: snap out of the sexy voice, Abby, what are you doing?

'OK, have it your way. I just wanted to touch base with you, make sure you're alright. Some of the comments at the coffee machine made me wonder...'

Abby's eyebrow shot up alluringly. Damn, she just couldn't help it.

'Well, the guys were saying that you've 'got it going on' and the girls didn't look impressed. You're an attractive woman, Abby,' Derek coughed. 'And I, er, don't want the other ladies to be rowdy. You know, squabbling women in the office isn't good for politics.'

'I don't know what you mean, sir,' Abby said slowly, grinning inside, unable to resist this part of the tease. She placed her fingertips on his desk and moved a little closer, arching her back the teeniest amount pressing her bra against her shirt.

'Really, sir, what could they possibly mean?'

'Well I'm not quite sure,' Derek said, moving uncomfortably in his seat, 'I can't put my fingers on it. You just seem ... slower than usual.'

'Slower?'

'Yes, well you're normally so direct and matter of fact, and yet you seem all ... and your outfit is ...,' Derek tailed off.

'I'll try my best to not let my sexuality distract people again, sir,' Abby winked and twirled span on her heels.

Oh my god, she'd just winked at her boss, this whole god damn role play had completely gone to her head. Time for an exit. She strode out but glanced back to see Derek mopping his forehead. She grinned inwardly. Tim was going to go insane if she could keep this up.

Must aim to walk faster as well, I can't believe people have noticed my speed. Barking out a few orders to prove she was still in charge and on the case, Abby strode as fast as she could in the tight pencil skirt.

God this lingerie was good. She felt she could lead the world – politicians should wear it, she giggled to herself.

Now to focus on Tim. She'd given him strict instructions where to go and what to wear. In fact, he was calling now.

'Hey, beautiful. I need to add a change of plans to the evening.'

'Oh no,' Abby felt instantly crushed, 'is everything alright?' The excitement of the last two days of planning slipping away from her. There was silence at the end of the phone.

'Tim? Is something wrong?' She could hear him breathing. This was unusual behaviour for him, she felt her heart quicken in pace.

'Yes, slightly. Can I meet you at yours? I need to speak to you. Will you be back by 6:30?' He sounded cold and tense.

'Yes, I'll be there. Is everything alright?'

'Yes and no. I don't want to discuss it now. It's not a phone conversation.'

'OK,' Abby tried hard to keep her voice steady. 'Fine, Tim, if that's what you want, I'll see you at mine in a few hours, bye,' she whispered and hung up the phone. He was going to leave her. The room was spinning. She felt the soft, rosy bubble around her heart bursting and sliding away.

No, she told herself, this wouldn't be like last time. Tim wasn't Charlie. She would force herself to concentrate. What was she doing again? Oh yes, she was proofreading a new staff member's contract.

Reading and rereading every single line twice to not miss a single mistake that could wind up costing the company a fortune, Abby focused. Derek would never forgive her for making a mistake due to guy problems.

Guy problems. She chewed on her pen. Is that what she was about to have with Tim? Her whole body shook and she felt sick she realised just how much Tim had changed everything. And he'd only been in her life for a month. One month. Thirty days. That was all it had taken. She hadn't questioned it because she'd never known anything to take her over so completely before. It felt like every waking moment she just filled with other tasks before she could be in his company again.

She managed to postpone the hotel booking for thirty days then distracted herself by staying at work until 6pm, figuring if she dawdled on the way home, she could get there for 6:25 and not have too long going insane waiting in her apartment.

As it was, Tim was bang on time, as usual. She said nothing at the intercom and buzzed him straight in. As she opened the front door to him, nausea flooded her stomach. She just wanted to put her arms around him and shriek desperately 'don't leave me,' and she couldn't help, it she started to cry.

'Abby, what's wrong?' His arms were around her, one hand pulled her into his body and the other hand nestled in her hair.

'Please don't break up with me.'

'God, no. You crazy girl,' he hesitated. 'Why on earth would you think that?'

'You were so serious and cold on the phone,' Abby said, 'and I thought you were meeting me here so if I was upset, you could just leave.'

'Good god, no! My boss came into my office when I was on the phone, hence the cold tone. Abby, I do need to talk to you, but my goodness, nothing like that. Haven't you seen how crazy I am for you?' He paused and looked at her. 'I think there are more people in the room than just us today, aren't there? Your ex is definitely here with a scar.'

Abby nodded. The effect of Charlie's abrupt decision to turf her out into the cold was just as scarring in the long-term as it had been that morning.

'Stop worrying, I *definitely* don't want to end anything with you at all. You are utterly scrumptious, in every way, and I hate to see you cry.'

Abby couldn't help it, she didn't even know where the tears were coming from, but they kept rolling down her face.

He kissed her nose and tried to wipe her face with his hands and got confused at the creation of more mess as the tears mixed in with her makeup.

'Oh dear,' he paused.

She giggled, 'Highly attractive now, I guess. But, phew,' she breathed out, utterly relieved by the news. 'Well that's good to know, Mr Mysterious.' She kissed him quickly on the lips before running off to the bathroom to fix her face. 'OK, you put the kettle on,' she shouted, 'and I'll be two minutes.'

In the bathroom, she had a word with herself: thank

god he wasn't breaking up with her. The relief was immense. 'Stay calm. He likes you. Don't panic he's not a Charlie. I'm sure of it,' she whispered to the mirror. But today had shaken her and made her wonder what was in store for them, after all it had only been a month. Perhaps she did need to calm herself and slow it down a bit … if only to protect herself. As wonderful as it was, she couldn't bear placing her happiness all with him to potentially have it taken away again and left hurt. Steeling herself, she re-emerged, ready to hear what Tim had to say.

'Tea's up,' Tim called from her room.

Pushing her pillows together so they could both sit up in her bed and chat, Tim smiled as she removed her heels, 'Comfy now?'

She nodded.

'Right, let me just say this Abby: I *really* like you. You've rocked my world. It's just the last time I felt like this I made a few mistakes and mucked up a perfectly good, or at least I thought it was good, relationship. Last night when I didn't see you, I was thinking about us and how we've become reliant on each other in a month. It's only been thirty days, Abby, and already I can't really remember what my day-to-day life was like without rushing to see you,' he grinned.

'I feel the same. Nuts! I was thinking that myself today. But it's a good thing isn't it? Having that feeling, it's pretty rare.'

'It is rare. But it's so special I think we should treat it with respect. With Catherine …'

'Catherine the not-so-great.'

'Yes,' Tim chuckled, 'well with her, we started off really strong and were with each other all the time

– granted it didn't feel as deep as when I'm with you – but that makes me want to protect this, us, even more,' He paused.

Abby reached for his hand to comfort him, 'I'm utterly crazy about you, Tim, I'm not going to hurt you.'

He looked deep in her eyes, 'It took me so long to let myself believe I would ever feel this way again about anyone, and damn it, I've only gone and met you and – if it's possible – I like you way more than I ever did her. It just feels right, you know?' Abby nodded. She did know.

Abby beamed. Good lord, she just wanted to kiss his neck, run her hands over his ...

Noticing her chest was moving faster and obviously sensing her plans, Tim grabbed her hands before she could start.

'I don't want to muck it up with you, Abby. I don't want to scare you off. I don't want to make the same mistakes again.'

'So, what do you propose?' Eek, maybe she shouldn't have said 'propose.'

'OK, so whilst it's the best sex of my life, and I could spend all day every day doing it, I want to make sure that we're spending enough time doing other stuff.'

'Phew. That's fine, my god, Tim, you had me worried that something was seriously wrong. We can calm it down a tad ... it might be frustrating at times, but ...' she started to kiss his neck.

He pulled back, 'No, Abby, you're not hearing me. I want us to abstain.'

'Completely? After the last four weeks of doing everything we've done?'

'Yes.'

'Don't get me wrong, Tim, I'm completely up for doing

good dates and getting to know you more, but sex is a big part of any good relationship. It's the difference between just being friends and, sometimes, it's the only way to show someone how much you're feeling.'

'Abby, this is crucial. I want us to last beyond the initial honeymoon stage.'

Abby was silent. Charlie had given her grand gestures, yet they'd been doomed at the honeymoon stage because they'd not built a foundation on anything that was real in everyday life.

'Tim, you're a genius! You're right! That's what went wrong with me and dick-brain Charlie. Well, either that or he just wasn't the right guy for me.'

'Obviously both,' Tim nodded.

'You're right. We're going to make it past the honeymoon stage just because we've realised this, you've realised this ... you're amazing...,' she beamed at him.

'Brilliant!' Tim looked relieved at their meeting of minds; he held his hands out to gesture her to come to him.'

'Oh no! No sex now, bucko. Not after all that,' Abby grabbed Tim's hand, pulled him off the bed in her energetic state and playfully grabbed his bum whilst pushing him out of her room.

'Right,' she said, 'I'm going to quickly change. The Agent Provocateur is coming off,' His jaw dropped.

'Well, I didn't know you were wearing that.'

Unable to hide his expression, he looked utterly crestfallen, as indeed he should. He still raised an eyebrow in hope. Abby grinned

'No way are you watching me change. We're not getting distracted. We have a bigger goal, remember?'

Tim held his arms up, defeated, 'I'll be in the kitchen

awaiting your command ma'am.'

'Cool, I won't be long,' Abby shut the door and realised her hands were shaking. She took a deep breath, she felt wired. Today she'd realised, just by the thought of losing him, how important Tim was becoming to her and apparently she was becoming to him. Now she was actively giving herself the best chance possible to ensure her past mistakes in love weren't going to creep up and scald her again. Shimmying out of her skirt, she changed her sex-charged lingerie to a still pretty-hot matching set and threw on skinny jeans, a floppy t-shirt that exposed the top of her breasts. She looked perfect for sitting down opposite him on a dinner date and driving him crazy whilst listening in earnest to whatever he had to say. Let the tease begin.

She strutted into the kitchen, opening her mouth, the noise that came out faltered to a 'oh.' There was nothing but silence. Tim wasn't there. Oh well, she thought, striding around the flat, he must be chilling out in the lounge.

'Tim!' Nope, he wasn't there and looking out to the driveway she could see his car was gone.

'Oh my god, he's done a runner,' she whispered. 'He's said all that stuff and my gushing on has freaked him out. Shit,' She grabbed her phone from her bag and tried calling him. No answer.

Abby sunk into the sofa, unsure of what to do. The clock ticking in the kitchen and her breath drawing in and out were the only sounds. She sank into the sofa, eyes wide open and lips parted in shock.

The intercom buzzed. She didn't even move. There was only one person she wanted to see right now and even Luce, with those 'I told you to take it slow' eyes she unfortunately did so well, wasn't going to move her.

Cutting through the silence, the buzzer sounded its hideously annoying tone again. It really did sound like a thousand blue bottle flies were trying to get in.

'Abby!' She heard someone call. 'Abby, it's Tim – are you in there?'

She grabbed the intercom. 'Go away, Tim. Stop playing with my emotions. One minute, you're fine, the next you're freaking out and leaving without saying goodbye. What is that called? Ghosting?'

Fuming she went to the window and flung it open. She couldn't see him. Damn, he must still be in the porch. Running down the stairs, she flung the door open with all of her might.

'Well, hello, Miss Abby. It wouldn't be a proper date unless I picked you up with flowers, would it? The woman in the shop took ages to get them done, I thought you might think that I'd left you. I tried calling but you didn't pick up. Are you alright?'

Abby held her breath as he placed a perfect bouquet of white roses in her hand and a perfect soft kiss on her lips.

'I thought you'd freaked out again,' her voice trembled.

'Abby what's going on today? You have to trust me,' he said softly, 'I wouldn't have said all of that if I didn't mean it.'

She was silent, mortified by how her emotions were playing her. Maybe she was hormonal. She needed to get a grip. She nodded and he held her tightly, somehow knowing she needed to be held until the wave passed her.

'The flowers are beautiful. I'm sorry, Tim, I don't know what's happening to me today.'

'Everything's been fairly emotionally charged, hasn't it?'

'Yes, expectations being dashed and thinking you were going to end it with me. I booked us a hotel.'

'What?'

'To celebrate our one month, silly I know-'

'Abby why didn't you say?'

'Because you said that you wanted to talk and I thought that was it, so I postponed it.'

'Oh gosh, what timing, I'm so sorry, I had no idea. And then me acting the way I have...' Tim smacked his forehead, understanding where the emotional outbursts were coming from.

'I need to believe you're not going to end it like Charlie did, out of the blue, can you promise me that if you're ever unhappy you'll let me know, so we can work at it? So that I have a chance?'

'Yes, absolutely. And that's what I've just done, Abby. I've been honest with you about how I want us to be, and you've respected it. The communication between us is good.'

'Yes, and as long as we've got that, we're going to be fine.'

'I'm not Charlie in any way, and that's exactly why we need to slow it down. I want you to feel safe with who I am so you know how I react to things. Come on, I think you're emotional because you haven't eaten yet, it's been almost eight hours since lunch ... we're not talking any more, we're going to enjoy tonight. Are you ready?'

Abby nodded weakly. Crikey my heart is going to be worn out with all these ups and downs she thought, before pulling herself up. You're doing this to yourself, she reminded herself. You were fine before tonight, so get a grip or you will scare him off.

'Tim,' she said halting him in his steps, 'thank you for

the flowers – they are absolutely beautiful.'

'Just like you. Now, let's eat.'

An hour later and Abby was full of the Irish pub's biggest and best burger. Tim had done the same, polished off her chips and was enjoying an Irish coffee with her now. She felt so much better. The food had soaked up their emotions and she moved to sit next to him, their bodies touching.

'Tim, would it be weird to have sex one more time before we abstain for a bit?'

'Well, it is our four-week anniversary...'

'Take me home now, Tim.'

Tim kissed her his answer. As his tongue sought hers, they kissed fervently, both of their hands on each other's bodies, forgetting where they were.

Tim pulled her close to him in their booth, one hand running up her sheer top and tightening over her nipple, the other hand clenching her thigh. Her nipple sent a burst of desire straight through her, and she gasped as she heard the cough from the waiter. They pulled away, Tim blushing.

Abby could have sworn the waiter deliberately took his time bringing the bill over and faffing around with the card machine.

'Remind me to bring cash next time,' Tim said, one hand still gripping her thigh, dangerously high.

She craved his touch – she had done all day. When they made it outside, she moved against his body, giving him a taster of what was to come. She felt him rise and urgency grew as she kissed him. Abby stretched on her tiptoes to wrap her arms around his neck, pushing him to lean on the nearest car, which happened to be a Porsche.

'I feel like Tom Cruise when he gets the girl, right

now,' Tim whispered and groaned as she moved her hips into his.

'God, if we were anywhere else, I'd take you right now.'

'Why did we walk? Let's hail that cab,' Abby whispered.

Throwing the money at the cabbie for the four-minute journey, Abby had the keys ready as Tim rushed round to open her door and scoop her up, grabbing the keys from her. Unlocking the flat, he expertly maneuvered her through the door, kicking it shut. Tim put her down on the stairs and knelt to kiss her, Abby unbuttoned his jeans and wriggled out of her own in record time, aching for him. Wanting to both devour him and to be devoured by him and as she rose her hips to meet him, he plunged into her. He took her over and over again, they moaned in unison, climaxing together. When their breathing had returned to normal, he smiled down at her, guided her off the awkward staircase, that had seemed so perfect when they got in, carried her up the stairs and laid her in her bed. Lying there alongside him with his hand gently caressing her breasts, she felt completely at peace.

'OK, so the 'no sex' policy starts tomorrow,' Tim whispered. 'Happy one month, Abby.'

'Yes, tomorrow it begins. Happy one month to you, too, lovely man.'

She smiled as he held her close. The entire day had been loaded with emotions she hadn't expect this morning. But somehow, she and Tim had come through it knowing they really did care for each other, and it was time to force those old ghosts out of her mind.

32

BRIGHTON HONESTY

'I CAN'T WAIT for you to meet him, Mum,' Abby said the next day. She wanted her mum's opinion on Tim as soon as possible.

'Well, we definitely want to meet him too. Come and stay whenever you like, dear.'

'Right, let me see what I can do. See you soon,' Abby signed off and looked at train times that day.

'Tim!' Abby yelled.

'Yes, Abby.' Tim came back from the bathroom.

'We're hopping on a train to Brighton. I think it's high time you met my parents.'

'That'd be great. I feel like I know Alice and John already, you mention them so much.'

'Plus, it will take our minds off everything else.'

Tim wriggled away from her, 'No more teasing. I can't take it. I'll run home, grab a bag and meet you at Clapham in an hour and a half?'

A few hours later their taxi carried them along the final leg of their journey and five minutes after hailing it from the train station they pulled up outside Abby's family home in Brighton. Walking through the door Abby saw a note resting on the side.

'Hi there, just zapped out to get some nice bits for supper and breakfast tomorrow, will be 30 mins - see you soon, Alice and John/Mum and Dad xx'

'Oh no,' she said, showing Tim the note, 'what could we possibly do that takes 30 minutes?' Moving up the stairs behind her, Tim grinned.

'Oh, I'm sorry, Tim,' she batted her eyes in a show of fake disapproval as she pushed the door open to her old bedroom, 'but we're not allowed to have sex. We're just getting to know each other properly remember.' Seeing him harden beneath his jeans, she knew her tease was working. Poor boy ... he had no idea what was coming.

'Now, will you promise not to get too turned on? It's just getting too hot in here.' With that she moved towards him and gestured for him to unzip the side of her dress. With one hand on her body, so close to her breast, he duly unzipped it, with a look in his eyes that said he was wondering how much he could get away with.

With that done, she lingered long enough for him to breathe in her perfume then stepped back letting the dress drop down to her waist to reveal a laced demi-bra, three quarters of her breasts were showing, her taut nipples pressing against the lace. Tim was silent, his heart hammering as he studied her form, waiting for what came next. Expertly pivoting round so her bottom was facing him, she glanced seductively over her shoulder at him and eased her dress over her hips. The panties were the best part about this combo she thought. They'd caught her eye because they were sewn with lace to match the bra but then the top half of them had a bondage criss-cross material design, showing off her pert cheeks perfectly. Stepping out of her dress but keeping her heels still on, she rested lightly on the side of the wooden cabinet.

Tim stayed rooted to the spot, clenching and unclenching his fists, appraising her.

'What next, Abby?' he whispered.

God, she loved having his attention. As much as she seemed to turn to goo whenever she was around him, this was a good lesson to teach him that she, too, could call the shots. Slowly raising her right index finger to her mouth, she licked the tip of it before wrapping her tongue around it and slipping it into her mouth. Tim's hand moved to his cock simultaneously. Abby trailed her finger south down her neck, between her breasts, snapping her left nipple with her left hand. She moaned naturally.

Tim pulled at his belt.

'No, no,' Abby immediately stopped, shaking her head until he rebuckled it. Tim's pleading eyes burned with desire as she continued her journey south with her finger. Slipping underneath her panties, she breathed loudly at the sensation. On fire, with her fingers in her panties, she walked to Tim, tugged his t-shirt and snapped her fingers, throwing her hand back over her shoulder as she did so. She stood there, legs apart, her left hand on her hip, right in her panties and waited for him to carry out her silent order.

T-shirt removed and Tim's hair looking pleasingly ruffled from the process, she gestured for him to move towards her. Only when he was ten centimetres away from her did she free him from his thick brown leather belt. She then glanced at the jeans, looked straight in his eyes and snapped her fingers to signal him to remove them. She raised her eyebrows when she realised he was commando. Horny bugger, she thought. Telling me we weren't allowed to have sex then trying to drive me crazy. I'm in control here.

She trailed her left fingertips over his balls, watching his manhood rise and ache for her, which she ignored as she slowly strode around him, running her perfectly manicured nails over his thigh, then clasping the cheeks of his arse before finally returning to face him.

Running her smooth palm over his shaft, she felt him harden fully, his hands straining at his sides, still clenching his fists, awaiting her command. Abby liked that. She started to focus on her own pleasure a bit more, her fingers quickening the pace as she leant on her chest of drawers and tossed her head back.

Bringing her eyes back to his, she pointed at his hand and then at his cock and nodded. Tim moved his hand straight to his manhood and began stroking it up and down, moving the foreskin back to reveal the smoothest skin Abby had ever tasted. It was a fucking phenomenal sight, and she held herself on the cabinet and gave herself to the moment, both hands in her panties, giving him a full frontal view. She furiously played and toyed with herself, bringing herself to the edge of satiation then slowing down to survey her man again. Tim never took his eyes off her, rhythmically moving his hand up and down whilst drinking in the sight of her. Abby plunged her fingers deep inside of her finding her g-spot instantly and pressing against it. She gasped.

Feeling orgasmic electricity rise and take over her body, she had absolutely no self-control. Coming this way felt insanely good. Writhing against the drawers, two fingers inside of her and her other index finger working her clit, she came hard. 'Tim,' she whispered through clenched teeth, knocking over the lamp and almost hitting her head on the wall, she rocked herself to more pleasure, knowing it would be about 30 seconds before she came again. Focussing on Tim, she withdrew her fingers from her wet pussy and tasted the wetness with her tongue.

Tim moaned. She let him lick her fingers then played again with her clit whilst forcing her hand underneath his so they could both touch his cock.

'I want your come all over my tits,' she said. He nodded knowing it wouldn't be long and reached for her bra unsnapping it with one hand whilst, speeding his rhythm with the other. She moved closer to him, running her tits against his chest.

'Now,' he whispered, through breaths. She knelt down and took his come, arching her back and rubbing it over her tits as he claimed her. Pure eroticism. Tim shuddered as his desire was released from his body. He stood, holding her, breathing together. Still not speaking, Abby curved her lips into a smile, smacked his arse and ran to the ensuite to sort out the damage.

When she wandered back into the room, Tim was spread-eagle on the bed. She tossed her head back and laughed.

'Abby... you've cast a spell on me,' he said grinning, trying to look reproachfully at her.

'No, I've been busy ruining the drawers,' she said, trying to restore all of the pieces to their former positions of glory. 'Besides, I'm just giving you what you wanted, dear boy. No sex policy, right?'

'Fuck, that was something else. You absolute tease.'

She got dressed grinning, selecting a jeans and t-shirt combo for their beach walk.

Tim sighed, dragging himself up and off the bed

almost tripping into the drawers, clattering the frames on to the floor again.

'It's not 'us' it's the cabinet,' he said chuckling.

Abby giggled. Brushing out her hair.

'Abby?'

She jumped out of her skin.

'Mum!' she ran down the stairs and enveloped Alice in a massive hug.

'You're looking really well, dear. And you must be Tim.'

Tim emerged wearing a cashmere sweater and jeans and with a natural smile on his face and moved down the stairs to give Alice a kiss on the cheek.

'Did you just have a nap dear?' Abby's mum questioned him with a wry wink and a smile. Oh god, she knows, thought Abby, realising she clearly got her teasing streak from her mum.

'No nap, just a quick change out of the city clothes. We're ready for a good beach walk,' Abby breezed past her mum's knowing smile.

'Well, in that case, you take Buster on his lead and we'll all go. Dad's still at golf but he'll be home soon.'

THE WAVES WERE fighting against the wind to crash on to the stony shore, and Abby grinned as Tim ployed her mum into giving her as many embarrassing stories about her childhood as possible. Alice giggled as she recalled them with her wicked sense of humour. Abby smiled at their chattiness and walked on ahead with Buster to lose her thoughts to the sea air for a bit. Gosh it was good to get away from the city for a weekend, just to breathe. She couldn't believe how much her life had changed in the last four weeks, let alone four months.

When Alice and Tim caught up with her, Alice

interlinked arms with Abby as Tim went off to find a stick for Buster.

'You've got a good one there,' Alice smiled to her daughter, pulling her close as if to emphasise her wish for Abby to keep Tim close.

'I know,' Abby agreed. 'It's weird though, you know I always thought that when I met someone I would be whooping and screaming and running around like a mad thing. And don't get me wrong, I'm overflowing with excitement, but after what I've been through, I almost want to be silent. It just feels so fragile, I don't want to muck it up.'

'Well, just let it carry on steadily the way you are and I'm sure it'll get better and better,' Alice said.

'Do you think he feels the same way about me?' Abby knew her mother's perception of people was always bang on; she hadn't liked Charlie from the start and had seen right through his loud gestures and was annoyed he was wasting her daughter's precious time.

Alice smiled back at her, 'I think he feels the same as you about everything. If you've both had your hearts trampled on, you're both going to be careful about letting your heart run away with you. But don't let that stop you falling.'

'I know, I was scared at first but now, well it's like I'm being drawn to him. I just can't imagine not being with him, and that terrifies me because it's only been a month. One month, Mum,' Abby turned, and Alice could see the fear in her daughter's eyes.

'What are you afraid of, dear? Being hurt or losing him?'

Abby thought for a moment, 'I'm not so afraid of being hurt, not only because I've lived through it once, but mainly because even if he hurt me now I'd still have all of these beautiful moments that show what love should be like ... I guess I'm already afraid of losing him.'

Knowing the words she said next would stay with her daughter long after she'd travelled back home to London, Alice ventured, 'Well if it's not about being hurt that's a good thing because it shows you have perfect trust between you. Abby, when the fear of *losing* him, overrides the fear of *being* with him, then you know that you have got over your past, which you have. You just really have to let it evolve naturally and be yourself in your most honest way, at all times. That's crucial, so you can learn how he reacts to you, so that *you* can then evaluate if you like him,' Alice paused and let her words sink in before asking: 'Have you had any disagreements?'

Abby filled her in on last night's conversation, to which Alice nodded approvingly.

'Well that shows he's a good communicator. Instead of keeping it under wraps like other guys do, he's made himself vulnerable and shared his true feelings and wishes with you in the hope you'll respect them. No yelling or egotistical tantrums?'

Abby shook her head.

'That's a massively positive start then.'

Abby beamed at her mother's words. Alice looked at her and smiled.

'Did you know that when you aren't looking at him, he's looking at you – it seems like he's trying to work out what you're thinking and how he can please you? He's held your hand whenever you've let him. He's so tender with you, I can see it in his eyes and all of his actions.'

'I wish I could just kick this insecurity that Charlie left me with.'

'He likes you for who you are, Abby, being fearful

will change your personality. If you have a doubt then communicate it with him, he might be worrying about the same things. Don't be afraid and paranoid. Be you. That's what he likes.'

'OK, if I have a fear about how Charlie treated me, I'll either voice it with him or you.'

'Yes. Other than that, just carry on being yourself and doing whatever it is you're doing.' She winked, 'Are my drawers alright, by the way?'

'It's fine mum, it was an accident and not what you're thinking.' Abby pushed her hip into Alice's for the cheek. Alice let out a loud laugh.

Tim turned around at the sound of her laugh, 'Got that on camera. Right now, let's get one of the three of us,' he jogged over to them. 'OK, the four of us!'

A slobbery loved up dog, daughter, boyfriend and mother all posed for a selfie on the beach before all walking arm in arm, laughing and sliding up the pebbles, to what Abby and Alice both swore was the world's best fish and chip shop, opposite the pier.

'I'm going to get ours and meet your father. He's just texted me to say he's on his way home,' Alice changed the plans slightly.

Tim nodded, 'How long have you been married?'

'Gosh, 38 years now. We met in school, he was the cool kid and I was the girl whose mum owned the cake shop. He used to come in and buy cakes until he eventually had the guts to ask me out. He ate a lot of cake,' she laughed at the memory.

As Abby waited in the queue, listening to them both chattering away, she realised she didn't know the first thing about Tim's family. How could she have let that slide?

With the food wrapped up, they walked outside.

'Are you sure you don't want to eat with us, Mum?'

'No, really, I want to see him. It's been a busy week.'

'OK, we'll see you in a bit for a movie, right?' Although they were going to see each other soon, Abby gave her mum a massive hug and kiss before she left with Buster to walk home. Abby turned to Tim and they moved quickly to get a bench overlooking the sea before a tourist grabbed it.

'So, you've never really mentioned your parents to me, Tim.' A flash of pain darted across his eyes. 'You don't have to tell me right now if you don't want to.'

Tim sighed and his gaze fell on the horizon, 'It's in quite stark contrast to your childhood, I'm afraid. I guess that's partly why I was up for coming along instantly this weekend: you always have so much pride and love in your voice when you talk about them, I wanted to see what it should be like.' He ate a chip and nodded, 'These are good.' He sighed. 'My parents are divorced; my dad wasn't that great a guy, he could never quite appreciate what he had and kept hurting my mum by running off with other women – literally, it could have been anyone.'

'What?' Abby was horrified.

'I know, I remember my mum's friends all saying to her that "at least it was with random women and not someone he'd actually fallen in love with". My mum would always disagree and say that she could have understood it better if he had fallen in love and wanted to be with someone else. But to ruin a marriage and break up a family for random people ...' Tim went silent and shook his head.

Abby took his hand, 'It must have been soul destroying to have grown up with that.'

He looked back at her, 'He would be so sorry about

it afterwards. Honestly, we'd end go on holiday, there were flowers in every room, he'd shop for her. All the kind of stuff that you should do because you're happy and in love and not do just because you're sorry. Tim turned fully to look at her and said solemnly: 'Abby, if I'm ever sorry for doing something, I won't buy you flowers. I will look at you and tell you honestly that I'm truly sorry for whatever it is, and I'll promise to do my best never to do it again,' Abby nodded. It echoed what her mum had just said about honest communication and that was fine with her after living a lie.

'I don't really plan on being in that position very much, though,' he said. 'Flowers should say you're beautiful and make you want to smile – they should express that, not be an apology. I'd quite happily buy you flowers every week!'

'Yay, that's fine with me!' Abby smiled, 'The ones you bought me last night are beautiful. So, how did she come to leave him in the end?'

Tim sighed and continued, 'With the flowers came the promises. He'd swear he'd never stray again, but he always did and eventually she got so fed up, she pushed for a divorce.'

'You turned out alright, though,' Abby nudged. 'Some people would be bitter and twisted, or worse, end up just like him.'

Tim shuddered at the thought of it. 'No, that was never going to happen. I just saw the amount of pain he caused my mum; her eyes were perpetually sad by the thought of what he was doing and trying to block out the memories of what he had done. I used to worry that they were staying together because of me and that was making her sad, but it wasn't even that. She honestly loved him and every time he let her down, the disappointment, rejection and hurt was ten times worse than the time before because despite everything, she lived in hope that one day he'd keep his promise to her. Even if he was just home late, her mind would start to wander. It ended up eating away at her. It almost destroyed her. She filed for divorce from a man that she still loved; I don't think she'll ever get her head around that. She couldn't understand why he'd changed so much or what had changed between them. She spent hours berating herself, wondering what she could have done differently.'

Tears rose in his eyes at the memories, and she welled up, too, holding his hand tightly for support.

Tim paused, 'Her whole life became all about how to keep her husband's attention. It was so sad. She just lost herself trying to meet his needs.'

I know that feeling, even on a minor scale in comparison, Abby thought. 'What made her realise enough was enough?'

'Well, I remember we went to stay with Gran and Grandad, my mum's parents, for a weekend when I was eleven. Grandad took my mum aside, and I didn't know what was said at the time, but my mum just started crying. Honestly, she was shaking uncontrollably, and the sobs were unlike anything I'd ever heard. They were heart wrenching. Dad had battered her confidence. She told me a few years ago what Grandad said to her that had made her cry. He'd said: "This wasn't the happy life we'd hoped for you, my dear. It's time to get you out of there." She told me after all of the debates with friends and feeling like she was going crazy in my own head, the simplicity of what he said, and the love in his eyes was just so pure and true that it broke through all of the excuses she'd been making for my dad. In that moment she just felt like a little girl that needed to be loved and protected unconditionally again.'

'It must have been a scary prospect from all angles to do, to break free and bring you up alone.'

'Yes, I think the guilt she felt about me not having a full-time dad was immense. She kept apologising for it. It drove me insane that she couldn't see I understood it was his fault and never hers. It literally took her years to stop questioning life, and the divorce was a painfully protracted process as my dad fought it all the way, saying how much he loved her, whilst of course sleeping with anyone else he could.'

'Crikey. How on earth could he justify that in his head?'

'I don't honestly know. I just remember Gran telling us both the way he treated us wasn't love. Love would never be unkind or disrespectful. Real love was quiet yet happy and strong. She told us to look at how her and my grandad treated each other and take strength from that. Which we both did. It was hideous for my mum though; it broke her to walk away from him, but it was killing her slowly being with him.'

'Has she found herself again since?'

'Yes, and it was such an achievement. Honestly as an example of perseverance, you just couldn't top it.' Tim's eyes shone with pride at his mother's mental resolve. 'So many of her friends had judged her for staying with him for so long that they had little sympathy when she eventually managed to leave.'

'Ha, it seems to be so easy for people to look on and judge, but when your confidence has been smashed to pieces you don't actually believe you'll be able to leave.

They should have been patient with her, though,' Abby, empathised with his mum, ever more grateful for how Woody and Lucy had been.

'Yes, they should. It's evil what he did to her really. Everything about her that made her beautiful and how she is today he slowly took away from her, replacing it with heartache and guilt.'

'So how has she dealt with it since?'

'Well I was twelve when she eventually moved out. She left everything in the house apart from her clothes, some of the photos and my toys, and we moved in with Gran and Grandad. I absolutely loved it. I missed my dad but then I guess from that moment on I had more of a normal childhood.

Abby beamed and squeezed his arm. Relieved.

'Grandad made me a treehouse, and me and mum would camp out in it sometimes and make shapes in the stars. My mum got healthy again; colour appeared back in her cheeks and little by little she slowly started to heal. I think it was just being surrounded by honest love that did it; waking up wondering whether her heart would be broken every day had absolutely drained her.'

'Did your dad contact her?'

'Yes, and every time he got in touch she dropped back to the starting point again. It was like that right up until the divorce, and after that, Grandad took me when it was Dad's weekends, so she never had to see him.'

'What was hanging out with your dad like?'

'It was really strange. At that point all I wanted to do was play football and go to the park, and he would oblige for a bit. Then he'd take me for some sandwiches and a milkshake and quiz me on how Mum was. We just hung out really. I could never hate him. I couldn't stand the way that he treated my mum, but then I could never understand how she put up with it for so long. Every time he'd upset her, I'd beg her to leave him and go and marry someone else, and I'd beg him to do the same. They were poisonous together.' Abby couldn't imagine it, a youngster begging his parents to divorce.

'I love him though. I mean, he's my dad. He's been in a relationship for four years with someone, and I think he's trying really hard at it. Which I think kind of hurts Mum – she wonders why he could never do that with her.'

'It's just time, isn't it? It took losing her, you and family life to realise he needed to change.'

'Yes,' Tim agreed. 'In terms of dealing with me, they manage it. I don't think either of them particularly enjoys being in the same room. Dad feels awful he treated my mum that way, and my mum is disgusted with herself for being such a doormat and wasting years of her life being so miserable.'

'Is she happy now?' Abby almost held her breath.

'She's really good. I'm so proud of her. She retrained as a midwife and works manic shifts at her local hospital, which is up north, by the way, Buxton. She's been dating a guy for seven years now, Andrew, who treats her beautifully.'

'Never had the urge to remarry?' Abby asked curiously.

'No, I think they've discussed it, but he went through a painful divorce as well, so they're fine just keeping things as they are. Maybe one day she will. I kind of hope she does marry him just because she deserves a proper marriage, the way it should be. She had a bad experience but that was so long ago now. It was lovely seeing the change in her though,' he smiled fondly.

'I remember it so vividly. When the divorce finally came through, it was two weeks before the end of the summer term, and when school ended, we went to the south of France with Gran and Grandad to a villa they rented every year when my mum was growing up. It was amazing, on top of a hill with a garden down to a massive lake. Mum was quite quiet during the first few days, processing everything, I suppose.

'Grandad always got up early, sat outside in his shorts to watch the 'morning light kiss the ground awake' as he'd say. It would make him smile this amazingly content smile and then, when he'd finished his cup of coffee, he'd set the cup down, stand up, stretch and then run full pelt down the hill straight into the lake. He did it every single day, and I'd watch from my room and giggle.

'One morning my mum got up with him, sat in silence beside him, stretched out, held his hand and they ran as fast as their legs could carry them down the hill and straight into the lake together.' Tim chuckled at the memory. 'She was laughing and splashing around like she didn't have a care in the world, like she was ten again.

'I think that trip reminded her of how happy she could be and steadied her. She realised her world didn't have to revolve around my dad. It was much better after that. I don't think until that point I'd *ever* seen her that happy. They came puffing up the hill ten minutes later, and she couldn't stop laughing. Every day after that, I did it with them. I thought my legs were going to drop off, I was running so fast. My childhood got back to a vague form of normality after that holiday, so I always remember it fondly. We went back there a few times, it's a beautiful old place,' he looked wistful.

Abby wiped away a tear, 'It's such a beautiful story,

Tim.' He smiled at the memory and Abby could see just how happy he'd been. 'I'm so relieved for her and for you. She must be so proud of how you've turned out.'

And they sat in silence for a few minutes.

'You might have to take me there, one day,' Abby said shyly, not wanting to impose on a childhood memory but share it with him. She was overwhelmed how freely he'd shared his memories. He'd been right, no sex and a larger focus on getting to know each other was turning out to be an incredible experience.

'Maybe I shall take you there. Maybe indeed,' Tim smiled that great smile of his and pulled her into his chest, kissing the top of her head. Abby snuggled in, the sun had gone down whilst they were talking and now the night air was chilly.

'Thank you for sharing all of that with me.'

'It was easy, you're a good listener, maybe you take after your mum more than you think.' His face turned serious, 'That's why, Abby, I need you to promise me now that if I ever, ever hurt you or you feel like I'm restricting you from being yourself then you have to let me know immediately. You don't need to yell at me.'

'I wouldn't anyway,' she said. 'My parents haven't brought me up to yell, we're a family of talkers. Tim, if you ever upset me, I would tell you what I didn't appreciate about the situation, you don't need to worry about that. I'm too impatient to dish out silent treatment.'

'I promise you now I will never treat you like that, Abby. I am not my father. I will spend every day of my life ensuring I don't turn out like him.'

Placing her hands on his face, she spoke softly, 'I trust you and I'm holding you to that. For the record, if you ever did act like that, I wouldn't accept an apology and stay. I'd be gone in a heartbeat because that's not the kind of love or relationship I want. But I know you're not like that,' she smiled honestly back at him, he made her feel so secure. Tim held her hand and looked shocked at how cold it was: 'You need gloves, me lady,' protectively holding it in his pocket. 'Come on, let's go back now. Movie and couch time.'

They gathered up a good pace walking home to find Alice looking pensive.

'Ah good, you're home. We didn't know if you'd decided to stay out.'

'You know we'd have called, Mum,' said Abby, rolling her eyes, reverting to teenage behaviour.

'Of course, dear,' Alice relaxed. 'Right Tim, you go and chill while I make us some of my famous hot chocolate.'

'Hurrah,' Abby heard her dad in the living room: 'Make mine a large one, please! OK Tim, ready to meet my dad?'

'Absolutely,' Tim nodded.

Abby grinned and ushered him into the lounge. She threw herself into her dad's arms for a big bear hug. He smelt like home to her.

'Tim, this is my dad, John.'

'Very pleased to meet you, sir,' Tim held out his hand, and John shook it warmly.

'Well she looks happy, so I think you can stay.' John replied with a welcoming smile.

'Dad ... seriously,'

Tim laughed, 'Phew!'

'So, do you like golf, football or rugby?' John enquired.

'You're more likely to find me watching rugby, but I secretly follow the football premiership when I have the time.'

'Mum! They're talking about sports. Get in here quickly.'

John rolled his eyes at Tim. Took a deep breath and obliged by changing the subject.

'Do we really have to watch a movie where you scream, dear, I find it quite unnerving.' Her dad asked pleadingly.

Tim chuckled. John looked at him, 'You clearly haven't heard how loud they are. How the neighbours haven't had the police round I don't know.'

Tim shot a look at Abby, 'You didn't mention screaming.'

'Well, how can you watch a horror movie and not scream? Surely you'd be more worried about my personality if I didn't?'

'Fair point,' Tim nodded, and Abby watched as he looked around. The lounge was warm and inviting and filled with memorabilia from her childhood. Pictures of them on holidays, graduation and the odd wedding, here and there.

Alice walked in brandishing four hot chocolates topped with cream and marshmallows.

'Yessss!' Abby exclaimed and went to grab hers.

Seeing Tim looking over the pictures, Alice placed the tray down and grabbed her phone for the camera.

'Come on, I want to have a nice cosy one of the four of us.'

'Mum!' Abby started, scared it was a bit full-on for Tim, but he held her close to him.

'It's fine,' he whispered and kissed the top of her head.

'Are you sure? Sorry.' They moved over to stand by John.

Clicking the timer and trotting back to the couch

before it went off, Alice elbowed John and, as the flash went off, hissed: 'Smile properly or else.' She got up to check how it came out and she pursed her lips at her husband, rolling her eyes in the exact same way Abby had done.

'All these years of marriage and you still can't smile properly. I look like I'm married to a maniac.'

'Who knows, after this horror film, maybe I will be?' John joked. 'But let's get watching.'

After yelling pointlessly for the characters to run away from the bad guys and screaming to the point where Tim looked more shocked at the level of noise than the content of the movie, the film ended and they all filtered upstairs to bed.

'Brunch tomorrow,' Alice called out, 'No early wake up here.'

'All good with us, I reckon,' Abby called back cheekily and ran into her room.

Grabbing her 'yes I always wear nightwear like this' bundle, she jumped into the ensuite first. Gosh I miss my comfy PJs, Abby thought as she slipped into the little shorts and silk cami. They had that cute but cool look. Seeing as she wasn't 'allowed' to have sex, she hoped Tim would still like it. She paraded past Tim, flashed him a pearly white, minty fresh smile and hopped into bed, but he disappeared instantly into the ensuite.

When he emerged, he strode out wearing her knickers, taking the mick by deliberately swaying his hips, pouting, walking around the bed before crawling over in fits of giggles. Forcing her to check out his arse, he flashed her the same smile that she had just given to him.

'Two can play that game, sista,' Tim grinned.

'Whatever,' she giggled and smacked his bottom. God

it was tight. He dived under the covers and tucked her under his arm. She hooked her legs over his and let the warmth of his skin on hers flood over her.

'Have you had a good day, Tim?' He picked up her arm and wiggled her around so she was spooning with him.

'I've had a better day than I could have ever imagined – your family is so lovely.'

'Good,' Abby smiled and yawned.

'So...?'

'So what?'

'Did they like me?'

'Ummmmm, we'll see.'

'Abby!'

'Yes, of course they did. You're lovely. Keep up the good work though – don't let it slip.'

'I won't. Tim stroked her hair and pulled her close. 'Sleep well, Little Miss Abfab.'

Abby drifted off, smiling as Tim held her tightly.

33

SURPRISES

ABBY COULDN'T WAIT to see Lucy. Both of their love lives were on fire at the moment, in completely different ways, and she was loving every second of it. Every time she'd messaged Lucy, she'd had a blow by blow account of whatever completely random thing Will had made her get up to, and she wondered what the latest one was. The door to the bar flung open and in strode Lucy, beaming, glowing with confidence.

She kissed her on the cheek and plonked down next to Abby, grabbing the bubbles in one swift move.

'Dive in and tell me everything,' Abby said with glee.

'Well, in the last two weeks, I've been chucked out of a silent disco in the Shard ...'

'How do you even get chucked out of a silent disco?' Abby was intrigued.

'We sang at the top of our lungs to the songs, and they escorted us out. It was hilarious and then last night he took me nude painting.'

'What, so where you paint someone who's posing?'

'No, everyone gets naked and paints their partner.'

Abby almost spat her drink out everywhere.

'What? Where on earth did you do that?'

'A private gallery in the depths of Vauxhall – don't

worry, it was warm.'

'Of course! Because that was my first thought. Hang on, though, Luce, I need a minute to process this,' this was all very different behaviour for Lucy.

'I know what you're thinking Abby, this isn't my usual self. And that's why I love it.'

Abby nodded, 'I can see that – you're glowing. But is it sustainable if it isn't really you?'

'All I know is that I'm in control of everything else in my life, so to be constantly surprised by Will pushing me out of my stupid old comfort zones I feel so much better about myself. I can let go and adapt. Before with guys, I'd be the one doing the organising and kind of controlling where the relationship went.'

'So, you don't have the urge to control any part of him?' Abby questioned.

'Nope. Not in the slightest.'

This was very un-Lucy like. 'And you don't want to know every minute detail of your plans beforehand?'

'Nope,' Lucy grinned back at her. 'I don't want to know anything. In fact, I LOVE not knowing. He surprises me daily, and then I surprise myself with my reaction.'

This flummoxed Abby; she'd never have expected this from her oldest friend.

'I've realised my control issues are just me wanting everything to be perfect. To perform perfectly at work, be perceived to be immaculately presented, always on time, perfect, perfect, perfect. But that doesn't exist and it's exhausting trying. Plus, you can only be perfect on your own. Will shakes my world up and my conventional view of perfection is totally different now. When something's typically imperfect I find myself letting go in a new way. I don't need to be perfect or perceived to be perfect to be happy anymore.'

'Wow!'

'So, I used to panic about the IBS all day, every day. Now if I need to fart, I do.'

Abby looked alarmed, 'But I don't want you to change too much, Luce.'

'I was just joking! You should see your face,' Lucy had a fiendish grin.

'Phew!' Abby was genuinely relieved.

'I'm just willing myself to be more chilled out, and I'm actually having a lot more fun.'

Abby paused, 'I don't want you to change or get hurt Luce.'

'I'm not changing; I'm doing what you said and evolving.'

Abby nodded, 'I can see that. So, you want to be with him?'

'Definitely. I'm done being independent and on my own. Happy to tick that off the list. I just have the best time when I'm with him. I want to feel more of that. And I think he feels the same ...'

'What? You looked like you were going to say something else then.'

Lucy looked shy all of a sudden. 'No, I'm all talked out. Talk to me about Tim, how are you and he doing? How was Brighton and the no-sex policy?'

Abby grinned, 'Nice change of topic, Luce, but I'll roll with it for now because honestly, my friend, I think that we have swapped personas here. Where I would normally be throwing caution to the wind, I am still staying very calm in my happy state. Well, apart from the burning 'L' word that still isn't being said.'

'Do you then? Love him?'

'Yes,' Abby nodded, welling up. 'I just can't believe my life, who'd have thought I'd be feeling like this four months ago?'

'Yes, it's nuts how quickly someone can spin your life around.'

'Crazy!' and Abby filled her in on Brighton.

'This is going so well because it's right for you both, after everything you've been through. You were absolutely slayed at the start of the year so to get to this point is amazing. I'm so proud of you.'

'And I'm so glad that I followed your plan.'

'Well, I'm not sure it brought Tim to you.'

'It kind of did – it fuelled the topics of quite a few conversations and forced me to see my life beyond Charlie.'

Lucy reached out and grabbed her hand, 'I knew you deserved so much more.'

Abby smiled, 'Thank you for making me see it, too. Now, how long should I wait before freaking out that he hasn't told me he loves me yet? I'm desperate to know he feels the same.'

'Have you created any perfect scenarios for him to tell you?'

'Now wouldn't that be me trying to control the situation and bring about a perfect ending – exactly what you were saying not to do?' Abby mocked.

'Yes, yes, it would. Scrap that.'

'Oh please! Of course I've done that. I've done indoor picnics, worn every type of lingerie known to man.'

'Maybe he likes a bit of, you know.'

'Christian Grey?'

'Yes, maybe he's into his bondage, and he's checking you out beforehand.'

Abby pondered this. Tim was an architect, so there might be some secret playroom she was not yet privy to .... 'No, his flat is too small for any secret rooms hiding that sort of stuff. Besides the sex is good enough anyway.'

'Just keep giving it time, Abby. I'm sure he'll say those words eventually, and it'll mean all the more when he does.'

'I love that you're happy too, Luce; I also love that I have no idea what you're going to surprise me with next.'

'It's so not the normal way I do things. But to hell with that right? If it'd been so right to do things a certain way, I'd have been married years ago. I'm done playing by my old rules. I've thrown that book out.'

'Well, let's drink to your next chapter.'

34

SO UNLIKE HER

'ABBY!' LUCY'S VOICE came on the line as a high-pitched shriek. Abby, cooking, almost dropped her spoon into her arrabbiata sauce.

'Crikey Lucy, you made me jump. What's happening?'

'Abby, we're engaged,' Lucy screamed down the phone.

'What?'

'We're engaged! Isn't it insane?'

Engaged. She felt instantly dubious.

'Are you really, Luce? Or is this a prank?'

'No, no, it's the truth. Will just proposed to me, well, actually it was 30 minutes ago, mid, well, during, you know.'

Abby left her sauce bubbling and sat on the edge of one of the dining room chairs, 'You're serious?'

'Yes, we were having sex and, my god it was good, he was on top of me and so deep. I just ...'

'Look skip that part.'

'Well, no, I can't because that's when he did it. He told me that he loved me, loved every part of me, how my mind and my body turned him on. Then just before he came, he said 'marry me' and let's do this forever. Of course, I said "yes".'

'Luce, you can't ...'

'Obviously, we'll come up with a different story for our parents,' she giggled. 'But essentially that's how it happened. Not one knee, Abby, but both. I couldn't wait to tell you,' she giggled again.

'That's awesome,' Abby said slowly, not believing what she was hearing. It was a golden rule: you never believe a guy who tells you they love you during sex. Let alone one that proposes.

Her best friend was engaged. To a guy she'd met a month ago. Focus on what she's saying Abby, focus on being excited.

'Do you have a ring?'

'Yes, it's gorgeous. He bought it last weekend when we were in Hampstead Heath.'

'So, did you suspect then? Lucy! You're engaged to someone I've barely met, how is this happening?'

'Yes, I know, I know, and we've discussed rectifying that. We're doing engagement drinks tomorrow night, can you make it?'

'Of course I can. I wouldn't miss this for the world.'

'Amazing!' Lucy was practically singing down the phone. 'Can we get ready together at yours? Dresses and heels?'

'Of course,' Abby said blankly, Lucy was clearly too busy flying around cloud nine to notice her tone.

'I'll come over straight after work. I can't wait to see you. Right, I'd better sign off for now as I've got to call my mum. Eeeek, I'm engaged!'

'Love you, Luce, bye.'

Abby sat in the kitchen in complete silence. Damn Woody for being out. He'd know what to say right now. Loved and engaged. Shit, why can't I be happy for her?

Is it my own feelings of wanting to be loved by Tim? No, Abby scrapped that thinking straight away – this was about Lucy, and all she wanted was her friend to be happy, more than anything. Lucy deserved it. It was just so god damn soon. One month in. She was terrified for her. Who even was this guy?

And during sex. Jeez, she would say anything during orgasm. This was so un-Lucy like. She dialled her mum, she would know what to say. She rang three times, but there was no answer.

Tim, she needed to speak to Tim. He picked up straight away and she let it all out.

'This guy could be anyone, they barely know each other, Tim.' She ranted down the phone, not realising she was crying until the tears fell on her hands.

'Abby, breathe!'

'It's Lucy. I should be happy for her – I want to be happy for her and I feel like a horrible person because I'm not. I just ...'

'I know. You're worried about her. Listen Abby, I'm coming over now. Calm down, it's going to be OK. Gosh, what a shock.'

That was it. A shock, not a surprise. Abby remained rooted in her seat in the dark until Tim arrived 30 minutes later. She flew down the stairs to let him in and he held onto her for a long while.

'Are you worried about her being engaged, or losing her to this guy and her changing because she's with someone so unexpectedly?'

'Both maybe. He's a lawyer. I thought he would be more level-headed than this.'

'Maybe ...'

'Do you think I should say something to her?' Abby

asked. 'She sounded so happy I don't want to kill her buzz. I don't want to be that person,' She looked at Tim in despair.

'Abby, your concern comes from a place of love. Nothing else, right?' Tim looked deeply into her eyes.

'No, of course not. She doesn't know him. I don't even know him. How can that be?' she raked her hands through her hair.

'Look,' Tim took her hands and held them, calming her, 'Gosh, your hands are like ice.'

'They always go cold when I'm stressed.'

'And now I know that,' Tim whispered, slipping them under his jumper and holding them close to his chest to warm them. He looked tenderly down at her and she moved closer, resting her head on his shoulder.

'It's moments like this I realise just how kind you are and learn even more about you,' she smiled up at him and kissed him. He looked relieved that she'd calmed down.

'Lucy hasn't had a chance to have this yet. Who knows if Will would even care if her hands were cold.'

'Look, their story is very different to ours,' Tim reasoned.

'What do you mean?'

'Well from everything you've told me, their crazies seem to match.'

'What if she gets hurt? I don't want her to go through what we've gone through.'

'Well, you and I are turning out alright,' Tim reasoned, 'and it's her journey, her life. You just need to be there for her.'

'I'm always there for her, no matter what. Do you think I should speak to her?'

Tim sighed, 'OK, let me think. If the situation were reversed, would she speak to you?'

'Oh my god, yes,' Abby said without hesitation. 'She'd be the first to make sure I was doing it for all of the right reasons.'

'Then you're justified in raising your concerns with her, too – and remind her of that, just be honest.'

Abby nodded in agreement.

Tim continued, 'But, Little Miss Abby, you may just have to accept they both love each other and that's OK.'

'We'll see, I certainly hope so. I'll be able to tell from how she is tomorrow ... Thank you, Tim,' Abby reached up and kissed him again, glad to have his support her in this moment of uncertainty. She needed to steel herself for tomorrow, whatever it may bring.

35

BRICK OF FLOWERS

'LUCY, I NEED to talk to you. Can you sit down for a moment?' Abby took Lucy's hand as they perched on the edge of Abby's comfy bed. 'I know if things were the other way around, you'd be saying this to me because we are absolutely the best friends in the whole wide world.'

Lucy's eyes blazed instantly at her and pulled her hand away.

'Abby, I already know why you're sitting me down and you need to know that right now I'm battling the 'why can't she just be happy for me' after all I've been there for her ... vs. the 'she's only doing it because she cares,' right now.'

'Woah, Luce, one month, though ...' It was so rare for her friend to be fired up like this, Abby knew she had to tread incredibly gently. Lucy was happily floating in the stars but she wouldn't be a friend if she didn't make triple sure she was doing it for all of the right reasons, 'You told me in that café how scared you were of losing him because of how he makes you feel.'

Lucy nodded, 'And now I don't have to worry about that.'

'But you can't marry someone because you're scared.'

Lucy protested indignantly, 'I'm not marrying him

because I'm scared, is that what you think?'

Abby was silent.

Lucy's face changed, lightened, 'I'm marrying him because somehow the universe, or God, or whatever you believe in, brought him into my life and made it, and me, ten million times better. Every inch of my skin comes alive at the mere thought of him, let alone when we're together. And it's not just the sex.'

Abby looked sceptical as Lucy took her hand, 'You have to trust me. I'm trusting every instinct I've got on this one. I wasn't born yesterday; I know how I feel and how I want to feel and, most importantly, how Will makes me feel.'

'But what if he changes in six months? What if he lets you down or hurts you?'

'What if *anyone* lets you down or hurts me?'

Abby shut up, but Lucy grabbed her hand and spoke gently.

'He's not Charlie. You can't keep equating everything in *my* life to that. That was your experience.'

'Luce, you know full well that if it was me getting engaged, you'd be telling me one month was just the honeymoon period ...'

'Abby, I'm so crazy in love with him that even if it doesn't work out we'll figure it out. Love is a risk. But it's one I'm totally willing to take. He knows me. He's only just come into my life, but somehow, he knows how I'm going to react to everything. He's incredibly astute and caring. He's seen me at my most horrific worse and just dealt with it. He knows what I don't like, and what he doesn't know, he wants to find out in the best way possible. I trust his morals, and I trust his attitude to life and to me. You need to get to know him, and you'll see you can trust him, too,' Lucy glowed, grinning as she spoke. 'You've always told me to let go of the fear and the order and the organising and just enjoy my life ...'

'No, I meant relax, don't lose what makes you you,' Abby exclaimed.

'*No* that's how I am when I'm around you and how I coped with being by myself. I *had* to organise my time so I wouldn't feel down or lonely. When I'm around Will, he takes away all the negative stuff I got used to blocking out. He fills my time with loveliness and that enables me to be the best version of myself, all the time. He makes me so happy,' she shrugged, smiling. 'He's so interesting, and everything he does appeals to me. And now I know he feels the same back.'

Abby took it all in. It made sense, but it wounded her that Lucy hadn't mentioned feeling so lonely.

'I can't wait to marry him and explore the world with him and live with him. I just can't believe it's finally happened. It's hit me like a brick,' and she smacked her hand hard on the table, punctuating her point, making Abby jump.

'Well, if there was such a thing as a pretty brick of flowers, if you know what I mean,' Lucy giggled.

Abby, silent, took a moment to survey her oldest friend. Everything about her did seem different, and in a good way. Lucy was in a short floaty skirt with a silky top that cut low over her breast and a Hermes scarf looped around her neck. Her eye makeup wasn't the normal safe brown with black mascara and eyeliner but shimmering pastel shades. She had a crazy cute grin on her face and her eyes ... her eyes were massive and brown and sparkled with flecks of gold. She looked like she was permanently blushing.

'Oh my god, Luce,' Abby pulled her into a massive hug before holding her shoulders and looking at her, 'you've found it, you've found someone that makes you ten million times yourself.' Lucy was right, whatever happened she would always be alright in the end, so taking the risk and hoping and praying it would all work out for her friend was really the only thing she could do. 'I'm with you 100 percent, the same way you are for me,' her voice broke and tears tumbled down her face. 'Does he really make you feel that way? To your bones?'

Lucy's smiled widened, 'Yes, I feel I'm capable of anything. Like I'm growing into new possibilities somehow ...'

'Someone who sees you for who you are, loves you for it and makes you even more incredible. That's THE DREAM.'

They both shrieked as Abby recited something they'd talked about when they were 19, trying to figure out what love should be like.

'Lucy, marry him now. Immediately.'

They were both in tears. 'Oh Abby, I'm so glad you're happy for me,' Lucy admitted.

Abby hugged her, 'I'm so sorry I was so concerned. I slipped into your worrying role. I really am happy for you.'

Lucy jumped on to the bed and bounced around, whooping: 'I'm getting married, I'm actually getting married.' The bed made a hideous crack: 'I'm also buying you a new bed.'

'Whoop to both of those,' Abby joked and jumped on the bed with her: 'Come on if we're going to do something, let's do it properly.' They both sucked up their chests and jumped and hollered, utterly euphoric.

They didn't spot Woody appear, and when they saw him with a look of complete confusion standing in the doorway, they were crying with laughter on a bed considerably lower than it had been. Abby stood back as Lucy held out her left hand and pointed to the finger exhibiting a rather large rock.

'What?' Woody asked.

She nodded.

'Are you?' He looked pensive.

Lucy nodded.

'Will?'

Lucy nodded.

'Oh my god, that's amazing! Come here!' Woody engulfed her in a massive hug. 'Does that mean that I can't do this anymore?' playfully grabbing her arse.

Lucy screamed and laughed, 'Well, maybe not in front of Will, but you, Woody, will always be able to grab my arse.'

Abby giggled, still on the bed.

'Champagne!' commanded Woody, beaming. But as he'd hugged her, Abby could have sworn she saw a flash of pain cross his eyes. Knowing Woody, he'd deny it forever, but Abby had always wondered if he carried a bit of a torch for Lucy. He shouldn't have hung around she thought, you snooze you lose. Still he and she needed to be in this together, so she bounced over to Woody and put her arm around him.

'She's deserting us, Woodster.'

'Ah I'll never desert you two. Don't make me cry!' Lucy hugged them both into her, 'I love you guys.'

'We love you, too,' Abby choked, in serious danger of getting emotional. She couldn't imagine her world without Lucy in it, and she was desperately trying to push her thoughts of 'will she remember me when she's married' out of her mind.

'Where will you live, it won't be far away will it?' I need you, she thought silently.

'London, definitely, we haven't thought about where yet.'

Abby nodded. Phew. One question down.

'Right, where's that Champagne?' Lucy clapped her hands, 'I put some in the fridge earlier,' she said cheekily.

'That's why we love her,' Woody grinned, 'I'll pop the cork, you grab the glasses.' Arm in arm, Abby and Lucy followed Woody into the kitchen and got ready to clink glasses.

'Oh, we should text my mum and tell her to Facetime us, you can share the good news.'

'Good idea,' Lucy said.

Abby grabbed her phone to send a text:

'Hey Mum are you around? We have some exciting news?'

The reply came back, quick as a flash: 'Can be online in five, see you soon x.'

Abby was intrigued to see how her mum would react to Lucy's news. Would she react in the same way she had?

Glasses in hand, Woody said: 'To our wonderful Lucy, who has found someone that makes her eyes light up. And is probably setting a new record for quick engagements! We love you, congratulations!'

Woody's voice was slightly higher pitched than normal. He looked slightly wired. Had Lucy noticed? Abby looked at her quaffing bubbles and laughing, nope, she was oblivious.

'So how did he propose?' Woody clapped his hands

together. 'Tell me all of the details.'

Clapping? Very un-Woody, she made a mental note to talk to him later. Cutting into Lucy's babbling story, Alice's FaceTime request pinged on Abby's phone. She nudged Luce and handed it over.

'Hello Alice, so what do you notice that's different about me today?' Holding the champagne glass with her left hand in an exaggerated fashion towards the camera.

'Well, you're positively glowing, dear ...' Alice peered in closer at the screen, and they all heard her draw in breath, 'Oh my goodness, is that? Arrgghhhh,' Alice squealed.

'OK so I definitely take after my mum,' Abby grinned at Lucy, waving at Alice.

As Lucy began to tell a slightly less sexually graphic version of her shock engagement all over again, Woody grabbed Abby's arm and dragged her up the spiral staircase to his room.

'How can you be so fine with this? Aren't you worried about her?' Woody demanded.

Abby looked at him, his composure gone, his face red and his breathing ragged. Shit, she thought, in every way, she wanted to be proved wrong on this one. She had to get him to calm down and quickly.

'Woody, of course I was worried, it's all happened so quickly ...'

'Way too quickly. Do you think I should have a word with her?' He was physically shaking.

Abby took his hand and said gently. 'No, I don't think you should do that, I already have,' she spoke softly, calmly: 'It's not our place to, Woody. We just have to be the best friends possible and celebrate her decisions and hope to god she doesn't need us for any more than that.'

'Can you imagine if it all goes tits up? She barely knows this guy. He could really hurt her. He could be a maniac!'

Abby saw Lucy glance up mid-sentence to where they stood on the mezzanine outside Woody's room before carrying on her chat with Alice.

Woody was pacing around now, and Abby raised her finger to her lips, telling him to keep it down. 'Woody, you need to get a grip,' Abby hissed.

'I'm going to speak to her,' he said. 'Abby, no-one gets married after knowing someone a month. How can she honestly expect it to last? It's the honeymoon stage.'

'Well, maybe she's thinking that mutual love, craziness and respect will grow, and they'll fashion something deeper when they're actually married.'

'Seriously, how can you be OK with this?'

'Woody, my reaction was exactly the same as yours, OK? I had *exactly* the same thoughts as you. When she came round earlier, I sat her down and talked to her about it and said *all* of this.'

Woody looked doubtful.

'Honestly. I justified saying it because we both know full well she would have said it to me if the situation had been reversed. She's so happy. I couldn't say any more. She's going to do this regardless of what we think.' Woody stared at her; she'd caught his attention.

'Bottom line, Woody: it's such a special time for her, and we are the two people she wants to be happy for her more than anyone or anything else in the world. We can't be the two that ruin it for her. Period,' Abby gave Woody a look that told him that was an end to it. Woody huffed, running his hands through his hair again.

'Just look at her. She's glowing, from top to toe. Just

do what I did and take a bit of time to get your head around it.'

'Pah,' Woody huffed again. But Abby could see he had relented.

Lucy had come off the call with Alice.

'Look, are you going to be cool?' she hissed at Woody.

'Yes, of course I will be, but ...'

'Look she's off the call now, you and I can talk about this later. Just come down now and let's get through tonight.'

Woody nodded, 'I'm just going to the bathroom and I'll be down.'

'Right, see you down there. It's going to be alright,' she gave him a quick hug and buzzed down the stairs.

'What did she say?' Abby beamed at Lucy.

'Oh, she was very excited. She very subtly asked me questions about Will to make sure he sounded like a good guy,' Lucy was laughing. 'I guess I'm going to get that a lot huh?'

'I'm not going to lie, Luce, yes you will. But at least you know people care, *and* it's what you would do if it was the other way around. Then when they see you literally glowing, they'll shut up straight away – the same way I did.'

Lucy nodded thoughtfully.

'Let me see that ring again.'

'Yes, I want to see the ring properly, too,' Woody was back, changed and ready to go out for drinks. Abby smiled and winked at him as he made his way over. Lucy did a little jump again and held her hand out. It really was extraordinary. It was a deep purple oval diamond and surrounding it were tiny pale-yellow diamonds laid into a deep yellow gold ring.

Woody held her hand to the light and the ring dazzled, 'Wow. It's incredible, I've never seen one like that before. Did you choose it together?'

'Yes, completely unexpectedly. We were on our way to Hampstead Heath for the day, after you and Tim had been, and we hopped off the bus in the village. We were meandering around and popped down that side street of vintage shops, you know the one? Well there's an old-school jewellers tucked away in there that I hadn't noticed before. I saw this in the window and wandered in to take a closer look.'

Abby raised an eyebrow at the classic tactics displayed.

'I swear I wasn't thinking any more than that – it was just so intriguing. I tried it on my right hand because I've been looking for a dress ring for ages, then I saw the price and put it back down. I was gutted, though. I went back out, and Will was in the street, wondering where I'd gone. I guess I was a bit quiet, you know the way you are when you can't buy something you want, and he got the story out of me. He just turned around, marched in and bought it, just like that. He said he'd choose when I could have it as a present, so I didn't think anything else of it other than 'oh my god I can't believe it!'

Abby was gobsmacked, 'You were just a little quiet and he did that?'

'Yes, he said "I never ever want to see you looking unhappy," simple as that.'

'Oh my god, Lucy, you must take him to Harrods, immediately. Just stand in the middle of the staircase and sob. He'll think you're unhappy and buy you everything you want. It would be incredible!'

Abby was psyched for her friend, 'I'll have to try that shopping tactic with Tim.'

Lucy grinned. 'You should. How is he today?'

'Heck, Tim!' In all the excitement, she'd forgotten to call him back. 'Right I'll call him back now, where are we all meeting?'

'Let's go to San Juan's, they've got a beautiful courtyard and roof terrace, we can have a nice view and good wine.'

'Sounds perfect to me. Shall I tell him we'll be there in 40?'

Lucy nodded her approval.

Abby quickly phoned Tim before dragging Lucy into her room, 'Right, what do you want me to wear?'

'Oooo, something sparkly and pretty.'

'OK you choose and I'll revamp my makeup.' Being careful to keep her makeup quite different to Lucy's, not wanting to take any attention from her at all tonight, Abby opted for a simple smoky eye with matching eyeliner and nude pink lips. Turning around, Lucy had selected a dark bronze knee length backless dress covered in sequins.

'You always look fabulous when you wear this,' and held it out to her.

'Alright,' Abby approved, 'nice choice.'

'Right,' said Lucy, 'I'm going to borrow your bathroom.' Abby changed into the backless dress. Tim is going to love this, she thought, checking herself out in the mirror. How had she forgotten about this little number? Good ol' Luce for remembering it. She'd worn it on a wild night out with her on a weekend trip to Valencia, so it held good memories.

Lucy emerged wearing a stunning white sequinned dress that hugged her figure apart from the cowl neck, which draped over her full cleavage. Abby literally was silenced for a moment.

'Wow, Lucy, you are literally showstopping.'

'I treated myself to this for tonight.'

'Seriously, you look red-carpet worthy. My god, I'm in love with you myself. Will is the luckiest man on the planet.'

'I can't wait to see him now and celebrate together. Are we ready?'

'Yes, I think so.'

Lucy smiled wide with her newly painted red lips.

'Brill, lots of photos tonight, please. You're in charge of the camera.'

'Ooo, is this a hint of the bossy bride you're about to become, huh?' Abby teased, wondering where the hell she'd left her phone, then pulling it out from under the clothes she'd just taken off.

'Well, lucky for you, you might not have to endure me being too bossy for too long.'

'What? Have you started to think about venues already?' The kind of places that she and Lucy had always talked about were the sort that got booked up months, sometimes years in advance.

'All will be revealed at the bar,' Lucy somehow managed to grin even more than before.

Abby spun round, 'Have you planned it already?' Abby knew she looked anguished, but she didn't care. They'd been talking about planning and doing this their whole lives.

Sensing her distress, Lucy hurried to calm her down: 'No, not planned it as such. All of the fine details need to be organised, don't worry – you'll be able to help me with that. But the venue, yes, we've got it all sorted. I can't wait to tell you.'

Abby felt mortally wounded that she didn't know. A lifetime of being the closest person to Lucy, and in one tiny month, she'd been usurped by a guy. *Good lord, this is what it's going to be like.* It was just all happening so fast.

Lucy had walked out and was chatting to Woody.

Abby felt shaky and texted Tim:

'Just about to leave – can't wait to see you.'
'Same. I've gone for smart casual is that alright?'
'Yes, we're in dresses, I'm sure you'll look fine xx'

She'd never seen Tim looking out of place once. She took a deep breath and willed her brain to process the change a little quicker.

'Photo please, ladies,' Woody called out, and she left her room.

'Woody she's booked the venue, and she's going to tell us everything at the bar – we need to there, immediately.'

'We've got time for one photo, my dear, the cab isn't even here yet,' and Woody nodded approvingly at Lucy's outfit – she really did look utterly fabulous. She seemed to have grown an extra few inches, and with the sequins, she was literally dazzling: 'I hope Will realises how fortunate he is, you are heavenly,' he said.

Lucy nodded, 'He does.'

Abby dragged her into a big hug, and they posed for a few silly pics before Woody set the timer for a group one.

'Epic shot. Epic night,' Lucy breathed.

Abby's breathing was getting quite shallow now, and she just needed to talk and let it all out, but she knew she couldn't do it now, not in front of Lucy. Watching her best friend skip down the stairs to the waiting taxi, she placed her hands on her hips for a moment.

Obviously catching her hanging her head as Lucy bounded out of the door, Woody wrapped her in a big hug. They were clearly both dealing with their own issues right now. 'Big change huh?' he said softly.

'Oh my goodness, Woody,' Abby whispered, 'I feel like I'm losing her so quickly.'

Woody hugged her tight, 'I know. Look, let's get through tonight, and we can always talk about it tomorrow. I feel like watching *The Notebook*,' he said, only half joking.

'Oh gosh, Woody. She's found her Noah.'

'I hadn't even thought of that. This is a big deal.'

When even Woody paused to reflect the gravity of her observation, Abby welled up, but determined not to ruin her makeup, she padded away the tears. What an emotional night. Her phone was pinging with a text from Lucy, 'Er, where the heck are you? I'm in the cab!'

'Crap, we've got to run, Woodster.'

'Deep breath and let's go,' she held his hand as they walked down the stairs as if holding it tightly would dispel both of their inner fears.

'Be happy for her, Abby,' she whispered. 'Come on. Buck yourself up.'

36

CHAMPAGNE PROMISES

LUCY CHATTED TO the taxi driver the whole way there, literally non-stop. It was like she'd just drunk five Red Bulls. Abby filmed her for 30 seconds, giggling at how hyped up she was. Woody remained in a thoughtful silence. At the bar, Tim was waiting with a bottle of Champagne and was chatting to Will.

'There she is,' Will said as Lucy strode in confidently in her heels walked straight to her fiancé and gave him a kiss, pressing her hands lightly on his shirt. He spun her around admiring her dress.

'Wow, I've never known anyone to dress like you. Mind you with the amount of shopping you do ...' Will pulled her in for another kiss.

Abby's eyebrow lifted, since when had Lucy shopped more than she did? Ah, since Will, of course...

Abby paused for a second, watching Tim who was shaking Woody's hand with a welcoming smile and handing him a glass whilst looking over to see where she was. He looked gorgeous with his two-day stubble. Everyone in the room must think so – it couldn't just be her. His great physique was emphasised by his dark jeans and heavy white cotton shirt, which he'd kept open at the top, and a chunky leather belt and matching brogues that completed his look. She made her way over to him and slipped her arms around his waist as he kissed the top of her head and whispered: 'What took you so long?' and placing the glasses down for a second he wrapped her into a deep kiss. 'I've been waiting to see you all day.'

He looked over at the newly engaged couple, 'Fast and furious, huh?'

Tim smiled, 'Look how happy she is; it's like she's had ten spa days and has somehow grown an inch.'

'Well, that's a woman in love for you,' Abby smiled, wondering why on earth he wasn't saying the 'L' word to her if he could see how happy being in love made people. She pushed aside a sinking feeling in the pit of her stomach. Tonight was about Lucy and Lucy's happiness alone. Withdrawing her arms from Tim, she made a beeline for Lucy and put her arms around best friend and nodded back at Tim who held up the Champagne.

'Right Missy and Mister,' quickly incorporating Will, 'It's time for a toast.'

She glanced at Woody, who had a somewhat glazed smile on his face and remained silent, staring at Will.

'To my beautiful friend. You've found a man that sees the best in you and loves you for it. May that continue to blossom on your journey together. Here's to planning an amazing wedding ... and to you, Will, congratulations on getting the most amazing woman on the planet to sparkle and be yours. Welcome to the family,' Abby almost choked. 'Raise your glasses to the newly engaged, Lucy and Will.'

Everyone clinked.

'Group hug,' Lucy yelled and everyone piled in laughing.

Abby couldn't take it any longer: 'Now you have to

tell us what you've got planned.'

Abby sat on Tim's lap. Will sat down, 'this could take a while,' he joked. Lucy remained standing to deliver her next bit of news.

'Weeell...?' said Woody and Tim, both also dying to know now as well.

Lucy's left hand glittered with her ring and she placed it on Will's shoulder, who automatically held it with his. 'We'd really love for you to join us in Singapore for our roof-top wedding at sundown, overlooking the city and bay.'

Everyone's mouths dropped opened. Abby almost screamed. 'Wow! How come Singapore?'

'Well, two reasons,' Will spoke as Lucy looked adoringly down at him. 'I know the manager there really well, and the last time I was there, I saw an event and it just looked stunning. I told Lucy she could get married wherever she wanted in the world and after looking at some images online, she fell in love with it, too, plus ... I'll let you finish, my love,' patting her hand.

'OK,' said Lucy excitedly, taking a deep breath, 'the location is perfect and fell into place because it's a stopover before our honeymoon ...' she waited as Abby let out a mini yelp of anticipation, 'in Thailand.'

'But you were thinking of going there in a month, weren't you?' exclaimed Abby, her brain whirring trying to recall the conversation that Lucy had mentioned about an IBS Clinic holiday, She'd dismissed it at the time, thinking that the plane journey and indeed the whole trip sounded like a recipe for disaster. Lucy beamed and nodded as Will tightened his hand on hers, waiting for the penny to drop.

'We're going to Singapore in a month. A month?

You're getting married in one month?' Abby leapt up, excited, her mind exploding with literally everything they would have to do in a month. She hugged them both again. 'You're getting married in a month,' moving some hair off Lucy's face.

'I know,' she bubbled. 'Will you help me organise it?'

'Of course. It's going to be amazing. I'm in shock right now, but I'll kick that into touch. Come here, you fast mover you,' Abby dragged Will into another hug. 'Oh my goodness, you two, what a night.'

Tim and Woody moved in to shake hands with Will and kiss Lucy on the cheek again.

'More Champagne!' Will said, heading to the bar.

'Ah you're going to have to take some photos now before I carry on like this and wipe all my makeup off,' Abby said dabbing at the tears around her eyes. 'Am I smudged?' she asked Lucy.

'Nope, I've never known how you do that. Although you're right, I do need pictures. Tim could you get a photo of me and my bridesmaid and bridesman, please?' She coyly turned back to Abby and Woody and laughed at the looks on their faces: 'Well, who else do I love more, huh? I need my best friends there on the day, and I'd be honoured if you were my wedding team.'

Abby squealed, 'Yes, oh my goodness. Is it just me and Woody?'

'Yes, of course.'

'Wow,' Woody looked seriously surprised and impressed.

'Well, you may have to do me the honour of giving me away if my dad won't travel,' said Lucy.

Woody stood tall and proud, 'Lucy, that's incredible. I'll do anything you want and be utterly honoured to do so.'

Tim looked at Abby surrounded by her friends and overwhelmed by all the hugs and emotion, 'Right now, get together quickly before Abby loses it and wells up again. We need some good pictures,' and they all huddled up together, fiercely tighter and prouder than ever before.

Abby smiled at Tim and they grabbed a quick selfie before munching through the smoked salmon blinis the restaurant had brought out, assuming correctly that none of the party had eaten supper and were consuming large amounts of Champagne.

After an hour of excited planning talk and many glasses of bubbly, Abby finally saw Will step away from the group. This was the opportunity she'd been waiting for. She downed the rest of her drink and placed the glass down firmly on the table.

'Right, Will, you and I need to have a little chat.'

Tim swung around; the emphasis she'd put on the 't' in 'chat' told him she intended it to be fairly one-sided. Will clutched his whisky on the rocks, ensuring it didn't overspill on her dress and obliged as she moved him across the patio.

Lucy looked concerned, 'Is everything alright Abs?'

'Yes, fine Luce, just secret wedding stuff. For Will's ears only,' Woody cocked his head up and followed them, moving the three of them out of view of the main bar where Lucy was drinking with Tim.

'Right, SssWill,' Abby hissed at him, slurring her words a tad, 'I don't know you that well. I sincerely hope in the next two weeks we can get to know each other a whole lot better because I want to trust you with my best friend.' She poked his chest with her finger. 'Ah, don't say a word because I haven't finished yet,' she kept her finger on his chest, 'Right, that woman in there is our ultimate best friend.'

'She doesn't have a big brother, but she has me,' Woody interjected, stepping up behind her.

Abby nodded, 'All of this is happening so quickly, and we want to know your intentions are good? Are you after her money? And how on earth are you planning on facing life's problems when you haven't had to deal with any situations together yet?'

Will opened his mouth to speak, but Abby hadn't finished. She poked him with her finger again with every question. 'Will you stand by her no matter what she decides? Will you support her? Will you be faithful to her?' Finally finished, Abby waited for his response.

'Can I speak now? Or is there more?' Will asked cautiously. Abby nodded. He breathed a sigh of relief.

'Look, I know this seems like a rushed affair. But I've waited all my life – and I'm 42, by the way, in case you didn't know – '

Abby and Woody looked at each other, admittedly they didn't.

'to find someone like her... wow. Lucy came along and excelled every single notion I had about marriage. I just fell in love with her, in about a week I knew I didn't want to be with anyone else. Ever. I'm very selective with my friends, I live quite a quiet existence and she makes me come alive.'

It looked the same for Lucy, Abby thought, she did seem reborn.

'And as for dealing with situations together, you've heard how we met right? Well, we can cope with that.' He grinned, 'I've already seen her looking at what she believes to be her worst and at her best, like tonight. We both feel the same, and we just want everything to be official so we can get on with starting our life together. Why wait?'

'Well I suppose when you put it like that,' Abby agreed.

Woody remained silently suspicious, so Will directed his next comment at him: 'And I do love her. I love her more every second. I know she's the best woman in the world, and I can completely see where you both are coming from, but you don't need to worry. I guess that is the only downside to everything moving so quickly; we haven't had the normal time to build relationships with each other's family and friends yet. But all of that will come in time. She talks about you all the time.'

'What is it you do?' he asked suspiciously.

'I'm a solicitor. I specialise in the sale of large corporations and companies. Mainly in the UK, but I'm starting to see more work in Asia.'

'Hence Singapore as the destination,' Woody confirmed.

'Yes, hence Singapore as the wedding destination. But I think you're going to love it.'

'I just want to know that if I'm not going to be her first port of call, then I can completely trust and love the person who is going to take my place,' Abby blurted out.

'Abby, you have nothing to worry about there. She's made it very clear that if you ever need her, no matter where we are and what we're doing, she has to leave immediately to be at your side. I've been briefed,' he smiled.

'Really? She said that?' Abby relaxed a little knowing she was still a priority.

'And as for you, Woody, well she said you were one of the best guys I could hope to meet and her big protector.'

'I will kill you if you hurt her,' Woody said, not blinking, to Will.

'I think I'd kill myself first if I ever hurt her,' Will's voice softened and lowered, 'I couldn't hurt her. I couldn't possibly.'

Woody levelled his steely gaze with Will's until they both evidently reached a silent-man-moment of understanding. Abby realised she still had her finger on Will's chest, and they had backed him to the edge of the balcony like some old school Mafia movie.

She released her finger, 'Good, well I'm glad we got that straight, Will. Now on to more happier things, have you sorted out your suit yet?' Woody rolled his eyes and turned to walk back inside.

'It's going to be hard work getting him on side, isn't it?' Will stated watching him walk away.

'Well give it time and keep making Lucy glow and I'm sure he'll calm down. Look, I'm sorry all of that came out the way it did, it's just been a big day. I would quite literally do anything for that girl in there. She is my absolute number one, so if she tells me that you're a stand-up guy and you're making her this happy then I need to get to know you pretty quickly, don't I?' Abby suddenly felt really embarrassed. Here she was judging someone who, for all intense purposes had been making her best friend ultra-happy, and she was somehow having a go at him about it.

Will relaxed his face into a big smile and said, 'Yes you do. However, I think we should make our way inside as you're cold, and they're probably wondering what's going on.'

Abby only noticed the goose bumps on her arms as she followed Will back indoors. The first thing she saw was the dual look of relief on both Tim and Lucy's faces.

Lucy turned to Tim and rubbed his arm, 'Thank you for telling me about the different types of brick needed when building a house,' before quickly scarpering into Will's embrace.

'Oh my god, don't ever do that to me again,' said Tim, pulling her close to him.

'Bricks?' Abby giggled.

'It was all I could think of when put on the spot. I knew you needed me to keep her occupied whilst you were 'talking' to Will. I saw Woody go out as well, how did it go?'

Abby put her hands on her hips and tossed her hair: 'He knows not to mess with her.'

'Ooo, you're sexy when you're feisty. Would you mind giving me that kind of treatment later? It's kind of hot.' He nuzzled his face into her neck and ran his hands over her back, enjoying the exposed skin of her dress. Abby shivered and moved in closer to him, feeling him begin to rise against her groin.

'Fuck, I want you right now,' she whispered.

'Right you two, none of that,' Woody cut in, obviously back from the men's room. Tim swivelled Abby around, partly to hide his hard on and partly to pull her arse into it.

Woody, oblivious, carried on: 'If I'm going to be surrounded by two girls and two extra guys now, the least one of you can do is be my wing-man.'

'Fair enough, Woodster, do you want me or Tim to do the opener?'

'Either, I don't care, just do it' before nodding his head to a gaggle of girls that had moved into a large space at the bar.

Tim looked confused, 'You show me how it's done,' he said to Abby, 'I'll just buy the drinks. Woodster what are you having?'

'I'll have a Jack and coke, cheers,' and Woody watched Abby as she walked over to the group of women and announced that it was her brother's birthday and would they mind ever so much giving him a kiss on the cheek? All of them glanced over and Woody raised his glass and delivered his winning smile, charismatic but emphasising his playful dimples. They waved him over and cheered. He finished his Champagne in one gulp, put the glass down and crossed paths with Abby on the way over.

'Some people are getting married. Me, why would I take myself off the market? It would cause far too much distress to these ladies ...'

Abby giggled at him before grabbing Tim at the bar. He grinned down at her. 'What are you two like?'

'We're dangerously brilliant, of course, it works every time. In about ten seconds, he's going to order a bottle of Champagne.'

Sure enough, moments later they watched Woody mouth to the waiter, 'Champagne.'

'And that's how it's done,' Abby smiled. 'Those ladies are in for a good night!' She turned back to Tim, 'As for you, you handsome man, order his Jack and coke and have it sent over,' she whispered, 'I've got plans for you at home.'

NEVER COMPARE

THE NEXT DAY at work was a daze for Abby. Slightly hungover, she tried to keep herself to herself, guzzling bottles of sparkling water while she waited for lunchtime, when she piled her plate with staff canteen beef bourguignon and chomped her way through it.

'Right, what's up?' Claire sat down opposite her, 'The bourguignon is not that good here, you'd only ever eat it out of necessity, so you're either hungover or something's bothering you.'

Not wanting to risk slipping up at work again after her 'women's problems' earlier in the year, she didn't mention the hangover. Instead, she was relieved to have a viable excuse for the beef shovelling. She shared Lucy's news with her.

'Wow, how exciting. But gosh, yes, it's all very fast,' Claire exclaimed. Abby nodded relieved to have the understanding.

'And Singapore, how expensive will that be?'

'Well, Lucy said that Will's covering it. He's booking our flights this weekend.'

'Oh my word, that's amazing. What a guy!'

'Mind you, I would have taken out a bank loan, there is no way on this planet that I'm missing that wedding.'

'Can everyone make it at such short notice? What do her parents think?'

'Well, her parents are very religious and had always planned to give her away in a church, which I think she grew up expecting, but she seems hell bent on going her own way with it.'

'Well surely, if you believe God created the whole world, surely you'd also believe he wouldn't mind where you got married on it?' Claire reasoned.

'Good point! I'll have to tell her that to say to them if needed. It's fair enough to do it her way, though. After all, it's her big day, but I know but she never wants to upset anyone, least of all her parents. It would absolutely gut her if they didn't go, just because it wasn't what they were expecting.'

'Oh well, you'll just have to be as supportive as you can. Maybe she could have a blessing in their family church when they return?'

'That's a good idea, Claire. Gosh you're full of them today,' Abby forced a smile.

'Are you sure that's all you're worried about?' Claire enquired quietly.

Abby looked away.

'Is everything alright with Tim? He obviously loves you to bits.'

Abby's head perked up at that. 'Really? How can you tell?' she demanded.

'Well, just by how he's treating you, going on everything you've told me, of course.'

'Really? You can tell by that?'

'That's what's really bothering you, isn't it?' Claire probed. 'Tim hasn't said he ...'

'Don't! Don't even say it,' Abby interjected. 'Gosh,

I know I'm pathetic, but if everything was *that* great between us, as everyone seems to think, then why hasn't he said it yet? Lucy's engaged in less time, for crying out loud!'

'Why do you need him to tell you, anyway?' Claire posed to her. 'If he's treating you beautifully, why does it matter?'

'Um, I dunno, maybe to prove that he's not just using me, to prove I mean something to him, to prove I'm special ...'

'To prove you're the one for him?'

Abby grimaced and put her head in her hands, 'Yes, to prove I'm the one for him.'

'Is he the one for you?'

'I don't know. I really think he might be, but I'm just too scared to let myself go fully and find out if he's not feeling the same way about me.'

'Love is a risk, and at some point, you're going to have to make yourself vulnerable and take that leap.'

'But he'll only catch me if he feels the same way.'

'Not necessarily, he might still catch you then set you down gently,' she winked.

'Oh great. Here's hoping for that ending!' Abby joked. 'Why do I have to leap? Leaping sucks!'

'Because half-hearted love just doesn't work, it doesn't last.'

Abby nodded.

'Look, I can't really comment as I've never met Tim, but what I do know is that you've seemed lighter and brighter since you met him, your work has excelled.'

'Thank you!' Abby raised her glass of water as a mini toast.

'And from all accounts, he's treating you really well,

in and out of the bedroom.'

'True,' Tim had slowed down on the sex so they could get to know each other properly. 'Look, I know it might seem like I'm worrying unnecessarily,' Abby said, 'but it's not just the insecurities from my screwed up head, it's also because I keep *almost* telling him. I can't wait to be able to tell him how much I love him. He's amazing and he's made my life seem somehow worthwhile.'

'Oh, Abby, I'm sure he'll tell you,' Claire clasped her hands together. 'Right, when did I tell Pete?' she mused.

Abby grinned, Claire and Pete had been childhood sweethearts, so she'd been spared all of this angst.

'That's right, outside the cinema and then we tongued for about 15 minutes, the way you do when you're 16 and crazy passionate.' She nodded to herself, 'And yes, he did tell me first.'

Claire looked up at the clock to see it was almost time to get back to the office. When she rose, she put a hand on Abby's shoulder: 'Just exercise some patience.'

'Ugh,' Abby scrunched her face in disgust. 'You know that's my least favourite word. What about asking and getting what you want?'

'Doesn't apply to emotions.'

'You sound like my mum...'

'Well you do give birth and suddenly know everything.'

'And you've got two kids.'

'Trust me, I'm a genius.'

Abby giggled as she handed her plate in before they made their way back to their desks. She felt marginally better.

*****

As much as she wanted to see Tim, she felt exhausted from the past 24 hours, so she made her excuses and fell into a long bath before throwing her pyjamas on and clambering into bed. Maybe she could just chill and watch a movie on her laptop.

'Argh, why can't I shake this feeling?' She pounded the bed. Should she just text Tim and ask him outright if he loved her? She grabbed her phone. No. She bid herself, don't wreck it by being impatient.

'Mum, can you Skype?' she texted instead.

'Hey honey, how are you doing?' Alice came online immediately and looked for her daughter in the darkened image on the Skype video.

'Oh sorry, I was in the dark.' She clicked her bedside light on, 'Mum I'm exhausted and so stressed out.'

'Are you comparing Lucy's relationship to your relationship with Tim and wondering why, if he cares about you, he hasn't moved so quickly?'

'Um. Well, yes.' Gosh she knew her well. 'I know I shouldn't because everyone's relationships are completely different, and I know that what happens for her might not be right for me, but Mum it's been over two months with Tim. We have this amazing connection and we're progressing everything a sensible way to create a good foundation for a lasting relationship, blah, blah, blah, but have we been too organised about it? In doing that, have we killed the romance?'

Alice sighed.

'Come on, Mum. Lucy can meet a guy, let herself fall in love and him with her and they're engaged after four weeks! Four weeks, Mum.'

'But you and Tim have very different pasts compared to Lucy and Will. You and Tim entered your relationship both having been utterly floored by your exes. It takes time for the heart to trust again, even if your mind is certain. You're slowly building a foundation of trust that works for the both of you. Lucy doesn't necessarily need to do that because she hasn't had the same mental and emotional battles you have.'

'Then why hasn't he told me that he loves me yet?' she asked quietly.

'Abby, from meeting Tim, I can see he's the considered type of guy that makes sure he only speaks what he knows to be solid and true. Maybe he's still getting to know and trust you and he's just making sure. Maybe he's waiting for the right time, maybe he's different to Will, maybe he thinks you might say it first?'

'All good points, I guess. I know you're right, Mum. It's not the fact that Lucy's engaged, I'm not bothered about Tim proposing so much, I'm just more concerned that he doesn't love me.'

'For goodness sake, Abby, it's easy to see the man adores you. And in most cases love – the true kind that trumps lust – takes time. You've barely been apart since you met.'

'But you don't think it's one of those blow hot and cold affairs, do you? Maybe I've seen too much of him and now he's going to get bored and dump me again.'

'Woah, woah, woah. What has brought this spiral on? You haven't said any of this to him, have you?'

'No, not yet.'

'Abby, you're just transferring all of your fears from Charlie on to Tim. You're only human to think that, but please don't compare them because they are so totally different.'

'But how do you know that? You loved Charlie until

the last six months. What happens if Tim changes?'

'For the record, I warned you about Charlie when we first met him. I asked you what he was like when he wasn't spending money on you. Abby, Tim *is* different, he's not showy with his affection, he's thoughtful and quiet and he does things just to make *you* smile. Charlie only did things for you to make *him* look good in front of other people. He's selfish. Tim is selfless. Don't forget the difference.'

For the first time all day, Abby felt her racing heart and stress levels truly begin to calm down.

'Look, if you're really that bothered, you should talk to him about it. You've got to be able to share your fears. All I ask is that you consider where these fears are really coming from first.'

'Would you speak to him if you were me?'

'No, I wouldn't. I would just enjoy that I'd met someone who treats me so well and that you care so much about. Six months ago, you couldn't have predicted this, could you? You can't hurry love, Abby.'

'Alright, Diana Ross. You've calmed me down for now.'

'Next time, I'll sing it to you...'

'Heavens above, no!' Abby exclaimed in mock horror.

'Now Abby, you need to focus on the good things in your life with Tim and Lucy. Be yourself around Tim because you don't want to act neurotically and scare him off, do you? Because that really would be awful.'

'Heck no, you're right. Thanks, Mum. I think I'll sleep now.'

'Call me again if you need me and happy wedding planning tomorrow.'

'I love you, Mum, good night.'

She was right, she didn't want to wreck a good thing by thinking about negatives that were in the past. It was paranoia not instinct in this instance for sure. She sent Tim a super positive text then rolled under the duvet and finally let herself sleep.

38

DECISIONS, DECISIONS

AFTER A MUCH better night's sleep and day at work, Abby started the post-work wedding planning session decisively: 'Right let's start by checking out this the wedding venue.'

'Will did suggest maybe we could go for a riverboat wedding in the marina but I'm not sure all of the guests' stomachs would manage that,' Lucy giggled.

'So are all of the IBS clinic members coming, too?'

'Just the ones that were there on the night we, er, met properly.'

'Brilliant,' Abby rolled her eyes. She still didn't really want to ever talk about their issues, so she skipped over it quickly. 'Well, yes, that might be a tad dodgy on a boat.'

'No, we definitely don't want any drama of that kind on the day,' agreed Lucy, her fingers flying over her iPad to bring up the Palace Dreams Hotel in Singapore.

'Wow,' Abby said, taking it in for a moment. They were staring at a skyscraper close to the waterfront. 'Grandiose doesn't come close, does it?'

'I know,' Lucy said with glee.

Abby looked at her, this was so far from her conversations with Lucy about this in the past, which always came back to the church in the village where she'd grown up as the number one choice, followed by a reception at some National Trust stately home close by. This option was way more exciting.

'So, is it all a hotel?' she asked.

'No, I think up to floor 50 is offices, the bottom has restaurants and a mall and the atrium...' Lucy brought up a picture to show the giant waterfall cascading over 50 floors down into the atrium.

'Gosh, talk about making an entrance – it's stunning.'

'So, the hotel covers the top floors and the revolving roof terrace ...'

'Well, it wouldn't be a roof terrace unless it was revolving, now, would it?'

'Exactly, and this is where we'll be taking our vows,' Lucy took the iPad back to quickly flick to the exact image she wanted.

'Eeeek, you're about to show me where you're going to get married, Luce. This is a mega moment.'

'OK, close your eyes and I'll tell you when to open them.'

'In that case, find an image showing it set up for a wedding and not just an empty space.'

Pure silence filled the room while Lucy tapped on the screen.

'Can I open my eyes yet?' Abby was itching to see it.

Lucy grinned, paused for suspense ... 'OK, now.'

Abby took in the magical rooftop terrace that pointed in a triangle to the horizon, like the front of a yacht. The building's height and clever positioning meant you couldn't see the city at all from the top, it just looked out to the bay where the sun sat low in the sky.

Abby couldn't help it, she welled up, 'Oh, Luce, it's going to be stunning. It looks like the edge of the world, where dreams take flight.'

'I know! It was when I saw this I knew it was the right decision to go to Singapore. It will be extraordinary.'

Abby and Lucy hung their heads to the right, both deep in thought imagining how it would look.

Abby snapped into gear. 'Right, so, we know they've got a gazebo ...'

'They have three to choose from, actually.'

'That floaty one might be a mission if it gets windy.'

'Maybe, although they do have automatic glass wind breakers to deal with that, you know, to keep everyone happy.'

'I'm impressed ... they've obviously thought of everything. Let's have a look at the other gazebos.'

Lucy drew her head up. 'Oh my gosh, we've been at it for two hours!'

'Blimey, let's have a break and a drink, I'll put the kettle on. We've made good progress though.'

They'd designed the themes and drawn rough sketches of where everything should go to make everything run as smoothly as possible in the space. Despite that, Lucy looked vexed.

'What's bothering you, Luce?'

'The logistics are great, but I just don't know what colours to have. I always thought I'd go for pink roses for the traditional wedding, but somehow, they just don't seem right here. It's driving me crazy because until I have the colours in my head, I can't visualise anything else.' She looked down at her ring and smiled. Abby followed her gaze.

'That's it, Luce.'

'What?'

'You've solved it,' Abby grinned. 'Your ring is stunning, let's model the colour styling on your ring.'

A slow smile grew on Lucy's face again.

'Go on ...'

'Well, I can either wear pale gold or a lilac, and the flowers can be ...'

'Ivory with maybe hints of lilac or lavender, if it's done properly?'

'Yes, let's look at that.'

'You make the tea, I'll get online.' Abby smiled. This was ace.

Abby would be wearing either a champagne or deep purple dress, the men would either have classic morning suits or whatever suit Will fancied, 'In my theme, of course,' said Lucy.

'Of course,' Abby agreed.

'Oh my gosh, I can completely see this now. And that makes the decision for my dress easier, instead of white. I'll go for ivory.'

'Gorgeous on your skin with your hair colour. I absolutely approve.'

'It would be nice to have a bit of a tan, how many days will we be out there for ahead of the guests?'

'I think it's two days before. I'm hoping that nerves will override any jet lag.'

'Gosh, I'm sure they will. Nope, not like that,' seeing Lucy's eyebrow raise. 'I meant the adrenalin will keep you going. We just need to stay hydrated and not nap on the day we arrive, go to bed at midnight and rise at 8am the next day and carry on as normal. Maybe we could have a spa session every day as well, as a treat.'

'Definitely, let's check out the treatments.'

Abby pulled her chair closer for this one.

'So are you alright choosing your own bridesmaid dress?'

'Yes, absolutely. I'll take Woody with me. He's gut wrenchingly honest and knows my style.'

'Plus, you can sort him out with his suit at the same time and tick two things off the list.'

'So romantic aren't you, Luce?'

'My spreadsheet is what's keeping me sane through this, I can't even joke about it. But I am excited to have a surprise on the day and see which dress you've chosen.'

'So I'm basically excited about ... um everything,' Abby joked. 'So are you dress shopping with your mum? Have they decided whether or not they can come yet?' Abby added softly.

'Yes, I'm dress shopping with her tomorrow, you don't mind, do you?'

'No, my lovely. You've always said that you wanted it to be just you and her, so I was expecting it, plus this way I get a beautiful surprise on your big day as well.'

'Thank you for understanding,' Lucy squeezed her hand. 'You and I do everything together, so I need to make her feel special. Gosh, I hope they can cope with the flight, I just assumed being an only child that they'd go anywhere.'

'Is it your mum?'

'Yes, she doesn't like long-haul flights.'

'Lucy, I can tell you this right now. There is no way that she's missing her daughter's wedding. I don't care how upset she is that it's not in your local church with all of her friends, she's just being mean and putting pressure on you to do what she wants.'

Lucy nodded.

'Well, this is your big day and you need to do it your way. She'll be on that flight and the proudest person in the room, or the rooftop, on the big day itself.'

'Yes, I'm trying not to worry or let her ruin my excitement in any way. I just want her to be on board with it all. The whole thing has been a shock for her.'

'Well let's see how tomorrow goes. Focus on having a good time, Champagne, cake and wedding dresses – you don't get a better day of shopping than that!'

'I can't wait. We're going to Richmond because apparently it has loads of bridal shops,' Lucy shook with glee.

'Have you made appointments for them?

'Yes, Mum did.'

'See – she's into it really. You're going to have a lovely day, Luce.'

'I'm going to try every single style on in every type of material, just to see!'

Abby laughed, 'The poor shop owners don't know what's coming, do they?'

'Well if they want me to spend thousands with them then they're going to have to work for it. But I genuinely don't know which style will suit me, modern or vintage lace.'

'Will you send me some pictures?'

'Obviously.'

And the two of them dived into a session of Googling dresses. Abby found a selection of floaty bridesmaid dresses that looked like an absolute dream. Lucy had her eye on Claire Pettibone and Jenny Packham but was keeping an open mind. At this late stage, it was more a case of what the bridal stores already had in stock and could alter.

'Right, I'd better go. I've got to go to the gym for a swim before going to Will's. Thanks for this Abby.'

'Oh are you not going to stay over?'

'Well, I've got to meet Will now.'

Abby nodded, 'Of course. You'll have loads to discuss.'

'Brill, see you soon,' and with that, Lucy flew down the stairs.

Abby's phone started to ring, she grabbed it.

'Mum!'

'Hi there, Abby! How are you?'

'Excited, I get to choose my bridesmaid dress, which is a relief, not that Lucy would ever have let me wear anything horrible.'

'Well, you never know ...'

'No, she wouldn't do that to me.'

'How is everything?'

'I don't know, it's just so not Lucy, you know? But she's so happy ...' Abby tailed off.

'Well it was always going to take a bit of adjusting to when you both met guys, wasn't it?'

'Yes, I guess so.'

'It's just odd hearing her talk about decisions she's made with Will and I haven't been part of. Six months ago, that wouldn't have happened. We used to discuss everything.'

'But it will be the same for you and Tim.'

'Yes, I know I think you're right, it's just the time to adjust. Anyway, I'm not sad in the slightest, just noting the change.'

'Good to hear.'

'So, I've found some bridesmaid dresses that I like.'

'Oh how exciting!'

'I'm going to get Woody to meet me tomorrow and try some on ...'

'And how is Woody?' Alice enquired.

'He's fine. Why wouldn't he be?'

'No reason, just glad to hear it.'

Abby chatted to her mum, whizzing over images of different dresses. Trying to narrow them down was hard, but it would be easier with someone else standing right there. Tomorrow would be fun with Woody at her side.

39

WOODY'S HEART

'WOODSTER, I'M HOME are you here?' Abby yelled. She was really annoyed: he hadn't shown up in Bond Street and she'd waited around for an hour, not really wanting to try anything on without his instant gut reaction.

'Where were you today? You could have called.' She yelled up to his room. But silence met her. She yawned. It had been yet another long day, and she hadn't seen Tim since the night of the engagement party and was missing him like crazy, but he was tied up at a work function, so it would have to be tomorrow. She paused on her way to the kitchen, hearing a muffled sound in Woody's room. He must have met a girl and dropped their plans. Not cool.

Sticking the kettle on, she leant on the kitchen worktop and flicked through the post Woody had placed on the side from earlier. All bills.

'Ugh, no mail is exciting once you move out from home,' she mused.

'ABBY!'

She jumped out of her skin at the sound of Woody yelling her name.

'What on earth is going on?' she exclaimed turning around to see Woody standing on the mezzanine leaning over the banister staring at her. 'Oh my goodness, Woody, what's happened?' Shocked at the sight of him, he looked completely dishevelled and red faced. His hands were clenching the banister as if to stop them from shaking. She ran quickly up the stairs to him. He turned to her, looking almost haunted.

'I've been calling you since you came in and you didn't come.'

'Woody, I'm so sorry I didn't hear you. What's happened? Are you sick?'

'No, sick would be easy,' he said, shaking his head.

'Well, what ...' Abby cocked her head to one side, what was that she'd just heard? She knew that sound anywhere. *The Notebook* was playing in Woody's room. She raised her eyebrow at Woody.

'You didn't.'

'I've been at home all day, and I've watched it three times,' he choked. 'It gets worse every time. Every time I watch it, I wonder if I found my Ally and she got away. I can't seem to turn it off, help me.' He was sobbing now. Abby got exactly what he was saying.

'Woody, come here,' she said drawing him into a big hug.

'I love Lucy. I should have told her ages ago, but I never thought ...' he breathed through his sobs. 'I never thought ...'

'I know,' she said soothingly holding him tightly. 'If it makes you feel any better, I didn't see this coming for a second, either. We're going to talk this out, and we're not going to stop until you feel better. But one thing I definitely *do* know is that you can't watch this film on your own. Come on, press pause, let me jump in my PJs, I'll order us the works from ...'

'Dominos, please,' Woody suggested.

Abby studied him. He held himself so confidently around women, and he had every reason to, he had a loyal heart of gold, great prospects, well educated, was brilliant at what he did and yet he was used to being in control. So feeling any less than his normal level of confidence must really be shaking him. It had clearly taken a lot for him to admit what he'd just said to her.

'Shit, Luce,' she whispered, 'do you have any idea what an emotional spin you've put your friends in?' She had no idea whether Woody was actually in love with Lucy or whether he was panicking that she may have turned into the one that got away, but either way it was a horrid state to be in, especially when so unexpected.

'Right,' she said curling up on his duvet five minutes later, 'I've briefed Dominoes to be as quick as possible, and I thought we'd wash it down with this bottle of Haut Médoc.'

'Don't spill any of that on my sheets. They're Egyptian Cotton, 800 thread count.'

Abby rolled her eyes, 'Well now you're making me nervous I'll probably slip on your ultra-smooth sheets and spill it now, won't I?'

'I'll take comfort in the fact you're unlikely to waste alcohol,' he retorted.

She nodded – it was true.

'I dunno, Abs, I've always been happy with just dating and going from one calamity to another. Especially after Delilah.'

Delilah had been before Abby's time, but they had been together for four years and she had utterly broken his heart when she turned down his proposal. That's when he'd needed a housemate and she'd moved in.

'I guess it's just that lately... well I feel like my lethal sidekicks have deserted me and I actually feel quite ...'

'Alone?' Abby nodded, acutely aware of the feeling of desertion. It was sickening. 'My gosh Woody, I'm so sorry, after all, you've been there for me, no matter what. The last thing I ever want you to feel is alone.'

'Don't get me wrong,' Woody quickly interjected, 'I'm so glad you're happy, I never want to see you the way you were after Charlie ever again.'

'All the same, I hereby promise to go out with you at least one day every week, I should never have let that slip.'

'But it's more than that, Abby, I don't just want to go to random bars and keep having the exact same conversations with different women. Seeing how Tim treats you and how you love him back, well it kinda makes me want to get squishy with someone.'

Abby melted, 'Aw Woody, well now you know you're ready to feel that again, you'll let yourself open up to someone a bit more.'

'So, do you think I need to go speed dating and do the list?'

'Um, not necessarily that just yet, maybe start by treating the women you naturally talk to as if they might be here for a little longer than a week.'

'I can do that,' Woody nodded thoughtfully.

'And here's the big one,' Abby grinned, she couldn't help herself. 'To find someone special, someone you can talk to a lot, you need to not sleep with them on the first date.'

'Why?'

'Because instead of sex, you'll be talking.'

'Does it really make that much of a difference?'

Abby laughed out loud. This was classic.

'Yes, it does make a difference because then you'll be finding out if she really gets you, up here,' Abby tapped her head. 'Trust me, when you have that mental connection, the sex is so much better. It goes up quite a few notches.'

'Is that what you and Tim did? And you don't need to go into your usual levels of detail about my cousin, thank you.'

'Yes, that's what we did. And it's been incredible. Yes, I know him, and he knows me, but I trust him implicitly now to tell me the truth.'

'OK,' Woody nodded, 'I think I get it. I might go out for a beer with Tim soon as well.'

'Yes, and if I'm not here for whatever reason, and you freak out again, just call my mum. You know she loves you.'

'God bless Alice!' and he raised his glass.

Woody looked thoughtful, 'Do you think I love Lucy, then?'

Abby also paused, acutely aware of how her words could potentially affect both her two friends' futures.

'I think that you love Lucy in the best way possible: for what she represents. She represents everything good in the world. She's kind, she's selfless, she's funny, she's intelligent and, to top it off, she's stunning. She's shown you you're ready to love again, be it with the next girl you meet or the 15th.' Abby paused again, giving him a chance to take it all in. 'Would it have worked with Lucy if you'd have given it a go? Who can tell; you wouldn't have realised what you know now without her relationship with Will, so chances are that you'd have acted in the same way that you always do. It wouldn't have worked, and you might have ended a perfectly good friendship.'

'But now I've realised, should I tell her?'

'Woody, it's not just up to you in a relationship. Lucy hasn't flirted with you to give you any hope, has she?' Abby crossed her fingers, sure this was the case, but, thinking about it, the two of them did have quite a bit of flirty banter going back and forth. She pushed it out of her mind. 'Whatever happens now, you need to realise you don't have an option. If you love her, which I think you do, you'll support her decision and continue to be her friend and protector.'

'But what happens if she's the one?'

'But what happens if you're just doing what I did and attaching feelings to someone who's unattainable so you know deep down it's never going to happen to protect yourself from actually having to gamble your heart on something real?'

'What?'

'It's easy to say that you love Lucy the moment you know you can't have her. Doing that means you avoided taking a risk with your heart, and it's easier to stay miserable, lamenting, rather than plucking up the courage to go out, make yourself vulnerable and potentially risk getting hurt by someone else.'

Woody pondered her point, 'Oh, that sounds quite true actually ...'

'Look, instead of focusing on someone you can't be with, why not look for someone you *can* be with and, remember, just don't sleep with them straight away.'

Woody wrinkled his forehead at this new tactic. 'What just go down on them?'

Abby laughed, he was comparing it to her and Lucy's old BJ before sex rule. 'Just go out, flirt, get to know them, chat. Talk.'

'How did Tim do it? Come on, you can elaborate a little bit.'

'He drove me crazy, well actually we drove each other crazy because we just wanted to get to know each other more and more. Restaurants, bars, walking in the park, cinema, markets, do anything but just wait a bit before jumping into bed and see what the girl is like outside of the sheets.'

'Mmmm, I'm going to need to mull that one over.'

'I'm here and I can always help you devise dates and strategies that will get her begging for you to sleep with her and if you like her personality, you will.'

'She can still be hot right?'

'Yes, of course! I don't mean you don't fancy them, you just have to consider their personality as well.'

'Interesting.'

Woody was obviously over his intense state she'd seen when she got home, thank goodness.

'You liked Sofia, didn't you?'

'Yes, but that was bizarre.'

'Bizarre! You had me bottling sweat for you. That's bizarre. I deserve a medal for that.'

Woody grinned.

'What really made you finally realise you didn't want to be with the armpit sniffer of the south again?'

'I became dangerously dehydrated and lightheaded due to a lack of salt.' Woody replied so solemnly that Abby laughed even harder.

'She was bad for your health. I did enjoy the flat being so warm for a certain amount of time though ...'

'Oh gosh, yeah, I meant to mention, the heating bill came in.'

Abby raised her eyebrow.

'OK, I've got this one.'

'Yes, you have,' digging his ribs with her elbow, thinking it would be wise not to ask exactly how much it was right now.

'So, are you and Tim good?'

Abby nodded and smiled. Should she tell him he hadn't said "I love you" yet, and it was driving her crazy? No, she decided, Woody had enough to deal with.

'Honestly, the thought of not being with him makes me shudder. You should've introduced us years ago and saved us the heartache.'

'Ah yes, but would you have appreciated each other though?' said Woody

'Good point.'

'Maybe the point of all of this heartache is to make The One seem all the more special?'

'I'd buy that,' Abby agreed, 'it's got to be good for something. It stands to reason that you just have to work hard and not to let paranoia from your past overshadow a relationship with a new person.' Knowing Woody's past, she knew he would be able to identify with that.

'I really mean that, Woody, I know it's tough, I have to continually remind myself that Tim doesn't mean what Charlie meant when he does certain things. And he doesn't, he really doesn't. That's where the whole no sex rule and getting to know a person really works because then you can trust them. I know now when a negative thought comes into my mind about love that I need to ask myself: is it my paranoia from Charlie or is this how Tim intended me to feel? More often than not, it's an issue from Charlie, so I let it slide because it's not relevant.' Shit she needed to take her own advice and not be paranoid about Tim not saying the 'L' word yet. Instead of being paranoid, she needed to be patient.

'Last chicken dipper?' Woody asked.

'You have it.' Knowing that was the signal for the deep chat to be over. 'Blimey, it's 1am, are you going to be alright, Mr Woods?'

'Yes, Miss AbFab, I'm good. I'm going to sleep and contemplate the idea of talking more to women. You're a weird breed and I'm going to have to figure out what else I can possibly say before sex.'

'God help us all,' she said seriously. 'On that note, goodnight. And I'm taking this DVD with me, I don't want you to catch any more feelings. You've got enough to be dealing with right now.'

'Night, Abby. Sweet dreams.'

Mocking how dramatically he'd taken the DVD out of the player to get it away from her earlier in the year, she grimaced and held it far away from her, grinned and went downstairs. She made a mental note to keep her promise to Woody and spend more time in the flat and hanging out with him, especially in the lead up to the wedding.

40

HOW MANY BASIL?

HEATHROW AT 4AM was surprisingly busy. Abby's spirits were high despite having risen at 1am after only three hours of sleep to check-in with plenty of time because there was an issue with the luggage – well, one piece of it. Lucy was determined to take her dress as carry on.

After granting Lucy anything she had wanted in the short build up to the big day, Abby had finally witnessed Will's eyebrow raise for the first time amidst all of the chaos when Lucy had asked him to book an extra seat for it.

'I can't check it in, Will. What if it gets lost or damaged? I'll just worry for the whole flight until I get it back in my hands again. I don't want to start our married journey together consumed with worry. I don't like myself like this ...,' Lucy was almost hyperventilating.

Abby watched as Will picked up her hand and kissed it, 'I'm so sorry I didn't realise how worried you were about this. Look, you go through with the others, I'll stay here and, one way or another, your dress will be with us on the plane us. They won't be check it in, I promise.'

Abby mouthed 'phew' to Tim, and they both remained silent, smiling politely at the immaculately dressed check-in clerk as Lucy refused to move and explained twice that she'd wrapped the dress in three waterproof bags.

'Let me see what I can do for you, madam. Believe me I understand the importance of the package. There might be a spare seat we could use. However, we won't know until we close the desk, I'm afraid. Let me see what I can do though.'

Team Wedding held its collective breath as the clerk tapped away on her machine.

'Breathe, Luce,' Abby whispered.

'Oh please,' Lucy dug her elbow into her chest, Abby grimaced. Thank god this process had only been one month – her patience couldn't have stood a much longer engagement.

'Good news,' the woman smiled, 'there's potential for it on this flight, but one of you will need to remain here with the dress until we close check-in as it will need to go through security.'

Lucy looked panicked, 'But I need to buy my makeup before I fly.'

'I'll stay here with it, Luce,' Will spoke up.

'But what if it needs to be checked at security? You'll see the dress! You're not allowed to see it,' the lack of control was finally getting to Lucy.

'I promise you, if that happens, I'll look the other way.'

Abby refrained from joking that she'd better get the class-A drugs out of the seams as Lucy looked like she was borderline psychotic.

Lucy flung her arms around Will, 'I could cry, I've been so worried. Thank you,' and she saw Abby.

'Sorry, Abs. I know you must think I'm such an idiot, but it's been the one thing stressing me out for weeks.'

'Best to get the bride-to-be distracted, me thinks,' Will

looked at Abby as a cue to help keep her calm.

'Yes, on to the shopping.' Thanking the lady and after Lucy giving Will the millionth kiss, Abby sped her best friend off in the opposite direction to get her away from the busy-ness of her family and friends all checking in.

'I need coffee and breakfast,' Abby moaned to Tim. He had been strangely quiet but it was only four in the morning.

Lucy grabbed Abby and, apologising to Tim, dragged her to the front of the security queue, 'Sorry Tim but we've got a list of shopping to do here.'

Abby groaned as Lucy gave her a printed list, 'Please can I have a coffee first?'

'Nope,' Lucy said, 'afterwards.' They piled through security and Abby read down the list.

'OK, there's not that much on here,' she couldn't see why Lucy was stressing out. On reflection, maybe that's what being a bridezilla meant, taking a normally fun procedure and making it stressful. L'Occitane hand cream, Chanel nail varnish in a pale pink and a YSL skin primer. She whizzed around and met Lucy by the till who was checking off all of her items.

'All good?' she enquired as Lucy double checked her list. Not a sound returned – it was a serious moment. Abby knew better than to roll her eyes, doing so could spark a war. Instead she wondered where Tim was. She scanned departures for him, but when Lucy smiled, Abby looked back at her fondly.

'I'm back in the room.'

Abby raised her eyebrows. So, she did know how neurotic she'd been. Still, bridezilla back to loveable Lucy worked for her: 'Yay! She's back,' Abby exclaimed, truly grateful. 'Can we have breakfast next? I'm starving.

I can't believe how much I've done without a coffee.'

There was still no sign of Tim either.

Lucy was joking around with the cashier, 'Phew, I don't know how brides handle this stress over a year. Just a month of one critical decision making after another has been enough for me...' Lucy prattled on until Abby finally spotted Tim looking rather pale in the pharmacy. By the time she'd paid for the makeup bits, he'd clocked her and was waiting.

'Coffee now?' she said. Tim steered her away before Lucy could resist.

Abby looked at him, 'Tim, what is it? What's wrong?' She was impressing herself with her new-found levels of patience on zero caffeine.

'Abby, I've got something to tell you.'

'Can you tell me in line for Pret?' she asked hopefully. Tim looked away. Nope, this must be important. She grabbed his arm and smiled, 'Sorry Tim I was joking; I didn't realise you were this serious. Of course, tell me anything.'

His breathing was quite heavy now and he looked down at her, 'I don't want you to judge me.'

Abby told herself to be patient even though every impatient bone in her body wanted to scream 'just spit it out so I can eat breakfast.'

'I'm afraid of flying.'

Abby was far too close to blurting out 'Is that it?' but just managed to catch herself. Be nice and empathetic, not everyone is like you. She wasn't in the least bit afraid of flying, quite the opposite, in fact. She marvelled at the physics that got planes into the air, she loved getting the in-flight meals and pulling the lids off each dinky pot and don't get her started on the mini TV screens with

160 movies ...

'So, what would you normally do to make yourself feel better?'

'Well, that's the problem,' Tim was distraught, 'my normal sleeping pills for flying were out of date, I only realised last night when I was packing and didn't have time to replace them. The pharmacy has run out, so I've bought the next best thing, which is a herbal sleep fix. But what if they don't work?' Like Lucy before over the dress, Tim was now working himself up into a frenzy.

'Fear is a state of mind. Just calm down.' Tim looked like he was going to explode in front of her. She spoke quickly before he could, 'OK, never in the history of me being told to calm down have I ever actually calmed down. It's early and that was the wrong thing to say,' Abby admitted immediately.

Tim nodded, incredulous.

'I'm sorry, Tim, let's think about this logically. What is it specifically that you hate?'

'I just hate take off, and any turbulence makes me want to scream. It's an absolute nightmare. Why do you think I like Europe so much? I can get there by ferry or train. I was just really trying for you, Abby. I didn't want to look like an idiot.'

Her need for a caffeine hit evaporated, 'Hey, come here,' she said, drawing him into a hug, 'You couldn't look like an idiot to me if you tried. I can't bear the thought of you not being happy. Let's go for breakfast and we can plan a list of distractions, kissing me might help to take your mind off any turbulence for starters.' And Tim finally managed a smile.

They grabbed a few bits and met Lucy in the line, then, finally, after sipping her brew and savouring every bite of her almond croissant, Abby felt a whole lot more alive.

'Oh good, so you've clicked into gear now I see,' Lucy registered.

'Well, there's no point clicking into gear if you can't start the car. I needed fuel,' Abby retorted. 'Besides which, I've done everything you asked for.' She was fiercely indignant.

'I know, chill out!'

Gosh all of these flying and wedding nerves were contagious, Abby thought. She heard a cough behind her and saw Lucy's face light up.

'Can my flying companion and I join you for a coffee?' Will said holding up Lucy's dress. Lucy squealed and kissed him. 'You're amazing! Thank you!'

'It's in economy,' Will said. Lucy looked instantly distressed, 'but next to Hilary,' Will hurriedly added, 'not next to a stranger.'

'Yeah, it's not like your dress was going to get first class was it,' Abby jibed.

'Well, they might have upgraded it,' Lucy joked. Will's eyebrow rose again, and again Lucy was oblivious.

After another coffee, they headed to the pre-flight lounge. Abby scanned the room; the wedding party was gradually getting acquainted. But where were Lucy's parents? She needed to say hello. She looked around, but they were deep in conversation with another group so she thought it best not to interrupt. Abby realised she hadn't seen Woody either since they'd arrived at the airport, but looking over at him now, he seemed fine. It looked as if he was bonding with Will's mates. That was a good sign. She felt herself finally relax.

She beamed at Tim, 'This is a once in a lifetime flight, isn't it?' Tim paled instantly 'No! Not because we're going to die!' she added hurriedly, 'Because it's for two people we love. We need a wedding group hug.' She called out. Whooping and hollering, everyone squashed Will and Lucy in the middle. Tim then pulled away to stand by the floor to ceiling windows overlooking their aircraft.

Abby joined him, 'I'm sure they're doing everything they need to be doing.' Tim nodded but didn't take his eyes off the plane outside.

She held his hand, 'Listen to me, Tim, however you're feeling right now, I want you to focus on the fact that six months ago, we hadn't even met and now look at us, we're taking our first trip away together. This is exciting.'

Tim turned a whiter shade of pale. Staying silent he continued to watch the workers busying themselves. Abby nodded her head and went and took a seat.

Lucy had obviously seen the exchange because she plonked herself next to her: 'Are you OK, Abfab?'

Abby whispered, 'He's afraid of flying.'

'Oh, is that all?'

'Well, I have to admit I thought this would be a bit more romantic than it is,' Abby's vision of them running around duty-free buying Champagne and kissing excitedly was clearly not going to happen and more likely the stuff of movies. Gosh real life could be a let-down.

Lucy took her hands and said firmly. 'He's scared of flying, and it's 4am ... give him a break!'

'Can I remind you of that?' Abby said playfully. Lucy pretended not to hear her.

'Just let him have some time with his thoughts and he'll come back over and be himself. The more you fuss, the more you'll make an issue out of it and the more frustrated he'll be instead of being calm.'

Abby breathed, 'OK. Men huh?! Shouldn't *he* be the

one making sure that I'm not scared?'

'Well, their vulnerable sides can be quite cute, just look at him now,' Lucy giggled.

'Oh my word!'

Tim had pressed his face and body up against the glass and was star fishing his arms out to each side.

Abby snorted, 'I need a photo of that, that's too hilarious for words,' She grabbed her phone.

'You can't take a ....' Lucy chastised her, 'Nope, you're doing it anyway.'

'Lucy it will be good for bribery one day,' Abby checked the photo then looked at him again, 'I wonder if he does this every time he flies.'

'You've got yourself a thinker there, girl.'

Abby grinned at her, 'Love you, Luce. So ... we're flying off to get you good and married.'

'AAAARGH' Lucy stood up and screamed with all her lungs in excitement. The whole lounge looked round in shock.

Tim threw himself to the ground in terror as if he was in mortal danger. His eyes were wild, looking around him. His reverie was well and truly broken.

'Sorry everyone, I'm just really, really excited and it came out,' Lucy said. Everyone but Tim smiled back at her. Shaking like a leaf, he looked totally traumatised as he dusted himself off.

'You go and talk to him,' Abby nudged Lucy. 'Come on, I've heard it's a bridal duty to your bridesmaid.'

Whatever Lucy said got Tim smiling again. She turned and winked back at her as she walked to Will. Tim's eyes flickered over the plane one last time, before he beamed and joined Abby.

'What's up with you and that amazing smile?' she said.

He bent down picked her up, placed her on his lap and kissed her, blissfully unaware of everyone's eyes on them.

'My goodness me, Tim you're going to drive me insane. Where did that come from?'

'We're going on holiday.'

'Yes, we are,' Abby said 'I'm glad you've noticed.'

'No more work and lots of sex in a hot country with a fit chick.'

'Fit chick?' Abby mocked 'since when are you calling me that, hey?' pinching him.

Tim breathed out hard. 'Well it's worth the flight...'

'Call me what you like if that does the trick...'

He nuzzled her neck and Abby felt her body respond. He could turn her on within seconds, it was borderline embarrassing.

'Do you know how hard I'm going to fuck you when we land?' she whispered in his ear, playing him right back and feeling him harden beneath her.

They hadn't had sex last night as they were too busy packing and organising. She just let the closeness of her body press against his as they breathed in each other's scent.

'I'm not sure I can wait that long,' he muttered. 'God, you're beautiful.'

Abby whispered: 'What the heck did Lucy say to you?' her hands were in his hair.

'Oh, I couldn't possibly tell you,' he looked very proud to have shared a secret with her best friend.

'What?' Abby looked back in mock horror, 'You can't have a secret with my best friend! Let me go and talk to her.'

'No chance,' holding her back, laughing and tickling her. She tried her best to get it out of him but he managed to hold his own until the flight attendant announced boarding was open. Hopping off in excitement, Abby grabbed her bag. Woody shook his head in mock disapproval.

'Sorry man,' Tim muttered.

'I just hope we're not sitting next to each other. And if we are, I'm swapping seats.' Woody muttered.

Tim changed the subject: 'What are Wills' mates like?'

'They're alright, thank god.'

'Yeah, good,' Tim agreed. They had a lads night planned, so knowing the other guys seemed cool to party with was a relief. 'Right, if we're about to board, I'm off to the bathroom to take my pills.'

'See you on board,' Woody said and moved to chat with Will.

Abby looked up to see Lucy chatting with some of the girls from the IBS clinic. Hilary was in full swing: 'Now just remember ladies, the vital points we discussed on how to survive a plane flight with IBS. What is the overall golden rule?'

'If you need the loo, go immediately in case there's a long queue. Don't leave it until the last minute,' her group chanted back to her.

'Duh, obviously,' Abby whispered to no one in particular but got an instant frown from Lucy, 'Well, surely that's a "golden rule" for life.' Lucy pretended not to hear her.

Hilary continued: 'Stay hydrated, we've all got our water bottles to be refilled, haven't we?' And finally and crucially, eat everything but the egg for breakfast.'

Dodgy stomachs could be brought on by eating anything on board a non privately chartered flight Abby thought, should she suggest that with a bit of salt the eggs could be alright? No, once again it was easier to remain silent in front of the ladies that had her down as a quiet type anyway.

As they all clapped and did a final roll call, Abby pulled Lucy to one side, 'Luce, I still haven't told Tim about the IBS clinic, do you remember asking me not too?'

Lucy looked shocked, 'Wow, I didn't actually think you'd be able to keep that a secret.'

'Of course I can. I hide all of the important stuff.'

'Well, of course you can tell him. He might already know from Will.'

'Really? You reckon guys talk about that stuff? I think he would have mentioned it to me, unless he was being polite to you, of course, no offence.'

'None taken,' Lucy replied through slightly gritted teeth.

'OK, well I'll find a way of working it in to the conversation.'

Lucy raised her eyebrows, 'Good luck with that. Oooo, we're boarding...'

Will gestured for her. He'd bought seats in first class for Tim, Abby and Woody as well as his best friends, Luke and Davenport. Lucy spun back to Abby, who was looking for Tim.

'Where's Tim gone?'

'He went to take his pills, but that was ages ago.'

'Oh no, you don't think he's done a runner do you?'

Lucy looked perplexed. Will was gesturing wildly at her to join him.

'Luce, you get yourself and the dress on the plane and I'll find Tim,' Abby said.

'See you on there.'

She suddenly felt nervous, Tim wouldn't have bottled it, would he? She walked towards the bathroom and as she peered around the doorway he walked out looking as though he was finding it hard to co-ordinate his feet. Scraping his hair to one side, he was in a complete daze.

'ABBY!' He yelled at the top of his lungs. Everyone looked, he grinned. She walked quickly over to him.

'Tim, are you alright?'

'Yep,' he staggered. 'Just took my pills is all.'

'What the …?'

Tim studied the wall, leant on it carefully, then pushed himself off as if it was a game. He laughed loudly.

'Do your pills normally make you like this?'

'Like what?' Before tickling her and almost falling over in the process. The flight attendant looked over disapprovingly at the commotion.

'Seriously, Tim, snap out of it. She's going to think you're drunk.'

'I'm not drunk. You are.'

'Oh god. Do you know what … Oh sod it, just follow my lead.' She wrapped her arm around Tim's waist, trying to wedge him fully upright against her as she smiled at the flight attendant.

'Is everything alright, ma'am?'

'I'm fine, thank you very much, pretty lady, for asking. Jus' had me a tablet to get me on the plane,' Tim confidently answered before she could get a word in.

'Nervous flyer,' Abby mouthed and pointed subtly.

'OK, madam, well here you go,' she handed Abby back their boarding passes and passports and studied Tim, who was welded to the spot, staring out of the window at the plane.

'We're going on a plane!' he exclaimed and pointed, before making a large nosedive and crashing noise. Abby pinched him.

'Ow,' he yelled, 'that really hurt. You're mean.'

She smiled as sweetly as she possibly could and shunted Tim down the ramp.

'Tim, you're cute, but if you mess this up, I will kill you.'

'You're mean. I say it cos it's true. You're very pretty, though. It's confusing.'

Abby giggled, grappling her phone out of her bag to film this. His steps were like a four-year-old's, plodding and stumbling.

'Tim, how many pills did you take?'

'I think - six.'

'Six?' She looked at him in horror.

'Or maybe eight,' he started counting on his hands and lost track.

'Eight? Shit, Tim you could overdose. What were you thinking?'

'They're herbs.'

'They're not herbs.'

'They're herbs.'

'Tim, they're not herbs.'

'They're herbs that make you sleep. I've had six. I remember now. I've basically eaten a load of basil and now I'm going to get on a plane. How stupid is that?' He started to giggle.

'Well, when you put it that way ...'

'Did you eat basil, too?' He smacked his forehead and blinked before being distracted by the couple in front.

'You, sir,' Tim yelled, making the man in front jump out of his skin.

'Have you eaten any basil before this flight?'

'Er, no.'

'Well, I have,' Tim said very proudly. 'I have had more basil than I've had in a while. I've had six.'

'That's nice, dear,' the man's companion patted Tim's arm.

Abby closed her eyes appreciatively and pretended that, yes, Tim was in fact a little bit special.

'Wait, I've forgotten my helmet. Do I need a helmet?' Tim yelled to the flight attendant as they stepped on board.

'Not in first class sir.'

He nodded, that seemed to make sense.

'Hope you've got your helmets back there, then,' and guffawed at the rows of people in economy before making nosedive and crashing noises again.

Abby was mortified. Blushing, she kicked him in his leg.

'Oooo. You again!' He looked down at her, 'Are you following me, you meany?'

'I'm with you, you pillock, now sit down and let me strap you in.'

He looked fearful as she said it but followed her instructions. 'You're bossy,' he said before kicking the seat in front of him and laughing. Lucy turned around.

'I'm so sorry,' Abby whispered, 'he's high on those herbal tablets. He took six or eight apparently.'

'Six?' Lucy mouthed back and nudged Will to look back at Tim. They both chuckled. 'Good luck!'

'Hello,' Tim beamed at them, 'I'm stuck in here and she just kicked me. But anyway, we're nearly off,' and started making train noises.

'No, we're on a plane,' Will said, unaware of Tim's nerves.

'Lucy,' Abby hissed, 'fill him in.' She turned back to Tim, 'He's joking, Tim, we're on the best train ever.'

Tim nodded, 'Thought so. It *is* the best train ever. So

I don't need a helmet?'

'No, Tim, you don't need a helmet.'

Tim nodded again before sighing and placing his forehead on the window, slumping against it drooling. 'Basil,' he whispered.

Abby breathed a sigh of relief and placed a tissue under his chin. Will captured the moment with a quick photo. 'Oh my god,' she mouthed to Lucy who was in stitches. 'I didn't think they were going to allow him on the plane.' Why oh why was nothing in life like she imagined it. Ever.

41

CLENCH AND HOLD ON

CRUISING AT 36,000 feet, Lucy cupped her hand over her mouth as she finished eating and gasped.

'Oh no.'

'What?'

'I've eaten the egg.'

Abby blinked.

'Hilary specifically told us *not* to eat the egg.'

Abby laughed 'I'm sure it's fine.'

'Abby ...'

'Lucy, it's never given you a problem before has it?' Abby cut in, trying to prevent a full-scale panic from sensitive Lucy.

'Not overly, but then Hilary did say ...'

'Well then don't worry, sometimes that poo-lady ...'

'... Hilary'

'Hilary, sorry, can be a bit over the top.'

'Mmmmm,' Lucy was pondering her words.

'Look, Luce, maybe the one technique you haven't tried is the mind over matter one. If you normally eat the egg and are fine, then you're just overthinking and making things worse than they are. If poo lady, sorry, Hilary hadn't mentioned "steer clear of the eggs"' said Abby, in her best matron-mocking voice, 'you wouldn't have thought twice about it and you wouldn't be having this problem now. Come on, think with me.'

'Can I hum?' Lucy asked.

'Well, yes, if that helps.'

Lucy began to hum to herself whilst tapping her fingers. It began to get louder and louder.

'Lucy, we are on a plane, though,' Abby said, nodding at Tim. 'Don't wake him up! Mind you, he's high on basil apparently.' Tim's head was bobbing around with his mouth partly open. 'I've just eaten his breakfast. You snooze, you lose pal,' Lucy giggled but looked at Tim's empty tray in horror.

'Oh my goodness, we had orange juice as well, it's all going to mix, and it's so acidic.'

'Look, it's going to mix with whatever the juice is that you produce when you stress out *unnecessarily*.'

Lucy began to pant like she was giving birth. Abby's patience ran out.

'Lucy, you have eaten an egg, you are in first class, now get a grip.'

'Oh Abby, will you shut up, you've never taken my IBS seriously. Now stop talking crap to me about how to think. The food isn't in my mind, it's in my stomach and I'm going to kill you in a minute. I'm a sleep deprived bride-to-be, so don't push it.'

Abby held her hands up at Lucy's tirade, adamant she was right, and they all made too much of a fuss. 'Will's eaten an egg, too. Are you going to wake him up and make him panic unnecessarily?'

'Maybe, we are sitting in front *and* upwind of you. Think about that.'

Abby grimaced and stopped in her tracks. She heard Lucy's stomach turn. It made a noise like cake mix falling from one side of the bowl to the other.

'Oh no,' Lucy groaned.

'Well, in that case, you'd better remember what poo-on-the-brain lady Hilary said before we got on the plane,' Abby paused.

'Well? Don't stop! I only really listened to the egg bit. What else did she say?' Lucy hissed through clenched teeth.

'She said that if you need the loo, go immediately before there's a massive queue.'

'What?' Lucy looked harried, 'Why didn't you tell me before? Oh my goodness,' and as she moved to take her seatbelt off, her stomach rolled again. The plane started to shudder, so she had to grapple and hold on to the headrest tightly to get past her sleeping fiancé. 'Oh my god I need to clench my ass already, this is bad,' she said almost hopping on the spot to get past him. 'I've never seen him sleep like this.'

Abby couldn't even hide her smile, 'Do you think he's faking it? Lucy, you look so stressed. Calm down, I'm sure getting this het up doesn't help.'

'You'd be getting het up if you thought you might shit yourself in first class. Jeez.' Lucy finally manoeuvred herself into the aisle. 'I thought first class was meant to be less complicated.'

Abby looked towards the loo, 'Ah, for once there's no-one in the queue. Quick, go and sort yourself out while you can.'

But as she turned towards the toilet, the flight attendant approached Lucy, 'Madam, could you please return to your seat? We're experiencing a bit of turbulence, which might get worse and the pilot will put on the fasten your seat belt sign.'

'But it isn't on just yet, is it? And believe me, I will be quick' Lucy smiled courteously and with as much stature as she could muster, squeezed past and ran up the aisle and into the loo, clicking the lock just as the order came from the pilot warning them of turbulence and to make sure their seatbelts were fastened.

This was way better than watching a movie, Abby thought. Lucy was always one to follow orders to the letter, what would she do? Right on cue, Lucy poked her head out of the toilet door and mouthed: 'What should I do?'

'Go to the loo,' Abby mouthed back.

Lucy's stomach must have turned again as she let go of the door to grasp it. Going pale, she slammed the door. Just as she did, a bash of turbulence rattled the plane violently.

'Gosh that was a bad one,' Abby thought, clutching the armrest. The shaking continued, Will's head jerked forward, awakening with a start. After looking directly at Lucy's seat, he spun around, 'Abby, where's Lucy?'

'She had to run to the toilet. I'm sure she's fine.'

'Do they let people in the toilets when there's turbulence?' and as Abby was waiting to respond, he glanced at the demolished breakfast tray and clocked the egg was also missing. 'Oh no, was it critical?'

Abby nodded her head as the plane jumped them up and down, this time more vigorously than the last.

The jolt caused Tim to bang his head against the window and he woke up, in some kind of half sleep, half reality state. Deliriously swinging his dazed and confused head around to Abby, 'Did you just hit me?'

'No, I didn't just hit you, when do I ever do that?'

His head lolled slightly, and he took a moment to

register where he was. 'If I'm asleep next to you,' pointing almost drunkenly at her, 'how come we're sitting up?' He held his hands up in confusion. He looked slowly down at his lap, seeing the seat belt he immediately looked out of the window and registered that they were in the air. He sucked in a breath of fear as his mouth opened in sheer terror.

'AAAARGHHHH,' he screamed. 'We are not on a train.'

As more turbulence shook the plane, he clutched both arm rests, covering her hand in a vice like grip.

'Owwwwww,' said Abby. 'I'll put my hand on top of yours if that's OK. It's going to be fine,' she tried to calm him. 'It's just mild turbulence. Would you like more basil?' The effects of the herbs had clearly and very instantly worn off. Tim looked at her as if she was mental, obviously not remembering his proclamations earlier. The plane dropped for a few seconds and their stomachs were caught in mid-air until it rectified. Tim looked at Abby as if she was somehow to blame. 'OK, that was a bad one' Her hand was now sweaty and gripping his just as tightly.

Will unlocked his belt and stood up to go and see if Lucy was alright in the bathroom.

'Sir, you must sit down, please,' the flight attendant was buckling herself in.

'But my fiancé ...'

'Sir, please sit down.'

Will sat back down, looking concerned for Lucy.

The plane continued to bump and roll and tip. Overhead baggage doors flew open and a few screams emanated from further down the plane.

Tim looked at Abby, 'Give me the herbs. Anything.'

Abby grabbed the packet from her bag and chucked it to him. He split a load into his hand and shoved them into his mouth, crunching them like peanuts. Wide eyed, they both looked at each other waiting for the turbulence to stop or the tablets to work. Suddenly there was silence. Abby breathed out.

A gargled farting noise exploded from the bathroom, taking everybody by surprise. Confused, Abby looked at Will. He closed his eyes.

'Oh dear god, Lucy,' Will whispered.

The long rippling fart was accompanied by a distant wail of shock then quickly met by another jolt of turbulence. The initial fart must have been the gates of Lucy's hell opening. With every subsequent turbulent shake of the plane a sorrowful moan came from the bathroom along with thuds and banging on the walls. Not knowing what to do for best Will twitched in his seat, the eyes of the flight attendant on him.

'Well, can I at least go and see if she's alright?'

Another fart sounded out again from the bathroom. It lasted a good few seconds and seemed to rise up a note in the end. The flight attendant visibly cringed before obviously remembering where she was: 'Let's give it a moment, shall we?' she said tactfully.

Abby remained seated with her hand over her mouth, wondering what was happening to Lucy in there. It sounded like she was holding on for dear life whilst exorcising all her demons at the same time. She looked at Tim to see how he was.

His eyes had glazed over again as the 'basil' took effect. His head bobbed around to Abby's with a slight smile. 'Where's Lucy?' he had gone back to his loud childlike voice again.

An enormous guff from the bathroom with a muffled 'dear god' answered his question.

'Is Lucy shitting herself?'

'Don't even go there, Tim.'

'We could buy her a nappy!'

A thump came from the bathroom. 'Or a helmet.'

Abby started to giggle. Will looked round at her crossly. 'Sorry,' she whispered trying to stop.

'Tell him to shut up when she comes out,' Will whispered fiercely.

'I'll try but ...'

As another fart trumpeted and the flight crew did their best to politely pretend it wasn't happening.

Tim opened his mouth in awe, 'What did she eat?'

Abby shook her head, 'I don't know.'

'Well I'm not hungry anymore. Do you wanna know why?'

'Why?' Abby squeezed out, desperately trying not to laugh.

'Because I had me some basil.'

'Yes, well done you.'

'I don't think basil will help Lucy though.'

'No, dear.'

'Do you know why?'

'Why's that Tim?'

'Because she needs a cork.'

Abby gave in to uncontrollable giggles, tears rolled down her face despite Will's look of fury.

'I'm so ... sorry ... Will ...,' she tried to breathe as another alien sound emerged from the bathroom, followed by a moan.

Will turned around, and it was clear he was now also trying his best not to laugh. 'Look when she comes out, she can't know we've heard her. She'd be utterly mortified.'

Abby nodded in agreement.

'I can't smell anything,' Tim offered.

'No, you can't *hear* anything,' Abby corrected him.

'But I can hear everything. I can hear it all,' He blew a long raspberry.

'Oh good lord, sort him out,' Will begged through giggles.

'How?' Abby said helplessly, holding up his herbal sleeping pills. 'I lost count of how many he took. He may be asleep by the time she comes out.' Will crossed his fingers.

Tim sniffed, 'Nope, still can't smell anything. And she'd been brewing that last one.'

Tim lolled back in his chair, pushing it all the way back, looking at her boyishly before he laughed as loudly as he could. She couldn't help but laugh: high-on-basil kid-Tim was hilarious.

'Hopefully, she'll come out and Tim will be like this, and we'll just blame our giggles on him.'

Will nodded.

'Do they have seatbelts in the loo, though?' Abby wondered.

They heard a loud thump.

'Doesn't sound like it,' Will said.

Suddenly they all heard the lock slowly slide back. Will turned around and shot Abby a warning gaze. Tim was a lost cause, laid back giggling and drooling.

Lucy, looking like she'd just survived a tornado, emerged from the bathroom with her hair mussed up and plastered to the side of her face in sweat.

'The water in the basin kept flying out over me,' her skirt was wet through. 'It was a race to flush the toilet before the turbulence threw it up at me. I feel disgusting.' She looked so upset that Will ignored the crew's protests and reached his overhead locker for the extra blanket. Wrapping it round her, he pulled her into a hug partly to comfort her and partly to hide his unmistakeable grin.

Abby bit down on her lips and tried not to make a sound as fits of giggles took over her body.

As the cabin continued to shake, Will sat Lucy down.

'Seriously how long is this bloody turbulence going to go on for?' Lucy fumed.

With another rattle, Tim sat bolt upright and noticed Lucy: 'You're back!' Happy as an eight-year-old at Christmas, he looked from left to right like a duck crossing a road. Seeing Lucy in her seat, he grinned at Abby, who was gesturing wildly with her hands not to say anything. Tim placed his finger up to his lips as if to say 'shhh' – *yes* Abby nodded '*shhh.*' Before she could stop him Tim calmly leaned forward so his head was between Will and Lucy's seats. Taking the deepest breath, he then exhaled and blew the world's biggest raspberry in Lucy's face. Cracking up and slapping his knees, he leaned back.

Abby couldn't hold it in any longer, the laughter flooded out of her noiselessly now as she bent over, struggling to breathe.

Lucy leaned around the chair at her in pure anger, or was it horror?

'I'm so sorry, Lucy. He's high on the herbs.'

Thinking Abby was deranged, and Tim was clearly off his face, Lucy slammed herself back into her seat, clearly pissed off that her flight was not going the way she imagined.

'Don't even think about it,' Lucy raised a finger to

Will who was about to console her. He bit his lip and turned towards the window where Abby could see his shoulders shaking. They were all failing miserably at holding their chuckles back.

'Only five more hours to go then,' Abby whispered to nobody in particular.

'Do you want some basil?' Tim offered her the packet.

'Um, no thank you. I think one of us needs to be coherent on this train.'

'Ah, yes! Choo choo. Choo choo,' He sang, waving his arms. She giggled again. This was great, they only had five hours left and plenty of 'basil.' All would be well.

42

PANIC STATIONS

FINALLY IN THEIR room, Abby moved towards Tim, grateful to be alone with him at last. He smiled at her. A knock sounded at the door and she switched direction to open it. Woody wielded her dress bag.

'I just wanted to give you your bridesmaid dress as soon as we got here, that way I can't be held responsible if ketchup lands on it or something.'

'Thank you for bringing it. I can't believe it was the one thing I left at ours. Thank you also for keeping it quiet around Lucy!' Abby winked, unzipping it whilst Woody poked his head around the door to see Tim.

'Hey man, nice room.'

'Not too shabby, eh?' Tim grinned. He'd upgraded them to a suite as a surprise for Abby.

'Woody, what the heck is this?' Abby demanded holding up one of her summer dresses.

'Er ... your dress?' Woody looked none the wiser.

'Woody!'

'What?'

'This isn't my bridesmaid dress,' Abby caught her breath. She must have swayed a little without even realising because Tim moved over to steady her.

'What do you mean?' Woody looked shocked.

'It's not my bridesmaid dress – what else could that sentence possibly mean?' Her breathing was getting panicky. 'Oh my goodness, Lucy's going to kill me, oh and my dress is just so beautiful. Woody, you were with me, how could you not remember the right one?'

'Wait. The purple one?' Woody asked. 'Oh well, I have that one too, I just thought you'd like to wear this one tonight.'

'You absolute jackass!' Abby yelled, jumping out to dig his ribs. Woody tried dodging but didn't move far enough.

'Ouch!'

'How could you do that to me?' Abby was totally flushed. 'I almost passed out!'

Tim shook his head.

'It was too easy. I just couldn't resist. Sorry man,' Woody said looking at Tim.

'Er, hello! Why the hell are you apologising to him?' Abby exclaimed. 'Go and get my dress now.'

'You've definitely got the right dress?' Tim enquired, eager to calm Abby down.

'Yes, I'll grab it in a bit,' Woody grinned. 'Hey, no stress, we're at a wedding!'

'Ugh. I'll see you in a bit,' Abby slammed the door.

AN HOUR OR so later, there was another knock at the door. Tim had meant to take a shower but was passed out cold on the bed, probably from all of the basil and stress of the flight, so Abby muted the TV and went to the door.

'About time, Woody just give me … oh,' swinging it open she found a newly showered and refreshed Lucy, beaming at her.

'Give you what?' Lucy asked.

'Oh, nothing much,' she grinned right back.

'I just wanted to give you this to take care of.'

Abby's eyes widened as Lucy handed over the giant box containing her wedding dress, 'Are you serious?'

'I may have been a *little* highly strung before.'

'Well, only a little, and I promise I'll take great care of it. Eeek, I can't wait to see it!'

'Is Tim here?' Lucy asked.

'Oh, he's sleeping,' Lucy looked beyond her to see Tim chest down sprawled naked over the bed.

Lucy nodded approvingly and giggled in slight embarrassment, 'Nice butt.'

'I know, I could just stare at it all day,' Abby said proudly. 'In fact, I may just take a picture' and she grabbed her phone.

'Well, let's get a bit more light on the subject.' A stickler for perfection, Lucy angled the bedside lamp over his back a bit more, creating some dramatic shadowing.

'We do this for the houses we show,' she whispered.

'OK here we go,' Abby took ten shots. 'Almost a calendar,' she winked.

'Maybe from this angle,' Lucy hurried her around to the other side of the bed, anxious to capture the shot before Tim awoke. As she moved, she caught the end of his feet which tickled him awake. He stirred and rolled over, smiling at Abby who managed to take the photo.

'What are you ...?' Then seeing Lucy, he grabbed the sheet, covering himself up. 'What the hell is going on here, ladies? Should I be alarmed?'

'Ah, December's shot will just have to wait,' Lucy winked at Abby. 'Don't worry I've got my own man, but nice work my friend, on the butt.' She high-fived Abby as she walked past.

'Are women really like this? I thought it was just guys,' Tim said in mock horror.

'Don't worry, she could only see your arse. It was nice to show it off,' Abby said.

'Oh, I'll bet it was,' Tim pulled some model poses whilst Abby grappled with her camera trying to shoot them.

Lucy laughed, then as her dress bag snapped into view, she clicked straight back into wedding mode.

'Right, I'm trusting you two to look after this. You need to hang it high enough to drop ...,' she said, her eyes darting around the room, 'that curtain pole over there. That's perfect for it.' Abby nodded.

'Tim not one word of what it looks like to Will or I'm be slicing your balls off, and sex with little Miss Fab Tits over there won't be nearly as pleasurable,' Lucy threatened.

'Well, I'm learning a whole lot more about you two on this trip, that's for sure,' Tim tucked in the sides of the sheets, ensuring they could block off any of Lucy's attempts to access his privates. He then covered his eyes and said in his best mock fashionista voice: 'Tell me when it's out, darlings.'

Bending down to unzip the dress bag, Lucy carefully tugged at the hanger, and with Abby's help, she pulled the dress out of the bag and walked it over to the curtain rail.

'It will hang just off the floor if we can put it on the top rung,' Lucy pointed out.

'It's surprisingly heavy,' Abby exclaimed, having never worn one before. 'Gosh, every bit of it looks amazing.'

Smoothing out the kinks and arranging it perfectly, Lucy stepped back and sighed. 'It's a work of art, isn't it?'

'Yes, it is,' Abby agreed. 'Rosa Clara has done you

proud.'

It was a one shoulder dress that clung to her curves, cutting away to a small, elegant fishtail. In ivory satin, it had a split over the left leg and detailed roses that ran over her right shoulder.

'OK I can't wait any longer,' Tim said, 'Wow. It's literally stunning, Lucy you going to knock Will's socks off in that.'

Abby nodded, approving of her boyfriend's words. 'He's right, it's utterly incredible. And more to the point, it will match what I'm wearing perfectly.'

'Yay!' Lucy clapped and gave a little jump before turning to leave. 'I'm just going to check the menu choices and make sure there are no egg-based surprises on there.'

'Good call. Hilary will approve,' Abby stuck her thumb up.

Lucy nodded, 'You two enjoy... this room. See you later for some food.'

As Lucy shut the door, Abby took a running jump and landed on Tim.

'Oumph,' he huffed as she knocked the air out of him whilst whipping her top off and throwing it on the floor.

'Do you want to wear it?' he said, eyebrows gesturing towards Lucy's dress.

'No, it's not my colour,' she joked. 'You on the other hand are ...'

'You're not going to let me leave this room, are you woman?'

'Nope, plus why ever would you want to?' Drawing her tits over his chest, she watched as he smiled coyly.

'Good point, Miss Abby. Could you go to the fridge for me, though, there's something in there I'd like you to have.'

'Ooh, what is it?' Abby moved off Tim quick as a flash and started opening random cupboard doors. 'Where even *is* the fridge?' she said confused.

He pointed to his bedside cabinet.

'Genius, with it that close, we never even need to leave the bed. We should do this in your flat.'

'Just open it woman,' Tim grinned.

Abby tilted her head, 'You're waiting for the cool air to hit my nipples, aren't you?'

'It's dangerously close to making them as hard as my cock just watching you stride around the room.'

'Excellent answer,' she reached down to open the fridge, and he grabbed her thigh, whispering, 'Remove your skirt before you open it. Let me see you.'

Hell, one touch and her pupils dilated. One touch and a whisper and she was tingling all over in a crazed, almost hypnotically sexed up. Wordlessly, she turned towards him, his hand still clasping her thigh and slowly unbuttoned the tiny clips that held her skirt together. It slipped on to his arm before falling to the floor. Her French satin panties emphasised the peach shaped curves of her perfectly formed arse, and Tim ran the back of his hand over it on to her stomach and down to her thighs again, pausing ever so gently over her crotch.

'Damn it, woman, how do you do this to me?' Pulling back the covers and revealing his fully hardened cock. Abby remained silent, wondering if he could hear her heartbeat and whether it would give her away. He moved across the bed, his lips touching her thighs making their way around to her front, kissing her through her knickers. The heat of his breath pulsed through her skin.

'God Abby, when you're clothed, I'm in a constant quandary of wanting to talk to you and find out what's going on inside your head, and just needing to rip your clothes off. I want to be able to read your mind, but I can't. You constantly surprise me. But then when you just stand so simply in front of me ... my god you're just so beautiful.'

Abby held her breath.

He continued to run his lips over her skin and then paused.

Abby followed his gaze ... 'Tim, is that putting you off?' The big wedding dress had the potential to turn into a massive elephant in the room.

'God no, it's stunning. A tad unusual,' he cocked his head to the side, looking at it, before hurriedly moving on, clearly not wanting to discuss weddings right now. 'Anyway, I digress.' Pushing himself up and kneeling on the bed, he kissed her belly. Abby bit her tongue, put her hands in his hair and kissed his forehead and focused on his touch. As her mum and everyone said, she just had to wait until the right moment to ask him all the questions she just wanted to scream about.

Fortunately her desire for his body overtook her desire for answers. He teased her, playing with her panties, running his fingers around the seams at the top of her thigh and around her waist. She waited impatiently for him to pull them down and place his lips on her. In the past, she had very rarely craved a man going down on her, but the way he worked her made every nerve in her body scream. Fingering her lightly, he made her groan and she felt her wetness engulf him.

'You still haven't opened the fridge yet,' he said, teasing her. Extracting his fingers, he threw her into frustration at the distraction. Abby snapped: 'You've got to keep your hands on me at all times, and I'll open that god damn fridge. What could be so important in there anyway?'

Yanking it open, she saw a perfectly chilled bottle of Dom Perignon and two Champagne flutes. Tim's fingers ran over her breasts and down her spine. Finding her wetness again, he artfully played her. As she struggled to focus, he whispered: 'By order of the management, I order you to pop that bottle and have sex and Champagne with me.'

Abby pulled out the bottle slightly clumsily, ripping off the foil as Tim moved to take her breasts in his mouth, still working her, he rubbed her clit through the satin panties and she instinctively arched her back and moaned.

'Get it open, woman.'

'Fuck you, you want Champagne so badly? You get it,' Abby was enraged. Here she was craving sex, and he wanted to drink? Feeling fiery, she wrenched off the metal casing as Tim placed his fingers inside her once more, moving on his shaft with his other hand.

'Holy fuck, just take me,' she begged. The sight of him touching himself where she should be touching him was too much. Pointing the bottle into the bathroom, she popped the cork shattering something behind her, enjoying the jump that Tim's shock had on his fingers inside her pussy. 'Champagne?' she smiled.

He forced his fingers deeper inside her harder, nodding. Clenching her pussy instinctively around them, she kissed him, opening his mouth with her tongue, and poured the Dom in. He gulped it back before withdrawing his lips, whispering: 'Now you.'

She duly lifted the Dom to her lips, took a mouthful and let the rest run down over her tits and seep into her panties.

'Oh my god,' Tim groaned, instantly going wild with his tongue. Abby stopped pouring for a second to let him catch it all with his hands, rub it over her tits and take his tongue and lick the elixir off her nipples. He ripped her panties and she poured again, this time enough for the bubbles to trickle down her body, and Tim homed in on them.

'Best fucking Champagne ever ...' Tim whispered skilfully finger-fucking her pussy whilst tonguing her clit. Reaching beneath her, she found his cock and heard him gasp as her hands, wet from the Champagne, worked their magic up and down his shaft. He paused, losing himself in the moment for a second. She grabbed his hair pushing him back on the bed, releasing more Champagne over his chest. Their bodies were now only separated by thousands of tiny bubbles of liquid gold streaming between them.

Her pussy was screaming for him, and as she rose her hips, he grabbed her bottom with both hands, angling himself perfectly into her. Moaning in unison as he took her finally, Abby felt every nerve come alive in her body. Pulling him closer to her, she felt the Champagne slide over their bodies as they moved together. She straddled him on the side of the bed and rocked his cock deeper into her.

Tim paused, rose, picked her up, her legs clasping around him, and carried her to the wardrobe. Her back against the cool wood, he drove his cock into her hard and fast, breathing raggedly as they screwed. Abby screamed as they came together. This was all she wanted, more than anything in the world: him taking her and making her his. She never wanted to let go. This was it.

Sex had never been like this with anyone before. No-one had ever taken her so completely before. He had her mind, body and soul. She knew she wanted to spend every waking moment with him.

'Abby. What are you doing to me?' Tim whispered with her legs still wrapped around him. 'I had planned a sedate glass of Champagne to toast our time away and instead you just rocked my world.'

'Well, I think you had a little something to do with it as well,' she said breathlessly.

He carried her back to the bed, and she lay with her head on his chest listening to his heart beating, kissing him. She ached to be able to tell him how she felt. Instead she did the next best thing and kissed him for as long as their ragged breathing would allow.

'This holiday was a great idea,' he said softly stroking her hair.

'Yes, thank you Lucy and Will for getting engaged,' she averted her eyes from his for fear she would let it slip just how much she felt for him, instead she kissed his chest some more: 'Mmmm, you taste of Champagne.'

'Speaking of which,' he rolled over, 'is there any left?' He reached for the bottle, 'Mmm, still half full.'

Abby hopped off the bed and grabbed the two chilled glasses from the fridge, 'Let's rectify that.'

'To my beautiful girlfriend and our first holiday together. Hopefully the first of many,' he added. Abby clinked her glass against his, 'I'll drink to that.' That sounded hopeful, she beamed and sipped.

'Cheers!'

As they finished off the rest of the Champagne, the phone rang. It was Lucy saying they were all a little tired, but did they want to meet in the hotel brasserie for some food? Realising they hadn't eaten since the plane, Abby whispered the idea to Tim who gave her the thumbs up straight away. 'We'll be along in five.'

Hearing 'five,' Tim jumped up. 'Five? Heck I don't know what to do with myself. Quick shower?' He dashed to the bathroom. 'Shit, Abby, the cork shattered the mirror. There's glass everywhere.'

She peeked over his shoulder. 'We'll sort it out after the food.'

'Good priorities!' He covered the floor as best he could with a towel then hopped in the shower for a quick dousing. Abby did the same and then they towelled each other dry, giggling and pushing each other over on to the bed like school kids. The holiday feeling was certainly setting in.

Tim opened her bag and threw over a random selection of clothes to wear, she duly obliged and did the same for him. Laughing their heads off at their random attire, they strolled into the bar, arm in arm.

'Over here' Lucy waved, appraising their attire. 'Nice. You remembered your outfits for the wedding, right?'

Abby shot a look at Woody, who grinned and nodded. 'Yes, ma'am, of course,' she replied sweetly.

Not quite realising what was going on, Lucy smiled. But Will sensed something was afoot and wisely distracted his fiancé with the cocktail menu.

'Tomorrow,' Woody mouthed.

Abby slide in next to him: 'It'd better be because otherwise you're buying me something from over here, and I promise you it will be an expensive shopping spree. I don't think you have any idea how much dresses cost.'

'I do, and that's why it got its own seat on a flight over.'

'Wait, so you actually didn't bring the right dress?'

Tim cracked up.

Abby's jaw dropped.

'You don't want to know the strings I've had to pull in the last hour to sort this mess out.' Woody looked woebegone. She rubbed his arm. Her last hour had obviously been considerably more enjoyable than his.

'Thank you, Woodster. You're a star. I'm sure all will be fine. Let's just enjoy the hotel until it gets here and not waste time worrying.'

He grinned, 'OK, deal.'

Abby looked around. They had 24 hours before the big day to relax, explore and have spa treatments. It was going to be brilliant.

43

TRUE BEAUTY

'I FEEL OVERWHELMED,' Abby choked, trying desperately to hold back the tears of love that were forming as she looked at her friend. Seeing Lucy so happy removed all Abby's doubts. She was glowing.

Lucy's stylist delicately looped up her buttons whilst Abby held Lucy's hands. She could tell Lucy felt the same. It was such a momentous occasion, one they'd dreamt of and discussed for half their lives. Lucy and Will were getting married at 6pm, just before the sunset, so the day had been relatively stress-free. Now the enormity was beginning to hit them both.

'Abs ...,' Lucy gasped, not able to finish. Abby fanned her face with her hands.

'Lucy, don't you dare smudge your makeup – it's perfect. You're perfect, Luce. You're the most amazing person in the world, and I love you so much. Will is the luckiest man on the planet to be getting you.'

'Abby, focus now, you're not losing me.'

Abby gulped, Lucy was voicing her worst fear.

'You could never lose me. You're just gaining a Will, the same as I'm gaining a Tim.'

'OK,' Abby whispered, 'I'll hold you to that. You are my truest friend, Lucy, I couldn't do 'life' without you.'

Lucy air kissed her to not smudge her makeup, 'Can you believe I'm getting married?'

Abby whooped and jumped for the both of them. Lucy squeezed her hands. And they turned to see the dress in the mirror.

'It's stunning, Lucy.'

The boutique in Richmond where she'd found it had done an amazing job of altering the dress to fit her frame perfectly. Her left shoulder was bare, which Abby had caught Lucy's mum raising an eyebrow to but she seemed to have got over it.

All that was left was her veil. With her hair down and perfectly curled, inspired by the women in Jack Vettriano paintings, Abby raised the veil and pinned it artfully to shape Lucy's face. Kudos to the hair stylist because it had come out exactly as planned. Abby held her breath as she did it, not wanting to ruin the lady's hard work.

'Maybe we could get Will to employ her and she could style our hair forever,' Lucy joked.

'Do it,' Abby nodded seriously. Trying not to touch her hair which took the same inspiration.

'Right, time for *your* dress, missy,' Lucy said.

'And time for your lipstick ...' Abby came back holding a towel which she gently placed under Lucy's hair and around her to act like a bib. If any of the red lip stain and lipstick spilt on the dress that would be a nightmare. When they were sure it was set, Abby ran off excited to finally put on her dress, which had arrived twelve hours ago thanks to a very apologetic Woody.

It was beautiful, a full-length lilac gown also with one shoulder delicately accented by tiny roses running over it. The rest of the dress had intricate bead work, making it heavy to hold and luxurious to slip on. She'd been so lucky to find it in the sale. She zipped it up at the side and smiled at herself in the mirror and hoped Lucy would like it.

'Are you ready to see my dress yet?' she called out to her best friend.

'The suspense is killing me,' Lucy yelled back. Abby moved back into the room.

'Oh my goodness, Abby! You're sensational, spin around.'

Abby showed off the low back before swivelling round again to see Lucy's face.

'Oh my goodness, Abby you've done me proud,' Lucy openly marvelled at her dress. 'That's amazing with the roses on the shoulder matching with mine – how did you know?'

'Same taste, I suppose,' Abby said, welling up again.

'Don't you dare ruin *your* makeup. Grab a tissue quickly.' Abby hoiked her dress up and ran, making it to the tissues just in time.

Lucy spun around in front of the mirror. 'I think we're ready!' And there was a knock at the door. Woody's voice sounded out: 'Can I see my favourite girls now?'

'Yes, come on in. Wow, Woody you look awesome, too.'

Woody stood in the doorway, his jaw open, staring at Lucy. He shook his head and tried to say something but was completely speechless.

'Oh my god,' was all he could muster as Abby snuck past him and quietly pushed the door closed.

'Lucy, you're the most beautiful bride I've ever seen. I'm welling up!' In sheer shock at the tears forming, he coughed and retrieved a tissue from the bathroom. 'I do apologise, ladies. I hereby promise to man up.'

'Maybe you should get another tissue for when you're standing at the aisle,' Abby suggested.

'I shan't need it,' he clicked his heels and spoke like he was in the military: 'You both look sensational. I came to report that everyone is in position. We are ready when you are.'

'Oh my word, Luce, this is it,' Abby whispered.

'Where's my dad?' Lucy asked tentatively.

'I'll go and get him and give you two a moment. Come on, Woody,' she dragged Woody away, conscious that he might have a last-ditch attempt at emotion with Lucy.

Lucy's dad Gregory was waiting just outside the door. Bless him he looks so nervous, she thought. He was a sweet and quiet man, bossed around by his wife, but he had always adored his daughter. Gregory pulled Abby to one side, 'Abby dear, you look so beautiful.' He gestured for her to talk to him quietly for a moment: 'It's all so rushed, Abby. Do you think she'll be alright?'

'I think that no matter what happens, she will always be alright. She's got a good head on her shoulders. You brought her up well.'

He nodded his head. Abby continued: 'Will's lovely and I think he just wanted to start their life together properly as soon as possible.'

'Alena isn't happy about all of this,' he said, gesturing at the hotel.

'Just focus on how much your daughter is glowing with happiness, if that doesn't calm Alena down nothing will, believe me.'

Gregory looked doubtful that anything would ever calm his wife down when she had a bee in her bonnet. 'Yes, well we can but hope. You do look lovely, dear. What is going on with your arm, do you need to find the other shoulder?' He looked quizzically at the swag of material on Abby's shoulder.

'It's a rose. It's meant to only have one shoulder to it. Anyway, it's good question to ask. You'll see why.' With that she opened the door to Lucy's room and let him enter. Hearing him gasp, she smiled and quietly shut the door behind them, giving them a few precious moments to themselves before the celebrations began.

Minutes later, Lucy's door opened and her father led her out. She glided like an elegant princess, smiling and walking tall, quiet now, as if savouring every moment. They all processed to the terrace, where from the behind the congregation, they could see the guests and, of course, Will.

Abby watched Lucy as she breathed in deeply. Gregory kissed her hand, and Lucy shared a smile with her and Woody. They all stayed silent, none of them wanting to break the spell.

'Whenever you're ready, my dear,' Gregory said, his voice shaking with emotion. 'I bet your groom can't wait to see you.'

Lucy nodded and kissed his hand. She turned to face the aisle, took another deep breath and the procession started walking. The satin of Lucy's dress caught the sunlight, magnifying her radiance as the violinist serenaded her walk towards Will.

'She's beautiful inside and out, isn't she?' Abby whispered to Woody, clutching his arm as they kept pace behind Lucy. Woody nodded, his lip trembling a little. Abby's heart pounded and she willed the tears to stay away as she smiled at the crowd of people gathered around them. She suddenly realised she hadn't seen Tim for hours.

She caught a glimpse of Will grinning from ear to ear

as Lucy made her way towards him. He held his hand out to shake Gregory's then Abby caught her breath as she watched him bend down to kiss her best friend lightly on the cheek. 'You're utterly beautiful,' she watched him whisper to her. Abby smiled broadly, Will's tenderness was exactly what she wanted to see.

Lucy turned and kissed her father then took Will's hands to stand on the steps in front of the registrar.

'Keep breathing,' Woody whispered to her, she hadn't realised that she'd been holding her breath.

She turned her head to the right and finally caught sight of Tim, who was sitting on the front row, completely oblivious to what was going on in front of him – his eyes were fixed on her. She beamed back at him.

'Wow,' he mouthed, she wished she could have him on one side and Woody on the other. Damn he looked handsome. Wearing a light linen suit with an unbuttoned shirt, he had acquired a pale lilac rose as a buttonhole to match her dress.

Woody nodded at his cousin, but Tim was still staring at Abby.

'Tim needs to blink,' Woody whispered to her.

She giggled slightly. He did look transfixed.

'Ladies and gentlemen, we are all here today to bear witness ...'

Abby tore her eyes away from Tim and focused on Lucy. Sending every positive vibe that her bones could muster. 'Gosh, she is so calm,' Abby thought, pride flooding over her.

*****

DESPITE HER CALM persona, Lucy's heart was racing as

she looked straight into Will's eyes, knowing she would be looking into those kind eyes forever. She couldn't wait. She grinned widely at him, delighted they hadn't waited a long time to do this. She just wanted to be his wife and start their life together so they could start enjoying forever as soon as possible. She'd never had many boyfriends, knowing that when she gave her heart away, it would be like this. Any nerves she'd had were stilled as he gazed at her. Together, they were whole. She knew deep in her bones he was the man she was meant to be with.

A slight breeze caught a wisp of hair and carried her fragrance to him. He looked giddy as he drank it in. She squeezed his hand and he placed his other hand on top of hers protectively.

'I love you,' he whispered.

'And I love you too,' she said right back before beginning her vows to him.

'Will, I may not be perfect, but I can promise you I'll never stop trying to make you happy, understand your needs and put them before mine. I've waited my whole life for you. I love you. You are my truth. Through good times and bad. From now, until forever.' She said the vows slowly, not wanting to rush them. Wanting him to know she meant every syllable.

Will cleared his throat. 'My darling Lucy. I promise you that I will spend the rest of my life making you as happy as you make me. I will never stop trying to understand your needs and putting them before my own. I love you, too. I will take great pride in the honour of being your husband, for you are my truth. Through good times and bad. From now, until forever.'

Will slipped her ring onto her finger, a simple yellow

gold band to match her engagement ring. She smiled and turned to Abby who smiled back, wiping a tear from her eye. Woody stood strong beside her. Looking back at Will, she took the ring from the best man and placed it on her husband's finger. Sliding it on, she looked directly into his eyes.

The registrar smiled. 'I now pronounce you husband and wife.'

'Finally, I can kiss you.' Will exclaimed.

Lucy grinned.

Will pulled her into him and kissed her. Moving her swiftly he bent her across his knee like in the old movies, and she kissed him back to the of cheers and clapping from their family and friends.

'Oh my goodness, we did it,' She beamed before melting into his kiss again.

'Yes, indeed we did, my love!'

Lucy turned to face everyone, her father, quite overcome with all of the emotion, was sitting down, while her mum, who she was relieved to see was smiling, walked towards her, arms open.

'Congratulations, my darling girl. You look sensational,' and Alina turned to Will: 'It was beautiful, Will, welcome to the family...'

Phew Lucy thought, she's finally got into the spirit of it. She beamed at Abby, who drew her into a massive hug, before quickly whispering: 'Can you check that my dad's OK?'

'Yes of course, leave him with me.'

*****

ABBY HUGGED LUCY back then whispered to Woody what

she was going to do. Woody moved automatically to congratulate Lucy and Will while Abby knelt next to Gregory, his hands were shaking uncontrollably.

'I can just see her growing up ...' tears streamed down his face, 'giving her away, that was the hardest thing...'

Her heart went out to him, and she pulled a tissue from her clutch.

'Hey, come here,' she said, softly holding his hand. 'I was terrified how this would change our friendship. I've known you all as long as I can remember.'

He nodded.

'So, I'm just going to say to you what Lucy said to me, not even 30 minutes ago. We're not losing her, we're simply gaining Will into our family.' She held her breath, hoping it would do the trick. His breathing calmed, slowly.

'Go and give her a big hug. She's radiant, isn't she?'

Gregory took a deep breath, 'Yes, she is. I'm so very proud of her.'

'Go and tell her,' Abby whispered.

'And you are a true friend. You look lovely, too, with your matching one shoulder thing. I quite like it.'

'Thank you,' she giggled and rose.

Suddenly she felt a warm hand at the base of her spine, and she glowed at Tim's touch.

'My god, Abby, you're breath-taking,' Tim leant in and kissed her lips. 'Come over here, I need to speak to you ...'

'Ladies and gentlemen, please gather round as the bride and groom take their first dance,' a voice boomed across the terrace,

'Blimey, Lucy and Will are going straight into it. Oh gosh, Tim, it'll have to wait, sorry.'

'Well I suppose it can wait,' he murmured, standing

behind her and swaying with her to the strains of Frank Sinatra. With the sun setting, fairy lights and candles flickering everywhere, Lucy and Will gleamed as they danced and spun around to *The Way You Look Tonight* sung perfectly by a Rat Pack tribute band.

'What a perfect day,' Abby breathed.

'Perfection indeed,' Tim agreed, nuzzling her neck.

'Whooooop,' Abby called out as loudly as her lungs would let her as everyone whooped and cheered them along. As the happy couple paused and gestured for everyone to join them on the dance floor, she turned up to Tim, 'Come on then.'

He obliged, twirling her around three times before drawing her close.

'Gosh, how much love is there on this rooftop tonight? You can literally feel it, can't you?' She gazed up at him.

And Tim stopped. Abruptly. Right in the middle of the dance floor.

'What's wrong?' She was confused.

'Abby, I need to speak to you,' he pulled her a little way away from the dance floor.

'But ...'

'Abby, this is important,' his face blushed and his eyes flickered with an intensity that she hadn't seen before.

She nodded silently; heck had her use of the 'L' word freaked him out?

He drew her to the side of the terrace.

'Abby, I haven't been able to take my eyes off you ...'

'You like me in this dress?' she said playfully.

'I more than like it. I love it, but that's by-the-by.'

'Well, we'll have to work on that ...' She leaned in to kiss him.

'No, Abby you need to let me speak. Please,' Tim

kissed her forehead and held her hands. She quietened down finally sensing the solemnity of the moment.

'Abby, I know deep down that you've been wanting, expecting me to say three particular words to you, and I haven't,' he paused.

She blinked. Her heart was pounding as he spoke.

'Well truth be told, I wasn't waiting for the perfect time, I was waiting for the perfect moment when those three words meant enough. Do you know what I mean?'

'No,' she whispered. 'You're going to have to guide me through this with you.'

'OK,' He paused. 'I don't know how to say, "I love you", Abby. Those three words don't seem like enough, they seem trite compared to how much I feel for you. You want me to say only *three* words to describe how I felt when I first met you and now how that feeling has grown and gone beyond love and anything else I've ever known. Only three words for all of that?'

He held her hands tightly, fixing her gaze. He looked at her earnestly.

'I've told people that I love them before and, genuinely, at the time, I thought it was real. Yet with you, it's *so* real it consumes my mind, and I have to be in your presence to feel whole.

I know right here, right now, that my love for you is infinite. They could send astronauts to the edge of space, and they'd look at each other, rub their beards and say, "there's something carrying on here, this isn't the end." Galaxies expanding on and on, and they still wouldn't find the end of my love for you.'

She felt tears slipping down her cheeks. Tim leant down and kissed them away, one by one.

'You have nothing to fear with me, Abby. My love for

you is the strength of my character. I will make every good decision I can to ensure you are safe and happy in everything you do. With every breath, I love you more. You saw it before when you were standing in the aisle, I thought I was going to combust if I didn't tell you as soon as possible. I literally don't know how to express myself because I feel this way, and it's only been three months, and yet in that time, I can't even imagine my world without you in it. I don't want to for a second.'

Turning her face up to look at him, she placed her fingers against his cheeks then ran them into his hair.

'You must know I feel the same, Tim. I love you with all of my heart and soul. You are my one true love. My gosh, I can actually call you that now.'

He breathed out in relief. 'Thank goodness for that,' he whispered gruffly and as he kissed her, he drew her into his arms.

'I'm not going to let you go for a single second.'

'That's fine with me,' she said, kissing him again. 'I've wanted to tell you for so long, I think I've driven my mum and Lucy insane.'

'Is that why you were a bit quiet when Lucy got engaged?' Tim asked.

'Yes,' she nodded. 'They'd shown their love for each other so quickly, and it made me wonder if you loved me, or if ...' she felt silly and shy voicing it now.

'You wondered if I only wanted you for sex and good times. God, no. I mean it's insanely good, don't get me wrong. But no, Abby, I wanted to take it slow so you could trust it and I could be honest and trust myself.'

'My mum was right about you,' Abby smiled.

'Yes, she is. Abby, I love you, of that I am absolutely certain. In fact, you are the one thing in my life that I am utterly certain about. That's why you feel calm when you're around me because you know the essence of who I am, and deep down, you know you can trust me.'

'Gosh, I love you Tim, this has been the best day of my life. I feel as though you've given me the moon.'

'You have no need to worry or fear that I'll leave you Abby. In good times, I want to celebrate with you, and in bad times I want to help you smile again. I never want to cause you pain. I love you so much.' Tim was whispering now.

'Oh my gosh is this actually happening to me?' She whispered back. 'I feel as though I'm dancing across the stars.'

He twirled her around, and she laughed.

'Tim, you've shown me the kind of love I've only heard people talk about truly exists.' He twirled her around again, finally pulling her back into his chest. She reached up and brought his face next to hers again to kiss him. Giddy from his words.

'Everything about you in your world is beautiful, and I'm honoured to be a part of it,' he said.

'Tim, you *are* my world. I know that and I've known that since Greenwich.'

He smiled immediately at the memory. She continued. 'I will never hurt you or betray you, Tim. I might be headstrong at times ...'

He grinned, 'You're passionate. That's a good thing.'

'But I can promise you, right here, right now, I will never stop trying to make you happy. Lucy and Will's vows make so much sense. You make my soul sing. With you, I feel more alive than I have ever felt in my life. There, I can finally say it: I love you with all my heart.'

With tears in his eyes, he kissed her. Slipping his arms

around her waist he held her close into him.

'I'm going to kiss you forever, Miss Abby,' he whispered. 'Just you wait and see...'

ABOUT THE AUTHOR

CHERRY MARTIN WAS born in a Sheffield hospital in the hot summer of 1980. She was not fully bathed for a whole week in some kind of experiment to see what that might do to a baby's temperature*. Needless to say, she cried for the first seven days of her existence and has spent the following years obsessively washing her hands and giggling her way through life to make up for it.

After graduating in 2003 from Greenwich University with a LLB Honours in Law, she moved across the Thames to Canary Wharf and has since worked as a local and national journalist, international writer, editor, copywriter and ghostwriter.

Nope, she didn't realise that there were so many facets to a career in writing either.

Her pen has taken her all over the world to experience things she never thought she would and meet people who have definitely made her life better. Never far from a pen, notepad and her latest book, she knew some day that the time would come for her to have her own name on the cover after ghostwriting for so many others. She now lives by the sea with her ginger ninja tribe and is beyond excited for the release of this novel after plugging away at it in her spare time since 2012. She's on a personal mission to do her bit to ensure that the world is a friendlier place where no one feels alone.

She's now typing away at book two of the BESTIES trilogy, *All the Vows*.

Find out more about Cherry, the Besties Trilogy or to join the Blossom Besties Book Club, head to bestiestrilogy.com

🅞 @CherryMwrites
🅞 @BestiesTrilogy

*If anyone knows the results to this trial, Cherry would be keen to find them out!

Dedicated to Lesley ...

One of my favourite people.

Aside from showing me nothing but kindness and love my whole life, she managed to find humour in any given situation and exemplified to me the sheer power of laughter when mixing it with love.

I could never put the phone down on her because I didn't want her to go. The last time we spoke, I prepared and cooked an entire casserole, ate it and we were still talking and giggling as I was washing up.

If you look up and see a star twinkling, it's her legacy of laughter and love beaming back down reminding you to try, however hard it is sometimes, to laugh through the tears and get to a point where you're making plans again.

RIP wonderful lady. You will always be with us.

WS - #0076 - 011221 - C0 - 197/132/26 - PB - 9781916895812 - Matt Lamination